MICHAEL S. VISCHI

outskirtspress
DENVER, COLORADO

This is a work of fiction. The events and characters described herein are imaginary and are not intended to refer to specific places or living persons. The opinions expressed in this manuscript are solely the opinions of the author and do not represent the opinions or thoughts of the publisher. The author has represented and warranted full ownership and/or legal right to publish all the materials in this book.

The Phoenix Gate
All Rights Reserved.
Copyright © 2015 Michael S. Vischi
v1.0

Cover Photo © 2015 Michael S. Vischi. All rights reserved - used with permission.

This book may not be reproduced, transmitted, or stored in whole or in part by any means, including graphic, electronic, or mechanical without the express written consent of the publisher except in the case of brief quotations embodied in critical articles and reviews.

Outskirts Press, Inc.
http://www.outskirtspress.com

ISBN: 978-1-4787-4453-5

Outskirts Press and the "OP" logo are trademarks belonging to Outskirts Press, Inc.

PRINTED IN THE UNITED STATES OF AMERICA

This book is dedicated to
Thuyvi Thi Nguyen.
*She has been in my life since
the first word was written;
she has been my inspiration
for every word that followed.*

And to our 4 munchkins
Arianna, Monica, Keola, and Aidan
*Our four greatest dreams
brought to life.*

"Man will one day discover the essence of God and, in doing so, give birth to their destruction."
~ Book of Prophecies; Junah 7:3

"And he shall come in the humblest of forms, only to unite the world through death."
~ Aurorian Chronicles

PROLOGUE
~ AD 2017 ~

The room was not very big and, although it was full of lab equipment, somehow appeared void, hollow. In the center rested a medical bed, a patient sitting in the inclined position. As he looked around the room, his wondering eyes took in all the minute changes no one else ever cared to notice, along with the rest of the medical equipment: monitors, computers, printers that never seemed to run out of paper. The far wall contained shelves lined with bottles. The labels were too far away to read, but the contents of each were of different colors, some translucent. He wondered if they would ever be used again or remain as they were, collecting dust. As faint footsteps echoed throughout the room, the boy turned his head to watch a nurse walking toward him, her hands holding the electrical sensors the boy knew by memory.

"Tests AGAIN?! Every day it's tests, tests, tests. Yesterday, tests. Tomorrow, more tests," Evrikh repeated as his eyes carefully scanned the room. "I'm TIRED of all these tests."

Arianna sat on the stool that rested beside his bed as she placed one of the sensors upon his chest. She looked up at his eyes, her own carrying a sense of monotony. "You know how he can be sometimes, Evrikh. He just wants to make sure you're all right," she continued as her gaze returned to the work at hand.

"If he cares so much, why doesn't he spend more time with me?"

"When you put it that way, you make an exceptionally valid point, Evrikh. And so, when he returns, you and I both will bombard him till he promises to spend more time with you. You do know he loves your company; it's his job that keeps him from you. And, Evrikh, you know that it has to be extremely important; otherwise, all of his time would be spent with you, right?" the nurse finished, as she placed the last sensor upon his body.

"Who matters then? I don't care for his job," Evrikh blurted as a look of anger rippled across his face.

Pieces of plastic, wood, and metal were instantaneously flung into the air as the desktop computer on the other side of the room, along with the desk it rested on, exploded; the sudden eruption momentarily deafening. The nurse immediately ducked instinctively. Moments after the room regained silence, the nurse looked from the small blast radius back to Evrikh.

"This is why it's so important for you to control your anger."

"I didn't mean to!" Slowly he sank further into the bed.

"And what would Kendrick have you do?"

The boy's head turned toward the shattered computer and desk as his eyes slowly lifted their gaze, tiny echoes of silver light shimmering throughout. As he sat there, his thoughts became extremely focused, reaching out with lives of their own. The debris slowly began to move across the floor and seconds later, left it, floating into the air. The nurse watched expectantly as the broken pieces started to realign themselves on the desk from which they came. Everything in the room disappeared as the pieces became Evrikh's only door of thought. Invisibly asking them to help, the pieces floated toward each other effortlessly, bringing themselves together and reforming their original shape, the computer. Colliding in a mesh of liquid, it all began to reshape and harden; seconds later, the corner of the room remained as it did before, untouched. The computer, as well as the desk, almost appeared brand-new.

Arianna looked back at him. "That is amazing. And each time I see it, it shows me how amazing you really are, Evrikh. But that wasn't so hard, was it?"

"Doesn't mean I like doing it, either," he quipped, as the door of the lab suddenly opened.

A man stepped in, dropping a folder of papers along with a bag, on a desk. As he turned in their direction, a slight smile spread across his face. "Hey, Evrikh, what's up with my little guy today?"

Arianna shot off the stool, her lab coat snapping into the air as she turned. "Kendrick, Evrikh and I have already decided that if you don't spend more time with him, then he's going to make your head explode, here and now. What say you to this, good Doctor?"

Kendrick's arms immediately flew up beside his head as though he were being held at gunpoint. "Innocent, I declare myself INNOCENT . . . wait, what're we . . ."

". . . guilty," Evrikh's gaze was ablaze with boyish passion.

"GUILTY . . . Yes, I'm definitely guilty! I'm guilty, be . . . cause . . ." Slowly he let his eyes roll back to Arianna.

"Because you made a promise to our boy here, that you'd spend more time with him, right?" Her eyes now reflected the same passionate gaze as Evrikh's did.

"Yes, yes, of course! A promise that I have made and, no doubt, you will hold me to, Evrikh!" A small smile began scrolling across his mouth as he witnessed the same smile etching its way across Evrikh's. "Hey, how'd you like to go grab a pizza with me later? Maybe even a movie, if you're feeling up to it?" he finished as he slid into the other chair next to the boy's bed.

"Pizza Hut! Do you promise?" Evrikh queried as he failed to erase his rapidly growing smile.

"Do I promise?" he asked while looking up at Arianna. "DO I PROMISE?" His gaze returned to the boy's face. "Tell you what, Evrikh. If I break it, then you can run the tests on me, and Madam Arianna here will be your witness." A slight look of concern broke through his features. "How's that sound?"

Arianna scoffed at the sound of "Madam" coming from Kendrick's mouth.

"All right," the boy responded, crossing his arms over his chest as though the game had been set, checkmate.

"I just need you to do this one last test, then that's it

for today." The doctor continued, "I need you to go back to that place."

Evrikh cringed at the idea. "But that place is so messy! Everything is always . . . together, it's never alone." His eyes trailed downward. "Sometimes I feel like I get lost there."

"I'm sorry, Ev, but for you to help everyone, we need to know more. Besides," he continued as he stood back up, walking toward the readout machines and computers, "you won't need to be there very long, AND . . . Pizza Hut awaits!"

"Well, let's get this part over with," Evrikh said as he uncrossed his arms impatiently.

Arianna stepped over to the computers as she started prepping the equipment for the phase shift. Kendrick leaned over the medical bed as he ran his hand through the boy's hair.

"Don't worry, son. If anything should go wrong, we'll pull you out," he reassured him. "The only thing I want you to do today is find out who they are. Can you do that for me?"

As the boy lay there, he looked up at Kendrick. "I'll try, but they don't like me very much." His eyes reflected a hint of sorrow.

"Nothing will happen to you; you have Arianna and me watching over you, and we haven't let you down yet, right?" Kendrick replied as he stepped away from the bed.

Walking toward Arianna, he turned to help her with the last of the preparations. His inner concerns carved their way onto his face.

"We need to get results quickly," he quietly told her, eyes fixed on the work at hand.

"The committee obviously doesn't see the potential this project could have," she said, stopping her work to look at him.

"The committee doesn't care for potential; all they care about is where their money's going, and right now, they're not seeing it. If Evrikh doesn't find something soon, I'm positive that they'll pull the plug." Kendrick turned to look at Arianna. "I want you to lower the protection barriers. I want his shift to go completely through."

Arianna's eyes slightly pivoted as her mind finally registered the sentences he had spoken. "We can't do that! Evrikh's never done a complete shift before. If we lower the barriers he'll be completely vulnerable. He might get hurt—or worse!"

Kendrick stopped his work as he stood up straight, looking directly at Arianna. "And what if the committee pulls the plug? You know what'll happen to him then. We have no choice. This is for him just as much as it is for us, for all of mankind." Kendrick's eyes returned to the boy lying on the bed. "I'm just afraid that he's not ready for what lies ahead—let alone us."

~ ~ ~

2017—the same year the world was forever changed by a single man: Kendrick Savari, the first scientist throughout the history of man to reproduce cold fusion. However, this discovery did not bring forth the result everyone had hoped for. The world slowly went into ruin, as countries became bitter toward one another. The world had become hungry for power and hungry for control. When one country couldn't purchase cold fusion from another, they turned to other means to achieve their goals. And so a few short years later it began . . . Everybody started fighting one another, treaties disappeared, and allies became only an idea. In the end, this four-year conflict was renamed the "War of Ruin." A blackened scar the world would never forget.

A species can often smell its own extinction, and man was no exception. Because of their current state and where it was headed, Kendrick Savari made one last contribution to our way of life: the Phoenix Gate. A fail-safe to ensure a future for the human race, and to preserve our way of life should we ever need to rise from our own ashes. After Savari overlooked the completion of the project, something had gone wrong and the project was seen as a mistake. The decision was made to bury the project in a location never to be found again. And so the Phoenix Gate, like so many others, was to become a fairy tale; the truth only known to Father Time.

By 2023, everybody had gone nuclear, and the United States, Russia, Japan, China, and Australia had sent their bombs toward the heavens. And in that one brief moment in history, the sky was said to have been so bright and beautiful that it would have left the far reaches of the universe breathless. But this beauty grew to an angry gray very swiftly and began to spread throughout the world, smothering out the sunlight and consuming the world in blackness. The smeared sky dripped its poisonous fluid upon the earth and became known as the "Black Rain," scorching the ground and changing the face of the planet. This period in history became the Great Darkness, and it changed the fate of all humanity for the rest of time. Millennia would pass before the world would heal.

Though there were not many who survived the Great Darkness, there were some. Those who survived were supposedly spared by Miriam, the goddess of life. It was said that toward the end of the Great Darkness, a woman shrouded in clothing traveled the land, helping people rebuild what they lost. The Aurorian Chronicles state that in times of turmoil, the goddess will return to the people she loves so much, to unite them once again until a day she is no longer needed. Upon that day, she would return to the heavens. She became our savior, humankind's only cornerstone for hope. An odd aura surrounded that woman; she was different from most people. They say that in the beginning, she founded the Council of Aurora. Even now she continues to cleanse the world, until that day when the heavens beckon her to return.

Many years would pass before man would return to the surface and begin anew. Groups of people began to reform and rebuild. Villages began to pop up all throughout the world, and these villages became governed by Guardians. The Senate, the House, the president, it had all been replaced by the "Council of Aurora." The people needed faith and spiritual enlightenment, not governments or representatives, so the Council grew, very swiftly and very powerfully. The Council maintained order and peace throughout the land by Guardians, who represented the Council to the people and formally spoke to the Council for the people. Members of the Council were not chosen; it was their destiny, ordained by Miriam. To be of the Council was to be above the commoners, the rest of mankind.

Then there are the Unfamiliars. These are the people that had supposedly been affected by the "old-time" in some way, whether it was the Black Rain or tainted soil. These people possessed strange abilities and were not accepted by the Council. Instead, they were outcasts, banished to the "Outlands." They were rarely seen or heard of. Most of them were said not to have survived. To be declared as an Unfamiliar by the Council meant that you were a creation of sin or conspiring against them. Either way, your name, your existence, would be removed from society, and you were to be banished or sentenced to death, whichever the Council felt necessary.

At the dawn of this new era, this new millennium, the world was given a new name in remembrance of the old one, "New Terra." Nobody knew what year it was, just that we had lost track sometime during the Great Darkness. So it was decided that if humans had to start all over, that time would have to also. All of humankind was once again united, and for the human race, this new age had become "Evolution."

* * * *

PART I
The Journey Within

CHAPTER 1
~ Present Day ~

HIS MIND WAS racing, surrounded by an unfamiliar world of green trees and plants; a forest. His senses were on their fullest alert. He was running. His hands still steaming of hot blood that was not his own; oily, enticing. Images vaguely remembered, yet so vivid he thought they would forever burn themselves into his retinas. An empty city, engulfed in darkness, limbless bodies lay everywhere, and the only light came from street lamps that flickered on and off. The images hinted at what had happened to him, yet his body was too exhausted to remember. As he sat there, catching his breath, he realized that whatever he was running from was getting closer. Instinct was alive within him, filling him with the primal knowledge that if he remained here, it would mean his death; so he ran.

The rain had made it hard to determine exactly which direction he was headed. *FUCK!* His mind twisted with fear and confusion, yet one thought remained clear: survival. More images. The city was covered in a dense fog, and the street lamps now looked like smoldering fires. Looking ahead he could see the faint silhouette of a child in the distance. The image flashed, and he was back in the forest. Moving again, as he proceeded through the forest, the ground grew harder to tread due to the rain and the already decaying leaves and moss-covered dirt. He slipped, and his head burst into flames. It felt as though someone had shot a stiletto of ice into his head, momentarily freezing all conscious thought. Looking up, he cursed the tree he had stumbled onto. While looking at it, the tree's shadow loomed over as though it were mocking him. Rising to his feet, he looked down once again, but this rusty soil of the forest was gone, replaced by the city. Turning to look around, his body froze. Holy Christ, the child was standing right in front of him, the skin of his young body as pale as death and as thin as a corpse. The raw scent of bloated flesh churned in the man's gut. Blood began to run from his eyes, and as they opened, the man stumbled backward in repulsion. The boy's eyes were gone; cavities, empty holes that oozed blood running as thick as oil remained. He screamed and grabbed his face with his hands, ripping at his flesh and peeling it off; the faint sting of bile rose in the man's throat. Please, God, make it stop! The boy screamed, and his neck split open just as the man tripped over a rock and landed on the forest floor. Water dripped from the sky above, and his body shivered from terror. The sounds of his chaser were not far behind. *Get up! Get on your feet, dammit!*

Struggling to his feet, he continued to press on, noticing that not far ahead of him the forest grew amazingly darker and that darkness seemed to call to him, keeping the man locked in its gaze; drawing upon him. Coming to the edge of the darkness, there was a clearing, an open area that went both north and south, with a wide river that ran to the left. The bushes rustled not far behind, and he would soon be dead if he did not act swiftly.

As he ran into the river, the water penetrated his body and brought numbness much faster than the rain ever could have. Voices were whispering throughout the air, tormenting him with their agony. Reaching the middle, he became confused and didn't know what to do, where to go, or which side this hidden tracker was coming from. He slammed his palms to his ears in hopes of shutting out the endless whispers. The man's heart began to race harder and deep down in the bowels of his mind he could feel something growing, something immense; something primal. Looking around, his vision flashed between the city and the forest. He didn't know what was real. How could he when it felt as though his mind was being ripped apart from within? Things began to change. Shadows became lighter, and all colors turned to reddish amber. Shapes began to mold together, and as he looked around, the previous images faded slowly. While witnessing this mirage changing, the realization of it came not moments after—not the world that was changing, but his vision. He looked down at himself and stared in astonishment, as he didn't know whether to be afraid or let this change take its course. *This is insane; why is this happening?!* A change that was both intoxicating and terrifying. There was also something new and small. He almost didn't notice had he not been so aware; something intimate.

The man's body began to lose all color as well, as though an oil painting had been set afloat upon the river. The water began flowing up his legs, covering his entire body. As he watched in wonderment, something within him knew it wasn't the water running up his legs, but his body that was adapting to mirror the water. His pigment began dissolving as his body became more and more translucent. Then, just before his hands faded away, there was a moment he noticed his fingernails had turned as white as ivory, almost perfect. Overwhelmed with fear and rage, he knew he could not control this other half. It was at that moment the man screamed in terror not knowing what was to come. His cries waked the forest, shattering the silence, and the water waked as though a tremor had hit; his attention stolen to the edge of the river.

From the edge of the forest leapt a ragged figure, shrouded in clothing. No real identification was possible. The man's vision flickered; the city strobed in. There was an animal across the street, barely visible through the fog. It tore into a child, ripping his limbs from his torso, and mutilating the body, his little screams fading away into a bubbly gurgle. The boy's faint screams pierced the man's ears as he began to choke on his own blood and bodily fluids. The animal played with that small limp body like a child playing with its food. The sounds of rubbery flesh echoed throughout the air, as the beast stopped its indulgence and looked up at the man; the light reflecting off its eyes like fiery ashes. The man's vision flickered back. The figure hesitated at the edge of the water and knelt beside it, examining it through shaded eyepieces. Although the man could not see those eyes, he knew they were alive with instinct and wisdom.

After a moment, the figure rose to his feet. The man, frozen, thought that surely he was staring at him, standing there in the middle of the river, his transparent body revealing itself. Then, calmly, the figure lifted his hand to meet his face, and the man knew he was communicating with someone. With hearing as concentrated as his eyes, the man could somehow hear this figure's words. He was telling the others that he was dangerously close and knew that he was somewhere near.

Suddenly, the water began running thicker and running darker; blood. As the man looked down, bits and pieces of flesh started floating by, the gurgling sounds of waves tumbling over one another. The smell began to grow unbearable. Then a small dark form started drifting his way, rolling as the waves carried it to him. Just as it drifted beside the man, it slammed into a rock, staring up. Those empty eye sockets wide open. As this rotting face opened its mouth, maggots began oozing out as its skin began peeling off, exposing cheekbones; the stench of rot alive in the man's nose, his tongue swollen with disgust. The head began to smile, crunching its teeth into those maggots. Then another wave hit and carried it off further down the river.

"Holy DAMN . . . fuck no! NO!"

Screaming, the man's foot slipped on the moss-covered stones below the watery surface. Landing in the oily blood, he knew the other figure had noticed; he could sense his sudden alertness. The moments that followed, the man continued to scream beneath the surface of this thick, churning, rotting fluid. The figure took a defensive stance and aimed his gun in the direction the water had seemed to explode all by itself, knowing that he would only need one shot. He was proficient. Whatever lay out there beneath the water could sense it, and he knew it. The man's heart began to beat fiercer, and his fear grew stronger in itself. It gave him strength.

The figure slowly scanned the river's surface. "YOU DON'T HAVE TO WORRY!" His voice was deep and calm. "I'M SURE THEY'LL FORGIVE YOU IF YOU GO BACK! IT WON'T STOP! YOU NEED TREATMENT!"

The man's leap from the water was almost blaring, his body somehow hovering just above the surface. Water began dripping from lifeless air and outlining his body, making him visible for only a moment. Looking across the water that separated the two of them, he gritted his teeth while clenching his fists, lost to this crazed arousal stirring within him. His eyes squinted to an angry blue, burning like fire. Opening his fists, the water shot to life, building a wall of defense and surrounding him. This wall of liquid continued to reach up through the sky, drying up the land of where the river once flowed; the figure at the edge watching as the waterline receded from his feet; his mind absorbing this fleeting moment of awe. As the liquid swayed in front of the man, he could see the distorted figure far on the other side, waiting for his moment. The man began concentrating, a low growl, or rather tone, emitting from his mouth. Every muscle in his body rippled, drawing on the same power that first brought the water to life; his eyes growing brighter. As this tone grew into a hellish scream, the water shot out in a circular motion, waking everything in its path like a chain reaction. The ground looming below his feet suddenly cracked and spider-webbed in an outward motion, spreading across the land and blowing the rocks, brush, and rust-stained leaves along with it. Dust, rotting branches, dead trees, and solid earth—everything blew away with a great force, the man's body being the focal point. In the midst of this subair quake, the air suddenly ignited, creating an explosion that engulfed the two, expanding to the width of the river, but more importantly, having a head-on collision with the stranger. The man could feel the heat tingling his bare skin, singeing the hairs on his body, his mind completely absorbed by something nonearthly; something inhuman.

The air was filled with smoke and debris, enabling him to see no more than a couple yards in any direction. As he sat there, hovering, he suddenly felt a presence, and he knew who it was although he did not want to believe it. As the smoke cleared, the stranger held his ground, his gun locked on the man. The figure was struggling just to stay up, and then he heard him giggle under his breath.

"No! It's not possible ... WHO THE FU—"

"My, my. It seems the unfamiliar has discovered a little part of himself."

At this point, he didn't need to see the stranger's face,

for he could sense his burning grin in his own thoughts. The man froze in fear. This stranger pulled the trigger, and the world seemed to stop. The bullet floated toward the man endlessly, and he, too scared to stray from its path. Then, just as the bullet pressed his neck, images of a bedroom flashed across his eyes. The grin on the stranger's face grew more demeaning. The images streaked through his vision again, only this time they seemed more real. Then the images of the forest faded away like a strobe light, and the man was in a room; his room. Breaking free of his momentary paralysis, the man launched himself off his bed and half collided with a dresser against the side wall. For a moment he caught his breath, and then reached above the dresser to turn on the lamp resting there. As he sat up with his back against the dresser, his body soaking in sweat, his vision slowly returned to normal. All those feelings of fear still fresh in his mind, the taste of the wild still fresh in his mouth. He could remember the brutality of it all, and yet, there remained a small hazy stint of arousal within his mind. It took him a few solid moments to gather himself and realize that this was indeed reality. A dream, a series of dreams that has plagued him for the last several months, bits and pieces of it revealed over time, but the meaning had always eluded him. *That boy, who the . . . why the hell is he always dead?* His stomach began to knot up at the clarity of the lingering dream. Knowing that it wouldn't help to think about it in such a slumberous state he decided it would be best to wait until morning. After taking in a deep breath, he lay back in the bed and closed his eyes.

THE PHOENIX GATE

He slept.

~ ~ ~

Jillian Keashin had always been his best friend for as long as he could remember. He didn't exactly remember how he had met her, only that they've been together forever, or so it seemed. Anything major that they had experienced in their lives had always been together. Now, she had become a beautiful woman, with hair as red as the hottest flame, and eyes that could engulf your vision much like the sun's brightness. She is and has always been there for him, and he, the same for her. But when morning came, she felt obligated to wake him up in the same annoying manner every day. He always appreciated the hot breakfast she would bring over, but he could do without the bombardment of pillows from above while lying there helpless. She would always do this to the point where he would leap out of bed ready to bust out every foul word spoken in the human language. Then she would go into an apologetic, and slightly sexy, state and tell him how sorry she was. And as the sunlight came through the window, grazing her face and reflecting off her hair, everything would suddenly melt away, and he would remember why he would always be there for her. This morning was no exception.

The doorbell rang, and he managed to sound a very faint grunt, almost too silent to notice he had even done it; the door slowly swung open.

A young woman's voice filled the air. "Hey, Alex! You home?" Naturally, it was Jill.

She had let herself in and placed some fresh pastries and hot coffee on the table. The sweet smell of the bakery floated toward the bedroom. As she peered in, she mumbled under her breath, "Alex," in a very sly, dark manner, knowing her intentions and realizing her opportunity. She grabbed a pillow from the couch in the living room, and thus, the morning routine began.

~

As Alex walked into the kitchen, he pulled out a chair and sat at the table. Opening the box of pastries, Jill walked in and sat at the table, opposite of him.

"Why the hell do you have to wake me up in the same damn way every morning?" his voice echoed the morning gruff while sipping his coffee.

"Well, if I didn't, you'd probably think you were getting robbed or something," a playful smile caught the corners of her mouth.

Too tired to remark on her smartness, he simply told her, "I had another dream last night," and gazed up at her slowly. Alex could see in her eyes an expression of interest, though she knew he didn't like to talk about the dreams—rather nightmares. Looking down, he continued. "Nothing's changed much. I still don't know what the hell they're supposed to mean. I'll say this, though, for every day I have one, they seem more and more real. I can close my eyes and see them as clearly as if I were holding a photograph in my hand."

In a low tone that he almost didn't hear, Jill replied,

"What'd you see?" Curiosity had gained the better half of her.

"I don't know," he said looking down upon himself. "I'm always running from this dark-ass figure of a guy. Never know who he is, though." Alex hesitated for a moment. "... Why he is always in such pain."

"Who's in pain?" Jill said, interrupting his thoughts.

He continued as though he didn't hear her, "... always lost. I start to head through the forest, and then come to a clearing," his eyes searching for an answer. "I'm confused . . ." Alex looked up only to notice the puzzled look on Jill's face. "I'm sorry, I know this doesn't make a whole lot of sense to you."

"It's all right, Alex. I may not understand you half the time, but you know I'll always be here for you," she said reassuringly.

He looked at her queerly, but with thankfulness in his gaze. He then got up and left the table to get ready for the rest of the day. "So what's the game plan, Jillatinous?" a nickname he rarely used for her.

Her face momentarily flatlined from emotion, maybe the humor was lost on her. "You know that serum we gave Boon yesterday? Well, it reverberated."

Alex's head snapped out around the bedroom door. "REVERBERATED?!" he said astonished. "Are you sure?" He grabbed a shirt and reentered the living room.

"Yes. After the serum bonded with his cells, it went into repression. It began altering his DNA, but because we didn't know what we were looking for, it went unnoticed." Jill uncrossed her legs from her sitting position on the couch.

As Alex sat in the chair placing his shoes on, he looked up at Jill. Her miniskirt had been pulled tight by the smallest shift of her thighs, and her velvet thong had whispered its presence. "This doesn't make any sense," he said mumbling to himself.

"What's that?"

"Oh, I'm just thinking it doesn't make any sense. The new DNA strand has its own genetic structure. In order for it to bond with Boon's, it would have to reconstruct itself." On that notion, Jill had given him a rather odd look; as though she understood him, just couldn't place where he was headed with it.

"I don't know, Jill, we'll have to look into it."

"Well, then, I also have some other juicy gossip you'd probably like to hear," she added with excitement.

"What the hell this time? Real live sea monkeys lost in that oasis between your legs?" Alex laughed while slipping on the other shoe. *Wish I was one of those damn sea monkeys!*

"Well, look at you, the funny man. Do you remember the incident that occurred yesterday with Guardian Daniel?"

"Yeah, I was wondering what happened with that," he said, his mind recalling yesterday's events in the news.

"Well, this morning, the Council declared him an Unfamiliar." She noticed his eyes had nearly fallen out of his head. "And rather than sentence him to execution, they're going to banish him to the outlands."

Images of last night's dream began to flood his

mind, streaming across his thoughts. The activity of the Unfamiliars had never bothered Alex before. But why do they keep popping up so very often now? His vision of Jill faded to a watery blur, and soon he realized he was in a daze.

"I can't say I've ever really liked Guardian Daniel, but Alex, you know as well as I do there's no chance for him in the outlands. It'll be like throwing a damn rabbit in the wolves' den."

"That does make sense though," he replied as he sat back in the chair, buttoning up his shirt. "If the Council couldn't prove that he's an Unfamiliar and sentence him to death, they just found an alternate route." He finished, bringing Jill back into focus. "But with the extensive research the Council conducts on every Guardian, it's hard to believe an Unfamiliar would slip through; especially when Guardians are selected from birth."

"And the other thing is, what would create such a decision when he's of Aurorian blood? They betray themselves, Alex," she finished as a look of disgust brushed through her eyes.

Watching her for a moment, he jumped up off the chair and grabbed his jacket from the couch. "Come on, Jill, you've got me interested in this reverberation business!"

Grabbing her coat, she followed him toward the door. "You know, Alex, you should wear those pants more often. They really bring out your girlish figure." She laughed slightly as she swayed her hips in Alex's direction.

You ass-bump me one more time like that, Ms.

Gorgeous, and I'll bring out YOUR damn girlish figure!

"Today will be a serious day!" disdain was present in his voice as he pulled the door open, though his mind knew better.

"Oh, you know I'm only playing," she added, her hand making a slight cracking sound as it came across his ass.

~ ~ ~

The year was AGD 948, or After the Great Darkness. Alex's hometown, Norwynn, had been mostly rebuilt, but much of the old-time was still around. The city was not new, but rather built around everything that was left from the Great Darkness; a brilliant testimony to the architectural achievements of man. The parts of the old-time that had not been rebuilt had become the slums. This is where the beggars would stay. The city is so vast; he always wondered how people would have gotten around in the old-time. Supposedly they drove archaic vehicles that had all kinds of mechanical moving parts, and it all worked off of something called gasoline. Now, most people drive speed bikes. They look like motorcycles of the old-time, only instead of using wheels to propel forward, they use super-charged cold fusion power cores. Just yesterday, Alex purchased the new Toriama 900- X: Special Class, naming her Sakura. He could never explain why, only that he's always loved the name. Jill had purchased its sister bike, the Toriama 900- ZS Turbo. There truly was nothing quite like the unbridled freedom you have when you're riding a speed bike. Jill and Alex took off like the wind.

As Mr. Dansforth stepped out of his house to breathe

the morning air, the silence was broken by two oncoming speed bikes. While Jill and Alex flew down the road, the morning air felt refreshing in their faces. Passing Mr. Dansforth's house, Alex waved to him, as he did every morning. He looked up. The sky was remarkably clear. Today was going to be a good day.

Jill and Alex pulled into the parking lot of a building from the old-time that had been restored. It was a rather large building, and from the size of it, looked like some kind of colossal monument. But Jill claimed that in the old-time, buildings such as these were known as skyscrapers. She could be rather strange sometimes, with her fascination of the past, but Alex had grown used to it. Now the building had become a research facility for the Council of Aurora. Jill and Alex had both been there for roughly three years and are accomplished researchers in molecular bonding and DNA sequencing. Their pride and joy was a dog named Boon. He had become a steady project over the past year and a half, although it was the Council that was pushing the project. Through DNA reconstruction, they had actually managed to splice his genes and give him the same intelligence that humans have, though sometimes Alex thought his now old and wise mind possessed an intelligence that surpassed most humans. Oddly enough, however, he never did speak, although Alex wasn't sure if he could. Instead, he communicated through telepathy. Alex was ecstatic when he first found this out. He wasn't sure if it was a side effect of the DNA reconstruction, or if his small mind was truly more evolved than that of humans.

MICHAEL S. VISCHI

Jill and Alex proceeded to walk toward the gate.

"Good morning, Dr. Landari, Dr. Keashin. How are you today?" the guard said in a rather cheerful mood. "Any further progress been made yet?"

"Heh-heh, come on now, John, you know the rules." Alex almost laughed at his repetitiveness of that same question every day.

"Who knows, John, if you keep asking him maybe he'll tell you something someday," Jill said, making her entry into the conversation.

"Well, have a good day," Alex gestured while walking past him, Jill trailing a couple feet behind.

"You too, Dr. Landari." His voice slowly grew louder as they got further away. "I'll just be out here protecting the lab from the evilness of bad guys!" Although a relatively distant scream, that last part just faded away to their ears. John turned around and flashed a quick pose, his hand resting upon his sidearm, "Yeah, who's got this? That's right ... John! John's got this!"

As they approached the double glass doors, Alex placed his hand on the scanner to open the door. A thin blue light began moving in a downward motion scanning his palm, every print, every imperfection that defined the singularity of his hand. As it reached the base of his wrist, the light turned red, and began moving in the opposite direction. Now it was scanning his bone structure and DNA, a dual security measure to provide them with the isolation they need. After the mechanism had finished, a female electronic voice replied, "DNA not specified. Access is denied."

Alex paused for a moment. "Hmm, that's a first."

"Here, Alex, let me try it," Jill said while sliding past him.

The scanner began its job once more. Moments later, the same female voice responded, "Good morning, Jillian Keashin, are you feeling well today?"

"Why, yes, I am Phanisia." Jill turned back with a queer look on her face. "Well, I guess it just needed that touch of womanly love."

Alex looked at her with an expressionless face. "Great, we have the world's first lesbian building on our hands. Now, let's walk through the door and violate her." Jill laughed, knowing she walked right into that.

Alex's remark had brought to mind the women off the continent of Uluria. Although the land was also littered with males, it was the women who remained in the seat of power over there; women who believed they were direct descendants of the goddess. Their size was unmatched the world over, and they would tower any man side by side by at least two additional feet. Still, the idea of Alex diving between the legs of such a behemoth and getting lost to the pleasure of her Amazonian jungle brought a very special smile across his face.

As the doors slid open, they breezed through. The main hall always smelled of wildlife, due to the fact that they let Naomi do the decorating. As they turned to the left, they saw Naomi sitting at the front desk. She glanced up from the computer and noticed the two.

"Oh, good morning, Dr. Landari, Dr. Keashin," Naomi said as she stood up.

"Hey, Naomi, how're we doing this morning?" Alex's eyes glanced around slowly. "Do me a favor, would you. I think Phanisia's having problems with the scanner. You want to have Mr. Vera come down and take a look at her for me." *And holy damn, Naomi, you should wear a blouse that's not as form-fitting tomorrow . . . or any day, for that matter.*

"That's no problem, and here," Naomi handed him two holonote recordings. "Mr. Dellington called. He wants to know if you've made any progress yet. And some woman called, but the recording's a bit visually skewed."

Alex gazed over at Jill. "Ah, well, shall we?" his arm waving toward the elevator down the hallway. As they left the counter, Alex turned back around to face Naomi. "Oh, and, Naomi," she looked back up to him, "do us a favor and back off a little with the wildlife. I feel like I'm getting Ulurian fever."

A smile spread across Naomi's face. "Sure, Dr. Landari, that's no problem."

"Thanks." With a slight nod, he turned back around and continued walking to the elevator.

"You flirt," Jill said while nudging his shoulder.

"What are you talking about?"

"You know what I mean."

As they reached the elevator Alex curled his lips in the silly way that only Jill ever saw. "What can I say? I'm a man animal."

The elevator took them down to the lower levels, to where their lab was, to where the research was. Their newest project was a genetically enhanced DNA strand, donated to them by the Council. Its origin was unknown, but its rarity made them forget all that. After disassembling the strand into its bicomponents, they conducted some more research and found out that they weren't cataloged in their system. Its genetic makeup was so unique that Alex could only guess it was the first of its kind. Initially, they attempted to reproduce the strand, and were unsuccessful. That was when Boon helped them out once again. By injecting a form of the strand into him, the team was able to achieve results. Inside Boon's body, the new strand adapted to its new environment, and began to bond with Boon's DNA, recreating the original strand. This appeared to have no effect on Boon during the first few days of inoculation. Then this morning, Jill had mentioned that the DNA strand had reverberated. But in order for the new strain to resonate, it would have to rewrite its own genetic code. Meaning, it would be conscious.

How the hell could anything be conscious on the damn molecular level? Alex wished that they had known the origin of this DNA, but he had a feeling that the Council would not likely release that information.

Jill and Alex walked into the research lab, placing their jackets on a rack to the left, then headed to where Boon stayed in his cage, passing the main lab, and down the hall into the incubation room. As they drew closer to the door, a voice brushed through Alex's thoughts.

"Good morning, Alex."

As they opened the door, Alex looked around for a moment thinking he was hearing voices, but soon realized it was Boon.

"Boon, how are you doing, old boy?" he had said aloud.

Jill had grazed him a curious look as they knelt down beside his cage. "Alex, you still think you hear that old dog talking to you? I'm beginning to think this research is getting to you."

"Yeah, but it looks like it keeps him happy," he replied, keeping his thoughts to himself. This was pretty damn wild. Why the hell can Jill never pick up on Boon's telepathy? But then, Boon had always told him that he was a special human and that he had a future carved in so many stones, though it would be he who chose which one to first cast. Alex was never quite sure what Boon had meant, but he always managed to keep Alex curious about it; about everything.

Ever since they've begun communicating with Boon, he's told stories of his life, and things that have yet to come; his own prophet of sorts. He also said that this was the way all species of the world communicated; through telepathy. But because humans neglect other species, and consider themselves to be superior, they choose not to hear them. Alex looked at Boon and extended his thoughts out to him.

"Oops, better not let that happen again, eh, old boy?" Alex could sense Boon laughing, and began to grin with him. Jill just sneered at them and told Alex he was crazy. Just then, they heard the door open and saw Brian had arrived.

Brian Viseli. He was a rather social man who always liked to be the center of attention. He's always had a well figured body, at least for as long as Jill and Alex have known him. On his spare time he would play an instrument he has always loved from the old-time, once believed to be called a bass guitar. There were times when Jill and Alex would sit and listen to him play, believing that his instrument was answering the prayers of old. Nonetheless though, he was their biomolecular physicist. He's also the one who engineers their tests and studies the results. Brian actually has this theory that it was a virus, produced by the War of Ruin that caused the first of the Unfamiliars to obtain their abilities. And now that virus has been incorporated into their gene pool. So in the end, mankind evolved himself. Most of the time, though, they just let Brian keep his theories to himself.

As he stepped over to his desk, he looked toward the cages and noticed Jill and Alex. "Oh, Alex, Jill," he paused for a moment. "How are you doing? Actually, I'm glad you're here. I'd like to show you something that happened to a blood sample I took from Boon yesterday," Brian said as he walked past them toward the DNA thermal cycler. "Jill, it happened roughly an hour after you left," Brian continued as he turned around with a sample in his hand.

"So what happened?" Alex wondered, rising to his feet.

"Come on, Alex, I'd rather show you then tell you," Brian said while placing his briefcase on a chair.

The three of them proceeded back down the hall into another room where most of the lab equipment was kept. Brian began walking toward a prepped microscope as Jill and Alex followed him. "As you know, the foreign DNA strain was converting Boon's DNA to resemble its own, right?" They nodded agreeingly. "Well, last night, it altered his genetic code and went into repression," he said while bringing the lens of the microscope into focus. "Here you go, Alex, have a look."

Approaching the microscope, Alex peered down through the lens, carefully examining what was laid out before him. Brian's voice interrupted his thoughts.

"That sample doesn't believe it's in any danger; it still thinks it's alive and well within the original host, Boon. That's why it doesn't even resemble Boon's DNA anymore."

Alex looked up to Brian from the microscope, his voice almost lost to its own curiosity. "So it converted Boon's DNA, in its entirety, to its own?"

"And it doesn't even end there," Brian added with excitement. He walked over to the NASBA Apparatus and pulled a small vial from it. In returning to the other two, he replaced the first sample with a second sample. "Here you go. This is another sample I took, attempting to detect the presence of gene expression levels and the amount of retroviral genomes."

Once again, Alex peered down into the microscope, and what he saw shocked him. "The original DNA strain isn't even present in this sample."

"Oh, it's there," Brian added. "You see, this sample knew it was in danger. So in order to protect itself, it recessed within the original host's genetic makeup. Or more accurately, disguised itself as the original host."

"Did you just say 'knew'?" Jill said, cutting into the conversation. "Are you implying that this shit is conscious?"

Alex looked at Jill with both astonishment and excitement, and then back at Brian. He continued his explanation.

"This is what I think happened. After changing Boon's DNA into its own, the new strand has some kind of defense to hide itself, so it's untraceable. That's why we didn't notice anything before." Brian turned his gaze from Jill. "Alex, the Council denies us any further information on it, right? You know, its origin, where it came from."

"We have the sample, what does that matter?" he replied, not following where Brian was going.

"What does it matter? That's just it; it doesn't matter. This DNA strand could possibly exist in anything that's around us. That sample, the wildlife within the building, any of our projects, maybe even one of us. At the same time, these results show that it's quite possible the Boon we know isn't even really Boon anymore."

For a few moments Alex sat there expressionless, then he looked through the microscope once again. Brian's explanation might be true, but it still didn't describe the possibility on how this DNA could be conscious. This new strand acts like a virus, yet it's more advanced than anything they've ever seen. How in the hell can DNA determine if it's in danger or not?

Just then, Alex felt a serrated pain in the back of his mind. It felt as though a piece of him had just died. As his eyes glazed over with an icy realization, Alex knew it wasn't himself feeling that pain.

"OH, GOD," he erupted, stumbling away from the microscope. "BOON!"

"Alex, what is it? What's wrong?" Jill asked, while trying to steady him.

"IT'S BOON!" Alex roared while prying himself from Jill and running for the door. Jill and Brian quickly followed. As he broke through the lab door, his body flew across the hall and slammed into the wall on the other side, dropping to the ground. It had felt like his stomach just slipped open, his innards poured out like fatty soup. Grabbing his stomach and enduring the pain, he stood back up and continued to run down the hall. As he drew closer to the door of the "Lab Specimens" room, his shoulder suddenly blew open in pain, and he screamed as he grabbed it, falling back to the floor. *Jesus . . . shit! What's happening?!* As he looked at his shoulder, it was ripped open, raw bone exposed to the air. The pain was deadening, and he tried stuffing the muscle back in as he looked up at the door. Standing up, he grabbed the handle with his hand. Looking back down at his shoulder, the wound was gone, and his shirt untouched. Alex's mind began reeling in confusion, pain, and fear.

"Brian, I think something's wrong with Alex," Jill sputtered as they watched him running hysterically down the hall, holding onto his shoulder.

Alex could hear Boon yelping through the door, and as he turned the handle, the door wouldn't open. *Open! Come on, you door fucker, OPEN!* Boon's screams grew more painful and louder. Alex began to slam into the door, but it still wouldn't open. Brian joined him while Jill stood away. Both began to hit the door with all their combined might. Then suddenly, the door just broke open and Brian and Alex tumbled inward. None of them were prepared for the horror sprawled out before them. Jill slowly approached the room and stepped inside, confused by the image before her. Someone or something ripped Boon's body apart, like a small cluster bomb had gone off from within his body. Bits and pieces of his flesh ran down the walls as blood dripped from the bars of the cage. Some of his teeth embedded on the bars where he tried to gnaw himself free. There were all the signs of a struggle—with the exception of an assailant.

"What in God's name could have done this?" Jill squeaked while tears rolled within her eyes. Brian approached her and held her while turning her eyes from the mess. "Don't look at it," he forced out, while holding back the bile within his own throat.

As Alex closed his eyes, visions of Boon trying to escape his cage flooded his mind. He felt an intense pressure arise in his head, and seconds later, felt his eyes slip from their sockets; such a damned horrible way to go. Slowly, Alex opened his eyes again, trying to repress his thoughts and those unwanted visions. Brian had already walked with Jill back over to the entrance to hit the alarm for security and was also trying to reach them over the phone.

". . . I wish I could tell you, Jill," Alex spoke softly as he looked down and noticed Boon's ear next to his shoe. Bending down and placing it in within his hand, tears began rolling in his eyes. Why him? Who would've done such a horrible thing to a dog, to his friend? As Alex closed his eyes, Jill's sobs faded out. He stroked the fur on the back of Boon's ear, and his mind was filled with all the good memories he had of Boon. Alex felt the tears fall through and roll down his cheeks, and he whispered into that blackness, "I'm sorry, Boon."

Alex felt his heart rate pick up a little, and he then opened his eyes. He sat there kneeling on the marble floor and looked up for Brian and Jill, but they weren't there. Instead, they were replaced by large marble pillars and a large open room. He stood up, and stumbled backward. The ceiling was made of a glass mural which loomed at least four floors up. Just then, Alex heard a voice streak across the back of his mind, "... remember."

He whirled his body around in a circle, but noticed no one. Alex then saw two large doors at the far end of the room, and as he stared at them, his thoughts became overwhelmed with fear. *Shit, this is NOT the time for one of these crazy-ass dreams!*

~ ~ ~

He quickly descended the stone steps as he ran through another set of doors leading outward to the street. Alex didn't see any of them, but he knew they were close, he could sense it. He was wearing some ragged clothes and a trench coat. They left imprints in his mind, and he knew they didn't belong to him. He looked around for some sort of familiarity, but all he saw was a sign that represented the building he came from ... Carnegie Hall. What the hell is this place? Alex began walking down the street until he noticed a back alleyway and decided it would be best to stay away from other people.

As he got halfway down the alley, he noticed a wire fence which ran at least 15 feet up. "Damn!" He punched the fence with his hand. Just then, his heartbeat ran out of control. He could feel the presence of one of them.

"TURN AROUND SLOWLY!" a voice echoed from behind.

Alex turned around slowly to face a figure standing at the edge of the alleyway. He could sense the same burning stare that he's always known; could feel his body filling with anger.

"Well, now, it's been awhile, hasn't it?" With his weapon locked on Alex, he pulled the trigger.

"NO!" Alex screamed, and his eyes began radiating an immense white. Then he jumped, and his feet carried him to the top of the fence as though his body had wings. Just as he cleared the fence and landed on the other side, Alex noticed the bottom half of the fence was gone from the blast. He looked in the figure's direction and screamed, bringing everything in the alleyway to life. The old car he passed, garbage cans, tires, even the street trash began to levitate between the figure and Alex. Then, as his hair started blowing backward from this hidden force, he screamed again and everything flew toward the figure, consuming his body and the street in one massive detonation. It felt as if minutes had passed before the smoke finally started fading into flames. Alex stood up but didn't wait to see if the other had survived the explosion. Then he turned and ran down the rest of the alleyway.

Coming toward the end of the alley, he ran around the corner of a building. That's when he stopped dead in his tracks. Standing before him was a face whiter than any ghost and as expressionless as death himself. It'd be impossible to remember a face that deteriorated, but then he opened those empty holes of where his eyes once were. The sockets began filling with maggots, slithering like hungry snakes, rolling around one another as though they were his new eyes. The lips parted with a slight burst of blood as he clenched his teeth and began grinning, his gums leathery and pulled tight. The more he grinned, the more they split open and blood began to run from his mouth. It was then that he whispered . . .

". . . help me."

Alex's mind was racing for a memory of him. Then, within that same brief moment, a name.

Gavin.

* * * *

CHAPTER 2
~ Remembrance ~

"ALEX, HEY, ALEX!"

The voice became clearer and clearer as his eyes fluttered open. A flash of red, the color of skin, trembling lips, and then he found those eyes as the rest of his blurred vision came into focus.

"Where am I . . . Who are you?" Alex's face became uncertain as he jumped off the couch and fell to the floor. He quickly stood up and moved to the other side of the room, ". . . and who the hell is that?" His thoughts were like a maze unknown to him; the confusion of his vision still heavy.

"Alex, relax," Jill said, while standing up slowly. "Something happened to you in the other room, dammit, and you were knocked unconscious. That's when Brian carried you in here."

". . . How the hell do you know my name?!"

His mind started to become clearer, and he began to recall what had happened, but more importantly, the visions he had. Alex's heart began to slow down, and he caught his breath; a small calmness growing within him. He slowly walked back to the couch and placed his hand on the armrest while looking at Brian, both astounded and confused that he knew this man, and at the same time, didn't.

"How long was I out?"

"Alex? You feeling all right now?" Brian asked, as though Alex was not himself.

"Yeah, I'm fine. What exactly happened to me?" he said, using his hand to pivot around the couch and take a seat.

"Well, you bent down to pick something up, and a few moments later, you froze. Your eyes were racing back and forth and they looked . . ." Brian paused for a moment to look at Jill, and then back at Alex, "they looked as though you were someplace else. That's when they started . . . glowing white—"

"White?!" Alex sat up, cutting him off. "What the hell does that even mean?"

"As if they were lights or something. Anyway, I tried shaking you out of it, but I couldn't even budge you." Brian turned his attention to Jill. "Then Jill knelt down in front of you and tried snapping you out of it." Brian's gaze returned to Alex. "But it didn't work. Then, you just suddenly took off, as if you were hit by something—big! Alex," Brian's voice dropped a tone, "at any point, did you come in direct contact with that strand?"

Alex sat there, wiping his face with his hands, not sure of what to make of any of this. *What kind of garbage is this?*

The three of them were there all the time; any one of them would've known if he ever came in direct contact!

"Do you remember anything that happened?" Jill asked him.

Alex turned slowly to look at Jill, his facial expression remaining confused. Then he raised his eyes to meet hers. ". . . Another dream." Those were the only two words he had to say to her.

"You had another dream like the ones before?"

"It wasn't like that, though. I was running from someone or something, but," he paused, "it was like I was in another world. But it has never felt this real before!"

"Alex, maybe you should elaborate on that." Brian's interest was practically tangible within the room.

Alex turned to look at him. "Have you ever had a dream that you were sure was so real, that you couldn't determine reality from fantasy? When I was there, I felt so much more different, I felt powerful." His recent memories blew through his eyes like a breath of wind.

"Powerful?" Jill almost giggled, slightly confused.

". . . Yeah. I felt so alive; it was like I understood everything. Like I was a part of everything and everything was a part of me; one crazy hell of a feeling. But, you know how you can tell when you're having a dream?"

"Yeah," the other two replied in unison.

"Well," he diverted his attention to Jill, "I'm telling you, this wasn't a dream." He looked back at Brian. "It felt just as real as the three of us sitting here now."

"Alex, I don't like the idea that you're starting to have these dreams while you're awake," Jill said with concern.

"Well, then, what—"

"—do I think it means?" Alex said, cutting Brian off. "... Hmm!"

"I really don't know, just that I was there, once."

His head began to suddenly hurt, and he reached up to hold it with his hands; his breath becoming heavier, as though a weight had suddenly been pressed upon it.

"Alex, what is it? What's wrong?" Jill was immediately beside him, her hand falling to his shoulder.

"It feels as though there's someone else in my head," he told her, the pain worsening. A sound echoed through his mind. No, not a sound; a voice.

"Alex, the DNA! Were you ever in contact with it?" Brian winced.

"What? No! The fuck is wrong with you?" Such pain. "Who ... is ... it, who's there?" Alex yelled while standing up.

Jill stood up and tried holding him, hoping for Alex to sit back down.

"AAAHHHHH, GET AWAY FROM ME!" he screamed at her. Alex stumbled across the floor, tripping over a table no higher than his shin. The strange echo grew more intense, and he finally began to understand it. His head felt like a raging bonfire that had grown out of control, stumbling even further across the floor. He dropped to his knees and looked up into the lifeless air, his hands gripping the sides of his head.

"WHAT DO YOU WANT FROM ME?" Alex's screams were loud, almost deafening; almost impossibly human. "WHAT DO YOU MEAN WAKE UP?" The pain grew stronger. "AM I STILL SLEEPING, AM I DREAMING?" He screamed with confusion as his fist splintered the floorboards in his increasing rage and this intoxicating fear. Images of his dreams began grazing his mind like a broken strobe light.

"AAAHHHHH, I DON'T KNOW!"

Jill glanced at Brian for a moment, and Brian returned that same glance.

"Relax, Alex, don't fight it with your mind. Let your body remember for you. Let your body remember who it was," the voice told him. He sounded so familiar, yet Alex knew not who he was. *"You have something of mine, and I'm sorry, but it's time to give it back."*

"WHO ARE YOU?" he asked, his body slouching involuntarily over his hands.

"ALEX!" Jill yelled in her own growing confusion and helplessness.

"Jill!" Brian said, while holding her. "Let it happen. There's nothing we can do for him now."

"Brian!" Jill cried, turning to look at his face. "They never said anything about it hurting him this much!"

"I know, I know! It's not Evrikh causing this, it's Alex. Damn it, I told them it's been too long." Brian said, upset at this event unraveling within Alex. "Ultimately, we must maintain our façade until we are confronted by Evrikh."

At that moment, Alex opened his mind and very quickly realized who the voice belonged to: himself.

No longer a whisper within his mind, *"Please, Alex, return to me."*

Knowing that he could not fend off this hidden persona, he made the only decision he could. So Alex placed all of his defenses aside and surrendered to it, relaxing and taking deep breaths, placing his hands on his legs. As he inhaled and exhaled, his body began growing hotter, but it was a soothing heat. Images began pouring through his mind, filling it with knowledge, filling it with memories. His hair started to flow in an upward manner, and his clothes swayed as though there was a breeze.

"The hell's happening to him?" Jill said, her grip on Brian loosening.

Brian's eyes glinted with understanding. "He's beginning to remember."

Alex's aura slowly began to glow white, his body imitating some kind of generator. The wind grew stronger, and he left the ground, floating upward like an angel, his body limp of all tension. The reality around the three of them began to bend and shift, somehow tangible electrical energy started manifesting itself all throughout the room, passing in and out of their reality. Alex's aura began glowing brighter as the energy passed around him; through him.

"That's it, Alex, you can do this," Brian mumbled under his breath.

At that moment, a heat wave shot out from his body in all directions. The light started glowing so brilliantly that Brian and Jill had to divert their eyes, as it escaped out the lab, blotting out all the security cameras of the lower levels. Then the distortion followed in the same manner, waking everything in its path. The building structure began to tremble as the air was filled with the faint sounds of vibrating glass.

~

John slowly looked around as he felt the slight vibrations from the ground below. Alarms sounded throughout the area as speed bikes toppled over in the parking lot. *Must be a freakin' earthquake*, he thought to himself.

~

"LOOK OUT!" Brian yelled, pulling Jill under him. As the force hit the two of them, they were ripped from their position and thrown into the other room. Moments later, the room flashed and the light was gone; only dense smoke and dust remained.

The entire lab remained silent for more than a few moments. A broken desk slowly slid across the floor as Brian climbed out from under it. Standing up, his eyes scanned the room for Jill. When he didn't see her, he glanced over his body to assess his own injuries. Hearing movement not too far from him, his eyes followed, and Brian saw Jill pulling herself from under some loose equipment and broken glass.

"You all right?" he asked, stepping over to her.

"I think so," Jill said, dusting herself from the broken glass. "What about him?" Her eyes turned to the other room as Brian's followed.

They both looked into the other room. As the smoke thinned, they could faintly see the outline of where Alex's body lay on the ground. Immediately, Jill started to find her way back into the other room. As she climbed over the broken furniture and scattered lab equipment, Brian quickly followed. Just as they entered the other room, Jill halted her approach; Brian only steps behind her.

"He's not . . ."

"This doesn't make any sense. It wasn't supposed to . . ."

As the smoke finally cleared the room, Alex managed to slide his arm up beside his head. Exhaling painfully as he put his weight on his arm, he lifted himself from the ground. He sat up and placed his other hand on the side of his head, groaning from the pain that can only be described as a migraine. He finally applied the rest of his weight to his legs and stood up, swaying a little. Slowly, Alex turned to face Brian and Jill's direction. For a few moments, the room remained silent, their eyes lingering on one another. As Alex looked at them, he realized that this was not the truth. Instead, there was a deeper truth that was never explained to him, or possibly kept from him. His vision suddenly flashed to what could only be described as a strange kind of darkened infrared; their heartbeats, their heat signature . . . He knew they posed no threat.

"Alex?" Brian asked questionably.

Slowly turning in his direction, he replied, "It's all right, Brian. We are once again reunited. I'm no longer Alex Landari, though he is a part of me, and I, a part of him. How strange is it, to be curious and confused within

THE PHOENIX GATE

the same moment," he finished with a grin.

Jill stepped away from Brian and slowly began approaching Alex. Their eyes became locked with each other's.

"Evrikh," Jill paused for a moment, "is that you?" she asked as she ran her fingers through his now-silver hair, her face lingering only inches away.

"Jillian Keashin," Evrikh said while bringing his hand up to her face, using his fingers to place her fiery red hair behind her ear. "Alex thinks so very highly of you. His strongest memories are of you."

"Is he still . . . there . . . somewhere?" Jill asked, slowly scanning his body, searching his eyes for that unspoken answer.

"Yes, Jill, I am. Evrikh and I are one and the same," he said, placing his hands on her cheeks. "We are each other. It's not like I forgot who I was. It's more like remembering the rest of who I am."

"It looked like it hurt like hell. If I knew it was gonna be like that, hell, I wouldn't have let it happen."

He could feel the sympathy radiating from her, almost like a scent. "You would have, as there is nothing you could've done. It's all right, Jillatinous," he said, smiling at her. "What's done is done. But thanks for worrying."

"Sorry to cut in like this, but, Evrikh, you should know we can't stay here," Brian suggested from behind Jill.

"I'm actually amazed security hasn't arrived yet," Jill added.

"Ever since exposing us to that new strain, the response strategy has changed slightly," Brian added, surveying the room. "I don't suggest we stick around to find out what exactly those changes are."

"Before that, Brian, maybe you should clue me in on what the hell's going on first."

"I'll tell you what, take the day to recuperate, and then meet me at The Sunrise tonight at about 9:30. I'll tell you everything." Brian turned his attention to Jill. "You wanna take care of him until then?"

"Sure thing, Brian. Come on, big guy, grab your coat. I'll take you home," Jill said with a motherly expression on her face.

"Brian, what of . . . Thea?" Evrikh asked, momentarily lost to the confusion of his own mind.

"Tonight, Evrikh, I'll tell you everything," he finished with a questionable look on his face.

When Jill and Evrikh stepped into the elevator, Brian immediately grabbed a cart on its side that was home to a dozen glass vials and slid it back to the center of the room. Quickly he continued to kick and push all the other rubbish around the cart. Running back over by the phone and security call button, Brian finally grabbed a chair, flipping it right side up, and took a seat.

"Security should be here soon enough," he exhaled crudely.

Just then, Brian was interrupted by other thoughts in his head, a voice. "I know, I know," he replied, "I know what you mean. For a moment there I couldn't feel her presence either." Slowly his eyes looked around the now-chaotic room. "Who knows, maybe this will turn out to be just as much of a mystery to us as it is to him."

The doors ripped open and a handful of uniformed guards flooded in and around the debris. Brian slouched in his chair, breathing heavily, as he continued his mental game of chess and the explanation that would ensue to explain what lay before them all.

~ ~ ~

As Jill and Evrikh reached the upper levels, they stepped out of the elevator and began walking through the lobby.

The clerk at the desk looked up. "Dr. Landari, are you feeling all right?" she asked, concerned about his appearance. Jill's arms around him as if she were holding him up.

His head remained bent over as his eyes kept their path on the ground. Jill moved one of her hands on his shoulders. "Oh, he's fine, Naomi, just feeling a little under the weather."

"Is there anything we can do for him? Call or make arrangements?" Naomi asked delicately.

"No, but thanks. I'm just gonna run him home and keep an eye on him for a bit. We'll be back tomorrow," Jill replied, helping Evrikh to the door, ". . . so you can keep your damn eyes off him," she finished, practically in a mute tone.

"OK, well, good night, Dr. Landari. I hope you feel better." Naomi returned to her desk to continued handling additional measures for the security alert that had been called.

"Come on now, Jill, Naomi's the best receptionist we've ever worked with. You should cut her a little more slack," he managed with only a small laugh.

Evrikh went to place his hand on the scanner when Jill grabbed his wrist and stopped him.

"Whoa, maybe you should let me do this." She placed her hand on the scanner. Moments later the doors began to slide open. Jill walked beside him through the doorway while whispering, "The last thing we need right now is security asking a bunch of questions on top of the incident I'm sure they're looking into at this moment. Besides, hanging around here any longer will probably give way to Naomi showing you just how much tighter that shirt of hers can get."

Phanisia's voice interrupted Jill's. "Good night, Dr. Keashin. We'll see you tomorrow."

"Good night, Phanisia," Jill replied.

They walked outside to see that John had been replaced by the night watch, Aidan. They then proceeded to walk toward the gate that would let them into the parking lot.

"Hey, Alex, Jill, how're y'all this evening?" Aidan asked with a cheerful voice.

"Hey, Aidan, how're you doing?" Jill replied. "You mind letting us through? Alex and I are going home a little early tonight."

"No problem, Doc, just give me a sec." Aidan cooperated and walked inside the booth, opening the gate for them. Waving from inside, he said, "Have a good night."

Jill turned in his direction with a smile on her face. "You too, Aidan." Evrikh continued walking toward his bike, Jill beside him. As he reached his bike, he grabbed the helmet locked on the side. "You know, Jill, I still don't know what's going on."

Jill looked up at him from her bike. "Don't worry, Evrikh. Brian'll explain everything later tonight," she said reassuringly. "For now, let's go back to my place. It'll probably be safer."

Safer? What the hell could she possibly mean by that?

The bikes started up like the wind. Jill looked at Evrikh from her straddling position upon her bike.

"Come on, Evrikh, everything'll be revealed to you when the time comes. For now, I'll explain what I can when we reach my place. Let's go." She punched her quarter winder and her engine kicked on, carrying her away like a bullet. Evrikh punched his quarter winder and quickly followed.

"There has GOT to be some law that states doctors like Dr. Keashin, with an ass like that, are illegal!" Aidan said aloud to himself from within the booth as he watched the two bikes blur themselves into the streets.

They left the aurora sanction through the side roads and ventured into the slums; buildings of the old-time flashed by in a haze. There were fights between beggars, people sleeping in the streets, a woman being raped by a gang of men in some alley. But no one notices because no one cares. Evrikh sped up to pull alongside Jill.

"HEY," he yelled, looking at her, "HAS IT ALWAYS BEEN THIS BAD?" he continued, the wind cutting down his volume.

Jill began yelling back, "IN THE SLUMS, YEAH."

"HOW COME I DON'T EVER REMEMBER IT

BEING THIS BAD?"

"BECAUSE," she looked back at him, "THOSE ARE EVRIKH'S MEMORIES."

A man being brutally beaten by another one with a pipe . . . old cars crashed in buildings . . . and those same buildings crumbling apart from decay.

"LET'S GO, EVRIKH!" Jill yelled speeding ahead. They kicked on their static chargers and headed for Jill's apartment.

~ ~ ~

The doorknob turned as the traditional click unlocked it; the hinges crackling as the door swung wide. Jill reached her hand out to the left and flicked on a switch. Moments later, the apartment flooded with lights.

"I'm sorry about the mess, but I haven't exactly had the time to clean up," Jill said, while throwing her jacket onto a chair on her way through the living room. "Evrikh, just make yourself at home. I have to use the bathroom." Her voice faded off as she walked into the other room.

Evrikh walked into the living room and took a few moments to look around. There were crumpled up pieces of paper lying on the floor, old take-out boxes left on the table, and there was laundry lying everywhere. This was a little bit of a surprise, as he's always known Jill to be well kept. This was definitely a side of her he's never seen. Even stranger was that Evrikh had no memories of her, for someone he remembered knowing for so long. He decided to take a seat on her worn-out, rather comfortable-looking couch. Out of the corner of his eye he noticed a satin bra, lavender; it was transparent by light. Below that, a cotton thong. "What the hell is this?" he asked himself as he picked them up with his fingers.

"Maybe you should hire a maid," he mumbled, while placing them on the ground.

He heard a door open in another room. Moments later, Jill came back into the living room. She was wearing a short sleeved belly shirt and a navy blue thong. The shirt was glued to her breasts like a glove; her nipples, hard dimes pressed against the cloth.

"Damn, Jill!" he said, diverting his eyes to the ground.

"Oh, it's whatever," Jill replied while slightly laughing entering the room. Her breasts absorbed the shock of her footsteps, bouncing proportionately with her movement. She walked over to a chair in a corner on the other side of the room and leaned over it. As she rummaged through whatever it was that was back there, one of her legs came up in the air and her thong shifted with the additional movement of her thighs.

"You know, Jill, that's a bit revealing," he told her as he looked back down to the ground, "even for you."

"Evrikh, have you seen a pair . . ." She paused.

Undeniably gorgeous breasts? How could I not?!

". . . Aha, a pair of leather pants." She pulled them out from behind the chair and shook them out.

"Here we go," she said, as she started to slide them on. The pants glided over her legs very smoothly. They seemed to hug her body with a passion, and as she pulled them up to her waist, they defined her every curve.

"There, that's much better," she said, while sitting

down to put on some jet-black steel toe boots. While tying the laces, she looked back up at Evrikh. "So," his eyes finally found hers, as he managed to tear them away from this impossibly alluring vision, "where would you like to start?" she asked.

"Well," he took a deep breath, "how about my age. How old am I?"

Jill sat back and crossed her legs. "Well, let's see. I can't really tell you, because I'm not sure. But I can tell you that I was assigned when you began your research at the aurora sanction."

Evrikh looked at her disbelievingly. "Assigned to me? I have memories of you for as long as I can remember."

She continued, "There's a reason for that, at some other time, Alex. There was talk that the Council was conducting an undercover investigation, and that their work was leading them dangerously close to you."

A small smile etched itself onto his face.

"What's up with that?" she asked while crossing her arms.

"You still think of me as Alex, huh?" His smirk remained in place. "It's ok, Jill, I'm sure on some level I'll never really get used to this either."

Jill's eyes fell down upon herself. Had she called him Alex just then? Had she lost him, or was the man sitting in front of her truly the two of them at the same time? If Evrikh remembers everything, will Alex be forgotten?

"Why's the Council looking for me?" he asked in hopes of regaining her attention.

"Well, from what I understand, a man known as the

Elder concealed you a very long time ago, as a means of protection. I was assigned to you as a bodyguard, so to speak, to guarantee your safety."

Or to reassure my attraction to women, maybe?

His vision flashed again, uncontrollably, to that strange amber, and for a moment he felt an unusual kind of tension, almost threatened.

"So," he wiped his face with his hand as he sat back in the couch, "you're telling me that both this Elder and the Council are after me."

Jill leaned forward in her chair. "I'm telling you that the Elder must think you're pretty damn important."

How the hell is this all even possible? "So, who was Evrikh before he became me?"

"Sorry, honey, but you have to look to yourself for that answer," Jill replied.

"I've tried." Confusion endangered his mask of calm. "And . . . ?"

"I know who I am, but I can't remember where I came from or how I got here. I can't remember the past. The only memories I have left are of Alex's life. Now that I think about it, I don't have any memories before I began my research." He looked right into Jill's eyes. "I don't even remember how I met you." His voice grew steadily quiet as his gaze returned to the ground.

Jill sat back in her chair again. "You don't remember anything about your life before Alex?"

"I'm sorry but—"

Jill's attention became diverted, and she raised a hand to motion Evrikh silent. "Shh," she whispered. "Do you hear something?" Her lips moved, yet they produced no sound, but he could hear her in his mind. He sent a thought back to her and told her yes. She quickly looked at him and appeared to be surprised. Just then, the front door blew open and pieces of wood and metal soared past their heads. Smoke came bellowing in continuously.

"SHIT, THEY FOUND US!" Jill screamed.

"Who?" He looked at her confused. Evrikh could sense a growing hostility in her. Jill reached through the smoke and grabbed his arm.

"THE RELICS!"

She began dragging him through the apartment. Evrikh turned around to see red beams sweeping across the room. He could see figures, but not well enough to make a description. The two of them reached the bedroom and Jill released him as she eased the door closed and locked it. Her attention turned to him as she whispered, "Not a word now!"

She crossed the room to the window and looked out. They were on the seventeenth floor, and there was no way to get down out there. Jill quickly turned her attention back to the door as the handle began to shake. Slowly, smoke started creeping through the cracks of the door. It was then that the handle stopped moving. Seconds later, the bedroom door blew open, and one of the figures stepped in, his weapon shooting everything in his line of sight. Just as the barrel of his gun flashed white, the world around Evrikh suddenly transitioned into slow motion. He watched as the bullets dragged their way through the air, heading in Jill's direction. Stepping toward her, he blinked reality back up to speed, and then suddenly they caught Jill, grazing her leg and shoulder. That small impact alone was enough to knock her to the ground.

Dropping to the ground beside her, Evrikh looked back at the figure, his body filled with rage, and his eyes were radiating with light.

"NO!"

Moments later, reality bent all around them, surrounding the two in a transparent bubble. The figure was soon joined by another. Both of them were mere shadows, hidden by the radiating light of their weapons. He could hear the bullets whizzing by, but none could penetrate the odd, distorted bubble that now surrounded them. How the hell was any of this even possible? Was it all even really happening? As his anger grew stronger, his eyes grew brighter. Grinding his teeth, all the bullets froze in midair, and as he concentrated harder, everything in the room began shaking. The figures started looking around, and Evrikh began to feel their fear. He could somehow sense it, began seeing it.

"AAAHHHHHH!" He screamed again, and all the contents of the room flew with his voice toward the figures. The two figures were blown into the other room as the wave carried them hurtling through the air. All the furniture began slamming into the wall of where the door once stood, mashing together to create a blockade. He looked down at Jill. She was confused, and she was also in pain. Evrikh bent down and picked her up, moving over to the now shattered window. His body's aura shifted colors to a bright blue, and he looked down at Jill.

"Don't be afraid, Jill. Hold on."

Jill placed her arms around his neck. "Evrikh, if we make it through this, remind me to kick your—"

He jumped, cutting her off just as another Relic broke through the barricade. As bullets ripped through the air, his body became a fiery blaze of blue, and like a beam of hot light, their bodies shot toward the ground. That's when Jill started screaming.

~

As a child was walking down the street with her mother, she looked up into the night sky, marveling at the stars that loomed so far away. Seconds later, a high-pitched noise caught her attention, and she noticed a blue streak that rushed toward the ground. Grabbing ahold of her mother's pant leg, she looked up to her. "Mommy, what is that?" she asked as she pointed in the direction of the beam of light.

As the mother looked across the sky, she placed her hand on the back of her daughter's head. "Oh, that looked like a shooting star, Monica. And," she knelt down beside her daughter, "they say that every time you see one, you're supposed to make a wish."

While Monica walked with her mother, her eyes remained fixated of the fading streak of blue that had been left behind. "That's so cool! Mommy?"

"Yeah, sweetie," she replied, memorizing this moment of her daughter against the background of a radiant blue shooting star.

"Can I wish for Daddy to come home from the navy?"

Her smile was as beautiful as that now-fading star.

"Sweetheart," she began, pulling Monica between her legs with her arm around her shoulder, "you and I are going to make that wish together; right now."

~

Just as Jill and Evrikh reached the ground, the blue light that surround them expanded outward, flashing down the street for only a moment. Seconds later, the remaining light dissipated and the two had landed safely on the ground. Jill stopped screaming as Evrikh set her down. She looked around nervously, and then her head snapped back at Evrikh.

"WHAT THE HELL WAS THAT?" she yelled, raising her hand to slap his face.

Just then, the ground started exploding everywhere, and he knew these Relics were just shooting blindly toward the ground from the window they had leapt out of. He grabbed Jill by the arm and ducked into the alley behind the building. They stood against the wall of Jill's apartment building. She looked up at him while still catching her breath from their recent descent to the street.

"Leap out of a building? Leap out of the seventeenth floor of a damn building?! What the fuck are we gonna do now?" She bit back her temper.

Evrikh turned around and placed his hand on the wall, turning his attention to Jill. "I want you to run."

"Evrikh, I'm not leaving you!" she retaliated.

His expression took on a level of seriousness she had never seen in him before.

"Jill, you have to trust me. I'm not sure what's happening to me, but I know I have to handle this on my own. I'll meet you and Brian as planned. But you have to go." his voice hardened. "Now!"

Tears began to fill Jill's eyes, and as they did, he watched as the closest parts of her aura began radiating a faint greenish blue. She was surrounded by so much red, so much anger, but now, beneath it all, there was something more. Something that was speaking to him in a way he was just beginning to understand. She was afraid of losing him.

"I'll be there, I promise. Now go, and don't look back."

She darted out from under his arm. Evrikh stood with his hand to the wall, looking down to where her feet were standing only moments ago.

She turned and ran off, crying, the image of her fading into the night as Evrikh closed his eyes.

I'm not sure who the hell you punks think you are up there. One thing's for DAMN sure—someone's walking away from all this . . . and here's a hint . . . It's not you.

Intense heat started radiating from his body, his aura visibly glowing as if it were on fire. His hand slowly started sinking inward as the heat alone was causing the wall to burn and melt away.

Jill had reached the end of the alley and turned around for one last look before she left. That was when all the windows on the top floor of the building blew out in flames, filling the air with the shattering of crystal shrapnel. If you didn't know any better, the falling glass could almost be mistaken as rain. Soon after, each floor followed in the same manner. The air around the building had been filled with the reflection of orange flame off the tiny pieces of glass, falling slowly. The alleyway had been set ablaze as Evrikh remained at the focal point looking back at Jill. Pieces of brick and stone soared across the sky as the tears in Jill's eyes flowed uncontrollably, then she turned back to face the street.

We'll meet as planned, Jill thought to herself, wiping the tears from her face.

She ran.

* * * *

CHAPTER 3
~ Who Am I? ~

THE SUNRISE. IT was a place for people of all sorts. Women danced on translucent platforms that hung from the ceiling while an Apox echoed music from the back. The bar was crowded with people eager to drink, and waitresses walked around helping those who needed one. A waitress walked by a drunken man who stood up beside her while slipping his hand up her skirt. As he rubbed his hand between her thighs, he licked her face and whispered into her ear, "Hey, babe, youz wanna go upshtairs?" the alcohol thick on his breath.

Repulsed by the man, she yelled out a name. "HEY, RESHARD!"

Seconds later, a rather large man stepped over to the drunken one. "Come on, buddy, let me give you a hand." His voice was deep and almost charming. He dragged the drunken man over to the door, and as it opened, the man stumbled out only to fall on the walkway and knock himself half conscious.

The bouncer walked back inside while closing the door behind him. "You'd think the regulars would be the first to learn."

The second floor consisted of the private rooms. Anything could be conducted there; business deals, women, and other things that can only be concluded within these walls of privacy. The second floor was a safe haven for the underground network. On the first floor, in a booth toward the back, sat a man drinking a Tribulin Mixer. Brian.

The door busted open and Jill walked inside, wiping her face. She looked around for a moment before noticing Brian in the back. As she began walking toward him, a commoner from the slums reached out and grabbed her arm.

"Hold on a shec, baby," he said as she turned around to face him. "Youz wanna go upshtairs and talk with our privates . . . I mean . . . in privates?" His words were slurred as he stumbled his way out of the chair.

A grin spread across Jill's face as her eyes squinted to an intense yellow. "Sir, drop your damn arm, or in another five seconds it'll be *my* arm." She spoke in an almost devilish tone.

The man removed his arm, stumbling backward, and returned to the bar. "Youz damn freak! Why dont'cha go back to where youz came from!"

Jill turned her attention back to Brian and continued to walk toward him as she passed Reshard who was now apparently helping the drunken man back outside once again.

"What the hell happened to you?" Brian asked as Jill sat down opposite of him.

Jill leaned forward across the table. "They know."

"A bit cryptic, Jill, what do you mean they know?" Brian looked around for a moment. "How the hell could they have already found out?" he asked, upset.

For a moment Jill was surprised and almost mentally stunned, as this was the first time she had ever seen Brian close to the brink of being upset, let alone if this even was his brink.

"I took Evrikh back to my place, and we were attacked by Relics. I'm positive they were there waiting for us. How the hell did they get there before us, Brian? The hell did they even know we were headed there, for fuck's sake?" Accusation slowly rose in her voice.

"There's a chance they could've been hunters," he added, hoping it was true.

"No," Jill replied, "they were Relics, and somehow, they knew we were going be there; which means they knew about Evrikh."

"Where's he now?" Brian asked while sitting back.

"I'm not sure," Jill said while looking down at her hands. "We were separated." She mumbled under her breath, "I'm not even sure he's still alive."

Brian crossed his arms. "So, when were you going to tell him your real name?"

Jill looked up at Brian. "I never made it that far. Besides, we got bigger problems than that."

"Which would be . . . ?"

"Brian, Evrikh doesn't remember anything before he

became Alex. He doesn't even remember how he became Alex."

"I guess this does pose a problem," Brian said, looking toward the wall behind Jill.

The door opened again, and Jill and Brian both turned to see a man walk through. His shirt was stained brown from intense heat, and the sleeves were missing. His pants were jeans without bottoms, and holes throughout what was left. His feet bore no shoes, and it almost looked as though he had chosen to roll around in muddy water just prior to walking through the door. He scanned the room with his eyes, only to stop when they reached Brian and Jill.

"Fuck me," Jill said while standing up.

Brian concentrated his stare a little harder. "... Is that ..." he paused.

"Evrikh," Jill said, cutting him off. "Sure is!" she continued with a smile spreading across her face.

Evrikh approached the table as his bare feet left muddy little footprints along the floor. Even though the music continued, all other commotion had stopped at the sight of this apparent homeless, dirty man, walking straight through the club as if he owned the place.

"Jesus, Evrikh, you all right?" Brian asked.

"I'd like a damn shower. I don't care how much people say that rain's refreshing, it really doesn't clean you all that well." His attention turned to Jill. "I told you I'd be here." There it was; that damn smirk reserved only for her.

His mind eased up somehow as a reflection of the tenseness from within her. Crazy, but damn, he was catching on to this whole radiant vision, or empathy trick, rather fast. Her mind was finally at ease, and a new kind of warmth began spreading throughout her body, invading his senses. Seemed there's still a ways to go before he'd have complete control over it. Evrikh looked into her eyes, reversing his unusual ability, and pushed his own thoughts into hers. She could sense his presence floating around in her mind and moments later, shared his comfort of seeing her.

"Evrikh," Brian interrupted, "please have a seat," he said while extending his arm to the opposite side of the booth.

Jill sat down and scooted in while Evrikh sat down beside her; he looked at Brian. "So . . ."

A little girl came running toward the booth. She appeared to be about eight years old. Evrikh whirled around in the booth, his hand slamming down on top of the table as Jill quickly grabbed him by the wrist.

"Daddy!" the girl yelled in joy while jumping into Brian's arms.

Brian chuckled while holding her. "Emilia, sweetheart."

Hearing Jill, Evrikh stood down as he quickly looked back at her, and then across the table to Brian and the little girl now in his lap. Jill was rubbing her hand after nearly getting burnt from Evrikh's wrist. As the three of them looked down at his hand, it was slowly sinking through the table as his hand almost appeared like molten lava. While realizing the girl was no threat, the heat quickly left his hand as the skin color returned, and Evrikh removed his hand from the table, the impression left behind cooling swiftly.

"Emilia?" Evrikh asked, while rubbing his now seemingly normal hand.

Brian glanced toward him. "My daughter."

"YOUR DAUGHTER?!" The words were more blurted out than actually spoken.

"Come on now, Emilia," Brian said while setting her down, "run along and play." His eyes glanced up at the man that had accompanied her. "Marcus, she's not to venture outside the club."

"OK, Daddy," she replied in a cheerful voice. "Bye, Daddy, bye, Keona, bye, Evrikh," she said while turning to run off.

Evrikh looked at Brian, ". . . When the hell did you have a daughter?"

While watching her run along, Brian replied, "Evrikh, my friend, there are many things you don't know." He then sat back and turned to face the other two once again.

Evrikh's mind was shrouded in a blanket of confusion. "Damn, Brian, you have a daughter . . ." A moment later his mind finally wrapped itself around that notion. "You have a daughter, and who's Marcus? And who the hell is Keona?" His mind demanded answers.

Brian looked at Jill and took a deep breath, his eyes returning after only a few moments. "Evrikh," his voice was calm and steady, "I am not the Brian you think you've been working with all this time." He looked at Jill once again, and then back to Evrikh. "My name is indeed Brian Viseli, yet I am more of a messenger than your coworker. I was assigned to you when you began your research at the aurora sanction. The Elder thought it would be the best opportunity for our lives to intertwine."

"... Why go through all this trouble?"

"Only the Elder can tell you that. I'm sorry," Brian replied.

Evrikh turned his attention to Jill. She began to speak, but he cut her off. "So," staring at her for a moment, he said, "you must be Keona." A hint of betrayal echoed from his mouth. "When the hell were you gonna tell me?"

"Evrikh, I wanted to, dammit, but," she paused, "I wouldn't have been able to until a time like this." Her eyes fell upon herself. "Shit ... I'm so sorry."

He turned to look at Brian, attempting to restrain his inner anger. "Is my whole damn life made of lies? Can you tell me that?"

Brian's words resonated the sorrow he felt. "I'm sorry, Evrikh, but what was done had to be. There was no other way. And there was no way we could let the Council have you. The Elder did the only thing he could."

"I see." The increasing taste of betrayal teasing his mouth, "And no one bothered to ask me."

"Evrikh, it was for your own safety."

"I don't care about my damn safety. It's always been MY life, right? You all had no right! All the memories of my fuckin' life belong to a person who should've never been ... Someone who, as of just a few hours ago, doesn't even exist anymore." His head began to pulse with pain; he closed his eyes for a moment to endure it.

Keona reached up with her hand and turned his face to hers. "Evrikh ..." As he opened his eyes, he noticed hers were glistened with tears. "Not all of it was lies."

He grabbed her wrist and pulled her hand away from his face. "Why? Because your ass loved Alex so much—?"

"YES, I DID, DAMMIT!" Keona replied, cutting him off. Her face was hard with passion, a few tears rolling down her face now made of stone. "Maybe I didn't know you before, Alex, but that doesn't change the fact that we shared something. Feelings I know you still have inside you."

"Evrikh," he turned to look at Brian, "it was *you* who agreed to be sealed away."

"Well, then, why the hell don't I remember the two of you?" He leaned across the table toward Brian. "How come I don't remember any other part of my life?"

"You have questions far older than any answer I could give you. Only the Elder can answer the things bouncing around inside your head, Evrikh. Maybe even help you piece your life back together. We're only here to ask for your trust, but in order for this to happen, it requires a leap of faith on your behalf; a leap toward something that was *your* idea to begin with."

"Trust you? You and her?" his eyes glanced over to Keona. "Where the hell do I begin, Brian? I'm not even sure what the hell's going on. I just found out my life has mostly been a lie, and I just had a very strange group of people, that you," he looked back at Keona once more, "what? . . . *Relics?*" then continued on with Brian, "tried killing me!"

Evrikh sat back and took a long, deep breath. He had such fond memories of the two of them, memories and feelings he wasn't sure he was ready to give up just yet. So, where the hell would he begin? Screw this leap of faith! Whatever the hell this is, it's certainly a lot bigger than just a leap.

He turned his attention to Keona. "I—no, everything that Alex was, everything that I was—loved you. I can't help but feel like you've betrayed that."

Keona let out a whisper, and although he couldn't hear it with his ears, he definitely heard it in his mind. He didn't need her to look back up to him in order to know the truth behind it. Glancing down at the seat between them, he could see her tears bouncing gently against the fabric. All she had said was, "I love you too."

For a moment, as Keona sat there in silence, he relaxed. No matter how hard he tried, Evrikh knew how he felt about her. How he's seen the sunlight bouncing off her hair back in his apartment. *How fuckin' weird is it to love someone, and not even know them at the same time? It doesn't matter who's done what to me. You might've dreamt up Alex, but you don't get to dream this up.* He placed his hands on Keona's shoulders and raised her head up. He looked into her eyes and there it was; that same greenish blue hue buried beneath all that red. Keona took his hands into her own and just as she opened her mouth to speak, Evrikh placed his arms around her and pulled her in. The rest of his confusion and questions would have to wait. He knew how he felt about Keona and Brian, here in this moment; and for now that would have to be enough. Even though he held her as though she was encased in stone, he opened his mind and invited her in. For the first time,

Keona knew what she had meant to Alex, had somehow felt what he carried in his heart for her. She didn't quite understand how this was happening, only knew that it was. She slowly pulled her head back in wonder to look at his face; the tears had stopped, but this expression was entirely new for Evrikh.

"Is this real?" her mind had whispered softly.

Evrikh's eyes softened. "Of course it's real. That's how Alex has always felt, and in a roundabout way, both of us, I suppose." He smiled at her.

"Evrikh, we should continue," Brian reluctantly interrupted.

At that exact moment, a mental picture of Evrikh's backhand had blown across Brian's face, so real, Evrikh had almost startled himself. How could you just interrupt like that? Couldn't you see her just then? Even in dreams she's somehow not as beautiful, and here she is sitting here in real life, looking impossibly gorgeous . . . her lips, so inviting!

". . . Sorry, Brian," Keona said while sitting back down. She had kept Evrikh's hands within hers as she sat so very close to him; her sweet lips so equally very far away now!

"All right, Brian," he said, turning to look at him. The flames in his eyes so tangible Evrikh thought they might actually set Brian ablaze had he stared at him too long, ". . . Who the hell's this Elder?"

"Well," he sat back and crossed his arms, "he's the one who turned you into Alex. He's also the leader of the Resistance."

"The Resistance? You're telling me there's actually a Resistance?" He quickly glanced back and forth between Keona and Brian. "Who in the world would be dumb enough to rise up against the Council?"

"Well, for one . . . yourself included," Brian added with a sly smile.

Evrikh couldn't help but grin himself. ". . . And this Elder's basically the only person who can give me my life back?"

And this was supposed to be my idea? Why the hell would I even agree to some crazy bullshit as this? Whoever the Elder is, he'd better have some damn answers.

"Yes, Evrikh, and unfortunately, there isn't much time left."

Evrikh looked at Keona, and then back to Brian. "Why you say that? Is he gonna die or something?"

"No, nothing like that," Keona added.

"Better not! If he's the only one that can return my life to me, then he's got some damn answers to give."

"It would just be best if you saw the Elder as soon as possible is all," Brian finished.

"So, at exactly what point did I come into play?" Evrikh asked, rubbing Keona's hand with his own.

Brian took another deep breath and continued. "Do you remember a man by the name of Kendrick Savari?"

"Of course," Evrikh had practically scoffed. "He was seen as the man who ruined the world with his research." A name both blessed and cursed depending on how you look at it.

"At the time, Kendrick was seen as the world's most

brilliant scientist, whose discoveries altered the world. When he discovered cold fusion, he knew that the nations of the world would do what they'd have to, to get it." Brian sat back while sipping his Tribulin Mixer. "But there was a project before that, one that he had been working on for his entire career."

Evrikh turned to look at Keona for a moment, wondering where Brian was going with this. As she smiled in return, his eyes found their way back to Brian. He continued.

"You see, somehow, Kendrick had foreseen the problems that cold fusion would cause, and because of that, he hurried to complete his lifelong project. It was a fail-safe, one that would ensure the existence of the human race—"

"You're speaking of the Phoenix Gate?" he asked, cutting Brian off. "That's a freakin' urban legend and has nothing to do with this."

"Yes, but not by what you know," Brian returned as his eyes glanced over at Keona. The two of them now listened attentively as Brian spoke.

"The Phoenix Gate was a biological being. It began using human DNA. Because of how fast the world was deteriorating, Kendrick had to activate it before it was actually complete. At the time, it was nothing but a child in many ways, and because of its premature activation, it would have to learn how to control itself, rather than already have the know-how."

As Brian continued to speak, visions of a lab suddenly streaked across Evrikh's mind. His face slowly erased all expression as his eyes showed him the deepest of memories. The visions suddenly dispersed as he blinked himself back to reality, Brian's voice becoming clear once again.

"But something happened, causing Dr. Savari to make the decision to have the project terminated, or so that's what he wanted the world to believe."

"So what does a past that occurred so long ago have to do with me?"

"Evrikh," Brian looked at Keona as he began, "now that the Council knows about the Phoenix Gate, it's of the utmost importance that we keep it from them." His stare turned to Evrikh. "We have to keep *you* away from them."

The lab again, only this time he was staring out through a small window; nothing but blackness around him. As his vision lingered through the little opening of light he could faintly see a name on a table across the room. The vision was suddenly gone.

"No! That can't be true." Evrikh grimaced as the world around him came back into focus. "That's not possible!" His conscious denial was attempting to bleed into his subconscious, and failing miserably.

"Look within yourself, Evrikh. You know it's true. You can feel it in there, can't you? It's like a bad dream that your mind won't let you forget. The Elder's the one who's taught you everything that you now need to remember."

"Need to remember?"

"Yes," Brian replied. "He already taught you everything you need. Now the Elder is the only one who can unlock the secrets you have in that head of yours."

Keona placed a hand on the back of his neck and began rubbing it lightly. Brian continued. "You were the first of us to be known. Evrikh, you were the first known Unfamiliar. Sometime after the Great Darkness, we're not sure how, but the Council obtained a file on you. They saw you as a threat to everything they stood for, and so the search began. Entirely new laws were enacted at the behest of the Council, and a new military branch thrown together all for the safety of the people; the Relics. I believe you met earlier, while at Keona's place. It was at that time that the Elder did the only thing he could. He needed you to disappear, and when you agreed, it was at that moment that you became Alex."

"None of this answers the main question . . ." Evrikh added, his eyes staring down at the Tribulin Mixer.

Keona peered up at Evrikh. "And that would be . . .?"

"Why me?" *YEAH, why the hell me? This is crazy . . . and damn, Keona, seriously, you need to holster those lips! Do you ever wake up thinking why in the hell God blessed you with such a kissable face? Damn it, Brian, you are NOT forgiven for your earlier interruption.*

He could see a grin sprawling out across Keona's face. "That's what you're gonna find out."

Evrikh sneered at her, mimicking her words, ". . . Damn, guess this means I can no longer call you Jillatinous." He then turned to look at Brian. "So . . . those Relics, what are they exactly?"

Brian finished off his Tribulin Mixer and placed it back on the table. "They, my friend, are a select few chosen to be elite bounty hunters. Each one of them has been genetically enhanced by the Council; legal Unfamiliars, if you will. Originally, they were used as a means of population control; that was, until *we* started showing up. After that, the Relics went underground. They are mainly used to sniff out Unfamiliars, to bring them to the mercy of the Council. Since going underground, the Council has basically declared their disbandment. But, there's still a select few of us that know the truth."

Evrikh removed his hand from Keona's and placed it on her leg, rubbing it for comfort. "So, how is it that they find us?"

Brian looked at Keona and slightly nodded with his head. Keona turned and positioned herself sideways to Evrikh. "Well, our auras are different than normal humans, and the Relics have a way of seeing that. But, those asses aren't the only ones. Take that drunk sitting at the bar, for instance; nothing special 'bout him."

Evrikh followed her hand as it extended out past his neck, pointing to the select individual.

"How can you tell?" he asked, interrupting her.

She looked at him queerly. "Come on, Evrikh, concentrate a little harder than just staring at him."

He looked back at the drunk with a more determined glare. "Keona, I'm telling you, I still don't see anything."

"Good," she said with a faint laugh; her intimate taunt. "You shouldn't see anything. Now, take that woman talking to the man at the end of the bar. What do you see with her?"

"OK, no, we're done here," Evrikh started, turning back toward Brian. "You wanna crack jokes about this?"

Keona reached up with her hands and placed them on either side of Evrikh's face, forcing him to look back toward the bar, and leaned in next to his ear.

"Evrikh, *look* at her."

He looked through the crowd and found the woman. As she sat there talking with a man, he began to concentrate his thoughts. Suddenly, the room fell silent, and they were the only two in the room. Evrikh watched her lips move, yet they produced no sound. And as she spoke, she slowly rocked back and forth using body language. It was at that moment that she started to glow a faint yellow, like the edges of the sun around an eclipse. Keona felt the tension leave his body, watched the denial fade from his face. It was so amazing and beautiful; he became captivated by it.

"You see, Unfamiliars are more attuned to the world that surrounds 'em. She's obviously no threat to the Council, but it's her distinction that makes her who she is."

He turned his attention back to Keona. "HOLY SHIT!" he blurted out as he stumbled out of the booth and onto the floor, his eyes shut hard. Brian shot up out of his seat as he moved to assist Evrikh back into the booth.

The last few seconds replayed behind his closed eyes. As Evrikh was surprised by this *new* vision of his, he was turning back toward Brian when his left eye was consumed by a reddish hue. Turning his head further, that reddish glow quickly spread across his right eye as he stumbled out of his seat, shutting his eyes. His mind was slowly attempting to sort out its confusion.

"It's all right, come on, let me give you a hand." Brian was immediately beside Evrikh, helping him back to his feet.

With Brian's help off the floor, Evrikh slowly reopened his eyes, looking back at Keona and taking his seat beside her, his face returning in awe.

"That's some of the craziest shit I've ever seen." He then grabbed a napkin off the table and used it to rub his face a bit cleaner, his eyes shooting back up in the girl's direction. *Damn, how in the world can no one else notice her glowing like that?*

"That's nice, Evrikh, but stay with me here," Keona replied. "Our auras are not the only thing that give us away. Not all Unfamiliars have gifts; some of us are as normal as everybody else. Those of us who possess gifts are the ones hunted down by the Relics. Compared to people like her, our auras tend to radiate a stronger . . . frequency."

Evrikh's memory from only moments ago was ablaze within his mind as his memory turned from the girl to look back at Keona, her body enflamed in an aura of blood and fire. He'd have believed her a demon had this been the first time he'd ever met her. Is that what she means by a stronger frequency? Evrikh's eyes glanced back toward Brian. Better not try that garbage with *him*; otherwise, he might literally shit his pants right here!

". . . Those're what Keona and I faced back at her place?"

Brian leaned forward. "Consider yourself lucky to be alive. I never met an Unfamiliar who faced a Relic and lived. They are physically altered, sometimes genetically, from birth, to be stronger and quicker than any of us. They've also never been known to give up until their objective is complete. Somehow, the Council has bred the humanity almost completely out of them."

Evrikh looked to Keona and smiled. "Well, I guess they never met *my* ass!"

"Well, don't get your hopes up. I think the Relics you and Keona faced back there discovered you by accident."

"Accident?"

"They must have been following up on normal protocol. I did what I could back at the lab, but it didn't appear to sit well with anyone," Brian added.

Evrikh took a deep breath and placed his hands on the table. "So what's next?"

Brian stared at him for a few moments. "The Elder needs to see you."

"Good, I'd like to give him a piece of my mind as well. Where's he at?"

"Hold up, Evrikh. It's not that easy. I can only take you as far as Jurubian City. From there, you'll have to go through the eastern badlands to a place called Mehrond. We'll have people in place, waiting for you."

"Brian, you're coming with us?" Keona asked.

"The Council, they're still looking for me out there. If they should hear that I've resurfaced . . ." he paused. "Out there I'd be nothing but a burden to you two. Besides, I've got other plans to set in motion back here," he added cryptically.

Evrikh took Keona's hand again. "When do we leave?"

Brian picked up his Tribulin Mixer and looked into the bottom of the glass as if it held the answers and he was simply repeating them. "We set out tomorrow, early morning. This way we'll look less suspicious. Meet me just outside the slums, on the eastern side of town."

"Sounds like a plan." *Shit, it's the only plan for now.*

Brian placed his empty glass back on the table and stood up. "Now, if you'll excuse me, I have other business to attend to before we leave tomorrow."

Emilia came running almost as if on cue. "Are we leaving, Daddy?" she asked, looking up at him.

Brian looked down at her and picked her up. "Yeah, baby, we're leaving." He turned his head back to Keona and Evrikh. "I'll see you two tomorrow morning." He then turned to walk toward the door, Emilia yelling from his arms, "Good-bye, Keona, good-bye, Evrikh!"

Evrikh waved to her as he rotated to the other chair, placing himself opposite of Keona.

"How is it that Emilia knows my name?"

Keona looked at him smartly. "The daughter of an Unfamiliar? Her's might be different than Brian's, but you think it skips a generation or something?"

"You're right," Evrikh replied, looking down. "She probably inherited something from Brian." He looked back up at Keona. "What are our plans 'til tomorrow?"

"We'll stay here. Then we'll leave early tomorrow," she said cheerfully. Keona got up from the table and motioned him to follow her. She turned to look at the bartender. "Hey, Brooke," she yelled, "I'm going to take my friend here to room three. Mind if we use it for the night?"

"The *whole* night?" the bartender yelled. "Provided the room looks better than he does right now, in the morning!"

That's right! I must look worse than some homeless beggar right now to these people. Here I am dressed like I crawled out from some grave, and they haven't even kicked my ass out yet!

"Thanks!" she yelled, turning her attention back to the stairs. Evrikh just looked at her astonished.

As they approached the staircase, he looked around one last time. At that moment, he felt an odd sensation. He felt as though he was being observed. Just before his eyes finished scanning the room, when they reached the far end of the bar, they halted. As Evrikh walked toward the staircase, everything seemed to move in slow motion. Sitting across the room, at another table, was a man whose body was concealed by a hooded cloak that loomed heavily over his head. His face was concealed by shadows. Evrikh sent out a probe with his mind to see who this stranger was, but all his attempts failed. His mind must be similar to his own in order for him to resist. A trick he would definitely have to learn himself.

Then without any notion, without any warning, this hooded figure looked up. Although Evrikh continued to follow Keona, his attention remained on that man. His face was still too dark to make out any certain definition. But then, through all the people, the chaos, the noise, this figure stared in his direction. Evrikh didn't know what to do; he felt discovered. Fuck! Could this guy really feel his presence, the same way Evrikh just picked up his?

The two of them reached the staircase, Evrikh only

steps behind Keona. His attention turned back to her as he followed her up the stairs. When they reached the top, he turned around one last time to see that hooded figure. Peering down to the first floor, he noticed he was gone. His eyes and his mind quickly scanned the room. He was nowhere. Evrikh couldn't even feel his presence. Was it just his imagination, was he just a vision Evrikh had? How in the hell could he have just vanished that quickly?

"Evrikh," Keona called from behind him.

Suddenly realizing he was almost walking back down the steps, Evrikh turned to look at her as she was leaning against an open door. One hand held the door while the other slowly rubbed the back of her neck.

"You comin'?" she asked looking down at herself.

Evrikh immediately began thinking that maybe if he concentrated hard enough right now, he might be able to blast the clothes right off her body. His left eyebrow rose. How could he refuse such a woman? He walked up to Keona and took her inside, closing the door behind them. Shortly after, the faint sound of running water could already be heard from the shower.

~ ~ ~

Evrikh opened his eyes to see Keona lying beside him, still sound asleep. His eyes turned to the clock on the other side of the bed. Four a.m. Slowly, he removed the sheets from his body and kissed Keona's neck as he rose from the bed. She smiled while exhaling, and turned over. He decided not to wake her just yet.

As he walked across the room, an invisible shock ran

through his body, with goose bumps quickly following. It literally set him on his toes as he suddenly felt some presence outside the door. Evrikh snapped his head around and looked at the crack at the bottom. Two shadows, feet most likely, stopped in front of the door. It looked as though they placed something at the base of the door, then they left, a small shadow remaining on the other side of the crack. Evrikh slowly crept over to the door. Kneeling down beside it, he peered through the crack to the other side. There remained a single envelope. This had better not be some damn game of Brian's! And who in the hell would come to visit Keona in the middle of the night?

He stood back up and placed his hand on the door. The hallway was deserted, there was no longer the feeling of any presence. He slowly turned the handle and opened the door as quietly and carefully as he could. Evrikh stuck his head out cautiously and glanced up and down both ways. It was empty. The club must have shut down some time ago, with nothing coming from downstairs except for a bit of radiant light. He looked down, and at his feet lay a single envelope with one word written across the front: EVRIKH. The sudden burst of laughter made him jolt back into the shadow of the door as a man and woman came bouncing off the top of the stairs. Their bodies slammed into a door a few rooms down as they probed each other and slid inside.

Evrikh knelt down and picked up the envelope, opening it and removing a small piece of paper. He unfolded it.

Evrikh, get away as quickly as possible. There are many

things you don't know and even worse things you couldn't imagine. You're in grave danger. When you reach Jurubian, go to a place called "Divine." Ask for Thea. She'll be expecting you. Please, Evrikh, you must trust me.
~ A Friend

He tried probing the note, much the same way he had shared his thoughts with Keona earlier, but whoever wrote it left no imprints. At least none of the kind Evrikh would be able to pick up on. He folded up the note and looked around once more before walking back inside, closing the door.

"Who was that?" Keona mumbled, sitting on the edge of the bed.

Evrikh looked up while slipping the note into the back of his shorts. "Oh, I didn't hear you get up. Who, that?" He began to cross the room to her. "Just some other couple starting a little party of their own; that, and I just wanted a bit of fresh air." He decided not to tell her about the note just yet.

Fuck, she's quiet . . . and he didn't even want to know where the hell he was going to stick that note had he not put his underwear back on!

Evrikh smiled as he placed his hands on her face and bent over to kiss her. "You about ready to go?"

Keona opened her eyes and bit her lip. "Mmm, yeah, I'm ready, but," she stood up placing her arms around him, "do we have to go now?" she said while pressing her breasts up against him and wrapping her leg around his own. She began kissing his neck. Evrikh could feel the faint bluntness of her nipples pressing against his chest. Just then, a whisper breezed through his mind, m ... i ... r ... i ... a ... m.

He laughed and separated himself from her. "Keona, as much as I'd like to, if we don't leave now we'll be late for Brian."

"Damn you," she said, giving him one last kiss. "Just remember, I might not be so willing next time." A grin spread across her face. "You have to get it while you can!"

WHO'RE YOU SHITTIN'! He *would* take it, Keona ... take it in such a way she wouldn't ever recover! Taunt *him* like that!

Evrikh laughed out loud to Keona's remark as she walked over to the chair and began putting her clothes on.

Just before he closed the door, he looked around the room one last time to make sure he didn't forget anything. Then he closed the door with only one thought in his mind, which added to the mystery of everything else: the note.

~ ~ ~

When they reached the edge of the slums, they saw Brian standing at the corner of an intersection and approached him.

"Keona, Evrikh. You're both ready to go, I take it?"

Evrikh looked at Keona, a flash of her naked body writhing below him had brushed across his eyes, and he immediately felt the blood that rushed to his face. He looked back at Brian in hopes he wouldn't notice. "Yeah, man, we're ready. Did you take care of your business?"

Evrikh noticed a sudden blush roar into Keona's face as she sat there staring at him. For a moment, he sat there thinking if he had accidently projected that image he had into her mind as well. *Oops.*

"Yes, everything's taken care of. Once we reach Jurubian, I'll give you instructions on how to reach Mehrond."

Evrikh looked at Keona and smiled. "Let's do this."

"We'll go on foot carrying as little as possible. I don't want to raise too much suspicion when we get there," Brian added, regaining his attention. "Evrikh, here, I got you some new clothes," he finished as he handed him a bag.

Evrikh took the bag and pulled the clothes out preparing to put them on; leather pants, jet-black, along with rugged boots with what . . . steel-coated heels? Aside from looking pretty cool and gaudy, why the hell would he even need these? Lastly, he pulled out a gray tee shirt which was remarkably soft, but somehow reflective in color. *Brian, are you secretly escorting us to a fashion show? Can't complain, though, these new clothes are far better than what I just took off.*

Now Jurubian City, this place called Divine, and is this somehow the same Thea he vaguely remembered, written about in the letter? Could Evrikh possibly trust someone he feels he might remember but also doesn't? Unsure of what the hell his future holds, Evrikh would be damned if his destiny wasn't carrying him to it.

With Norwynn to their backs, they headed out for

Jurubian. Maybe Evrikh's answers lay there; then again, maybe the only thing Jurubian would bring is more questions. With Brian in front and Keona by his side, they left. Evrikh slowly watched as Norwynn faded in the distance behind them and began to feel the full force of this crazy adventure that had been thrust into his life . . . his life that was already so full of lies. It was then, at this exact point, that Evrikh had decided he would leave the lies of the past behind and live only for the truth. He wasn't sure what truth the future had in store for him, but he would invite it . . . within reason, of course.

* * * *

CHAPTER 4
~ The Watchers ~

ELDERLYNN FOREST. THIS was a place where people spent little time. The Council declared this place a dead zone. From a religious standpoint, they simply proclaimed the forest void of Miriam's presence, and that this forest concealed a darker religion, governed by an unholy will. Though it is never spoken aloud, there has always been talk around the city that the forest is somehow within the control of the Resistance. Now, interestingly enough, it seems Brian and Keona are both somehow connected to the Resistance. Thinking about the relationships the three of them shared over the past years since working at the lab, it seemed impossible for them to be in bed with the Resistance. Evrikh would've noticed something, would've picked up on *something*.

As they reached the edge of the forest, they stopped their progress to observe the surroundings before proceeding; who knows what kinds of secrets this place held. Parents have shared ghost stories with their children; the

Council has publicly warned about the danger; hell, even survivalist junkies have entered here to challenge themselves. The tree line stretched as far as the three could see in both directions, and as Evrikh looked within the forest, the light dimmed out remarkably fast. A forest, for all that's known, has been left alone since the War of Ruin. A slight breeze picked up, and for a second Evrikh thought he sensed a presence, but that feeling was gone before it went any further.

Brian turned around to look at the other two. "Come on, let's go."

Stepping through some thick and tall grass, they began to enter the forest. Evrikh watched Brian climb up onto a fallen tree, and when he reached the top, he looked around for a moment before disappearing to the other side. Moments later, Keona followed. Evrikh grabbed the closest tree limb and placed his foot into a little hole and continued up the side of the tree. Upon reaching the top, he stood up to look around.

The ground was covered with old leaves and moss; a ruffled sadness lying beneath them. Knee-high grass only grew where the sunlight broke through the canopy. The trees had trunks bigger than most houses, whose branches seemed to reach for the heavens. The tops loomed so far away that they didn't even look like leaves anymore. Instead, the sky above them was a pool of cascaded colors, which all ran together; green to yellow, yellow to orange, and orange to red. Every time a wind blew through, the colors seemed to somehow sway like water, occasionally allowing the sunlight to break through.

The air was cool, and the plants almost appeared to move, yet there was no breeze, no breath of life. As Evrikh looked deeper into the forest, there were spots in the canopy where the sunlight reached through, stretching for the ground. Beyond that, the sunlight grew dimmer as the density of the forest practically squeezed it out altogether. Evrikh took a breath, allowed his mind to stretch out into the area around them. He pushed it out as far as he could go, taking in a sharp breath as his mind slightly collapsed in on itself. *Damn, guess that's it for now.* Evrikh allowed himself to mentally hold that position, feeling the trees that grew within the miles around them, scanning the forest floor for their would-be assassins. He could hear the forest talking, whispering its secrets; almost weeping for its own loneliness. Evrikh could actually feel the minds of others all around them, their eyes somehow on the three of them, monitoring from a distance. The longer he probed and felt them out, the more they felt more curious than harm bearing. What the hell *are* they? Is this why the Council ignores the forest? Maybe all the damn ghost stories are true. They might be the inhabitants of the forest, but those stories had better *not* be true!

He jumped down to rejoin Keona and Brian while taking another nervous breath, and they pressed on, his mind still aware of those watching them. *All right, Evrikh, time to psych yourself out! Who knows what crazy shit is out there . . . Hell, who knows what crazy shit is in here!* He extended his hand, palm up, looking down upon it, studying it, turning it back and forth.

Brian remained a few paces ahead, and Keona, a few

feet. Stepping through some dead plants, something out of the corner of Evrikh's eye caught his attention. Not more than five feet away was a small pool of water. They might've just entered the forest a little while back, but he couldn't remember them passing by any source of water. As Evrikh looked around, as far as he could tell, they still weren't near any source of water. How strange for a small pool of water to just be sitting there all by itself. As Evrikh stepped closer, it became more mysterious that there was no reflection of any kind; not even a single blade of grass from the very edge. Evrikh stepped over to the pool and knelt down beside it. Leaning over to peer inside, he didn't even see his own reflection. Now *that's* a little crazy. For a moment the water was amazingly still, and then quite suddenly it shimmered as if a pebble had been tossed in. It was actually so sudden, Evrikh had jumped back a foot. The tiny ripples screamed across the surface, colliding with one another until the whole surface became a small web of confusion. Then, almost as a reflex, the shimmering abruptly stopped, and Evrikh realized he was now looking at a reflection. As he stepped back up to this small pool, he saw that it was of a destroyed city, and everything was on fire or crumbled to pieces. Kneeling down, Evrikh could see himself in the reflection, and the point of view was all correct. It was as if he was looking up from the group on the other side, his mirrored self looking back at him.

Hey, Brian, is there some kind of freaky shit in the air none of them knew about? Were the three of them inhaling something that was drifting throughout the forest from the outlining badlands?

"Hey, you two, come take a look at this." As Evrikh looked up, Keona and Brian were gone. Evrikh jumped to his feet and realized that the ground had become sturdier, and when he looked down, the forest floor had become replaced with broken cement and other stone debris. He looked back up and the forest was gone as well. He was surrounded by buildings crumbling apart, and the air was stale with the palpable taste of rotting flesh; a tart that his mouth could only associate with death. His heart began to beat faster, and he could sense a growing fear within himself. "KEONA, BRIAN, WHERE THE FUCK...!"

"What're you talking about?" Keona's voice filled the air.

"Where the hell are you?" he asked nervously. "I can't see you!"

"We're right in—"

"Hold on a sec, Keona," Brian said, cutting her off. "Evrikh, calm down. What do you mean you can't see us?"

"I'm not in the damn forest, I'm in a city I've never seen before." He started waving his arms wildly around. "Why the fuck can't I see you?"

"Evrikh, relax. We're right here. You must be having some kind of vision. Don't push it away, let it happen," Brian added. "Tell us what you see."

"This city's in ruins, man ... shit! I don't know what the hell happened, but it smells real bad; *real* bad. Looks like the aftermath of some huge bomb!"

Keona and Brian saw Evrikh's face look up toward the sky, his eyes panning across the horizon. "The sky's dark, no sun, only clouds ... and the air's pretty damn thick."

"What about the city? Are there any clues as to what happened?" Keona's voice cut in.

Evrikh's head lowered to their level and began looking around. He was definitely looking out past them, somewhere in the distance maybe. Whatever Evrikh was seeing, it certainly wasn't the forest the three of them were standing in.

As Evrikh looked around, buildings continued to crumble to pieces, and he could hear the low toned whine of the other buildings soon to follow.

"What in God's name? I can see bodies laying everywhere ... fuck, they're dead ... every one of 'em!" he practically whispered, slightly recoiling. "It's like the life of this entire city has just been ... removed. Wait a minute," he paused for a moment. "I can hear something."

"What is it?" Brian asked, placing his hand on Keona's shoulder.

The fuck should he know? He didn't want to find out. Why don't you jump your happy ass in there and investigate that shit! Why would you even ask him that?

"Seriously?" shaking his head in his own disbelief, Evrikh turned to the left.

Brian and Keona watched as he began walking, climbing over empty spaces, and navigating this invisible world. When he reached the end of a building, he walked around the corner. "Come on, it's down this way," his voice was almost a whisper. Keona and Brian began to follow him as he walked around a tree and continued deeper into the forest. "Wow, it's disgusting! I think the smell's getting worse!"

Just as Evrikh reached halfway down the alley he saw shapes moving in the distance. "I can see them," his voice almost mute now. He raised his hand to his mouth in hopes of somehow filtering out the increasingly sour taste.

"See who?" Keona faintly breathed out from behind him.

"Damn it, Keona, shouldn't you be saying something like, 'Be careful, Evrikh,' instead of asking who the hell I'm looking at? Well, let me see. Oh shit, it's my dad . . . Hey, Pops, long time, no vision," he finished, looking around for Keona like a blind man.

"Right now? You wanna get into it right now? Tell you what, I know you had this ass last night, but check . . ."

"HEY, you two! There's something happening here right now that's a LITTLE more pressing than the two of you trying to enjoy each other's after-party!" Brian threw in.

"OK, hold up, let me get a bit closer," Evrikh began, as he slowly sidestepped in the figure's direction. "Not really sure, they're just shadows now," he drew closer still. A woman lay by the side of the building. She had no legs, and her stomach was disemboweled. As he drew closer, the bodies grew more grotesque; a face whose head looked as though no bones remained within it. Passing a garbage can, he looked inside it and noticed a compact shape. As a light flickered by, Evrikh realized it had been a body, compressed so much that its innards had begun to liquefy. He looked toward the shadows to keep his mind off of the horror that lay all around him. Brian and Keona could both see that his face had gone flush and could only imagine how much worse his vision actually was.

What in the goddess's name could have done this to these people ... to have deserved this?

Evrikh's feet kept stepping through the grass and over the fallen tree limbs, and just as they reached a small clearing, he came to a halt. Brian walked around in front of him.

"Evrikh, what's going on?"

His face was absent of life, the sheen of death pulled tight over his head from ear to ear. Keona stepped beside Brian. "What in the hell's happening to him?"

Neither Brian nor Keona had ever seen Evrikh in such a state. It was as if he had passed out, yet remained conscious at the same time. At this point, neither of the two were sure they wanted to see what Evrikh was currently witnessing. Whatever it was, God help him, seemed horrifying enough to wash the life straight out of him, from this vision alone.

"I ... can see ... it," his voice was almost as ghostly as his appearance, crackling like a fading storm. At the end of the alley, a woman was screaming as her hands held onto a low hanging bar of an escape ladder. As she hung there, what the hell was that moving behind her? Suddenly, the other shadow pulled her from the ladder and stepped into the light; forcing her to place her hands on the side of the building. This other figure was massive in size, and it brought to Evrikh's mind those women of Uluria. His hair was long, defiantly long, and as the light refracted throughout it, it flowed like rippling water; the sheen of metallic color. The fuck are those tails, tentacles coming out of his lower back? They were all at least six feet in length, flailing wildly yet with precision to their movements like something Evrikh had never seen before. His feet were high arched, and his entire body had to have been coated with a very thin layer of . . . hair? Either that, or oil or some shit. He scanned the body of this hellish beast upward, and as he reached the face, it pivoted and Evrikh could see his eyes. They were white, glowing. They were somehow haunting, and it wasn't like he was a product of this place . . . no. Evrikh knew, when he saw those eyes, this was *his* playground. Whatever the hell happened here was all *his* doing, and Evrikh had somehow stumbled right into it.

It was magnificent and horrifying at the same time. Had all this destruction been caused by this grand beast, straight from the depths of undreamt nightmares?

"What the fuck is this?" Evrikh groaned, stepping backward. A slight smile had etched its way onto his face, and *this* was a look that Keona had never seen upon him.

"What's going on?" She walked around to his side and watched carefully as his mind journeyed through that foreign place.

Evrikh stepped a few feet closer and could then see everything clearly; immediately regretting that he hadn't. As the woman held her hands on the wall, the strange creature wrapped his arm around her stomach and lifted her waist into the air. When he did this, he placed his legs between hers and spread them apart as far as he could. Doing so caused the woman to scream out in pain, but

THE PHOENIX GATE

as Evrikh looked at her face, into those eyes, he couldn't tell if she was experiencing pain or pleasure; maybe some crazy mix of the two? Then he lowered her waist onto his, and she screamed out in agonizing joy as his member slid into her body. He then reached up with both his arms and gripped her exposed breasts, kneading them like two loaves of dough. Her clothes had been shredded, and she seemed somehow oblivious to the mounds of other dead bodies lying all around them. She continued to moan in pleasure as he slid her up and down, going deeper into her with every movement, feeling the intimate curves of being within her. As Evrikh stared at this event occurring before him, he could see her legs shuttering, vibrating, getting lost to these waves of uncontrollable pleasure being thrust over and over again into her body. Suddenly, the aura of this crazed animal began glowing white, and he started moving the woman faster; eagerly. Unable to withstand the pleasure, the woman's arms gave out and she rested her head and neck up against the building; her face was looking in Evrikh's direction. It was still impossible to tell if she was moaning or screaming. As her arms dangled freely, he could see in her expression that she was lost to a world of ecstasy, a half-smiled dead stare whose only thoughts were of the high being forced into the deepest parts of her pleasure. This was one of the most disturbing images Evrikh thought he could ever be exposed to, and there was still some small part of him that kept thinking, damn Keona, you'll be screaming like that too someday. His little smile grew a little broader.

Suddenly the name Thea flashed through Evrikh's

mind, but for the life of him, he couldn't remember more than just the name. As she sat there, convulsing from the pleasure, the creature placed his hands on her waist and began sliding into her even faster; his member growing in size. The woman attempted to wrap her legs around his, like he was a drug her body couldn't live without. She needed him now, depended on him, this raw pleasure being thrust upon her. As she did this, she replaced her hands on the wall and began pushing herself down onto his erection. The woman's screams became louder, and they nearly resembled pain now, her body quivering with every movement. She immediately grew out of control and began thrusting herself onto him, until all control was lost. Why was this even happening? Why would she even have sex with that thing? Will somebody please explain what the fuck is going on?! While this was happening, the creature's aura grew brighter still, and hers started glowing as well.

"OK," he whispered to the other two, "and *why* the hell are they both glowing now?"

Brian glanced over to Keona and simply shook his head in confusion.

". . . who? Who's glowing? Evrikh, what are you seeing?" Keona blurted out in frustration.

As Evrikh concentrated a little harder, he could see that the creature's hands began to be absorbed into her breasts, and as she thrust herself onto him, their waists no longer separated; they were becoming one. Her stomach started growing in size as her waist was slowly being absorbed by his. The creature pulled her back up to his chest, gripping her breasts even harder. Then, just as their bodies became a jumble of living flesh, she turned her face back in Evrikh's direction, and within that moment he knew she was looking right at him.

". . . and as the great veil is lifted, he shall be given dominion over the world; the devourer of life."

Keona and Brian jumped away as Evrikh screamed suddenly and stumbled backward, falling. After hitting the ground he looked around nervously, wiping the sweat from his face. The sunlight almost hurt his eyes as he looked up into those small openings in the canopy. He heard voices in front of him, and as he looked up, Keona and Brian knelt down beside him. Evrikh looked at his hands; they were still shaking.

"Hey, you all right now?" Keona asked from beside him.

Evrikh turned to look at her, his face still blanketed with confusion; her eyes were scanning his face for any kind of discomfort. "I'm back. I don't know what the hell happened, but I can see you now," he looked at Brian. "That's never happened before. As Alex I can remember nearly every dream I've had similar to this, but never had a waking dream before. Never like this!"

"Can you walk?" Brian asked.

Evrikh looked down upon myself. "Yeah, can't imagine why I wouldn't be able to. Just a little light-headed is all." He slowly stood up. "We should keep moving." He looked up through the canopy. "It'll be getting dark soon and we'll have to find a place to camp."

"You're right." Brian turned to walk in their original

direction. "We have to keep moving," the concern for Evrikh and this new vision of his practically glued to his face.

Keona took a step back from Evrikh and stared at him for a few moments, then looked at him up and down multiple times. She took a deep, slow breath, brought her face back up to meet his, and said, "Will be nice when we see the Elder and get some damn answers. All right, let's go." She turned to follow Brian, with Evrikh a pace behind her. Evrikh was just happy to know he wasn't the only one looking for answers now.

As they continued through the forest, his mind kept flashing through images of that woman and that creature raping her; absorbing her. What in the world was that even about? It seemed so real, but what did it mean, and what happened to that city? Was it even real . . . Had he really just seen all that? Suddenly Evrikh felt a slight breeze and that same feeling he had earlier, only this time the presence remained. He slowly looked around the trees, near them, in the distance, and realized that there was more than just one presence out there; dozens—even hundreds more. That was the moment he felt one staring right at him. Evrikh quickly twisted his head to the left to look at a tree in the distance. As he walked along, he stared into those shadows; it was watching him from there. He sent a probe out to discover their shy new friend, along with a thought. *I see your ass too!* Then, before his probe made it any further, the presence was gone. Evrikh could no longer sense anything from those shadows; it was like snapping out of a trance and noticing at the same time that the breeze had left as well.

He turned to look at Brian, who had just stepped up onto a dead tree limb. "Hey, Brian!" He stopped and turned back to Evrikh. "You should know we're not alone out here."

Brian raised his eyes and slowly overlooked the forest. "We're not. You can feel it too then?" Brian looked back to Keona and Evrikh. "I can see a clearing up ahead; we'll camp there." He turned and continued to move forward. Keona started to climb over the dead limb as Evrikh proceeded to pass under it. As he stood up on the other side, he could see where the forest opened up into the clearing, a hundred yards or so, maybe less.

~ ~ ~

Brian began setting up the second tent as Keona started unrolling the thermal blankets. "Hey, you think Evrikh's gonna be worth it? What if the Council discovers any part of this? You know what'll happen to us."

Brian grabbed the left side of the wire frame and lifted it up, bringing up the left side of the tent. "I think that if we're to have a future without the control of the Council, then he's required. I believe he really can end all this."

Keona grabbed another thermal and looked up into the flames of the fire. "That's good to hear." Just as she rolled out the thermal, she heard a noise. Her head whipped up and looked to the other side of the fire.

As Evrikh looked at Keona through the fire, he dropped the bundle of dead wood. "Relax, it's only me." A smirk spread across her face, and then she looked down to continue with the thermal.

"Hey, Brian, how's them tents coming along?" Evrikh asked as he stepped closer. Brian had just finished putting the last two parts of the wire frame together when he looked up at Evrikh.

"You had good timing asking that question. They're both done," he said as he pointed to each one.

Brian and Evrikh walked back to the fire as Keona left them to place the thermals inside the tents. "I think we should post watches. I'll take the first one; you and Keona should get some sleep." After stoking the fire twice, he looked back up to Evrikh. "And by that I mean actual sleep. We still have quite a ways to go and no idea how long it'll take to get there."

"Are you sure? Brian, placing Keona and I in the same tent at the same time . . . isn't exactly telling us to get some sleep."

"Maybe so, but you definitely need some downtime, and I'm sure you and Keona have your fair share to talk about," Brian added.

Just then Keona stepped out of their tent and joined the other two at the fire. "So, what's the deal?"

"Posting watches; I'll take the first one so you and Evrikh can get some sleep."

"Sounds like a plan," Keona said while turning to look at Evrikh. "Well, now, isn't your face just bloated with tiresome, baggage beaten emptiness."

Evrikh's face twisted, and he could feel his left eyebrow rise. Keona began to nod her head up and down.

"Don't be nodding your head up and down like that.

You just get your happy little ass in that tent."

Keona turned and jumped into the tent with glee. He then turned to look at Brian. "... Remember, not *my* idea."

That was the first time Evrikh had seen a smile crack itself into Brian's iron jaw.

"I'll take the next watch," Evrikh said as he walked toward the tent.

When he stepped inside, Keona was just slipping off her leather pants. She looked up noticing him. As she pulled the pants down over the curves of her hips, she knelt to the ground, and they slipped off in a fluid motion. This was the first time Evrikh had a really good look at her scar. She had a few here and there, but this beast had run from her right side, clearly halfway down her thigh. Someday he was going to sit down and have a real conversation about that scar, and what the hell happened. But for now, she was just so freakin' sexy. Her skin was as pure as ivory, with the scent of a morning blossom. She lifted her eyes up to meet his, slowly crawling toward him. When she reached Evrikh's feet, she began standing up, probing his body with her hands. He felt the softness of her breasts press through the cloth of his shirt. Just as her head reached his, he leaned forward to embrace her, their lips meshing together in an explosion of passion. As their lips remained locked together, feeling the pleasure of her moist tongue, a craving grew from deep within him. A feeling barely strong enough to even notice, but one that he knew was a part of his past. He wrapped his arms around her and pulled her body to him, fully embracing her. Seconds later, their lips separated, and she looked into his eyes.

"Still wearing that, huh?"

Evrikh laid Keona down on the thermal and lifted his shirt over his head. As he slid it off his arms, Keona sat up and their lips embraced once more. The warmth of her breasts pressed up against his now-bare chest, and they descended back down to the thermal, together. As he rolled over bringing her on top of him, she pulled the other thermal with her, over them. She lay there, her gaze lingering above him for a few seconds, and then leaned forward, bringing their bodies back together. In that instant, she had appeared more beautiful than the many women that he'd seen in his life, or could remember. Her hair drooped down over their faces, and as it fell, the light of the fire slowly dimmed out.

~ ~ ~

Red-hot ashes began hovering throughout the air as Evrikh adjusted the fire with an old tree limb. The light of the fire illuminated the area around the tents fairly well as the moonlight that descended through the canopy lit the trees around the camp like that of a pool. He reached over and grabbed a couple more branches to place them into the fire. Just then the breeze picked up a little, and for a moment, Evrikh thought nothing of it. But then, the breeze carried with it a familiar feeling. He looked up into the night and began probing the forest with his eyes, his mind able to see farther, for the light of the fire would only stretch so thin. Suddenly, another breeze picked up, and a voice was carried by it.

"Lun shea bae rien."

Feeling this presence within his mind, Evrikh continued to probe in return. It was as if this presence was absorbing their language, and sharing its own with him.

He stood up, stepping back from the fire. "Who are you; who's there?" he said with eyes that darted around, and a voice not loud for the sake of his companions who lay asleep in the tent not far behind him.

"Relax." The voice had to have been female. "*Gan owie* you *ua* harm. You humans *uvi* outcast *sien*. Yet you *pheswa* through our forest; why?"

Evrikh was amazed how her presence had learned the language of their race so quickly. "We are travelers," he began; the reflections of the fire alive within his eyes as they continued their scan of the area. "We're on our way to Jurubian City, and this is the quickest way we know."

Another breeze picked up. "We see through *sheai* words." Her voice came from beside him. Evrikh whipped his head around, but she continued to elude him. "You were meant to be the chosen one."

He suddenly had the uncomfortable feeling that she knew more than he certainly did. "If you don't mean to harm us, then why mask your presence?" Clearly she either knew him, or thought she knew him.

Just then, the wind stopped blowing and he could feel her there; upon the other side of the camp. The flames danced around the air like a wild curtain, teasing his vision with their radiant heat as her silhouette approached from the darkening shadows at the edge of their site. Very slowly, her figure passed through the streaks of moonlight and into the light of the fire; a woman?

Maybe I should've taken a longer rest! Damn, I mean . . . How the hell do I decide if she's attractive or not? I mean, what the hell; half woman, half . . . tree? Flower? She almost looks like some sexy-demon collage of this damn forest! All right, Evrikh, time to play it cool.

She appeared to be slightly taller than Evrikh himself. Her hair was long, stretching almost down to her calves, and the firelight echoed an almost creepy kind of motion around it. She had a slender body, and as she drew closer, became more detailed. Hair . . . wasn't hair at all. It was a web of vines; an intricate, woven, stunning flow of leaves, soft grass, and blooming flowers; almost as if the beauty of the forest had been captured within her very folds.

Slowly taking in the rest of this forest-woman, Evrikh found himself caught in the middle of a breathtaking moment. For the lack of a better term, he simply accepted that what she was wearing had qualified for clothes, at least in her eyes. Her skin was remarkably smooth, almost marblelike, and he could faintly see rings along it almost in the same manner as a trunk when a tree is first cut down. Her breasts were encased in a thin layer . . . of soil? He could only guess it was soil because as the light refracted from its surface, it beaded like the freshest of dirt, enriched with the same kind of beauty as her hair. Small flowers bloomed and vanished all throughout this makeshift bra, and it appeared so fragile that the smallest of wind would blow it off her entirely; yet instead, there it remained.

A bra of dirt and flower buds, huh? Gotta give it to you,

though . . . breasts such as those would bring most men to their knees! Ah, and such a grand place that would be, your wonderful love pillows looming . . . WHAT THE HELL AM I SAYING! This is the Forest-Chick! Dammit, Evrikh, get your damn eyes off her breasts!

Allowing his gaze to move downward, he took in the rest of her that completed the image of this lovely creature. Her hands and wrists seemed to be gloved with the same kind of thin-layered soil as her breasts. Her waist was bare, save for the place that would truly deem her a woman; that soil, beading; rolling. Maybe a thong . . . a strapless thong? As the contours of her hips lingered downward, it all ran into the same soil just above her knees, boots; if that's what they were. As she stood there it almost appeared that her legs were rooted to the ground. Evrikh could see the small vines and roots that lofted freely from the soil around her would-be calves, gliding in and out of the ground as easily as two colors of paint that would run together. In fact, all of her clothing appeared that, had Evrikh simply screamed at her, it would all blow off like dust from a book. Slowly she left her place by the fire and ascended toward Evrikh. He was neither frightened nor alert of any threat, simply amazed that her soil-clothes remained in place. With each step her foot pulled loosely from the earth, and as she placed it back down, quickly rerooted itself with remarkable fluidity.

"You intrigue us, Evrikh."

He stood there staring at her for a moment, realizing that she was extraordinarily attractive. *And who the hell is us?* "What are you . . . some kind of forest nymph?" The woman's face was suddenly alight with mirth.

As calmness took her once more, their eyes met only inches apart now, and Evrikh almost found himself lost to her unearthly beauty. Her eyes, remarkably clear like large dewdrops found on the morning grass, her pupils the allure of roses. How the hell could anyone have roses for eyes? And now, here he was, caught in the rapture of this exquisite creature; her intoxicating presence. Evrikh knew he had to remain alert, but, oh man, how her scent had simply overpowered any attempt he could make at any form of guard.

"How is it you know who I am?"

Suddenly, the fire flared intensely, and she was gone. He looked around, only to find that she was beside him; behind him. He stumbled away from her, half confused as he fell down upon a dead tree limb. "Who are you?"

"We have had many names through the life of our mother, yet you humans have never seen us as anything more than a myth; a tale woven throughout the history of your children."

"Myth, I'd say?! Would have to be ... no human woman could possibly have this kind of beauty, this kind of ... rawness of life."

She looked up and scanned the forest with her eyes. "My name is Lorelei. I am a *Shuswu-lei*." Her gaze lingered about the air.

"... forest elemental ..." His voice was slight, barely audible.

Her eyes returned, and she sat down beside him. "Long ago you humans almost murdered my home, our home." He watched as she reached out and touched the ground with her hand. Remarkably, vines grew swiftly from the soil-glove of her hand and embraced the earth much like a lover would cup the cheek of her beloved. "She had cried then . . . she continues to cry, even now."

"Wait a moment. Lorelei? Does that mean that . . . Wait, FOREST ELEMENTAL?" he blurted. "You're a forest elemental?"

He now noticed *her* eyebrow had risen; was she mocking him? "Quiet your voice lest your friends wake."

"Not only are forest-nymphs, sex-spirits . . . damn, sorry. OK, not only are you mythical from the old-time, but back then, they didn't believe in them either," he gestured. Shit, who was he to make such claims? Then again, how the hell would he even *know* that? "You'll have to forgive me if I find it a bit hard to believe. Besides, wouldn't you then be . . . a bit monstrous in size? Try to bury us in our sleep? . . . Try to impregnate us with terran worms and plague us with disease or whatnot?" He paused for a moment, "OK. I'll give you the whole appearance thing, 'cause I'm not really sure how the hell that soil about your body manages to not fall off. You definitely have the crazy wild hair thing going on, and overall, you're rather undeniably sexy in an . . . unbridled, Greenpeace sort of way. But, Lorelei . . ."

Evrikh watched as her soil-clothes quickly spread across her body, and she actually began descending into the ground, as though she was returning home.

"So pigheaded you humans are! *Fel-un bor est latoh!*" Her return to the earth slowed momentarily. "Do you honestly believe you're the only sentient beings upon the earth?"

He turned his posture toward her, leaning to the arm between them. "Lorelei, forgive me. I didn't mean it like that. So much has happened to me recently that everything seems a little hard to believe." He found that his eyes were soul-bound to this wonderment of her being absorbed by the earth. "If I've offended you in any way, I truly apologize."

Lorelei slowly rose from the earth, the soil covering her body returning to the clothing effect it retained earlier. There had been moments as she stood there that Evrikh had pictured her writhing below him, her soil-bra falling from her breasts, his hands running freely across her marble skin. *Are you seriously thinking of this now?* Evrikh found himself in his own shock. How strange that he would think of the two of them being lost in pleasure at a time like this, but something within him stirred; growled for a taste of her beauty. Shit, if Keona were awake right now, she would definitely tell you where you can stuff that soil! Oddly enough, as Evrikh was entertaining his internal struggle, the intensity of her eyes upon him shifted, as though she had sensed what he was thinking. Caught in this moment of vulnerability, Evrikh felt his face flush red-hot, his eyes trailing away, fighting to fall upon her once more. *Come on, Evrikh, don't be such a guy.*

Suddenly, she ascended through the tree limb as if it were a part of her and straddled it beside him, for a moment her eyes glowed a bright blue; blue roses.

"This is all right because I like you, Evrikh. I can teach

you of the past, if you'd like. Time runs, however; we have more than enough."

As she continued to straddle the tree limb, Evrikh watched as fresh grass and moss slowly spread out over it, felt the brittle bark beneath him somehow regain its strength, its life.

"*Know* the past?" His mind had reeled over that very question for days now. *DAMMIT, EVRIKH . . . her face, her lovely damn face! NOT her cleavage!*

"*My* past; the past of our home. I can show you, but trust is the step in which we begin."

That flare in her eyes appeared again, accompanied by a slight wind. Her eyes appeared violet now; violet roses, and as she leaned closer, Evrikh could somehow sense the tension between them, as though she had been envisioning him the same way he had been envisioning her. She smiled; their lips only moments apart, the full softness of her mouth, the velvet touches of her plum lips. Had she entranced him somehow? Was this some spell cast over him that continued to bleed his mind of all thought, save for her? Why the hell would he be so enraptured by Lorelei without a single thought of Keona? She somehow had Evrikh at the edge of his seat mentally, but he just couldn't stop.

Evrikh looked around for a moment, and as he listened carefully to the wind, he could hear the faint laughter of the others lingering within the shadows, hidden by the wildlife. His eyes returned to Lorelei. As he looked into her indescribably seductive eyes, he probed what he had thought to be her mind and sensed no hostility within her.

"I'll trust you."

Lorelei's eyes suddenly shifted color again as her soil, roots, and her hair seemed to quickly fall to the ground; her face, enveloped in a glimmering hue, vanished like a breath of wind. A moment later, the fire flared outward as she reappeared, like a reforming dream beside the glowing embers.

"Come over here if you would," she requested as she continued to the other side of the fire, away from the tents. Evrikh followed her. As they reached the other side of the fire, she turned, her gaze lingering back at him. As she moved, the flames seemed to grow hotter, expressing her arousal, her eyes shifting yet again; a deep maroon, the same color slowly bleeding into the marble skin of her cheeks. Evrikh was captivated by her as more flowers bloomed within her hair.

"What about Keona and Brian?"

"They'll sleep for now and awaken tomorrow, with never a thought of tonight's endeavors." She waved her palm across the ground, small vines recoiling across the surface of her soil-glove, and all the debris floated away with the help of the now-rolling earth, creating a small open space. "Come, Evrikh, lie upon the mother here."

He wasn't sure of her motives, he wasn't even sure why the hell he was agreeing to this, but in the end, her beauty alone was enough to simply steel his will. Evrikh stepped into the little open area and lay down upon the ground. Looking back up to her, he said, "Lorelei, we're cool, provided this doesn't hurt . . . much."

Lorelei let out a laugh that quickly whispered throughout the forest. It was the first time he had heard her laugh, but it was a sound that flooded him with warmth he felt he had never experienced before. She looked back to him with an almost intimate smile across her face, her eyes somehow containing the concern of both a companion and a lover.

"Now is the time we relax, Evrikh; Lorelei will do the rest."

Holding out her arm, the vines of her glove came alive again and stretched beyond her hand creating an elongated staff. *OK, she is definitely a forest-something... You just be careful with that stick you've got there.* Slowly, she continued walking around him, using the other end of that stick to draw a circle upon the ground. As she began stepping around Evrikh, he could faintly hear her speaking.

"Sylph, spirit of the wind, let thy currents guide us to the truth. Shelter us through the currents of time as we descend through our journey." Her voice was soft, and it warmed his body like the sound of a lover who'd finally returned home. "Sylph, spirit of the wind, let thy currents guide us to the truth."

Just as she completed the circle, the ground flashed a bright blue, and he could see a change in the air around them. He could see the canopy lingering above, the breeze ruffling the leaves and brush, yet he felt no wind within this small circle. Slowly the circle lit up as if it caught fire, smoldering like ashes that echoed of the night before. The circle emanated this light no more than a few inches off the ground, and yet the light had remained within the line that she had created. Looking at the edges of the circle, he realized that as the fire burned, the ground did not char, nor discolor. Evrikh looked outside the circle and could see Lorelei looking down upon him. As he watched Lorelei for a moment, the light of the circle faintly illuminating her, the name Thea suddenly whispered through his mind again. He couldn't know if it was Lorelei, what was currently happening, or if her beauty alone had recalled the name. He simply knew that this moment of peace, of serenity, had brought to mind a name he could neither fully remember nor completely forget.

"What happens next?"

Standing above him, Lorelei let her arms fall to her sides. "Evrikh, worry not, for this is necessary." Within a flash, the soil-made clothes she wore shot across her body, engulfing her. Evrikh could still see the beauty that was her, yet she appeared to be carved from earth. As she raised her right leg, she began to step into the circle; the smoldering light glowing inches below her foot. With her foot passing, then her calf, followed by her thigh, a blue light outlined the surface of her earthly skin that was passing over the circle lying below; it was if she was passing through a cylindrical portal.

Damn, this is like some shit straight out of a crazy house! You're lucky though, Lorelei, had you been some ugly-ass shrub-master, he'd be damned if you had him lying there!

Just as her right leg touched the ground, Evrikh watched as it delicately rooted itself once again, her breasts emanating that same blue light as they began to pass through this invisible portal. He gazed upon her, almost aroused, as her earthly breasts bounced through, followed by her waist, her shoulders, her sculpted face, and then finally her left foot. Her hair had simply glided through, reblossoming and coming back to life as it floated to our side. Very swiftly, the soil had retreated across her body as it did before, and there was Lorelei, smiling down at him in all of her captivating beauty; the exquisiteness of nature herself.

"Once the circle is complete it will pass nothing, save for us," she whispered.

Kneeling down beside him, he realized she was now watching his motions. Feeling a flutter of blood leap into his face, Evrikh deterred his eyes from her in a little embarrassment.

"Our journey continues as we tune to the mother herself; seeing the past . . . together." Lorelei spoke as she motioned her gloved fist over his stomach. Speaking her words again, she slowly opened her hand, expanding her fingers as the purest of soil dripped from her glove onto his body like that of an hourglass.

"Is the truth you seek that of your heart?" Those amazing roses sparkled in the shadow of blackness her hair invoked.

Without warning or notion of any sort, Evrikh suddenly found himself in a very erotic situation, and he had to use all his concentration to stop himself from looking at such a wondrous creature as her.

"Yes, Lorelei . . . it is."

With the last of the dust falling to his body, the blue

light around them began to rotate, creating a gentle funnel of wind. He watched as Lorelei raised her hand to her mouth and exhaled; a greenish haze. Catching this breathy dream in her hand, she laced his body with it, settling upon him like some kind of foggy dream. As he rested in the greenish tint of her breath, his body was suddenly rushed with a distinct pleasure. Looking down, he could see the edge of his pants bulging from his member within. While Lorelei sat there speaking her words and breathing, Evrikh could see the silhouette of her breasts rising and falling beneath the lit sky. Such a marvel was this body of hers. As the light rotated faster around them, it began to emit waves of light across the ground, spreading like an aftershock to something that never occurred. He closed his eyes in wonderment of this experience, and the presence of her beauty brought his blood surging through his body. As he opened his eyes, a vision streaked by. A vision of a world he had never known, yet somehow more than just a memory.

Lorelei repositioned herself over his body and Evrikh could now feel her legs resting beside him, the weight of her body pressing down upon his member, nestled between her thighs. Leaning forward, her hair began to fall around their faces as her breasts pressed between them; velvet skin. As she lay above him, he welcomed her there, wanting them to do more than simply lie with each other. He could feel the soil of her makeshift bra and gloves spreading out once more, slowly ascending across her body and approaching her face. He watched with excitement and a hint of fear as the light was trickled away by her falling hair, until the last of the moonlight had vanished from this veil of hers; the soil reaching her lips just as she pressed them against his own.

"Sylph, spirit of the wind, let thy currents guide us to the truth. Reveal to us our desires and show us the way." Her face had become consumed by shadow; there was nothing. "Evrikh, chosen one, to know the past you must be born of the past. As you were, so it shall be."

As the last of her words whispered throughout his ears, he could no longer feel the weight of her upon him; just her presence all around him, as if he was within her. Her lips had felt locked with his own, her body caressing his entirely; his voice, a faint sound of her own. Evrikh felt as though she had become a vessel, to bring him on this journey of hers.

The waves of light suddenly returned brighter, defying the very concept of light, and as he looked he saw the sky through this funnel of wind; it began to change. Clouds sped by as if racing each other; light came . . . and went. Moments later he could no longer feel the presence of the campsite, or Keona and Brian. As the scent of Lorelei began to linger in his mouth, streams of light began jetting out in a circular motion. With every breath he inhaled Evrikh felt as though a piece of her had been drawn within him, stealing the memories he himself couldn't remember, and replacing them with memories of her own. Lying there motionless, he watched the sky continue to change as the blue light streaked outward. Suddenly, Lorelei appeared above him once again, their lips dangerously close.

"We are here," she whispered, her lips slightly resting

upon his. As she pulled away, he could feel her drawing from him; from within him. Her scent retreating from his body as he exhaled and she inhaled. Watching her retreat across his body, Evrikh saw that her soil had encased him entirely, as though the act of her leaving him was the earth itself giving birth to his body. Suddenly, everything was still.

Lorelei was breathing heavily as though this trip had exhausted her. Evrikh himself had somehow felt a little fatigued and couldn't help but wonder if whatever just happened had drained him a little as well. As a veil swayed around them, her body emerged from the retreating soil, her voice no more than a whisper.

"This," her breasts heaved up and down from exhaustion; her body beaded in dew, ". . . is the truth you seek." Within this moment, she had appeared more human than he had seen her before. Her skin was almost the tone of flesh, those odd rings ever present, no more earth as clothes; plainly a naked, vulnerable woman. He had wanted to hold her, to bring her some form of comfort.

Holding his hand within hers, he realized they were already standing. The circle of blue light had remained, moving all around them as if it were a dream. He reached out with his hand to touch it, and Lorelei had immediately snatched it back.

"If you touch it, you'll disrupt the flow."

Disrupt the flow . . . What the hell does *that* mean? He then looked through the wave of distortion to the world that now surrounded them. "What is this place?"

Lorelei placed his hand between hers. "This is the

time before your War of Ruin."

As he gazed out, they were standing before an unbelievably large chasm. Evrikh could see black smoke billowing from the industrial machinery far on the other side. Looking down, the hole before them seemed almost never-ending. Watching carefully, some of the equipment continued to operate as workers were spread throughout this mammoth dig site, almost appearing as ants before them.

"What the hell are they looking for?" Evrikh asked with an almost astonished voice.

"Pylorium, it was called back then . . . and these humans searched for it tirelessly, uncaring for mother or the consequences it would entail." Tears welled at the edges of her eyes.

"I remember that," his eyes turned from her back to the chasm before them. "Wasn't it the mineral that made cold fusion possible?" *Remember?* How in the world *did* he remember?

"Indeed . . . and only one way to obtain it. Deep from within the core of our mother." As she spoke, a very distinct sadness sprawled over her, and Evrikh took her into his arms. He held her close while the two of them peered out into this past dream—this past nightmare.

"During a huge earthquake in your year of 2017 was when your people made the discovery of that mineral here. It was after that, this gouge began; this rape of my mother." Her eyes shifted their color; molten ash. "Lake Tanganyika was once so very beautiful."

"And so they dug," Evrikh added, "as deeply as they

needed to go for more of that mineral, in hopes of learning how to create more. It continued for two years . . . continued until the War of Ruin in 2019."

The same sadness that gripped Lorelei now began to settle upon Evrikh as he realized the beginning of what was so very nearly the end. The humans were like some age-old virus, some endless disease that would eventually be the death of New Terra. Hearing voices, the two of them looked out over behind Evrikh, where a small crew of sentries were patrolling the edge of the dig site.

"I don't give a shit, man. Hey, at least we gettin' three grand a day while we'z down here, ya know!"

The other sentry pulled a cigarette from his mouth. "Tree weeks on, two weeks off, mon. I'm not saying da schedule's bad, brah, but damn! Look at dis damn ting . . . tis like a giant black hole, sittin' ere in da middle of de eart'."

Placing the cigarette back between his teeth, the mingling of the small crew stopped as they began their target practice back on the trees behind them firing away without a care in the world. As Evrikh looked back down at Lorelei, she was whispering something as though she were remembering the lyrics to a song. Moments later, Evrikh heard a loud crackling pop and his head whipped around to where the small band of sentries were performing their target practice. He had barely had the chance to hear their screams as they were all tumbling down the giant ravine. The ground they were standing on had, unfortunately, broken off, and they all went sliding into the chasm. As the dust was slowly settling about, Evrikh could have sworn he had seen small roots retreating back into the earth from the edge of the chasm where the crew had fallen. Slightly in awe, he turned back to look at Lorelei, still within his embrace.

"They deserved so much worse; every one of them." The color had returned to her marble skin, her soil hands encasing Evrikh's back, the small vines embracing him in return.

He looked back out over the chasm. "Why not study the mineral he already had? Why go through all this trouble just to obtain more?"

"Reproduction of the Savari Effect required the mineral Pylorium. Dr. Savari, much like the rest of your kind, was selfish, indulgent. Studied it, of course, but that was not to stop him from having more; from taking more." It was the first time Evrikh had heard a hint of disdain in her voice; of disgust.

"Mother, she cried your year of 2017, and it was here that I was first born; the very pit of this wretched womb." She shuttered at the memory of it, her soil armor waking across Evrikh's body, pulling him closer. "How very proficient the humans are at hurting our beloved mother."

He looked at her, and there was no denying the anguish resonating within her eyes. "I'm so very sorry for all of this, Lorelei. I'm afraid I don't understand what this has to do with me, but I wish I could've done something for you." He glanced back out to the black hole that disappeared into the core of New Terra. "For her."

The distortion shifted slightly and the view changed to a room. It appeared to be some kind of lab. The distortion faded for a moment, and then returned.

"The field grows weak, and so our time has nearly ended."

Evrikh looked around the room and could see a strange device that looked like a capsule. Its contents were of small stones and very fine dust that radiated a faint hue of violet, yet the light that refracted from its edges glowed a very bright white; Pylorium. Across the room he noticed another capsule. It had a small opening; a window toward the top, and above that, a nameplate. The distortion field faded again, and the image grew weaker. He concentrated his vision and a second later he could read the nameplate ... THE PHOENIX GATE.

Evrikh's eyes widened, and he looked at Lorelei. "What the hell is this?"

Lorelei looked around the room, and then back up to him. "The beginning."

The room faded one more time, and the distortion field was almost gone. He looked around the room one last time, and his eyes halted on the desk. Sitting on the other side of the desk was another nameplate. KENDRICK SAVARI.

Seconds later the distortion completely faded away and all that remained was blackness. He looked back at Lorelei. "What's happened?"

"If we had once left, so too must we return." She had spoken as Evrikh found her lips again within inches of his own. He could feel her breath caressing his face as she exhaled that greenish haze. Enveloping his senses, he could feel her beauty invading him once more, intoxicating his body with a primal lust. Entering his mouth and attacking his sense of taste, Evrikh began to feel a deep burn in the back of his mind. He watched through her beautiful haze as her hair came alive and stretched up around their faces. Wrapping around his head, it began to seal out the light once more, bringing their faces even closer together. Her face was truly a marvel, whose eyes were as soft as a lion's mane and twice as fierce. Then, just as the moisture of her lips connected with his, she was gone. Blackness was all that remained, the blackness of her soil . . . around him; within him.

~ ~ ~

Evrikh felt the comfortable sensation of a hand running through his hair, stimulating his head like the morning after an intimate evening. As he began to open his eyes he could see the canopy that lingered so far away, that familiar sea of colors. A slight breeze blew through the forest and brought the leaves and grass to life. They swayed back and forth, appreciating the cool wind. He faintly heard Keona's voice in the distance, then she suddenly leaned over him and a couple seconds later, came into focus. As that ocean of colors weaved around the silhouette of her face, he couldn't help but think of Lorelei.

"Hey, there, I thought you were supposed to be on watch?" a grin streaked across her face.

Evrikh sat up and looked around for a moment. "Damn, I'm sorry; I must have been more exhausted than I thought." He looked back to Keona and noticed that she was staring at his neck. She reached out and grabbed something that hung there.

"Where'd you get this from?" She brought her eyes back up to meet his.

He looked at her baffled, and then followed her eyes back down. In her hand lay a strange small pendant he had never seen before. He took it into his hand and held it closer, looking at the intricate detail carved into it. The strap came down from around his neck and ran right into what would be the circular edge of the pendant; into her hair. It was only a moment before Evrikh knew exactly who she was. Lorelei. Her amazing wild hair falling around the marble skin of her lovely face, eyes that radiated with life, that were still fresh; roses whose color was that of the sunset. As he watched her carefully, he could almost swear there were still flowers blooming about her hair, her gaze upon him ready to strike up a conversation at a moment's notice; her lips, poised as though she had waited for him there, waited for his lips, his kiss.

Damn, Lorelei, isn't this some form of invasion? Of course, he appreciates the gift, but maybe something a little more subtle would be better next time . . . But, wow, even as a little pendant, she's crazy hot!

"Ha-ha, Keona, funny," he snickered. "Wow, it's really beautiful. I'm not even sure when you slipped it on me, but thanks." He looked up to Keona and gave her a genuine smile. She stood up, looking down upon him for a moment.

"Well, let's go. We're burning daylight," she finally blurted with enthusiasm.

He looked over to Brian only to see that he had

already packed up the tents and most of the other equipment. Keona had started with the thermals. Evrikh stood up and looked around for a moment, running his hand through his hair. As he looked over toward Brian and Keona, his attention was drawn past them to a distant shadow almost to minute to notice. He stared for a moment before Keona interrupted, prompting him to give her a hand. He looked back to the shadow and knew that she was still out there, watching them. He would have believed it to be a dream had it not been for her presence out there. Who in the world would've ever thought beings like that even existed? Damn earthly spirits, elementals ... That's some damn crazy shit! It seems the world will always have more secrets then it would ever allow us to know. Evrikh turned his attention back to Keona and helped her with the rest of their things. Before long, they had packed up and were on their way.

As they trekked through the forest, Evrikh looked ahead and could see that the trees began to grow thinner. Brian and Keona had noticed it as well.

"There's a clearing up ahead," Brian said while looking over his shoulder.

Evrikh stepped up over a rock and landed hard on the other side. "I know; I see it also."

As they drew closer, the trees grew scarce. The sounds of waterfalls could be heard in the distance. The forest had opened to a cliff. Brian was the first to step up, looking out over the edge.

"Well, there it is." His head panned the horizon. "It truly is a beautiful sight. And in the distance you can barely see Jurubian City."

Keona jumped around Evrikh's arm and started pulling him along with her. Just as the two reached the edge of the cliff, they stopped. Keona's eyes grew wide with amazement, and even he was surprised by the beauty of this landscape. There was an impossibly large ravine—chasm—that separated the edge they stood upon from the other. At the very bottom, there was a raging river that flowed effortlessly along, as if driven mad by some unknown force. The water almost seemed like a blur of light, slightly reflecting this valley that encaged it. On the other side of the canyon was where the waterfalls sang their music, cascading from the walls of the canyon and falling to the river below, as it the earth itself was crying for its past losses. Looking beyond that, you could see where the land had become a lush green, riveting with life. As Evrikh took in the beauty of this sight, a very new memory was also thrust before him. A sight of a time immemorial, when this chasm before them was a raging scar upon the earth; a gaping hole as man dug relentlessly; the taste of that endless sorrow burrowing its way onto his face; this birthplace of Lorelei.

"Wow," Keona said while stepping closer to the cliff. "It's so beautiful."

"Or so very tragic, however you look at it," Evrikh replied, placing his arm around her. "Makes you wonder what could've happened here, and why the Council would fear such a wondrous place."

"Could've happened . . . Evrikh, nothing's ever happened here. Look at this place, as if it's forever gone untouched by the hands of man," Keona spoke, clearly captivated by the beauty of the scene before them.

"Us," Brian said, stepping to the edge of the ravine, "they don't know what's out there. They don't know if we're out there."

"I see," Evrikh said while rubbing Keona's shoulders. "Maybe they're afraid that there's more than *us* out here." An intimate smile etched its way onto his mouth.

"There," Brian said, pointing a finger way across to the other side, "do you see that glittering spire between those two mountains?"

Evrikh squinted his eyes, and suddenly it was as if he was standing on the other side of the chasm, the edges of his vision slightly out of focus yet there he was, as if he was standing 100 leagues closer than a moment ago.

"HOLY SHIT!" he grunted out as he fell backward. "HELL, YEAH, I FUCKIN' SEE IT!"

As Keona and Brian were both startled by Evrikh's actions, they whipped around just in time as his back hit the ground.

"What is it?"

". . . The hell's wrong, Evrikh?" Keona had finished.

Standing back up and brushing himself off, Evrikh realized his vision had returned, and he was once again on this side of the ravine with both Brian and Keona wearing worried looks on their faces.

"It's OK, it's OK." He began dusting himself off. "Sorry, it just startled the shit out of me, but I'll tell you all about it a bit later."

WHAT THE HELL WAS THAT? Some kind of

crazy-ass hawk vision? Shit, wonder if that can happen on demand. He'll definitely have to work on that one, and it was pretty cool. Talk about crazy dizzy though, maybe Evrikh should brace himself next time; felt like someone suddenly throwing up HUGE magnifying glasses in front of his eyes!

"That's the Aurora Temple. That's our destination; Jurubian City," Brian added.

Evrikh's mind was left to wonder about what was to come.

"Jurubian City," Keona murmured.

He turned around to the forest one last time and smiled, knowing that they were still watching, knowing that *she* was still watching, lost to the world in this sacred forest of theirs. Evrikh opened his mind to his newfound friend, to Lorelei.

"Perhaps in the future your precious mother will no longer need to cry; maybe she'll heal, maybe it'll all heal."

As he finished his words, he found himself kneeling, his hand brushing across the grass. With his hand gliding along, we watched as small vines slowly caressed his touch in return, the ground reflecting his emotion; her emotion.

He turned to catch up to Keona and Brian.

* * * *

CHAPTER 5
~ Do I Know You? ~

JURUBIAN CITY WAS like a world within a world. Even though Evrikh had memories sprawled all throughout his head of places he had been yet didn't remember, he still felt that this city was magnificent; a true contribution to the artistic endeavors of their ancestors. Evrikh felt that these insane cases of déjà vu would ultimately be what drives him crazy. How is it possible to walk into a city for the first time, yet somehow feel as though you were there when it was first being built? The streets were bustling with people of all sorts: Ulurians, Fiorenians, Tresarians, from what Evrikh could immediately recognize. Jurubian was definitely more culturally diverse than Norwynn could ever hope to be. Buildings of the old-time were refinished to look anew. It somehow gave the city the appeal of a modern artifact. Speed bikes weaved in and out of the streets, like some prey trying so frantically to avert its predator. A parade was heard in the distance as confetti spread throughout the air to honor the

Goddess Miriam, no doubt. As the three visitors walked on through the edge of the city, through all the buildings and the confetti in the air, at the middle of Jurubian sat a monument. Water ran from small windows, falling as if frozen in time, gardens of flowers growing along its sides; a monument that reached higher than the clouds and glistened like a mirror. The Aurora Temple.

While walking down a street, a man descended from a crowd and approached them. His pants bore a resemblance to dull leather; his shoes, boots with steel toes, laceless. The man's shirt was tucked in with the appearance of tedious work. His face was exotic, carved from the pleasures of a nightly life.

"Excuse me," he began as he handed Evrikh a folded flyer, "won't you come to our club tonight? We have drinks, dancers, music," the man invited with enthusiasm. "We even have women, or you can bring your own," he expressed, gleefully waving a hand at Keona.

"Come on, Evrikh, Keona. We haven't got the time for this," Brian cut in.

Evrikh took Keona's hand and thanked the man. Then he turned to follow Brian, the stranger's voice to his back.

"... Any time, friend," his voice faded away.

Evrikh looked down at the flyer in his hand and opened it, only to find himself staring. An orange neon symbol written in bold letters, accompanied with an invitation:

Visit the most exclusive club, more enticing than the forbidden fruit, and more enchanting than the gardens of Eve . . . **Divine.**

What the hell! There's no way this is a coincidence! Who was that? . . . Did he somehow know Evrikh? That's impossible, he couldn't know him!

Evrikh quickly turned around, his eyes darting through the crowds of people, searching for that random stranger.

"Evrikh!" Keona erupted as she wrenched her hand free from his firming grip. "What the hell! You know that guy?"

"WHAT?" His eyes quickly glanced toward Keona. "Oh, sorry." He noticed she was now rubbing the hand that was formerly within his grip. "No, no, Keona, sorry 'bout that." Evrikh reaffirmed his attention to Keona as he took her hand back between his in an attempt to rub the soreness away. "I was just thinking this club here sounds interesting, and I wanted to get directions for later, you know," he finished as he waved the flyer about apologetically.

"Well, Jesus! I mean, I love ya, but how 'bout you crush your own damn hand next time?" She gestured for them to catch up to Brian. "Come on, besides, you wouldn't wanna know people in that low a place," she added as their hands glided apart.

Evrikh watched Keona for a few moments as she stepped up beside Brian, and for a second he almost sensed a growing change within her, and then it was gone. Like a feeling of seeing something out of the corner of your eye, and when you turn to look, it's suddenly gone altogether.

". . . Yeah, you're right," he finished smiling; his mind

thought otherwise.

As they reached the inner city, the streets quickly filled with people attending the parade. They began weaving their way through the crowds. Evrikh looked up to notice a hovering platform in the middle of the parade. On top of the platform was a seat so crystal clear, so translucent, it resembled water. Then it happened, suddenly and without warning. Evrikh's vision had been stolen from him, and as he uncontrollably looked upon the woman embraced by her crystal throne, he fought to remove his eyes from her, willing himself in a failed attempt. Even though her beauty was unmistakable, there was somehow so much more, something Evrikh felt within him yet couldn't see. We watched as her gown swayed like a wind that nourishes the flowers of spring. Her hair cascaded in such a way, and her face so soft, so enrapturing, it was as if she had been ripped from the very threads of man's dream. Her gown loomed into a corset as it ascended upon her hips, sheathing the curves of her sides, her stomach, her breasts, hugging her like a love that hugs the soul.

"Hey, Brian, who is that?" he asked, waving his head in her direction.

Brian turned while maintaining his path through the crowd. "Don't you know? That's Miriam."

"...Miriam?"

"Yeah," Brian continued, "she's the prophet of Aurora. People say that she founded the Council, you know that. There's still many who believe she's the one who helped the people rebuild after the Great Darkness. Some even say *she's* the original, but that's a little hard to believe."

Miriam's body glowed as though she were a heavenly angel. How in the world was she so radiant like that? Evrikh looked at those who stood around, glancing up in her direction. Do they not see her glowing like that? It looked as though her purity was tangible, simply flowing out of her body in the form of light. Evrikh immediately felt he should've lived a more churchgoing life. No wonder these people think she's a savior . . . When you look like that, how the hell could you be anything else?

Just then, as she was looking around at the people, she stopped; her hand slowly dropping beside her. Through all the bowing priests and priestesses that gathered around her, their arms of praise . . . Through the noisy confusion and the drifting confetti, and the distance that separated them, Miriam was watching Evrikh; her lush green eyes staring, radiating as though the hunter had found its prey. Everything around them remained motionless, and after a few moments everything began to blur; the only thing remaining in focus were her eyes. Evrikh's crazy eagle vision suddenly kicked in, and he was visually thrust in front of her. As she looked at him, he could smell the scent of her flesh as though she were beside him, her eyes caressing the breeze that now consumed them. So close they were; he could practically feel the breath she passed between her lips. Suddenly, Miriam's body lay below Evrikh, writhing in ecstasy. Reaching up, she pulled herself to him, he taking her breast into his mouth; the softest shades of color, the most intimate tastes of sweetness. The image was suddenly gone as swiftly as it arrived, Evrikh realizing his normal vision had finally returned to him. Miriam's eyes grew wide and . . . was she grinning now? Her face suddenly twisted with pleasure, and their two bodies were closer than any physical moment he ever knew, almost like a longing to be whole; her radiant glow somehow invading him.

As Evrikh blinked the world back to life, the parade was moving once again and the dancers continued while the music played on; people cheered, praised, unknowing of the intimacy shared only moments ago. Evrikh looked around cautiously, slightly confused of where he was. His eyes fell upon Miriam once again; her hand waving as she looked about the crowds of those who worshipped her. It was then that he heard a whisper streak the back of his mind . . .

I've waited for you.

"Evrikh," Keona's voice interrupted, "you coming?"

He quickly spun his head to look at Keona, as though he was caught. "Wha . . . yeah, I'm coming."

As he began walking again, Evrikh turned back to look at Miriam. Her eyes continued to greet the crowd. Could he have somehow known her before, or is this the first time he's ever met her? Damn, this selective amnesia! With eyes that green, how the hell could Evrikh not remember her?

They all turned down a side street and walked in a little ways, Brian's feet bringing him about.

"Here's the plan," he stated very seriously, "raise no suspicion about yourself, and make sure you lay low. Now, I've got some items to attend to before we continue." Brian handed Evrikh a piece of paper. "Meet me at that

THE PHOENIX GATE

hotel this evening. We'll continue everything then. For now, why don't the two of you familiarize yourselves with the city? But at all costs, stay out of trouble," he finished, emphasizing the last part.

"Copy that. Should trouble arise, I shall run in the opposite direction, as though Keona were awaiting me with her thighs parted to the winds," Evrikh's arms gestured grandly.

"Can we . . . can we handle that," Brian continued, as Keona scoffed the back of Evrikh's head, "right . . . RIGHT?"

"Got it; damn . . . no trouble," Evrikh said, his hand quickly smoothing the backside of his head.

"Should anything happen, Brian, Evrikh and I will contact you," Keona reassured.

The two of them watched as Brian walked between them and back into the crowds of the parade, completely lost to them moments later. Keona and Evrikh slowly walked back toward the parade, halting at the edge of the alley. He turned to look at Keona.

"Hey, would you mind meeting me in a couple hours?" There was a small glow in Evrikh's eyes he knew would not escape hers.

"You serious? Were you having a brain fart just then? Perhaps an out-of-body experience at that exact moment when Brian mentioned *no trouble*?" Keona had crossed her arms as she finished.

Wait a damn second, Keona; you upset because you're worried Evrikh might accidently find some trouble? Seriously though, it's not like he goes looking for trouble, it's more like the shit just falls upon him ... maybe buy a shirt that says "Beware of falling shit zone" or something. OR, are you upset 'cause you feel like Evrikh's taking off and leaving you to your own devices?

"Thirty minutes sounds a bit rational, but a couple *hours*?" Keona's arms crossed a bit harder, and it immediately stole Evrikh's vision as her breasts just happen to bounce out on top of them. *Clearly* that was planned.

"Yeah, there's some things I'd like to check out," he said, his eyes mentally ripping the shirt from her torso. "Besides, you heard the B-Man ... Familiarize yourselves with the city," he finished in the most exaggerated tone he could possibly think of.

A small laugh escaped from Keona's mouth. "You sure about this, Evrikh? I mean, to have had these thoughts about each other for so long," she manipulated her arms so he could see her breasts shifting under that thin cloth.

Dammit, Keona, you'd better send those fiery serpents back to the abyss! Seriously, though, Evrikh takes pleasure every time he snuggles your sweet bosom ... but something else has arisen here, and dammit, he's going to get some answers.

"Maybe you and I should spend our time together while the advantage is ours," she finished, letting her arms fall and her hands clasping together. For a moment Evrikh had recalled her, the way she had been before this crazy adventure of theirs began.

"Keona, you have very little to worry about." He stepped to her so that their hands touched, their chests embraced, their noses grazed. "I'll find you." He then leaned to her and just as she began to speak, he instead inhaled her breath, their lips exploring each other's with the truth that their next kiss might not come for some time. He then took a step back from her as though a prince would bid adieu to his princess, and as his lips curled into that familiar silly grin, he descended into the crowds. After-images of Miriam still burned within his mind. Evrikh felt drawn to her, like each piece had glimpsed the whole. His body was aroused like the excitement of a lost child that had found his way.

Evrikh continued through the crowds, turning onto a side street with less people. He walked past onlookers to the parade as they watched this grand ceremony pass them by; an old pipe suddenly wretched to life as steam began spurting from its bottom. Evrikh continued past some apartment buildings, and then a small park, a small oasis from this large city. He stood there for a moment, taking in the glimmer of truth behind this façade of man. Walking farther still, he passed some shops when he noticed an orange glow out of the corner of his eye. When he looked up, his body quit its progression forward and turned to face that orange sign. The building before him was a club: Divine.

As he looked around, people lingered outside drinking and having a good time. He looked down the street only to notice a group of guards heading in his direction; perhaps a bit too far astray from the parade, if that's indeed why they were out. Maybe it would be best to avoid them. His feet carried him toward the club.

Evrikh opened the door just as a woman walked by,

empty glasses held in her hands. "Hey, sugar."

He smiled at her, his eyes scanning her body as she walked away. Evrikh walked in past the opening, and his ears shot to life with the rich tones of mesmerizing music, upbeat almost, screaming for his body to dance. The club was lit by a faint yellow, as other lights flickered through the air, reflecting off the leaves of tropical plants. The walls were lined with giant screens that displayed images altering to the beats of the music, almost acting as a medium to both the emotion of the music and of those who were lost to its hypnotic effect. The ceiling had at least a quarter inch of clear plastic suspended from it, containing water. With the ceiling above it emanating that faint yellow, it passed through the water like the gentlest of sonnets, setting the mood of the club's very name.

There was a bar to his right, the counter shifting colors from blue to red. At the far end of the bar were the tables. Watching the people enjoying themselves, Evrikh noticed the clothes they wore, the sophistication of their body language, the friends who remained at the tables. This club was definitely not intended for people like Evrikh, people of his class or stature. Well, damn, that doesn't mean every fifth person has to stare like that!

There was a staircase to his left, the railings carved from Eldridge trees, conveying the intimate high the owner must have felt during their creation. Women walked around sharing drinks with men, sharing pleasantries, teasing them with the ageless charms of women. Some of these girls had their shirts unbuttoned, the seams parting to allow the lure of their cleavage to rape the sight of male onlookers. Some wore no bra at all; their shirts pulled tight to forge the erotic static of skin against cloth. Evrikh stopped, scanning the room for danger in hopes of foregoing it before the onset; there was none. Curious minds loomed in his direction, knowing he didn't belong there. Oddly enough, some of them seemed a bit more than curious. Slowly, he approached the bar, and as he sat down the bartender immediately approached him.

"Personally, I don't care what'cha look like, long as you can pay," he said as he overlooked Evrikh's appearance, "so, what'll ya have?"

"I'm looking for Thea."

Their eyes locked gaze, and for an instant, Evrikh felt as though they had exchanged challenges. He was a tall man and rather stocky. His face was hard; lean. Bouncer or not, he gave off the aura that he could take care of a situation, should one arise.

"Thea doesn't see visitors," the bartender replied, returning his hands to the bar.

"I see."

Evrikh opened his mind to this man, and within moments he knew him better than this man knew himself. He first saw his wife and their child. His life blew through Evrikh's mind like a chaotic wind. He then saw his other lover, beyond that; his other job. It was there that his deepest pain had been uncovered, the darkest of his secrets. Evrikh continued coldly. "Well, my friend, wouldn't it just blow some damn goats if the Council knew this place was run by you and our kind?"

The bartender looked at him half-pissed,

half-determined, but ultimately defeated as he saw the truth that was ablaze within Evrikh's eyes.

"You think the Council scares me?" He gestured nonchalantly. "I must see 'bout a hundred of you clowns a day."

"Maybe not," a hellish grin nicked the corner of Evrikh's mouth as he snatched the bartender's hands from the air and placed them back on the counter. "But I promise, I could scare you."

The bartender's eyes grew wide from the realization his hands were somehow back on the counter. It wasn't any kind of motion, more like a strange blur he witnessed, and now his hands were pinned beneath Evrikh's. A moment later his look drew past Evrikh.

"Thea!" he yelled, his voice streaming by.

Evrikh turned around to see where his yell carried to, releasing the bartender. As his eyes loomed across the room, a woman turned around from a table of friends, their voices fading to soft whispers. As she slowly stood up, Evrikh suddenly felt very intensely, the beating of his heart drastically slowed; there was even a moment he had believed it stopped altogether. It was as though his heart had finished the puzzle his mind could never solve. For a moment she stood there, her eyes seeking a path to his, covering the space between them inch by inch. As Thea drifted in his direction, she moved with a grace that went beyond captivation, a gypsy lost to the music of her soul. The spell had been cast, the trap set; he was entranced by the motion of this wondrous being.

Her hair was as black as a moonless night and twice as

fierce, twice as consuming; each shimmer from the folds echoed a memory that was simply that, a shimmer. *Wow, Thea, huh? You approaching this way because you know him? But what's the deal, you work out? Exercise? Get regular tune-ups from the goddess's personal pit crew?* There was something in her eyes, something familiar that tore at Evrikh's sanity; a piece of him perhaps, a piece of his past. Her body could have been cast from porcelain, and who would've known the difference? Her top had been covered by a tight long-sleeved belly shirt, every reflection of light bouncing a glimmer of metallic off it. This V-neck revealed a tattoo of tiger stripes, running along her cleavage up around her neck; her doe-shaped eyes softly looking back at him; silver eyes that would steal his very soul had he let his guard down. She was definitely a Vinarian, the most beautiful damn Vinarian he'd ever seen. *But she's also mixed with something else; screw it, look at her!*

Allowing his eyes to fall further downward, he noticed her navel was pierced. The bottom half of her body bore tight, auburn leather pants, accompanied by a pair of jet-black high-heeled shoes. That tattoo continued around her hips and joined together below her navel, traveling downward into her pants, to the jewel only saved for her king of kings. As she drew closer, Thea seemed to radiate even more beauty.

Just as she reached Evrikh, he began probing her mind to foretell her intentions. Her eyebrows shifted, and she gave him the slightest look of disbelief.

"Now, sweetheart, you should know better'n that," she

began, while running her hand down his side, watching her own fingers glide along as though she were painting upon the very canvas of life. "It's been a while," her palm caressed his inner thigh. Thea leaned forward to kiss him, and Evrikh found his body drawing away from her, a tear spilling from the corner of his eye. She stopped her progression and looked at him oddly, and as he wiped the falling tear from his cheek, Evrikh found himself within his own puzzlement.

"You all right?" her lips glistened with the wetness of melted ice.

"... I don't know." For a moment he sat there, rolling his fingers with the moisture from this mysterious emotion that so suddenly fell from his eye.

"Come on," she took him by the hand, "let's go in the back."

As they departed the crowds, heading for a back room, the people around them finally began to lose their curiosity and carried on about their business. The two of them stepped into a room with a bed, Thea sliding the door closed. It was a simple room meant for pleasure, not business. She turned around and walked up to Evrikh, her hands hovering around his body as her face rested against his. The sigh that came from her mouth wasn't a sigh at all. It was an answer, an answer to a long-sought question hidden within the deepest beats of her heart.

"Damn you, Evrikh, I thought you died." There was a slight pause as she seemed to breathe in his scent. "We all did. Why'd you wait so long to make contact?"

He placed his hands on her shoulders and stepped

back from her. Evrikh couldn't understand why standing there, holding her, had felt so natural. He only knew that at this point he needed an answer, or answers. But every time he separated himself from her, a very distinct feeling spiked through his chest: loss. Another tear slipped from his eye.

"I don't remember you," although it almost sounded as though he was trying to convince himself.

"Evrikh, what're you talking about?"

"Thea, I don't remember you. I don't remember this place. I don't even remember this town. Have I come here before? I know when I see you, hear your voice, shit, even when I touch you, something changes inside me. And, damn, seeing you standing in front of me, with this look in your eyes, makes me wish that I had an answer for you."

Thea stared at him for a moment in a way Evrikh had imagined she had quite looked at him many times before. "He really did lock everything away up there," she said, nodding her head toward his, "and there's only one way for you to remember. The Elder knew the Council would come for you, we all knew, even you, Evrikh. So he hid you away." Thea reached up and placed her index finger on his forehead. "He hid you away in the pleasure side of your mind. He knew it would be impossible for the Council to reach you there. That was the last time we've seen each other," her voice hinted at what she must have believed to be a mistake.

Evrikh left Thea standing there and sat down on the bed, taking a deep breath. "That doesn't make any sense," he began, looking down at the floor. "So the only way I'll remember . . ."

"... is through pleasure; a very *specific* kind of pleasure. When you agreed to be hidden by the Elder, he sealed away your memories in such a way that only one person could ever free you." She gazed at him with a bit of triumph. "You ever find yourself aroused at the strangest moments? Look at something or someone you wouldn't otherwise look at and find attraction in it?"

You mean like right now? . . .

"Evrikh, it was never meant to be a permanent solution. We all agreed at the time it was the *only* way to hide from them. They were too close, *way* too close." Her hands had run along the contours of his arms and shoulders. Her mind was still trying to wrap itself around the idea of him finally standing before her.

"I received a note that told me I should meet you here, from someone I never got the chance to meet. Now you're telling me it's possible to get my memories back, so why?"

"Why take back your memories?" Her voice was the echo of pleasure.

"Why should I trust you . . . when I can see your secrets?" His gaze found its way to hers.

"Evrikh, whether you choose to believe me is irrelevant; doesn't change the fact that it's still the truth. And if nothing else, I *will* have you remember me. You don't get to forget me, not me."

She had changed now; her words were that of someone who had lost something so very precious to her, a tone of her trance-inducing voice that he believed had also been reserved only for him. *You don't get to forget me, not me . . .* echoed back and forth in his mind. Somehow it was a small echo that reflected a very similar loss.

"Evrikh, do you want your life back? Do you want answers to questions I know are burning inside you?" she continued, approaching him as he sat there on the bed, her legs bending, straddling, beside his own; her hands probing his neck.

"This'll only happen when you're ready, Ev. Just know, I'm the only one who can make this happen for you; for us." Her hands held him then, cradling his face, and as Evrikh looked up into her eyes, he had finally received part of an answer; even though it was to a question he had never thought to ask.

"I meant what I said about needing a very specific kind of pleasure. Because it's the kind that can only be felt between two people who have a very unique bond." Her voice was soothing.

Everything about her was familiar; the scent of her skin, the gaze of her eyes, the tone of her voice, the softness of her hands, even the beat of her heart. The BEAT of her heart! How in the hell, Evrikh thought as his eyes carried downward. He had been so captivated by just looking in her eyes that he hadn't noticed their bodies were touching, their stomachs, and their chests. Beneath it all, there it was; her heartbeat. As Evrikh looked back up he felt another tear slip from the edge of his eye. She had unleashed this wild lion within his heart, this untamable, powerful, alluring beast. Evrikh fought against it with his mind, but this unstoppable, ferocious beast was eating him alive. It had consumed his willpower before it even began, and all that was left within him he had already turned over to it.

There is a unique bond, and it was as tangible within the room as sure as Evrikh felt her heart beating against his own. He *knew* this woman once; Thea. Every piece of him had known every piece of her, and the only thing getting in the way was his mind. As he tried to think about it, only his mind had felt confusion, or didn't fit into this equation of theirs. But as he sat with her, so close, he knew his body had remembered her, his hands, his eyes, his taste as he inhaled her scent, even his heartbeat slowed to the pace of hers, longing to share her familiar rhythm.

As he looked up back into the depths of her eyes, he did all he could to put his mind at ease; the only warrior still standing from his internal conflict. His mind stood down, Evrikh knowing that whether Thea was or was not as she seems, he would still do whatever it took for the answers he sought.

"Whatever life we agreed I should've left behind, Thea, I'm ready to have it back."

Thea placed a hand on his chest, holding it there for a moment before pushing him down on the bed. As their heartbeats separated once more, there was a brief moment when he felt as though a black hole had opened within his chest, and Evrikh knew this emotional response was from the bond they did indeed share; his mind damning him for being so careless with someone he had hardly known.

"Evrikh, no matter what happens, stay as relaxed as you can."

~ ~ ~

He lay across the duvet, relieved of his clothes. Thea stepped up onto the bed and crawled over him, the brief grazing of her skin sending electrical waves throughout his body. Her breasts loomed above his face hinting at the secrets within her shirt, the velvet softness of a breath. Slowly, she lowered herself onto his waist, Evrikh's member resting between her thighs. His heart rate sputtered alive, and yet he could still feel hers maintaining the same rhythm. Thea began to breathe a little heavier.

"Now, Evrikh," she breathed, half-vulnerable, half-relieved, "this is going to feel a little unusual. But just let it flow naturally."

Thea began gently sliding herself up and down his waist, his erection rubbing against her. As she continued to move, he felt the contours of her vagina find their way around his member, her inner wetness massaging his flesh. What in the hell could possibly be unusual about this, other than it all feeling so familiar? Evrikh used his hand to brush her hair up behind her head and looked deep into her eyes. At the moment she exhaled, he breathed in her scent again, and a memory had momentarily projected itself onto the screens behind his eyes. She was above him; it was their bodies that had once intertwined. He had shared himself with her before, shared this bond of intimacy, of love. As Evrikh continued looking into her answering eyes, he knew he would regain his memories, but more importantly, he was beginning to remember what she meant . . . *You don't get to forget me.*

The gentle motion became easier as her fluids slowly lubricated them. Thea's body momentarily fluttered from the pleasure, and she dropped to her elbows, her breasts pillowing Evrikh's neck. Teasing her skin with his mouth, his lips had remembered her softness, her wondrous flavor. His hand teased across the skin of her legs until he had a firm grip of her ass, the other lay to the small of her back, and he repositioned her directly above him; their eyes a mere blink away from each other's. Their noses brushed, taking in each other's incense, their lips exploring like feverish tendrils. Thea began rotating her hips as her womanhood milked the edges of his member, teasing his mind with even more memories. Evrikh ran his tongue along her cleavage and bit down, his teeth marking her addictive skin. Thea groaned from the sensation, and Evrikh continued edging her up and down. That was when the next of the images came.

~

Evrikh was surrounded by darkness; his body restricted. He willed his body to move, but it was as though it was no longer listening. Lingering no more than two inches in front of his eyes sat a small window. Concentrating as best he could to look out from it, Evrikh was momentarily blinded by an immense flash of light, and then he was suddenly in a different room. As the radiant blindness dissipated, this new place was destroyed, furniture thrown about, the windows smashed, and the walls cracked. Evrikh heard a voice beside him and as he looked in its direction, there stood a figure out of focus.

"Evrikh, we can't keep running forever. There's only one thing we can do. The Council mustn't have you."

He tried to bring the figure into focus, but it just wouldn't happen. Suddenly, a loud noise erupted from the door across the room. The distorted figure looked back.

"They're still coming!" It glanced back to Evrikh once more. "They won't have you!"

The room flashed again, and he was lying on a couch holding a wineglass in his hand. He looked down and noticed Thea sitting beside him, her legs wrapped across his own, her head resting softly upon his neck. A fire raged in the fireplace before them, and the light illuminated the room like a reverie. Thea brought a glass up to her lips and sipped from it. She adjusted herself and placed her arm along his side. As Evrikh peered down into his own glass, he watched as the tears fell from his eyes, passing through the wine like the memory this was.

"I wish it didn't have to be this way, Ev. But he's right, I don't think there's any other way."

He could hear and feel himself moving and talking, although he wasn't in control. "Don't worry, Thea, no matter what happens or who I become, I'll always love you." Before he was even given the chance to think about it, he had already recited those words from this sacred memory.

She turned around and looked up to him.

~

The light returned, drowning out the vision, and suddenly, Thea was on top of him, her body quivering, her teeth clenched, as she reached her climax. She looked down at Evrikh breathing heavily, her hair cascading over her shoulders, falling, teasing the skin of her breasts, her nipples peeking the air as two dewdrops.

OK, now this is getting a little unusual. Those are powerful memories of the two of them, and for someone Evrikh loved so deeply, why in the hell would he ever abandon her? Such a deep sadness had begun to etch itself into his eyes as he held her like the reflection of water she appeared to be, afraid that even the slightest movement would ripple her away.

"Now it's time," her breasts pillowing between them, noticing that small familiar look within his eyes.

Thea sat up on her knees and reached behind her, grasping his erection and lifting it toward her. She eased back and the tip of his member burrowed into her. Thea groaned in pleasure and continued easing backward, his erection gliding deeper and deeper, filling her as only he could do. Evrikh felt the warmth of being inside her; *her* familiar warmth. More images.

He took in the world and how it used to be, before the Council of Aurora, before the War of Ruin. How the Council first rose to power, attempting to control and manipulate everything it could possibly get its hands on. Thea rocked forward, then back down, bringing another wave of pleasure and images as Evrikh involuntarily moaned. Her pleasure was a memory ablaze within him, something his heart had always ached for more of.

That distorted figure stood before him as it slowly began to come into focus. As images continued to streak across his mind, Evrikh suddenly remembered who the Elder was, why she concealed him, and why the Council would never rest till they owned him. He started to remember the past, but most importantly, the memory of who he was.

His palms glided along the contours of her hips, wrapping around; his fingers gripping the flesh of her ass. He slid his other hand up around her back, his palm resting between her shoulders as he indulged himself, sliding deeper within her. He moaned again as his muscles rippled, pulling her closer. Thea's breasts pressed firmly against his chest as he gently kissed her neck; her body quivering at this ancient, familiar pleasure that was only theirs. His thrust became more eager and forceful, as the past renewed itself within his mind. Thea had reached her climax again, and this new wave of emotion poured out from her, coating his member. She bit her lip and suppressed a groan from this delicious ecstasy, this irresistible ritual.

His eyes journeyed down while his mouth began caressing her breasts, his lips and tongue like wild tendrils lost to the erotic scent of her skin. Evrikh had barely noticed their bodies glowing where they were joined, and he could feel change occurring within him. As her lips found their way to his, he knew that same light was emanating from their mouths, as her nose cast a shadow above her eyes; eyes that held a look Evrikh completely, and forever, would remember. His mind was absorbing Alex and returning him to the place he had come from. With each thrust, the light intensified and the sensations grew stronger, more intimate; more eager. Suddenly he felt like this is where he's always belonged, inside her. His erection slowly grew bigger, and her body tighter, as her muscles contracted around it, holding him the way she has so many times before.

Evrikh's hair slightly lengthened, slowly turning silver, all color somehow bleeding out. His body shimmered, the vibrations thrumming from deep within him until every unnatural mark had simply vanished from his body; his perfect skin renewed. He could feel all his senses growing even more acute, and he immediately knew that he had never experienced this passion he shared with Thea before, so deeply, so completely, as he did right now. His eyes began glowing, and each thrust was more demanding. Thea was helpless now as his member continued to grow within her, her body quivering as if in answer. She moaned uncontrollably from this frenzied pleasure, this half-memory of his warmth once again inside her; the light brightening, consuming the air all around them.

"Oh my God, Evrikh!" Thea blurted, "Oh my God."

It was as though his mind had been a prisoner; a beast whose chains had finally broken. Evrikh could not see past this light that now enveloped him; he simply relished in that he shared this light with Thea; beside her; within her. As their moans were mere echoes somewhere in the distance, both his mind and body had finally reached their limit. It had all been restored, every memory, every emotion, every detail, as vibrantly as the very moments they were forged. With the echoes of their moans growing even further away, Evrikh barely noticed the light finally dimming, the softening hues bringing with it a numbing sensation. It was only then that he truly realized the extent of his exhaustion.

". . . My Thea," he let slip past his lips one last time before the blackness took him.

He fainted.

~ ~ ~

Evrikh awoke, to see the world through the eyes of who he was; the convoluted illusion of Alex truly removed. He looked to his side and the breath that escaped from him was one that only the heart can exhale; the very life of his spirit, all the threads of his fate, his soul mate. She rested while her body still quivered from their interaction. He could smell the exhaustion surrounding her body, the sea breezes of her sweat. Evrikh loved her before he became Alex, and the Elder didn't just conceal him in the pleasure side of his mind.

"You never told me who that one person was," he whispered into her ear, her body panting within his arms.

"It's always been me . . . your true love," her mouth slightly echoed.

The Elder made it so that Thea would be the only person who could revive him. He leaned over and kissed her softly; her skin, the haze of his dreams. Evrikh whispered once more, ". . . My dearest Thea."

As he sat up on the edge of the bed, Evrikh realized that he had forgotten about Keona and Brian. His second realization leaping in almost immediately following; he didn't even know who they were. What the hell . . . more lies? The Elder never mentioned them, and they were never involved until recently. He's only known them for a couple of years actually, yet he couldn't recall anything about their past, or where they came from. Evrikh suddenly wasn't sure if he could trust them anymore, wasn't sure of whom he could trust. He looked down at himself. What if he *did* go and meet Keona? Would she recognize him like this?

But in truth, Evrikh had already made up his mind. The room suddenly became filled with a faint glow as his skin lit up from the inside. It was a warm and gentle feeling. The light became so bright that he could no longer see his body, just its shape. Slowly, Evrikh witnessed the shape of his body changing, returning to the shape it once had; returning to Alex, and he suddenly remembered what Brian had said about Boon.

". . . after changing Boon's DNA into its own, the new strain has some kind of defense to hide itself, so it's untraceable . . ."

Brian was the one who gave Keona and Evrikh the DNA strain to work with. But where could he have gotten it? Wait, is it possible that there's another person like Evrikh out there?! He briefly looked at the clock on the wall. Shit; it's already 7:00 p.m.? He'd better get back to Keona or Brian before he goes off on another crazy tangent about *trouble*.

As he slowly rose, his body experienced a horrific sensation. His mind became erratic, his heart beating wildly. Evrikh became terrified, and he knew something wasn't right. He leaned back onto the bed and whispered into Thea's ear.

THE PHOENIX GATE

"Hey; hey, Thea," he placed a hand on her shoulder, "Thea, wake up."

She groaned under her breath and opened her eyes, turning to her side. "Hmm, what is it, Ev?"

"Shh," he motioned with his hand to his mouth. Then continued whispering, "I want you to get up and leave out the back."

Thea immediately sat up. "Why, what's wrong?"

"Something's not right, Thea, I *know* something's not right. Please, just go."

Just then he noticed a glimmer out of the corner of his eye. As he snapped his head around, the window curtain was blowing inward from a breeze. For a moment, Evrikh sat there, his eyes absorbing every detail the room concealed. The jemha beetle that skittered across the ceiling, the rodents that made faint noises behind the walls, the light dust that blew across the floor. His vision did not divert; instead, it remained fixated, continuing through the curtain and through the shadows, to the corner of the room. Slowly he eased off the bed, his eyes squinting to an angry glow.

"Thea, get out now ..." he ordered, motioning his arm toward the door.

She climbed off the bed and stood up with the blanket wrapped around her body. She bent down and picked her clothes up off the floor, her eyes filled with both questions and fear.

"Now slowly walk toward the door. When you get there, open it and run."

Thea could sense the gravity in his voice and reluctantly

complied. As she reached the door, she opened it, dashing around the corner, leaving the blanket to float to the ground like a heavy leaf lost on the currents of wind.

As the curtain blew inward, its shape became deformed by an unseen object lingering in the shadows.

"She plays no part, leave her out of this." His body was full of rage, yet he could feel an even deeper sense of fear. The figure stepped into the light, the curtains flapping around his body, like a half-seen memory.

Evrikh's eyes grew wide, and he suddenly felt more fear than he's ever known. THE FUCK?! Have his nightmares become real? As he stared at this man, into his face, into those makeshift glasses, he could feel him staring back. At that moment he *knew* who this was.

"Well, well, Evrikh," he paused. "It's been awhile."

Lowering his stance, Evrikh planted his feet into the ground. "Hey, Cazziel, still working for the Council?" His teeth ground together as his aura began glowing, the air within the room thickening with the taste of anger; the haze of madness.

Cazziel watched him in their stillness as a grin developed around the edges of his lips. "I've had over six hundred years to develop my skills. How long have you had?"

Evrikh slowly raised his arms in front of him, and as he did, the reality around them began to distort, resembling a large bubble of free-flowing water. He threw his hands out toward Cazziel, and the distorted reality shot out like a wave toward him. Evrikh's feet embedded themselves into the ground as everything exploded between the two. Bits and pieces of the building were flung everywhere, as

THE PHOENIX GATE

if hit by something that was not there, and crumbling to pieces as they collided with their surroundings. Smoke and dust quickly filled the room as he held his ground, his breathing growing heavier in anticipation.

Slowly, the smoke began to dissipate through the wall that was now missing. The details of his surroundings peered through the white fog as he began seeing lights from the street outside. Lightning streaked across the sky as it started raining. The corner of the room was gone and Cazziel as well. The room fell silent, save the rain and Evrikh's cautious breaths.

Quickly his eyes diverted to the floor before he had even thought to move, just as the broken floor started glowing red. Evrikh's mind became overwhelmed with danger as it all converged on a single thought—get out! As he leapt from the floor, the room burst into flames, his eyes watching as everything happened in slow motion. The floor spider-webbed out, as if the puzzle had fallen apart, and the furniture had leapt from the floor also, flying through the air effortlessly. The fabrics of the room sparked from the intense heat as the blast consumed the room, the hellish blaze spreading like a plague, devouring the air like a half-starved child.

~

Rain fell from the clouds smoothly, coating the ground with its renewing sheen. Thunder rolled throughout the sky, and in the distance the roof of a building exploded as a blue light shot up into the clouds. Debris from the building spread throughout the air, as the rest of it began to glow a bright red. Suddenly, there was an explosion, pieces of brick and stone flew into the sky as the remnants of the club lay burning in the streets below. The fire lit up the night as though it was day, and far up in the sky, there remained a faint blue light.

~

As his eyes scanned the ground, he found no trace of his assailant. Where the club once stood was now a roaring fire, bellowing its poisonous smoke into the air. He kept his mind alert, attempting to find Cazziel, but it was as clueless as his eyes.

"WHAT'S A MATTER, CAZZIEL, AFRAID TO FACE ME?" Evrikh screamed in anger.

"Not afraid . . ."

Evrikh whipped around to the voice so nearly behind him. When the hell did he . . .

". . . Just gathering information."

Cazziel's body levitated at the same height as his own a little distance away.

"Evrikh, are you and your kind still pursuing your stupid little cause? You are their hope, and once you have been eliminated, they'll have no choice but to obey the Council," Cazziel snapped his gun up and held him within its sights.

Evrikh's face contorted as he began grinning at him. "You forget one thing, old friend."

"And what is that?" the reply came slowly; bemused.

His mind became at ease, his legs coming together. He started raising his arms beside him, palms up. Evrikh really didn't want to go *there* so soon after his resurrection, but ah, what the hell. His eyes burned with concentration, glowed with fury, as the words he spoke sounded like that of something else; something inhuman.

"I am the alpha and the omega, the beginning and the end..."

The wind began blowing strongly all around them as Evrikh's voice bellowed throughout the sky. Cazziel's eyes glanced around momentarily before their gaze returned to his prey, levitating right in front of him. "What game are you playing at...?"

"I have dreamt of you, Cazziel, for many years now. If you plan to pursue me, you should be aware of something." His small grin grew wider. "As God once made man in his own image... man has made God in *his* image. What do you think awaits the man who challenges a God?" Evrikh's voice could almost be heard as absolution.

You've plagued his dreams, sent your "Relics" after him and his friends; hell, you even had him possibly researching himself! You don't deserve to be absolved, you should burn... It all should burn!

Cazziel eased his finger on the trigger, preparing to fire. The wind grew immensely strong, ripping Cazziel's weapon from him. Even with all his strength, his fingers were peeled from the handle like a fruit losing its skin. He struggled to remain in position as he watched Evrikh's body burst into flames; his eyes that of molten ash. Evrikh looked down at his hands as he rolled them over. Now that's more like it. His ivory skin quickly turned shades darker as his veins grew hotter until they seemed to contain the same molten lava held within his eyes.

"Are you seeing this?" Cazziel continued his struggle to remain afloat not more than twenty meters away from Evrikh. "He's not supposed to be able to tap into this side of himself yet! Where's this data at? Someone needs to get me an answer immediately!" He cut his own communication to listen a bit more carefully to the rising threat now floating in front of him, ". . . and someone needs to tell me how in the hell he knows the language of the ancients, right now!"

Evrikh's voice continued to echo throughout the sky. *"Demorandom norectu verahshea intravalia . . ."* The fire radiating from his body began burning as nearly bright as the suns, turning the clouds around them to a crimson orange. Suddenly the brightness flashed and the wind died down. He remained floating in the sky, hair and eyes in a fiery blaze. His body had become a cell for something encaged in this world, and the next. For a moment his body was motionless, and then his arms were slowly lowered beside him, his lips curling into that fiery grin. Eyes; eyes that were alive with two spirits, bound by the same body.

Well, now, look at this . . . Here I was hoping you had died this entire time. I certainly didn't expect to find myself back here.

"Quiet now, you!" Evrikh snickered at his side.

"I have more than the Council on my side, Cazziel," his breath came in wisps of fire, his hair, wild flames dancing around the silhouette of his face.

"You have never been what you believe yourself to be!" Cazziel gritted while lowering his arms. And *who* was

Evrikh even speaking to just then?

Cazziel screamed, throwing his right arm out in front of him. A blue sphere emerged from his hand, flying toward Evrikh with great speed as lightning rippled around its surface. He flinched to the left, only to feel a sharp pain in his shoulder. Looking down, Evrikh watched as his arm fell toward the earth dissolving into ash. He looked back up to see more blue spheres screaming in his direction, promising death had he not acted swiftly. He flew to the right to dodge the first two. Cazziel kept screaming, blue spheres erupting from his body. Evrikh turned into the sky, and his body hurled him away, radiated the majestic heat of the sun, his eyes echoing the smoldering abyss. Erratic flames pirouetted around his body from where his arm once rested.

~

As civilians walked down the street, a fiery streak jetted across the sky like a meteor, followed by a shadowy line of darkness. The two streaks headed farther into the city as the pedestrians lost them to the night sky.

~

Neither of us were ready for this, Evrikh. You know there has to be a balance between—

"HUSH UP!" Evrikh erupted.

The flames that were his hair roared backward from the force of the wind as he dived down toward the buildings, spinning in circles to evade the spheres of black mass that came from behind. He still hadn't figured out what the hell those crazy balls of energy were, but if Cazziel had *that*, what other skills might he have developed since Evrikh's disappearance? He looked ahead and saw a huge building heading toward him. He quickly rolled to the left and it blew by, barely missing him although catching the folds of his shirt. Evrikh turned his eyes back and caught a glimpse of the shadowy sphere that surrounded Cazziel, continuing his damn pursuit. Evrikh had been awake all of five minutes, and you couldn't even give him that; five damn minutes of peace. Evrikh looked forward once again, his aura visibly glowing brighter as he pushed himself faster. Cazziel and Evrikh weaved in and out of the buildings, the citizens becoming worried of the strange light that streaked throughout the sky.

Are you serious! You've only just woken up, and already you call me here? Evrikh, you cannot push yourself like this! Your body will...

"In case you haven't noticed, I'm trying to save our lives!" he yelled into the sky.

LOOK AT YOURSELF! You're not saving us, you're committing suicide! You can't go over six hundred years without being a vessel, and expect your body to hold up! It's giving up!

An immediate image of Thea thrust itself before his eyes, the flames receding from his memory. It finally dawned on him; Thea's urgency, Cazziel's comment from earlier. Had he *truly* been hidden within his own mind for over six hundred years? That was never the plan; what the hell had happened? Another electrical charge seared his ear as it blew by, his fiery hair lapping after its trail. His attention was regained, his mind resolved.

Evrikh's eyes looked up, carrying his body with them, leaving the city below and ascending into the sky above. He could see the Aurora Temple in the distance. Intense heat bellowed from within his shoulder, and suddenly it burst into flames, filling the space of where his arm once was, molten lava bubbling and churning with his own blood and bone. Seconds later, the flames retreated only to reveal a new limb. He flexed his arm while curling and uncurling the fingers of this new hand, looking back at Cazziel, smiling.

"IS THAT ALL YOU HAVE?!" he screamed to Cazziel, the wind carrying his voice backward.

Cazziel raised his hands in front of himself, exposing the palms and pushing them forward. As he did this he started to slow down, and his body became vertical. Slowing to a stop, he was now confronted by this retched prey.

"Ah, the rabbit would choose to face the fox," he quipped, bringing himself to a halt.

". . . Sorry about this, but trust me. I have a plan," Evrikh nearly whispered.

A plan? Evrikh, what the hell are you thinking about in here . . . ?

Evrikh flexed every muscle in his body and concentrated with all the strands of the two halves within him. Soon he felt his body becoming the focal point of his raging thoughts and emotionally used his deepest embers to fuel these thoughts. He screamed, as suddenly giant wings of fire erupted from his back, spreading out across the sky. Opening his eyes, an almost pained breath escaped his mouth.

Clever man . . . this might work.

"Hold it together just a little while longer," he breathed into the air.

Slowly marveling from side to side, Evrikh finally returned his gaze to Cazziel, watching as his face panned the air, taking in the immense size of those wings. For a few moments he simply sat there, staring at Cazziel, his eyes grinning with anger. The monstrous wings flapped across the sky, generating thunder as they moved.

Cazziel brought his palms together and a faint red light began to emanate between them. "*CONDUSIA VERALIA!*" he screamed. Suddenly, a ball of black lightning shot out from his hands and flew toward Evrikh with great force. As it reached him, he crossed his arms bringing them up to his face. The ball exploded as it hit an invisible barrier. Fire spread throughout the sky as black lightning streaked across the clouds, the vision of a nightmare come to life. Cazziel looked forward as the flames thinned out. Evrikh's wings stretched back as if in answer to the question his attack had made, his body glowing so brightly Evrikh almost didn't look human.

Opening his eyes, Evrikh lunged himself toward Cazziel with massive power and speed, his body jetting across the sky like a comet. As Cazziel looked at him, Evrikh was screaming, those wings, a wall of flame pushing him forward.

"I see," Cazziel grunted to himself.

Within moments their bodies collided, and the sky exploded with such intensity the clouds were pushed backward, opening a hole into the stars above. A shock wave echoed throughout the sky, generating a force that quaked the earth below. Seconds later, the air began to implode bringing the light and flames back in with it.

As terrified citizens looked into the sky, it erupted into a bright white and the focal point burst into flames, spreading out like a disease and replacing the clouds with smoke. The citizens screamed and ran for anything that resembled cover.

Now THAT was a show . . . well played, Evrikh, well played. I appreciate you not getting us killed.

"Is it over?" His voice was erratic, and it echoed throughout this cloud of smoke.

Evrikh bolted out of the flames, and the city lights below came into view as he flew out of this poisonous cloud. His eyes frantically scanned the area as his mind searched the sky, but he could not feel Cazziel's presence. As he continued to search for him, a figure remained in the shadows of the city far below, a thought too distant for Evrikh to hear.

"My, my, it seems the Unfamiliar has discovered a little part of himself." The figure vanished further into the shadows as thunder rolled throughout the sky.

~ ~ ~

The streets continued to pool with water as rain continued from the evening sky. People walked down the streets, their conversations uninterrupted, unknowing of the secrets contained in their city; the secrets contained at the "Phantasia Hotel."

Evrikh walked into the dining hall and looked around.

A waiter immediately approached him as a look of disgust overwhelmed his face, a smirk quickly attempting to mask his awe. "Ah, sir, is there anything I can help you with?"

"I'm here to see Brian Viseli and Keona Keashin, or maybe just Brian and Keona." *Shit . . . if that's even their real last names. No more lies.*

"Of course, right this way, sir," the waiter said while waving his hand to the room behind him. As he turned around, he motioned Evrikh to follow him, his previous look of astonishment immediately vanishing.

As the two approached the table, Brian and Keona stood up to greet them. Evrikh walked around the table and pulled out a chair to sit down.

"Is there anything you'd like to drink?" Evrikh could only guess that the gentleman's renewed composure was that reserved only for his ordinary days.

"Ah, I'll just have a water, thank you."

The waiter cleared his throat, and then readjusted himself. "Ah, I'm sorry, sir, but we're fresh out. Is there anything else you'd like?"

"You're fresh out . . . of water?" his eyes slowly arced upward.

"That is correct, sir."

Brian sat down and leaned over. "Evrikh, they actually don't serve water here," he whispered as he sat back up.

Looking back at the table, Evrikh readjusted his chair. "Of course . . . Why in the hell would they serve water?" The waiter's face continued to smile and remain content.

"Then why don't we make it a Moon Teaser?"

The waiter nodded. "An excellent choice, sir. It'll be

just a moment." He walked away as Keona joined the other two at the table. With Brian sitting back, his face winced as though he was pained, momentarily catching Evrikh's attention.

"What's wrong?" Evrikh asked, his voice bordering the edge of an accusation.

"Wha . . . oh, that," Brian said examining his shoulder with his head. "Nothing really. I had a meeting with some of our allies out here, and we encountered some Resistance, courtesy of the Council. Needless to say, we'll have to be more careful." He sat back, and his pain eased. "The Council, no doubt, knows of our being here, which has now hastened our stay," now having the look of something more concerning breaching his face.

Evrikh looked down to his hands, agreeing with Brian's words. *This may very well be revealed to him over time, but he'll get the truth from you . . . from both of you.*

"You're worried one of them is working for us? An 'inside' man?" Evrikh added, sharing in Brian's hidden concern.

"I was about to ask you the same thing. Evrikh, what's wrong? You seemed troubled," Brian asked, noticing his change in facial expression.

Evrikh's eyes blinked for a moment before he responded. *How in the world is he even supposed to begin?* "I encountered another Relic today." They both seemed to be listening more intently now. *Yeah, he'd bet* that *caught their damn attention.*

"He was different than the other ones, though, more powerful. There was something almost regal about him."

He paused, and then raised his eyes to meet theirs. "I knew him."

Brian sat back, his mind already set to work on how they might have to alter their plans. "I see."

"He calls himself Cazziel, and he's been hunting me since before the Elder introduced us all to Alex. He's been working for the Council for a very long time . . . perhaps since the beginning."

"Well," Brian said, exhaling, "it would seem the Council has played their next card."

The waiter returned with the Moon Teaser and placed it on the table. "Ah, there you are, sir. Is there anything else I could get for you?"

Evrikh glanced back up to the waiter in a dismissive manner. "No, thank you, I'm fine."

"Very well," he replied, and then turned, walking away.

As he looked back down, Keona leaned forward. "Evrikh, obviously you've heard of the Phoenix Gate, but have you ever heard of the legend that goes with it?"

He looked at Brian briefly, and then back to Keona. "It's a children's tale. Who the hell hasn't? During the War of Ruin it was supposedly man's last hope for survival, should we become extinct. But something happened, blah blah blah, and they hid it, hoping no one would ever find it."

Keona took a deep breath, looking at Brian, and then turned her attention back to his now-puzzled eyes. "Evrikh, according to Marcus's journal, Kendrick had successfully hid the Phoenix Gate. But not before the city had become devoid of life. Something happened back then, something that was left out of the journal."

"OK, so who's this Marcus guy?" he asked, leaning his vision to Brian.

"He was the closest colleague of Kendrick, and he documented all of his research into a series of journals; collectively, Marcus's Journal."

"Evrikh, the 'Phoenix Gate' has the ability to manipulate life and death. This was the first thing deciphered from the journal. It's a gateway to ... somewhere else, and all the secrets they hold. Kendrick and his people who created it knew what they had done, and they also knew that man wasn't possibly ready for such a thing. That's when they decided it *had* to be hidden." She paused, taking a deep breath, and then continued. "The Council wants you because they think you know where it is. And if they gain control of that, they'll control everything."

Evrikh sat back, absorbing everything.

"Is it possible my memories might lie somewhere in that journal?" he spoke softly to himself, the cracks left behind within his memories written down on some crazy old testament? It's like a spiderweb, everything's always connected, but there's just too many damn holes.

"It's possible, but the only place you'd find that answer is in the Annals of Eden, or perhaps one of the journals themselves," Brian finished, his words of hope appreciated. "Now you see why it's so urgent that you go with Keona."

"Where do we go from here?" Evrikh peered back up to Brian, his expression changed; determined.

"There's a town north of here called Gravenport.

You'll meet up with the Resistance; they'll be able to take you through the Eastern Badlands to Mehrond. That's where we're scheduled to meet up with the Elder."

"Well, let's not waste any more time then," Evrikh said, glancing at Keona.

Looking at her a few moments longer, he realized her gaze had not left him for the duration of their meeting.

"Evrikh, do you know where it is?" she spoke, her eyes searching for an answer she would not find.

As he watched her, his reply slipped from his lips. "No, I do—"

"Hold on a second, hero. To get there, you have to go through Pandora's Skyway."

Evrikh looked back at Brian. "And that would be . . . ?"

"That would be what leads to the Floating City of Eden. So you can expect it to be heavily guarded. Make sure you use extreme caution."

Evrikh turned his attention back to Keona. "There's no other way to get to that town?"

"Pandora's Skyway is the only path through the mountains. Think of it as one bus up, quick exchange, one bus down. Besides, we don't have the time to look for another way." Keona's remark was simply a fact.

"And where will you go?" he asked, looking back at Brian.

"Back to Norwynn. I have a few things left to tend to before we play our hand."

"Why are things never easy," Evrikh asked, his eyes trailing off into thought.

Brian suddenly erupted with a laugh, quickly relaxing

into a smile. "Life itself is complicated, my friend. If it isn't complicated . . . then it definitely isn't life."

Evrikh smiled at Brian's nostalgia, and then looked at Keona. "Well, then, my lady, shall we?"

Keona laughed while leaning over to kiss him. "We shall."

How could those lips possibly be more inviting? Strange that Evrikh would feel so strongly for her such a short time ago . . . only now to remember *his* Thea, who he would never again be without.

Although Evrikh had decided to continue traveling with Keona, his mind still dwelled on his one true love. She had finally found him, only to lose him once again. Evrikh feared for her safety, but knew that she'd remain safe as long as he wasn't with her. Besides, this was something he has to do on his own, to see this through to the end. Evrikh simply dwelled on the thought that although he had given her up once, it was a decision he would never make again.

* * * *

CHAPTER 6
~ Savior ~

A WOMAN SAT in a chair, in front of her loomed a fireplace so large that it dwarfed the room. The flames were the only source of light, the casted shadows dancing along the walls like marionettes free of their bonds. The walls were lined with tapestries that chronicled the past; the War of Ruin, the Great Darkness, the rise of the Council, and the closest history to what could have been known as the Phoenix Gate.

As she sat there, large doors whose size rivaled that of the fireplace opened from behind her, their ancient wood whispering, infiltrating into the room. The carvings of the doors were remarkably detailed; two angels reaching out to each other, their hands coming together at the center. In the background were many other angels and a world full of life. As the doors opened, a figure walked in, kneeling down as he reached the center of the room.

"Lady Miriam, everything is as you planned. He now heads for Gravenport with Brian and Keona." His gaze remained on the floor.

"Well, then," her eyes mirrored the flames like glass, "proceed to the next step, but stay cautious. Should he realize the truth, we would lose everything we are working for. And we cannot have that now, can we, Cazziel?" Her head turned to her shoulder.

"Of course not, my lady; we'll proceed as planned," he replied, rising to his feet.

Cazziel hesitated for a moment to watch as the firelight echoed off the features of Miriam's face, her eyes alit like smoldering embers, only to turn around as his cloak weaved into the air. As he drew closer to the door, he waved his hand and the doors opened upon command, only to shut behind him after he departed.

She sat in reverie for a moment, almost as if the door would reopen once more, the ashes of her eyes rekindling as she returned her attention to the fireplace.

"Don't worry, my dear Evrikh, you will be home soon," Lady Miriam began to exhale slowly, and as she did, the fire died, extinguishing the light within the room.

~ ~ ~

As Keona and Evrikh approached the clearing, they remained at the edge of the forest, kneeling into the shrubs. The trees and grass provided enough of a cover to conceal them from being sighted. It also provided them with a nice vantage point to clearly see the road that led to the gates of Pandora's Skyway.

"Evrikh, that's the skyway. Once we get through here, we'll be able to reach Gravenport," Keona whispered, observing the situation. "I don't know how many guards there are, but—"

"Nine at the front gate," Evrikh finished, cutting her off.

"How can you tell?"

"I can feel them. As for the rest, it's pretty heavily guarded." He looked toward the skyway, "Who knows, maybe they're expecting us."

"That's not funny," she continued her observation.

As Evrikh's mind continued probing the area, a voice echoed from behind him. "YOU THERE! STAND UP AND TURN AROUND!" it demanded.

As he stood up, placing his hands behind his head, Evrikh turned around slowly, noticing that Keona was no longer with him. Shifting his eyes toward the guard, he left his mind open to locate Keona; it returned with nothing. The man was simply a guard, and as Evrikh began to probe his mind, he discovered that he was a normal human; a human who had no idea what he was about to step into the middle of. He slowly approached Evrikh.

"What are you doing there?"

Well, hell, this could get a little complicated. Keona, where the hell did you go?

Evrikh looked around carelessly, and then returned his gaze to the guard. "I'm actually looking for my brother's fiancée. She's quite stunning, but also a little mentally sick. And violent. I don't know what in the world he sees in her. I mean, she's not the greatest catch in the world. I've been chasing her down from town where she left her clothes. You see, she's naked . . . and vulnerable. When I saw all those guards I didn't know what to do! Am I trespassing? If I'm trespassing I can leave!"

"It's a little late for that ... and no ... there's been no women running around here."

The man stumbled forward as his uniform suddenly caved inward and the skin of his chest split open, his body suddenly impaled by some invisible assailant, his blood spraying like some half-broken lawn sprinkler.

"HOLY ... fuck!" Evrikh finished in a whisper, quickly dropping to the ground. His gaze was madly looking around for some form of explanation.

The guard began choking on his own blood as his arms flailed about wildly. Directly behind him Evrikh noticed the air was a bit odd, distorted, and that same distortion protruded from the guard's chest. The guard looked down just as blood began to leak from his mouth. With all the rest of his strength, he raised his head up, those eyes full of questions; full of fear. Then, they slowly rolled upward and to the left, his limbs slowly going lax. Evrikh was momentarily blinded by an image of a dream he had what seemed like eons ago. Gavin.

This fluidic air began to take on color and shape, returning to its original state. Keona. Evrikh was astonished by both her abilities and her actions. As the guard's lifeless body knelt on the ground, Keona raised her foot to his head, pulling her arm from his chest as her foot pushed his body to the ground; not a predator that scored a kill, but rather a different kind of beast, one that triumphed over its sport.

Keona looked at him with a peculiar look. "... Your

brother's fiancée, I'm naked . . . and I'm retarded? What the hell were you thinking?"

Keona? How the hell can you stand there, like the man you just murdered isn't at your feet? Like you didn't just PUNCH that knife through his damn chest? Is this the side of you you've had to keep hidden for the sake of Alex? Maybe not retarded, but there's a piece of you that's definitely ill adjusted. Evrikh looked back up to Keona, the dead guard hunched over at her feet.

"He was just an innocent. He couldn't possibly pose a threat."

Keona sneered at the corpse, and then raised her eyes to meet his. "They're all the same, Evrikh. He's just one less human we have to worry 'bout."

Keona simply walked past him, back to the tree line, the tall grass providing enough cover to hide the doubled over body resting behind them. Never before had he sensed such coldness from her. It was as if she was someone else entirely. To avoid his growing suspicion, Evrikh carried on, rejoining her. It was time for him to take his earlier warning a bit more seriously.

Evrikh, I know you're getting as nervous about this as I am. Something's changed . . . There's a lot more to this than she's letting on.

"You just keep your eyes open and we'll take this one step at a time," he whispered toward the ground.

Keona let out a slight laugh. "How about you keep *your* eyes open."

"What? . . . Yeah, maybe a good idea for both of us." More like the three of us.

As the two of them lay there at the edge of the forest, his eyes remained fixated on Keona. Her face continued to scout the area, making sure their presence hadn't been compromised. While her attention was diverted, Evrikh decided to do a little scouting of his own. He sent a probe out to her mind, and all he could sense was a cloud of confusion, almost as if she had no mind at all. Her thoughts made no sense; they were intertwined like a maze he could never hope to navigate. As the initial bewilderment wore off, he noticed she had been looking right at him.

"What're you looking for, Evrikh?"

"I'm looking for answers," he retorted, suddenly very serious. "Why? What are you afraid I might find?"

Keona's eyes remained locked with his own; motionless. "I'm afraid I've none to give you, only an assignment to carry out," her voice deadened.

Keona turned her head back toward the skyway. "There lie the answers you seek, maybe answers for us all."

His eyes became thin and detached. "Who are you?" His stare remained on her, and slowly the hair rose across the whole of his body, his heart picked up a beat, his muscles tensed, and his mind was flooded with the ultimate realization. "I don't know you."

Keona exhaled in annoyance and stood up. "You've come this far on faith alone, and *now* you begin to wonder." She turned her face down to meet his. "You couldn't just wait a little bit longer could you? Shit."

His body was slowly becoming rigid as he felt a growing sense of danger lingering around him, an unforeseen danger. Keona began to step away.

Evrikh, get up; you need to stand up right now.

"My assignment is to take you with me—at all costs," her face became conflicted with a moment of hesitation. "Evrikh, whatever you're thinking, I promise, the 'cost' will be greater for you than I."

Her eyes bled free of color till all that remained was black, her aura lighting up her skin as though she had been encased within a shadow. Evrikh rose to his feet as his aura began to glow a color of its own; green.

What is she playing at? We need to get ahead of this, act before we need to react!

"What damn assignment, Keona? Who the hell are you working for, huh?"

"I'm sorry, Evrikh, but we do what we must. Given my shoes, you would've made the same choices."

We do, huh?! Keona don't make us do this; not us . . . How can *you* do this? Am I meant to be a puppet for *everyone*; for *YOU*?

Hey, whatever the hell happened between the two of you in the past, I could care less about. Whatever she's planning right now is bad news and . . .

Evrikh lunged his arms forward, bringing the forest to life. Grass and weeds shot out like an eruption of life to hold Keona where she once was. Immediately halting his attack, Evrikh looked around for any signs of her, his mind clouded in danger; clouded with betrayal. Why, Keona? With all the memories they have in their short life together, why would she betray that? A slight breeze picked up and through the rustle of leaves, he could hear her faint laughter. She was near.

Suddenly there was a sharp prick through his side and as he looked down, he noticed a syringe protruding from it.

How did we miss that?! Dammit ... How long is it gonna take you to realize, Evrikh, we still need more time?

"THE FUCK IS THIS?!" He half-retched, pulling the needle from his clothes, slipping from his skin.

A sedative, my friend; she means to take us ... the real question though ... is ... to where ...?

"THE HELL DO YOU WANT FROM ME ... DO ANY OF YOU WANT FROM ME?"

Evrikh was enraged at the idea that at this very moment he would be so torn between the obvious feelings he has for Keona, and this grand betrayal of hers. He knew from the moment this all began that there would be secrets, more lies, further deception. But this ... her ... no, this was something different; something more. A person is no more a puppet than a heart is a tool. But to her, to it ... You're not even human, are you? And you don't even have a heart; after this, how could you possibly? Evrikh's mind began to relax as the drug started working throughout his system.

"It's not I who wants you," Keona's voice echoed within his ears like that of a fading dream.

As he looked around, his vision became blurred, his concentration growing vastly weary. "Why ... would you ... do ... this?" his legs grew meager as his knees gave out; his magnificent anger dropping in defeat.

"They have my brother, Evrikh; imprisoned at Roinhein. They took him from me when they butchered our family, and I will see him freed no matter the cost. You were simply a means to an end. I'm telling you, because you deserve this much, maybe more. But I can't let him rot in there any longer." Her voice reflected nothing of the emotions he felt for her now fading within his heart.

Damn, was there nothing! The entire *life* the two of you had spent together was plainly—nothing? You will regret using him as a puppet, Keona . . . All of you will regret.

Falling to one arm, then moments later falling to the ground, Evrikh lay there concentrating his efforts only to see that distorted air running from her body as Keona faded out. Evrikh's eyes suddenly changed to a deep bloodred, his face void of emotion, and stood once more as if in defiance. There he stood, breathing, somehow gazing right at her. But that's impossible when she's cloaked. Was it not enough? Should there be more tranquilizer? A moment later, Evrikh's eyes suddenly returned as they were before, and he collapsed to the ground; unconscious.

~

As Evrikh looked around, he was in an amber field of knee-high grass, whispering as it caressed the edges of his legs; trees in the distance. Leaves swam by, carried on the waves of a calm breeze. The air smelt of sweet pollen, and the sky was a mesh of elegant colors, shades of red intimately mixed with light blues, and clouds that seemed to weave in slow motion. All he could sense was harmony; everything seemed to flow with perfection.

In the distance he could barely make out a figure

walking toward him. As it drew closer Evrikh concentrated his eyes, but its identity remained unknown, hidden by a blur that wouldn't clear. Even though this being remained within the haze of a dream, it also resembled a man. It came to a halt roughly ten feet away; only then did it speak.

"Evrikh, the rest have been expecting you." His voice was deep and soothing, almost angelic.

"Who are you?" His mind, although curious, came up with nothing.

"It's as I've said. You cannot go such a great length of time without being a vessel and not have consequences."

"Seraph . . .? How did I get here?" Evrikh asked as if in a half memory.

"You didn't. Your mind is here, and at least that's a step. It will become easier over time, as we attune to each other. When you have awakened, I'm sure the confusion will subside, and the rest of your memories will return to you. For now, who we are is of little consequence; spectators, perhaps. But it does matter who you are."

"Why? Who am I?"

"The woman you travel with, she works for the Council. Do not resist her; quite the contrary, you must accompany her."

"She doesn't care of me . . . She's betrayed me . . . me; she's no different than the rest of them. Why would I go with her?" His words gave rise to the anger swelling within Evrikh, even here, in this place of calm.

"You were born to be the chosen one for your people; whether you embrace this destiny is up to you. Your answers will come later, but for now, you have to wake up."

~

"WAKE UP!" A sudden sharp pain streaked across the side of his face. "Come on, you ass, I said GET UP!"

As Evrikh blinked his eyes, he realized the field was gone and he was in some sort of vehicle. Great. How long was he out for, and where the hell were they headed? Was Brian a part of all this? He raised his head and looked around, only to see that he was surrounded by guards; hands bound behind his back. He looked up and noticed Keona looming over him. She took her seat across from him, rubbing the hand she had no doubt used to get him to "wake up." Was she staring at him or analyzing him?

"Evrikh, glad to see you're back with us. We can't exactly have you sleeping where we're going . . . You had me worried I might have stuck you with the wrong needle."

Looking up, there sat two guards on either side of her and two beside himself. Keona was right there, her eyes staring at him with her legs crossed. The look of regret slowing etching its way into Evrikh's eyes.

"Where are we?" he mumbled as he attempted to shake the resonating effects of the drug from his head.

Hey, me? . . . I don't care where we are, as long as we make it in one piece.

"Pandora's Skyway, on our way . . . up." Her lips slightly popped as she glanced upward. "There's someone at Eden who'd like to see you."

He glanced up at the window slightly behind Keona, and there it was, the floating city of Eden.

We need to get our head back in the game. Every detail, every piece, it all gets memorized if we wanna make it out of this.

Evrikh turned his face to his shoulder as if to itch his cheek. "We don't even know what the hell *this* is! We wait . . . play it by ear."

Just as the glare veered from the window, Evrikh could see the spires of Aurora stretching up toward the heavens, monstrous in size. The city was remarkable. Enormous statues carved of the goddess Miriam lay everywhere, sprouting endless streams of water; waterfalls. The city itself rested at the bottom of the statues. As they drew closer, other vehicles were arriving and departing at the various platforms around the spires.

The buildings were made of stone, as were the streets. The sunlight reflected off the waterfalls, giving the city an almost heavenly appearance. How could such an enormous creation stay afloat in the sky? Where the hell was all the water coming from, for that matter?

Keona stood up and walked to the front of the vehicle where the driver sat. Evrikh looked out the window again, and they began to drift toward a landing pad on the side of one of the Spires of Aurora. As they started to land, a man wearing a long black cloak awaited them, along with many soldiers. Why the show? What in the world was all this for? Do they seriously need that many guards?

*Are you gonna sit here and say that we **still** don't know what **this** is?*

". . . Maybe. Only one way to find out though," Evrikh spoke softly as his eyes glanced back up toward Keona and the pilot.

Their clothes came alive from the wind as the vehicle landed. A door quickly rolled to life on the side of the vehicle, and Keona stepped out. Moments later the guards motioned Evrikh to stand up and walk out.

As he stepped out, Keona remained a couple feet away from the door, awaiting him. Evrikh stopped moving and looked around, feeling the breeze against his face, his jaw and cheek still ablaze from earlier. Using his eyes, he panned the area, taking in his surroundings for future assessment. One of the guards thrust his gun into his back, Evrikh nearly stumbling to the ground.

"Get moving!" he demanded.

After regaining his balance, Evrikh turned to look at the guard, whose weapon lingered on him.

". . . Ever touch me with that again," he stepped toward the guard until the barrel was pressed firmly against his chest, pushing the guard back a step, ". . . and I will erase you." He turned and proceeded to follow Keona toward the man wearing the cloak. As they got closer he realized who it was. Cazziel. When she reached him, he turned to walk beside her. Evrikh drifted more than a few paces behind them.

"Well, Keona, I'm glad to see you finally accomplished something." His face remained forward as he continued to walk.

"No thanks to you. Maybe he was just too much for *you* to handle!" Keona's eyes did not stray from their path.

"Remember your place, Keona," Cazziel's voice became that of a superior.

The small party proceeded inside, and their direction turned to the left. The drugs had fully worn off, and Evrikh was completely aware of everything. After reaching the end of the corridor, they stood before two very large doors. The carvings on the doors were simply amazing. Those two angels reached out to each other as if they couldn't exist without one another. Keona and Cazziel halted and turned around to the guards.

"Throw 'em inside." She had spoken without even a hint of emotion, void of the person Evrikh had always thought he knew. How could she just abandon him like this?

Don't look at me; I was just invited to this party not that long ago.

"No one's talking to you," he gritted.

The guard positioned himself to thrust his gun into Evrikh's back, and just as he did, Evrikh slid his legs to the side. Before the guard had the chance to realize what was happening to him, Evrikh spun around and caught his weapon between his arms and back, pulling the man in front of him. Catching his neck with Evrikh's shoulder, he fell backward, dropping to the ground in astonishment. Just as Evrikh raised his leg to the top of his head, his eyes focused instead at the point of the other weapon now resting against his chest.

"I wouldn't do that," came another voice from behind the barrel.

As Evrikh looked up, he found the other guard embracing the handle of his gun.

"GET INSIDE!!" The butt of the gun came raging in

against his chest, pushing Evrikh into the room, the doors quickly closing behind him.

Slowly Evrikh stood up and looked around, every fiber of his being pulsing, searching for any kind of immediate danger, Keona's betrayal a constant raw wound within him. At the other end of the room were large windows that stretched from the floor to the ceiling, consisting of nine panels each. Deep scarlet curtains draped from the sides, whose weight prevented them from moving even with the heaviest of breezes. To the right his eyes scaled a fireplace that put all others to shame. Seriously, if that fireplace were ever utilized to its maximum capacity . . . who in their right mind would want a forest fire raging in their home?! The fireplace itself was so large that Evrikh could probably walk right through it, perhaps if there was a hole on the other side; a clever plan for a hidden door . . . had there been no raging fire. Above rested a large painting roughly proportionate to the fireplace below it; immeasurably detailed. The painting was of the upper half of a naked woman.

Hey, now there's something I can appreciate. Let's take a moment to really appreciate this.

". . . Idiot," Evrikh snickered with a small smile of his own.

Her body was spread across the canvas like melted caramel, smooth and inviting. Her hair was flowing like a wild river, shimmering as though even now the sun was beaming down upon it. Her eyes were alive with such spirit that they practically took on a life of their own; or rather, would be willing to steal the lives of those willing to gaze upon her.

"I see you've found the goddess . . . I thought she would be forever lost to us."

The voice came from the corner of the room next to the windows. Evrikh quickly turned around to see who it was. Her vision remained out through the window, and the only view he had was of her side.

"You don't need those here." Her voice was soothing and relaxing.

Suddenly his restraints fell to the floor, and his hands were free. He slowly brought them up to his chest while rubbing his wrists, not a single piece of his body losing tension.

"She's the reason why the Council exists. She created it. She helped people rebuild after the great darkness, and, in turn, the people believed she was a goddess. So, she created the Council of Aurora to bring the people hope and faith; to guide them." She turned to face Evrikh. "Quite surprisingly, I'm amazed it's lasted this long."

He suddenly recalled the parade along with those vivid images. She was the prophet, Lady Miriam. She uncrossed her arms as her elegant body moved to a table on the other side of the room.

There'll be time to remember those images of her later; for now, let's keep our head in the game, Evrikh.

But how in the hell does someone move like that? It's easy to see how people would believe her to be a goddess; having grace like that.

"I've been waiting for you, Evrikh; a very long time." Her blissful face looked up at him and she genuinely smiled.

Yeah, I'll bet you have.

Evrikh let out an annoyed sigh. "And why me?"

She pulled a chair out from the table and sat down. "In all honesty, you're the last missing piece . . . just you . . . to complete the Phoenix Gate."

~

Suddenly Evrikh was lying on the table, relieved of his clothes, Miriam's naked body loomed over his own as she straddled his waist. The skin of her porcelain breasts erected themselves as Miriam arched herself backward. She was sliding up and down, her breaths coming in waves as his member slid in and out of her. Her breasts jolted with the motion. Then, within seconds the image was gone.

ENOUGH! Otherwise, you'll make us BOTH forget why we're here . . . maybe even make us want to stay!

~

Evrikh sat there blinking, his face expressionless, as he felt the small smoldering ashes of a fire somewhere deep within him. What the fuck was that? Why the hell does he see every beautiful woman he comes across writhing below him in an erotic vision? Could this have something to do with the Elder sealing him away in the pleasure side of his psyche? Or could Evrikh actually be more perverted than even he is aware of! He didn't want any part of it. His thoughts immediately shifted back to Thea and his love for her.

We need to focus; work on a way of getting you out of this. As his thoughts slid back into reality, Miriam motioned a hand for him to sit down. He approached the table and sat, his mind mulling away at prospective plans.

"If that's what this is about, the Phoenix Gate, then I'm sorry because I can't help you, dammit. I don't know anything about it. Besides, I'm sure Marcus's journals would give you infinitely more knowledge than I ever could . . . and then simply leave me out of it; out of *all* of it." Maybe he should just subdue her and brandish his escape now.

You need to clear your damn head! Think about this before you go jumping in, Evrikh . . . you're in their city; this is home turf to them. Whatever plan you decide to hatch has got to be the best plan.

"If I want your advice, you'll hear me ask for it," he snickered off to the side.

". . . Excuse me?" Miriam asked, her grace slightly offbeat.

Miriam shifted her head and smiled. "Funny you would mention that; the journals. Exactly how many people do you think are even aware they exist? Please, Evrikh, I would love for you to feel welcome here. Are you hungry? Thirsty, perhaps?" The sincerity of her voice never wavered.

"I'm fine, I wanna know why the hell I was brought here forcefully," his voice stern, demanding answers.

"I am truly sorry for that, but we needed to get you here as quickly as possible, before there was the chance of anything happening to you; before *they* were given the chance to interfere."

"You know, if you take those damn dogs of the Council out of the picture, your Relics, we would have eliminated danger from my life entirely!" Evrikh sneered obnoxiously.

*And **They** . . . Who the hell are **they** supposed to be?*

"Now, Evrikh, given our . . . history, there's absolutely no reason why you and I can't simply enjoy the company of each other. And by the way, now, I'm sure you're aware that the Elder, as you call him, is looking for you."

Surprise, surprise; of course, she knew that. She can have whatever information Keona feeds them, but it's highly doubtful she knows of Thea.

His eyes widened, but not at Miriam's spoken words, more at the thoughts he could see rising within her mind; the same thoughts he's hinted upon himself. Then it came.

"Evrikh, you and I both know the Elder is the self-appointed, no doubt, leader of the Resistance. They're looking for you because he has them all afraid of the Phoenix Gate. Brian Viseli is amongst them. He knows of the journals, and he has the Resistance believing that by eliminating you, the Phoenix Gate will remain unfound."

Is Brian in on this? How would she even know that he knows about the journals? And then, you have to know what the hell that leads to . . .

". . . Damn good question," Evrikh stated, listening a bit more intently now.

He could sense the truth in her voice, or rather, her perceived truth. Either Miriam was a good liar, or her mind was clouded by lies; with lies. Miriam leaned forward and placed her hands upon his. Evrikh suddenly becoming very aware of her compassion.

"With the Phoenix Gate we could finally eliminate every problem that plagues the human race; we could heal people, Evrikh, truly heal them. The Phoenix Gate would benefit us all." Her voice was full of sincerity.

He slowly slid his hands from beneath hers and sat back, crossing his arms.

"Shouldn't you people be asking, why in the hell was it buried and hidden in the first place?"

Miriam drew back and stood up, ". . . Oh, Evrikh, don't be so naive. People only see what they want to see. The Phoenix Gate was never hidden."

Miriam walked over to the fireplace and stared at the painting of the goddess.

He was suddenly very aware of the striking resemblance of the woman in the painting and Lady Miriam.

"At the time it was created, the Phoenix Gate consisted of itself and the key that would unlock it. Two parts, actually, though one and the same. The Gate has the ability to control life and death, even manipulate time itself. People have never found it because how do you find something when you haven't the slightest idea what you're looking for?" She had turned from the painting now, gazing back toward Evrikh.

Obviously. You should always know what you're looking for, if you ever hope to find it. But, damn, Evrikh . . . both of their eyes are exactly the same!

"The Phoenix Gate was never an object, per se. Biological in nature, yes, but also made to look just like us so no one would ever know the truth. It was to be our savior in mankind's darkest hour. With it, there would never be another War of Ruin. Why would you ever have to hide something like that when you could simply display it out in the open, for all to see?"

Evrikh took another glance back at the painting behind her.

. . . It's her!

". . . It's you!"

Miriam took a deep breath, almost hesitant, then slowly stepped toward him. Evrikh was bewildered at how her hair shimmered as wildly as the painting behind her.

"Marcus has written intimately about every detail he witnessed when Dr. Savari began his work when he finished it. Because of his knowledge and his fears, he felt he had to conceal *you*. Evrikh—"

You? Hold on a second now, Evrikh, we need to think about this.

"STOP . . ." he ordered as he stood up and stumbled backward, knocking his chair to the floor. "I've had enough lies . . . and I won't let you finish this one!" he gritted. "My mother died when I was born. I have memories of this; I can *see* memories of this."

"Marcus has indeed written of her as well. It seemed she would've been quite lovely. However, his journals make only a single reference to a name associated with the Phoenix Gate." Her voice was a soothing veil of mystery. "You can feel it, can't you? Lurking, somewhere in between the shadows of your thoughts maybe.

"Evrikh," Miriam continued, taking another step toward him, "look within yourself . . . You know this is true;

your body can feel the truth."

"Brian spoke to me of this!" he spat.

"Brian Viseli . . . What a very interesting name. Mentioning him earlier was no coincidence, of course. We used to have a Brian here with us. He was part of a team very close to Marcus's journals," she added.

"Why would he not tell me this?" Evrikh's thoughts were becoming increasingly chaotic.

"Evrikh, it is as I said about him, about the Resistance; you must see this. He only told you what he had to in order to gain your trust—"

And how in the hell is what she's doing now any different?

"NO!" he suddenly erupted, cutting them both off. "I don't know, I don't care what you people are trying to do with me, but I will not be controlled!" He shuddered by the intensity of his own voice; definitive, almost majestic. He pointed his hand at Miriam. "And you . . . You're just like the rest of them."

Suddenly that vision of the field flashed through Evrikh's head along with *his* voice; Seraph, *". . . whether you embrace this destiny is up to you."*

"STOP IT!" he abruptly screamed, his sudden change in demeanor catching Miriam off guard. "JUST LEAVE ME ALONE!" His hands grabbed ahold of his head as his eyes slowly illuminated like two hidden lights switched on from behind the skin of his face. He laughed hysterically, but the tone became dark and inhuman. Evrikh screamed once more, falling to his knees.

"I'M NOT THE PHOENIX GATE! Get out of my head, you shit! I will not have you using me any more than any of them!"

HEY, you brought ME here! I never asked for you to be a vessel! You want someone to blame, blame your damn father! If it wasn't for that last trip, I wouldn't even be in this mess.

Evrikh's head was suddenly filled with images of the War of Ruin, personal images; intimate images. Corpses lay strewn all around him. Gunfire echoed throughout his ears as it went off in the background. Blood splattered across his face, and as he looked down upon himself, his skin began to peel away, muscles slipping into the air. He felt the faint sensation of dripping on his head, and as he looked up, a body, came tumbling to the ground. Evrikh scrambled across the floor just as the body landed on his feet with a heavy thud, momentarily pinning his legs in place. He turned around and looked at the mangled jumble of flesh lying across him. He screamed again, more out of anger than of fear as he kicked it off. Then, just as it rolled away, its head turned in his direction, and his body froze in fear as he realized that it was Gavin. Suddenly the sky flashed and everything quickly faded into a white light. Then it was gone; everything was gone.

Evrikh fainted.

Rising to his feet, Evrikh's eyes shifted once more to that deep bloodred. His body limp of all tension, void of concern. He turned to Miriam as if on cue.

"... And so it begins. It is time for you to finish what has been started."

Upon finishing his words, Evrikh collapsed to the floor once more.

For a few moments, Miriam sat there watching him, as

if she had watched him in this way once before. Glancing toward the doors, as if by command, they opened. Two guards walked inside.

"Lady Miriam?"

Miriam's eyes fell upon Evrikh's unconscious body. "Take him to the chamber immediately; it's almost already too late, I fear."

The guards picked him up by his arms and legs, carrying him out of the room, Miriam following closely behind them. As she stepped into the hallway, she waved her hand bringing the doors once again back to life.

The doors closed, humming their ancient sigh, and moments later, the room was once again silent.

~ ~ ~

As Evrikh's eyes fluttered open, he was slightly blinded by the multiple suns glaring down upon him; lights hanging from above. He raised his hand to shield his eyes, quickly realizing it wouldn't move.

"What's going on? Was I drugged?" For a few moments Evrikh struggled with his restraints. "Why the hell am I tied down?"

Evrikh? . . . Welcome back. Calm down, and first things first. Check the legs . . . feet . . . toes . . . all right then. The hands now . . . then the fingers . . . Well, whatever the hell they're planning, they must not have started yet.

"Yes, well, I sure as hell don't care to stick around to find out!"

Evrikh raised his head to familiarize himself with the surroundings. He was strapped to a table, his shirt had been removed, and his arms were bound to the table by his wrists. He tried to free his legs; however, his bindings proved to be too much, all of his restraints were too strong. He then noticed wires connected to his chest and figured they must be monitoring him for when this party finally did get started. He could see more of those wires out of the corner of his eyes and knew that whoever was monitoring him was monitoring his whole body, not just his vitals. The wires ran off the table and sank below it; their destination would remain a secret; for now.

Looking to the left, Evrikh noticed a rather large window no more than ten feet away. Whatever, or whomever, loomed on the other side remained hidden as the brightness of the room brilliantly reflected off it. Closing his eyes, he probed the area with his mind and could sense the presences on the other side. Seconds later he heard the faint sound of an opening door from somewhere behind him.

One of Evrikh's oldest memories suddenly thrust itself into motion.

~

Arianna shot off her chair, her lab coat whizzing through the air as she turned. *"Kendrick, Evrikh and I have already decided that if you don't spend more time with him, then he's going to make your head explode, here and now. What say you to this, good Doctor?"*

Kendrick's arms immediately flew up beside his head as though he were being held at gunpoint. *"Innocent, I declare myself INNOCENT . . . wait, what're we . . ."*

"... *guilty.*" Evrikh's gaze was ablaze with boyish passion.

Evrikh's body relaxed as the nostalgia of this ancient memory settled upon him.

"*Dad...?*"

~

He felt a hand touch his shoulder. "Evrikh, please relax." Miriam's voice was soft as she walked around beside him.

Wherever his consciousness had been, it swiftly returned to his eyes. "Now what the hell is *this* all about?" he managed to calm his rising anger.

"We're not going to do anything to harm you; I promise. To you, Evrikh, this I would always promise."

"And what the hell is it you want from me?" He watched Miriam as she continued to walk around the table, approaching his feet, her fingertips running along the folds of his clothing.

It's not what she wants from you, Evrikh, it's what she needs to finish.

"Needs to finish? What the hell are you going on about?" He stopped as though his mind had finally come to a complete halt.

I told you earlier, it was up to you whether you chose to pursue this destiny. And . . . Here we are. It wasn't easy, Evrikh, and every detail had to be planned. From the very first time you and I have met each other, this destiny was set in motion.

"Seraph! You better give me some damn answers!" he exploded.

"Who?" Miriam asked gently.

Evrikh glared at her standing at his feet as if in defiance.

"I've had my suspicions for quite some time, Evrikh. And I'm aware there's no one else within the room," she reassured him.

"Seraph . . . It appears he's here to betray me as well," Evrikh sneered.

*No! Evrikh, this is not what's happening, and be careful of how much you say to this woman. She herself has a destiny that doesn't intertwine with yours much past this point. **This point, however, is crucial . . . to your survival . . . our survival!***

"YEAH? Then why all the betrayal, secrecy, and lies?"

It's not what you think! You'll understand afterward. Evrikh, you and I have been acquainted for a very long time. Every moment has led the two of us to this moment, this defining moment. I promise you, afterward, you will understand.

Crazy devil bitch! Yeah, Evrikh, we don't mean you any harm . . . Let's just send our small army after you, have your closest friends betray you, secure you to this hard-ass cold table, strap you to our machines . . . What the hell is next?? Harvesting my damn organs? How you like him now . . . zombie bitch?!

"Evrikh, I'm here to fulfill your destiny, because I'm the only person who can." Her voice remained smooth as she spoke.

"I don't understand!"

This could not have been a coincidence. First, Thea

is the only one who could truly reawaken Evrikh. Now, Miriam is saying only she can help him fulfill his destiny?

"I know that there is another within you; someone else with whom you speak, and I've known for quite some time." She placed her hands on his ankles and looked up. "Marcus's journals spoke of this concern for quite some time. They feared your mind had split from a journey you had made as a young boy. Some time later, they realized your mind hadn't split but simply returned with something more." Her voice reflected pure empathy, almost a longing to bring him peace.

"Think of it as a lock and a key," Miriam leaned forward, her hands coming up to his knees.

"I'm here to set you free. Evrikh, I've been waiting for you for over one thousand years. By doing this I will fulfill my own destiny as well, the destiny I was created for."

Miriam leaned back off the table and stood there for a moment, watching him. She then left, walking back up toward his head. As she walked around behind him, her left hand ran up along his neck and was placed on the side of his head. Seconds later, she used her right hand to do the same. While her hands held his head so delicately, her face suddenly appeared above his own.

"You're going to lead the world into a whole new era of evolution. Don't be afraid, Evrikh."

As he looked up into her eyes, Evrikh felt the faint sensation of something growing within him. Her eyes were like something of a world he so longed for. Miriam leaned forward and brought her face down to his, her lips lingering so very close.

"We're going to show the people a new world, the world you and I were meant to bring them." As she spoke, her lips probed his as if in discovery.

Miriam brought herself closer, and their lips molded almost immediately; a motion that could only be described as unity. As their mouths remained joined, lost to intimacy, these sensations within Evrikh continued growing. Visions of Thea immediately flashed through his mind. Miriam slowly pulled her head away, rising back up. As she held his head in her hands, she closed her eyes. Suddenly the sides of his face grew slightly warmer. It was then that Miriam began to speak, her voice echoing like a breeze.

". . . all that is life . . ."

Her palms slowly grew warmer as they started to emit a faint black light. Suddenly an image streaked across Evrikh's eyes. The universe, the world, why everything is, and why some things never were; it was knowledge, forbidden knowledge.

And here we go . . .

The light above him returned, and he felt the growing sensations within him shift, sensations he wasn't even sure he could control. Miriam continued speaking, her voice becoming a faint dream.

". . . Heed me now, thou who is as ageless as dust. In the name of that which has been lost within the ends of time, imbue me with power to free that which controls you . . ."

You free us! Take them beautiful glowing hands of yours, and you free us!

"Wait . . . Seraph, what do you mean by free us?" Evrikh's words almost couldn't be heard over the hum now emanating from Miriam's hands.

The light from her hands quickly resembled that of a mute fire as electrical arcs shimmered alive from where her palms hovered around Evrikh's head. That blue light started to flow from Miriam and into his body, and soon after, his aura began to mimic hers; a two-tone harmony. A murmur of wind blew throughout the room, Miriam and Evrikh being the heart. As she opened her eyes, two beacons of lights exploded into the room.

"Wait, stop! Miriam, something's not right!" Evrikh struggled to free himself, the metal of his restraints digging its way into the flesh of his wrists and ankles. "Seraph, this isn't right; not for either of us!"

Evrikh, understand, this has been set in motion since the day your father decided he'd rather have his Phoenix Gate than his own son.

The electricity grew stronger as wild lightning danced brilliantly around her body, striking the ceiling and the walls. Images continued to fill his mind as waves of distorted reality began emitting from Miriam's hands. So much knowledge was pouring into Evrikh's head it started causing him physical pain. He arched his back up, lifting himself off the table. His hands remained bound by the wrists, yet his fingers were erected from the growing pain; writhing for a helping hand, some way out. He flexed his entire body as the distorted reality consumed the room.

Miriam's hands were vibrating wildly from the force generating between them. Giving way to screams of her own, she gripped the sides of his head. Lightning jolted throughout his body, as if he were a metal rod tossed into a pool of electrical waves. His screams grew more horrified as his last bit of self-control gave way to frantic convulsions. As the waves of light passed through his head, the color of his eyes slowly became golden. Miriam's aura rippled madly, and it looked as though her body was surrounded in a similar golden flame, her grip grew tighter, and the waves of light passed through his body at an increasing speed.

Evrikh bit back another scream, closing his eyes, and as he did the lights around them began to explode; the other personnel within the room attempting to flee the falling debris. Moments later the only light within the room was radiating from Miriam and him; the surge of wild voltage had already fried all the equipment. When Evrikh realized he only had but one retreat, his screams continued, flooding the room with a deafening tone. Suddenly the large window spider-webbed, and seconds later, exploded outward. Figures on the other side jumped out of the way as glass flew through the air. The light flashed as bright as day, and then all was silent.

As the other scientists looked around, assessing their own injuries, they slowly stood up. Their eyes remained fixated on the hole of where the window once was; no movement was seen within that blackness. The lead scientist looked to the others.

"Bring the auxiliary power online."

"Just a moment, sir," one of the other scientists complied, as he ran to a terminal and started up the auxiliary power. A few moments later red light flooded both rooms as mist was bellowing in from the hole in the wall. While it was slowly dissipating, the lead scientist cautiously approached the gaping hole; the soles of his feet crunching the broken glass. He adjusted his glasses, then placed his hands on the broken windowsill. When the mist finally cleared, the scientist saw Miriam sitting on the floor, leaning against the legs of the table; she remained unconscious. Evrikh's body, strapped to the table, appeared to remain motionless.

Suddenly Miriam fell forward, leaning onto her arms. As she sat there, catching her breath, the scientist jumped back startled by the sudden movement. It had taken Miriam more than a few moments to gather herself. Slowly she found herself rising to her feet, stumbling as she progressed. She looked out the window at the other scientists, her chest heaving.

"Don't worry. I'm fine," her words were spoken softly.

Miriam turned back to the table and Evrikh lying upon it. She approached, placing her hands on the side of the table. For a moment she stood there, her eyes scanning his body. She then leaned forward, her face hovering dangerously close to his. She ran her hand through his hair, perhaps a morning routine had they both led drastically different lives, and whispered his name.

"Evrikh, it's all right. You can open your eyes." She plied her words soothingly; alluring, slowly trying to pry him from the world of dreams and back to this world of man.

Suddenly there was an explosion within the other room. As Miriam whipped her head around, Thea's voice faintly sounded in the distance.

As Thea stepped into the room, she thrust her gun forward preparing to fire at anything that posed a threat. After she emerged from the smoke, she noticed three scientists within the room.

"Don't move!" She aimed her gun at the scientist across the room. "You there, get away from that terminal!" she yelled as she turned her gun around to the other scientist.

Thea stepped further into the room. "Where is he?!"

"Whe . . . Where's who? Ah . . . I don't un . . . understand," the lead scientist stuttered nervously, his eyes glancing toward the open hole in the wall.

Thea noticed the movement in his eyes and stepped over to the window. "Don't move!" she yelled as she turned to peer inside. "Evrikh! Evrikh, are you in there?"

A woman stepped into the light as Thea scanned the room with her eyes. Noticing the figure, she whipped her gun around into the room, aiming toward it. "That's quite far enough! Not another step!"

"Foolish little girl. Why try to indulge yourself in such matters?" As Miriam stepped forward, she waved her hand at Thea.

Thea's gun was suddenly stripped from her hands and flew into the far wall, embedding itself into the surface.

"WHAT THE FU . . ." She looked beyond Miriam and noticed Evrikh strapped to the table. "EVRIKH,

EVRIKH, WAKE UP!"

Miriam continued to walk toward Thea. "Don't worry about him, young girl, you have bigger problems to worry about." Miriam squinted her eyes as they began resonating a faint white. Thea had seen this before, with Evrikh himself.

"PLEASE, EVRIKH, HELP ME!" Thea's voice was suddenly filled with fear.

Just as Miriam began to probe Thea's mind, she spoke. "What is it you hope to do here?" moments after sifting through Thea's mind, she continued. "Ah, yes, the undying affections of love. I'm sorry, child, but this love has been lost to you before you even had it."

As Evrikh first opened his eyes, his mind was still emerging from the throes of confusion. He wasn't exactly sure of what to make of this world around him; what exactly had happened? Suddenly he heard Thea screaming from across the room. As he turned his head, Evrikh noticed the window was gone, and she was standing on the other side. *Thea... When the hell did you get here? What the hell happened to the damn window? ARE YOU HURT?!* He tried to move his hands, but they were still bound to the table. He looked back to Thea and saw Miriam stepping toward her.

"You think he'll answer to you?" Miriam twitched her hand at Thea, and she suddenly left the ground, thrown to the other side of the room. As she flew through the air, Thea screamed, landing hard as her body crashed into the wall.

"THEA!" Evrikh screamed, and the restraints blew off the table, crumbling into ash before what was left hit the ground.

Miriam stopped her progression and turned around as he sat up on the table. Evrikh turned toward her and rolled off, staring at her. A smile began to spread across her face.

"Evrikh, I'm so glad you're a—"

He twitched his eyes, and Miriam's voice was suddenly gone. ". . . You don't speak to me."

Miriam's eyes grew wider at the realization of what he had done. She tried to speak, but her throat produced no sound. Evrikh started walking toward her.

An intense pain suddenly throbbed throughout his head. He raised his hand to the side of his face and wheezed from the sensation. The burning eruption within his head caused him to stumble forward a few feet, but moments later, he regained his balance. He looked back up to Miriam.

"You think you can keep me here?" The throbbing slowly grew past the boundaries of pain and into something maddening. Evrikh pushed it aside, willing it into remission, but this pain was something that wouldn't be forgotten. He suddenly dropped to his knees and grabbed his head with both hands.

As Evrikh muffled back another scream, Miriam watched in astonishment as something swirled around him, and within the time she blinked, he was gone; somehow vanished. After another moment of nothing, she turned her attention back to Thea.

"... you ..."

Another muffled grunt suddenly came from behind her as Miriam turned back around to where Evrikh once lay. There he was, stumbling as he attempted to stand back up.

Immediately Miriam went to his side. "Evrikh, listen to me, we have to start you on the serum immediately! Please, come with me!"

He managed to raise his eyes to look back to hers when the door across the room suddenly came to life as guards attempted to break in from the other side. Evrikh looked back at Miriam. "I don't need you!"

Regaining himself, a grin etched its way into the curves of his lips, his expression a cast of internal torment. "I'm leaving this place, Miriam, and I'm taking Thea with me," the rest of his physical duress seemingly cured, "and if you take even one more step in between us, you will end up as broken as that window."

Miriam's composure suddenly returned, and she stood up straight. "I see. I'm sorry, Evrikh, but I cannot allow you to leave."

One of the other doctors jumped through the window and into the room. He raised his hand and held a gun within it.

"Please understand," Miriam continued.

Evrikh suddenly burst out laughing, and as he heard the doctor's finger ease onto the trigger, his laughter stopped. Slowly, his eyes pivoted from Miriam to the doctor. Another pain erupted in Evrikh's head, and he fell to one knee. He looked up at the doctor as his face crinkled from the pain, concentrating all thought in that direction.

Miriam stared at his body, taking in Evrikh's condition. Seconds later the words slipped from her mouth.

"Shoot him." No sentiment, no emotion; nothing which reflected the emotional attachment she had claimed to share with him.

After a few moments passed, Miriam realized the doctor never pulled the trigger. Out of the corner of her eye she saw the doctor's hand was shaking violently. Glancing over at him, he dropped the gun. Evrikh shut his eyes, lowering his head as the pain teased him on the edge of insanity. He growled from the overwhelming pain, and suddenly, the doctor's body split open. His innards erupted into the air as his blood sprayed out; a refreshing burst of red rain. His limp, lifeless body dropped to the floor, nothing more than a bag of moist raw flesh. At first glance one would find it hard to even recognize it as being human. Evrikh managed to open his eyes and look back up. Looking around, he saw that Miriam was gone, her presence although close, was fleeting. The pain suddenly began to ease.

Finally standing up, Evrikh took a moment to gather himself and allow his feet to gain their balance before starting to walk toward the hole of where the window once was. Just as he placed his hand on the wall, he noticed Thea on the other side. She was stirring on the floor, in the middle of sitting herself upright. He climbed through to the other side. Placing his feet on the floor, his attention drew back to the door in the other room; the guards were still trying to get in. He turned his attention back to Thea, and as he walked toward her, she managed to rise to her feet. When he finally made it over to her, he reached out and took ahold of her arm.

"Come on, Thea, we have to get out of here," he said as he turned to walk toward the other door. Moments later he felt that she was hesitating, and immediately turned back around to look at her.

"Evrikh, you all right?"

"Are you kidding me? I have no idea, but we can figure out if I'm fine later."

"I thought I came to rescue you." She remained a little dazed.

He stepped over to her and took both her hands into his own. As he leaned forward, their lips embraced and a new feeling of comfort spread throughout her body, as though her heart had once again bloomed alive. This was their kiss; the only kiss he ever longed for.

"Then take me away from here," he said as he looked into her eyes.

A smile spread across her face, and then Thea stepped around him, proceeding to the door.

The hallway was filled with a slight whisper as she eased the door open. She glanced up the hallway but could see no movement. She turned back to look at Evrikh.

"What do you think? Can you feel anybody out there?"

He looked toward the door for a moment, and then back to Thea. "No, there's no one out there. It's a bit strange; this whole damn place should be lit up by now. Everyone else is on the other side still trying to access the room."

Thea slid the door wide open and stepped into the hallway. After glancing around, Evrikh followed. The hallway was incredibly large, and the walls were made of layered stone. Small windows laced both walls as light crept through, shining down to the floor. The ceiling loomed far above them, almost too dim to see against the contrast of the window light. As they looked down to the end of the hall, they could see another door. Running toward it, Evrikh's mind was still dwelling on Miriam; where had she gone?

Something's not right about this whole damn thing! Psycho bitch, you are here . . . but where? And why the sudden lax of guards, security . . . Where the hell's the cavalry, huh?

As the two of them drew closer, the door abruptly came to life as guards broke through from the other side. The red uniforms came oozing through as they began to fill up the end of the hall. A bullet came screeching by, grazing Evrikh's ear. Soon after, another one came, grazing Thea's shoulder and sending her spinning to the floor. He ran to her and picked her up into his arms. His eyes squinted to an angry black as he grinned through his teeth. The end of the hallway exploded into a red blur as bits and pieces of seared flesh soared through the air. The guards' mutilated bodies dripped from the ceiling and walls; Evrikh would allow no peace for them in this life or the next. He could sense Thea's pain, and instinctively he pulled her closer still. As he looked through the red fog that lingered at the end of the hall, more guards continued to pass through the door; the lingering pain in his head mentally pushed to the background of his mind.

"WHAT THE FUCK?" one screamed as he ran inside, his eyes looking in Evrikh's direction. The others quickly joined him, hesitating at the nightmarish loss of their comrades. Evrikh could hear their gasps in the distance, their stomachs churning, their hearts skipping; fear—raw fear. Attempting to recover from this wretched scene, they all pulled the triggers of their guns.

Evrikh looked to the wall on the opposite side of the hallway as the shadows around the guards quickly filled with smoke. He ran toward the wall looking down at Thea.

"I'm getting us out of here, Thea, just ... HOLD ON!"

Thea placed her hands around his neck and clenched his body, letting out a small grunt of her own from her bleeding shoulder. As he drew closer to the other wall, Evrikh screamed. He could hear the sound of the bullets ripping through the air as the wall shot to life, layered bricks exploding apart. Debris and smoke quickly consumed the hallway, the blast concealing them from the guards' sight. As he leapt through the hole, he could feel the air from the other side rushing in, the light momentarily blinding. As his eyes finished adjusting, Thea clung to his body as they fell from the sky, their clothes rippling from the force. Gaining momentum, their eyes quickly began to water, and Evrikh faintly saw the city far below.

Holy shit, they must've leapt from one of the spires!

"Thea, if we survive all this, please don't hate me!" The rushing wind ripped the voice from his mouth. They had better survive all this ... Aurora, the Council, they were getting theirs, every last one of them!

Their two bodies continued to gain speed as the air around them started to glow a faint blue. The sound of a distant thunder filled his ears as the spire continued to pass by, the two of them racing for the ground. There was no way to hide their arrival. They would have little time in planning their next move, upon hitting the ground.

A bolt of blue lightning struck the ground, sending pieces of brick and earth into the sky as the ground exploded. Civilians screamed as stones fell like small meteors, striking the ground. Evrikh quickly emerged from the smoke and dust and could feel the fear and confusion of the people around them. As dust continued to bellow out from the hole, Thea stumbled out shortly after him. After escorting her to a small wall she could lean against, Evrikh continued to look around, ready to engage. The people weren't afraid of what would happen to them, they were afraid of Evrikh; their fear practically overwhelming, intoxicating. He felt a new sensation wash over his body as he began to laugh. Stepping away from Thea, his eyes continued to scan the city. He looked at the people, absorbing their fear.

"ARE YOU AFRAID?" His laughter continued to grow louder. "WHERE IS YOUR COUNCIL NOW?" His voice echoed throughout the sky as the citizens cowered; his voice, the voice of someone more than just a man.

Thea fell upon him with bewilderment, taking a small step forward. "Evrikh, what's wrong with you? Get ahold of yourself!" Her voice was alarmed with concern, but seemed distracted by the current situation.

Evrikh snapped his head in Thea's direction. "What about you? Are you afraid?"

An uncontrollable pain suddenly snapped in his head, and he reached up with his hands, grasping at his temples, that searing pain was right there, so very close to the surface. Evrikh screamed from the intensity as this raw nerve had more control than he did, the feeling of his brain melting into acid, left to slowly eat its way out. He looked back up at Thea, his face knotted with both pain and anger. The veins in his arms started to pulse wildly, as though a foreign fluid was passing through them. He reached his arms around his body, holding his stomach. Sweat dripped from his face as he looked toward Thea.

"... Help me!"

Throughout the whole of their life together, never had Thea seen him so exposed, so vulnerable. She had experienced overwhelming compassion for him before, but this was something more, a silent despair to relieve him of this hidden torment.

Evrikh suddenly felt a familiar presence in the back of his mind. He looked around with weary eyes as Thea was ever still, caught in the small rapture of her own anguish. His eyes shifted to an alleyway a mere ten feet from where they stood now. Seconds later, a figure emerged from those shadows. As he stepped into the light, his head pivoted from Thea to Evrikh.

"It's as Miriam said, it won't stop unless you take the medication."

"Cazziel . . ." Evrikh gritted through his teeth, unable to shake the pain, "now's your chance! After all, this is what you want, isn't it?"

Cazziel took a few steps toward them, bringing himself to a halt. He looked from Thea back to Evrikh. "This is almost like before, isn't it?" he sneered. "I take no pleasure in killing helpless animals."

Evrikh began to laugh hysterically, the veins in his arms relaxing. The laughter continued to grow as his body had found its resolve, and he rose to his feet. Evrikh brought his head slowly down looking back toward Cazziel, his spell of laughter replaced; all that remained was of chaos and anger.

"Such pathetic existence! Tell me, Cazziel, throughout the whole of history, have humans always been this idiotic?"

"Evrikh, I would have killed you, but it seems that Lady Miriam has different plans for you. I'm here to take you back. Make it easy on yourself."

Cazziel pulled his weapon out and brought it up to aim. Evrikh started to step toward him as his face flared with hate. Cazziel eased his finger onto the trigger. Suddenly his weapon shot to life as a blinding light headed in their direction.

Thea lunged in Cazziel's direction, grabbing his weapon with her hands and knocking them both to the ground. As Evrikh pulled himself up to a sitting position with his hands, he looked down at his legs. The shot had taken out his left leg and all that remained were a few strands of wet flesh. Bits of muscle and blood stained the ground a vibrant red. His eyes were fixated on all that was left; a bloody stump. As his body continued to flare with hate, pulsing veins shot out of his thigh.

"My FUCKING leg! You shot off my fucking leg! Dammit, Cazziel, God himself won't be enough to save you from my wrath! DAMN, this fucking hurts . . ." He squeezed his thigh as he shot a thought out in Thea's direction, . . . *and you, Thea, I appreciate you saving my life like that.*

Thea rolled away from Cazziel, his weapon in her hands. Cazziel jumped back and his eyes left Thea, returning to Evrikh. Staring at him, he watched as the pulsing veins stretched down, reforming the interior of his leg. Running loose like wild animals, Evrikh's body raced to repair itself. He rose to his feet as the jumble of flesh below him continued to reform the lost leg. He laughed in Cazziel's direction. Suddenly, the air around Evrikh erupted to life as he was being assaulted from above. The bullets ripped through his flesh and passed through his body, into the ground. He screamed from the pain as the air around him started to cloud up from the rupturing ground below. His ears filled with the rippling sounds of his clothes, the cracking of his bones, and the rendering of his skin. Cazziel continued to stand his ground as the dust cloud quickly grew lifeless.

"NO!" Thea erupted, as she watched Evrikh's convulsing body disappear into the forming cloud of dust, her worst fears rippling across her face.

Cazziel slowly watched as a black sphere of light began to materialize within the clearing dust. Within seconds, the black sphere shot up into the sky, heading toward the spire that contained Evrikh's assailants. Just as the ball of black lightning struck the tower, cracks quickly spread from the point of contact. Cazziel could faintly hear screams resonating from within. Bits of stone came slamming to the ground as people ran for cover, Cazziel ducking backward himself. Dust clouds began forming high up in the spire as pieces of it blew out, their weight dragging them swiftly to the ground. But then suddenly, everything froze in midair, as though time itself had stopped. It was then that Cazziel noticed a ball of that same blackness emanating from within the spire. Lightning flickered throughout the sky, as everything began to pull itself back toward the center of that black mass. Suddenly, very quickly, everything pulled together with an immense explosion as a wave of black energy shot out across the sky, fading the sun for only a moment. The spire was gone; somehow erased.

Cazziel's eyes slowly trailed back down to the dust cloud lingering that mere ten feet away. As he concentrated his eyes, he could see jumbles of flesh and tissue moving throughout it. Seconds later it all retreated back into the cloud. As the dust dissipated, a figure began to emerge from it.

Evrikh's vision grew clearer as he departed from the dust. He halted his advancement as he looked in Cazziel's direction. Measuring their distance, he noticed Thea was the same from Cazziel's side.

"Enough of this! Cazziel, you and I both know I won't be going with you!" Evrikh turned to look at Thea. "Don't worry, Thea, he won't track you himself. Stay safe." He watched as sadness and confusion blanketed her face, ". .

. I love you ... I'm sorry." His face momentarily reflected his own sadness.

Evrikh leaped back, vanishing from their sight, his feet carrying him to the top of a building along the other side of the street. He sat there perched upon the edge of the roof, looking down to Cazziel and Thea. Far below he watched as she ran from him; she was no concern of his. What had Cazziel meant ... *This is almost like before, isn't it?* Evrikh stood up and turned around, almost stumbling at the sight of such green grass.

The roof was gone, no stone, no brick, only soft, feathery grass. As he looked around, a forest loomed in the distance. He turned back to look at Thea and Cazziel, but his eyes halted a few feet away, only to stare at more grass, swaying with such vivid detail. Evrikh was left thinking the city he just came from must've been the vision, the dream. He tried to calm down as he gathered his thoughts.

Shouldn't he be finished with the damn visions? Is it possible his mind had been fractured for so long, it would be impossible to put it all back together, and keep it that way?

"This shit should be over," he sneered toward the grass, "SO WHY THE HELL AREN'T YOU, HUH?" his voice echoed throughout the field.

The air around him flashed and suddenly there was a distorted figure standing right in front of him. He looked at it as his body naturally repositioned itself, bracing for an attack.

"You again? What the hell do you want?"

". . . 'You' again," the figure said calmly. "Evrikh, we're here to help you."

"A blurry image here to help me; thanks, but, no thanks! Look at you, you're blurry, YOU'RE FUCKING BLURRY! Let's just agree to leave each other alone; you don't visit me, and I won't visit you," he erupted as he waved his arms in dismissal.

"How often is it you believe that we visit you? Evrikh, if you do not let us help you, you will suffer the fate of your ancestors."

"YEAH? Maybe that's a welcome fate! What the hell do my ancestors have to do with me anyway?"

"We understand your growing contempt, but please, come and see for yourself."

The air around him began to fluctuate as images started flashing by, carried by waves of light. As the images continued to flash by, they filled his head with information, information that has been lost to time, erased from the histories of man.

The Atlantians were the first to make such a discovery, a discovery that would take their race to the next level of evolution; the lost city of Atlantis in all its glory. The Atlantians had damned themselves with their last contribution to their very way of life. The "$Ge\square t\ \partial v\ la\square f$," translated to "Gate of life." Upon its creation, the project lost control and consumed the very people it was meant to save. The Atlantians did what they could, but in the end it was their race that lost. The "$Ge\square t\partial v la\square f$" consumed all the life that existed on the continent of Atlantis, destroying

THE PHOENIX GATE

the symbiotic circle that existed there, causing a series of cataclysms. The continent plunged into the earth, sinking below the great oceans never to be found again. The very few who survived relocated to Egypt, sharing what little had remained of Atlantis.

Millenniums had passed before mankind would once again reach the level of enlightenment that had once been lost. The Polynesians were the creators of Stonehenge and Easter Island, and some believed that the Polynesians used Stonehenge to predict the future. Easter Island was their way to the gods. At the climax of their civilization, they beckoned the gods and used their advanced knowledge to create the "*do☐☐-we☐ əvla☐t,*" the "Doorway of light." The *do☐☐-we☐ əv la☐t* existed in the form of a man, a prophet who promised his people the enlightenment of the gods and all their glory. The Polynesians, clouded by deception, followed the *do☐☐-we☐ əv la☐t* into a tale that wiped out their entire race and deadened the island. There was no resistance, as they were blinded by their own ignorance. All that remained of their existence was their contributions to the land, Stonehenge and Easter Island.

The Incans, Machu Picchu, Huayna Capac, those whose fates had been unknown to the world of man all began to flip through Evrikh's mind like a picture book. In the end, the holes had been filled, the missing pieces replaced, and ultimately, an alternate version of history had simply been created, for such is the corruption of man.

The images quickly dissipated, taking that blinding light with them. The forest returned, and the distorted figure with it.

"And now your race is on the brink of repeating everything, all over again. Evrikh, you're the reason why it's going to happen."

"What the hell are you saying?!" he grumbled. The pulsating pain in his head returned and his hand raced to his temple. He looked through his fingers, toward the figure. "I'm not going to kill anyone!" The pain grew sharp, and his other hand shot up to his head.

"Look at you, Evrikh, you've already lost control. There's nothing you can do now."

"SHUT UP!" he blurted, as he eased himself down to a sitting position and looked back up through weary hands. "Who are you bastards, anyway?"

The figure looked down to him. "Evrikh, you are a miracle, and yet a mistake at the same time; you were never meant to be. We were not allowed to intervene in AD 2004, and this has been meant to happen since your birth. We are simply here to foresee, as we have been since that first visit you paid to us so very long ago. Unfortunately, there's nothing we can do now. We are so very sorry."

The figure took a majestic step back, almost as if he was standing before his king; hesitant, perhaps mourning. Slowly, he turned to face the forest and began to walk away. As he walked away, Evrikh could suddenly feel the presence of many others. His eyes scanned the edge of the forest, as it slowly revealed the shapes of the others. All of them, standing there, their figures distorted across the distance.

He peered up into the sky and thunder began to roll

throughout it as black clouds pushed back the blue sky. Within seconds the blue sky was filled with the ashness of brewing storms. Evrikh looked back down, only to see an old street as his clothes dampened from falling rain. His head cocked left, then right, assessing the street, as he stumbled out from an alley. The pain had subsided for now, allowing his mind to dwell on other things. It had felt as though the two halves of his brain were finally merging back into a single form.

Is this true? Were the others right? Was Evrikh truly here to destroy all this; the human race? All those races of people simply vanished from history. Was he to do the same?

"This is almost like before . . . isn't it?" . . . Fucking Cazziel!

Evrikh's thoughts suddenly shifted to Thea. What was to become of her? All he could do was pray that she had made it away safely.

As he continued walking further away from the alley, the rain started to come down harder, lining the streets in a rippled gloss. He turned, leaving the street lamps behind, only to be concealed by the shadows that followed. His stumbling body continued lurching forward as he slowly became numb from his internal pain; his internal struggle. The rippling sheen grew angrier as the rain continued; the street remaining ever lifeless.

* * * *

CHAPTER 7
~ Elijah ~

THE SOUND OF cascading water filled the air as two angels held each other, trapped within flesh made of stone; a water fountain. A large circular platform rested in the center of this open room, surrounded by a foot high marble wall. The wall itself was engraved with an ancient language, restraining the water from flowing out onto the floor. In the center remained the two angels, their wings carrying the burden of heaven. As they held each other, water flowed from their eyes, only to know that they would never be together again. Ripples cascaded across the surface as a hand stirred the water from the far side.

The sounds of footsteps glided throughout the air as a figure stepped out from a garden and into this enclosure. As he walked forward, sunlight pierced through the ceiling and glistened off the water. For a moment, it appeared as though it were a fountain of liquid gold. The statue shimmered along its silhouette from the light as birds were heard singing from the garden just outside. He approached the water fountain, only to halt at the marble wall. He looked across the water, to the figure sitting at the far side, her hand continued to stir the water.

"Lady Miriam, there's nothing we can do. He knows too much, and there's not much time before he'll become a greater concern."

The hand suddenly came to a stop as Miriam pulled it up, placing it into her lap. She looked across the room, to the doorway that led out to the garden. "After all this time . . . I grow tired of this game. Cazziel, you know our next option."

"My lady, are you sure this is the path you wish to take?"

"If there was another way, it would have already been chosen." Miriam's eyes fell down upon herself. "I've failed; him, you . . . perhaps us all, Cazziel."

For a moment, his eyes glanced down at her, absorbing her image as her reflection rippled throughout the water. "Everything will be done as you will. My lady, why don't you go and rest now."

Miriam slowly stood up and brought her eyes up to meet Cazziel's. "I'll do that. Inform me if any progress is made."

She crossed the water fountain and found her way to the door leading out to the garden. As she stepped out around the wall, her gown wisped as it followed along the ground. Cazziel's eyes followed her out as she faded into the garden.

~ ~ ~

A gentle breeze blew through the town of Norwynn, rustling the leaves and papers that lay about. People walked about the streets as the sun was nothing more than smoldering ash within the sky, hidden by an occasional cloud. A man walked out of a building, a child following closely behind him. As he held her hand, she looked around with curious eyes, awing at a world that's still new to her.

"Come on, Emilia," the man said as he whisked her up in his arm, placing her on his shoulders.

"Oh, but, Daddy, I'm having so much fun here," Emilia said as her eyes moved around with intrigue.

As they continued to walk forward, they approached the marketplace. The streets were always busy about this time of day, and it began to slow their progress. Noticing a cart of fresh produce, Brian stepped over to it. A little girl came out from some boxes in the back and ran up to the cart, placing her hands on a small table.

"Would ya like to buy thumthing, mithter? I'th all really good." She looked at Brian with eyes that resembled purity; a purity that he's witnessed within the eyes of his own daughter.

Brian looked at her and let out a laugh to her enthusiasm. "Sure, little missy, how about some of those Falussion melons."

The little girl, overjoyed, ran back behind the boxes and moments later a sturdy-looking man came out and approached Brian. "Good day to ya," he said as he wiped his hands with a cloth, "and what can the Azjran family provide for you today?"

While reaching for his pouch, Brian pointed to the

fruit beside the cart. "How about half a dozen of those Falussion melons."

The man grabbed a bag from the small table and walked over beside the cart. As he began going through the fruit, grabbing the freshest ones, he looked back up at Brian. "These things seem ta sell pretty well here. I guess ya folks don't see much tropical fruit around here, do ya?"

Brian looked over at the man as he steadied Emilia on his shoulders. "They are pretty tasty. Well, you know what they say, relish it the time you have. Who knows, tomorrow there might not be any more."

The man started to walk back toward Brian as he finished tying off the bag. "At the rate they sell, I wouldn't doubt it."

Brian chuckled as he handed the man the money. "Thanks for the fruit, friend." Brian nodded as he turned and began to step away. Just as he reached a few feet away from the stand, he stopped his progression and slowly raised his head; his eyes suddenly becoming filled with awareness. Slowly he glanced up and down the street, peering through the crowds. As he looked up the street, his eyes scanned the buildings, searching for something unknown to him. He turned his head to look down the street, his eyes continuing their surveillance. Brian's body turned and started walking, his head slowly turning with it.

As Brian and Emilia continued moving forward, Emilia noticed Brian's progression was a little quicker. As she bobbed around on his shoulders, she looked down at him. "Daddy, what is it, what's wrong?"

While stepping through the crowds of people, he spoke, his face, remaining forward. "We're being followed."

"Are we in danger?"

"I haven't decided yet."

Brian kept on pressing through the people. As he drew closer to the end of the street, he noticed an alleyway out of the corner of his eye. He looked around for only a moment before heading into the alley.

While standing beside a building, hidden by the crowds of people, a figure watched as Brian stepped into an alleyway, carrying a little girl on his shoulders. As he stepped out of view, the figure stepped away from the building and started to follow Brian's trail, making sure he remained no more than twenty to thirty paces ahead. The figure glided through the crowds of people as though it were a ghost, its identity hidden from the world by a hooded cloak.

As the figure reached the alleyway, it slowed its pace, being careful not to be seen. As it looked around the corner, it paused for a moment, only to realize that Brian was gone. Slowly the figure stepped away from the building and into the alley. While stepping forward, the figure's hood moved back and forth, scanning the surroundings and observing the situation. There remained no doors, no windows, and the rooftops lingered far up into the sky. The only thing occupying the street was a couple of trash cans and a couple of newspapers that rustled at the slightest breeze. The alley was too long for Brian to have beaten him to the other side, let alone the fact that he was carrying a child. The figure continued to walk down the alley.

When it reached the halfway point, he was coming up to the trash cans. A slight breeze blew through the alley, rustling the newspapers and shifting the contents of the trash cans. Suddenly the figure stopped as it felt the sharpness of something pressing up against its back.

"Who are you?"

The hooded figure remained hesitant for a moment before Brian pressed the blade a little harder. The figure reached up with its hands and grabbed ahold of the hood, slowly pulling it from its head. Brian became shocked as the hood revealed long hair, remarkably black. Brian's grip eased up a little. She turned around, her face revealing silver eyes.

"I'm sorry to contact you like this, Brian, but we need to talk."

For a moment, Brian stood there staring at her. After sensing there was no danger, he put away his blade and regained his posture.

"I'm sorry, miss, but I think you have me mistaken for someone else. Now if you'll excuse me, I have business to attend to."

Seconds later Thea noticed the little girl standing behind Brian. He grabbed her by the hand and turned to walk off. "In games like these, we never break the rules, miss. I'm sure you understand."

"Brian, please! Without your help Evrikh may die!"

"That's impossible!" Brian yelled back to her as he continued walking. "Unless they've found out a way to kill a god!"

"What about a god who'd kill himself and everybody else in the process?"

Thea paused for a moment as she realized that Brian had stopped moving forward. Slowly he turned back to face her. "Now, why would he do such a thing?"

Thea stepped toward Brian and Emilia as she spoke. "I fear that Evrikh is losing control of himself, and if that should happen, he would become the worst plague the world has ever known. This is why I need your help—he needs your help!"

Brian appeared to be weighing very rough decisions before speaking again. "I'm sorry, but there is nothing I can do."

"Maybe not, but I need to find the Elder. Only you can help me with this, Brian, and you know that. Whatever caused those chapters to be missing from Marcus's journal I'm afraid are going to be caused again."

After looking at Thea for a moment, Brian turned his gaze down to Emilia. Seconds later, his eyes returned to Thea. "Come with me. We'll speak in private."

As they exited the alleyway, Brian looked up and down the street once again. Moments later he looked toward Emilia and Thea. "Let's go."

Stepping out into the street, the three of them walked through the crowds of people, leaving the marketplace. As they continued walking down the street, there remained a restaurant unnoticed on the other side; lounge tables on the outside. A pair of eyes watched the three of them closely as she spoke across the table.

"Do you think he'll finally take her to see the Elder?"

As the other set of eyes continued following them, he spoke back, "The pages of time have already been written. What will happen will always happen; has always happened."

For a moment, the two at the table watched as the three walked off.

Seconds later, Brian stopped, Thea almost bumping into him. Brian slowly turned his head, scanning through the crowds.

"What is it?" Thea responded, aware of his alertness.

Brian's eyes fell upon a restaurant across the street behind them. The tables on the outside remained empty, "Nothing to worry about." Brian's head turned back, and he continued walking.

"So this is where it all started," the woman spoke as her vision remained concentrated on Thea.

"This chapter's finished, Lashara; let's go." The man's eyes turned to her, sitting across the table.

As Thea followed Brian, her eyes began to move as though they were controlled by something else. Her eyes carried their sight back to the restaurant. For a moment, Thea stared as a female and a male returned her look. As Thea blinked, she realized that the tables were empty and Brian was calling to her.

"Hey, you coming?"

"Oh, I'm sorry," Thea replied, looking back at Brian.

As they pressed on, Thea looked back once more, but the chairs remained lifeless. As she turned back around, she realized that Emilia was staring at her, as if she was hearing something that she didn't understand. A moment later Emilia began to giggle, and then let her childish eyes roam the streets, the crowds of people being left behind.

~ ~ ~

The sounds of footsteps echoed throughout the air as a woman descended a circular stone staircase, a man following behind her.

"We're still trying to coordinate the final settings for the last ring, but otherwise the alignment's almost complete."

". . . and what of the stabilization? Are you sure it'll hold?" Cazziel asked, steps behind her.

"All the specifications are exact, as written in Marcus's journal. You worry too much, my dear Cazziel. Besides, you're here now, aren't you?" Lady Miriam responded.

"Even so, the journal declares this to be an untested experiment; an idea never fully realized," he warned.

"Of course it's been tested," Miriam let out a small laugh. "This conversation couldn't have happened otherwise."

As they reached the bottom, Cazziel stepped ahead of her and opened a tall wooden door. The door opened slowly from its own weight as he stepped aside for Lady Miriam. They passed through the door and into a large chamber filled with scientists and researchers who continued about their business. Lady Miriam stepped up to the edge of the platform they had transcended onto, a waist-high wall lingering before her. She placed her hands on the railing that ran along the wall; Cazziel approached the railing beside her.

Both their gazes fell down to the center of the room. At the bottom there was a base at least thirty feet or so, by fifteen feet, rectangular in shape. Protruding from the sides of that base were two pillars that ran straight up another fifteen feet. Resting between those pillars was a large circular stone; a ring with two brackets connected to the inside of the ring. Within that ring remained another, held in place by those brackets. And within that, a third ring. Along the edges of each ring were engravings, a language that didn't exist to the rest of the world.

"My dear Cazziel," Miriam's eyes marveled at the creation before them, "I give to you, the Elijah Rings."

Lady Miriam stepped away from the wall and over to a small staircase that would take them to the base level. A scientist approached Miriam as she reached the bottom of the staircase.

"My lady, the initial settings for the last ring have been finalized. Translation of the language has been completed and the alignment's been adjusted accordingly." The scientist's voice was sharp and accurate. "If you'll follow me, I'll show you the RSAs we've developed."

"RSAs?" Cazziel slid a quick glance to Miriam.

"Return signal amplifiers. They'll be what allow you to return, in the end."

As the scientist walked away from Miriam and Cazziel, they continued to follow him, descending to the other side of the room where a clear box was being observed. The box was connected to electronic monitors, and within it were multiple organic life-forms. Each organism was no more than seven inches long; a half inch wide. Protruding from it were five very slender tendrils, sliding around within the box, feeling the edges of its confined world, exploring every intimate detail of its transluscent cage.

The scientist placed his hands on the box. "This. This is what'll allow you to come back, maybe even go anywhere else—everywhere else. Nothing's for certain, as it has never been tested yet."

Cazziel knelt down beside the box and peered inside.

"So you're the reason why I'm here." He remained silent for a moment. "And how exactly will I use something like this, Doc? From looking at it, almost seems our Lady Miriam would get more enjoyment out of it," he finished, with a small crack edging his lips upward.

Miriam noticed.

The scientist looked down to Cazziel. "The organism will be grafted onto your spine. From there it'll tap into your nervous system and start emitting signals until it aligns with your brain waves, till essentially every one of your body's electrical impulses are identical to its own. Once both your signals align with each other's, then, in theory, you should be able to use it at will; much like you would tell your arm to move, your legs to walk, your head to turn. That is, all with the exception of here, of course. You see," the scientist continued, his gaze turning to Miriam, "time, like everything else, works three-dimensionally.

The 'Frequency,' if you will, is the part that Marcus's journal takes in as the actual key." The professor raised his hand in front of him. "This Frequency consists of three different wave forms, or three-dimensional tones," his eyes returned to the box. "If you reproduce these tones, it would be like tricking time into believing that anything radiating the same complete tone would be a part of it."

Lady Miriam looked over at the scientist. "Its DNA patterns are holding, and its vitals have stabilized then?"

"Yes, my lady, she's been alive for . . . roughly seventy-six hours now. It took our team quite a while to decipher his algorithm for chromosome augmentation," the scientist laughed slightly as he looked up from the box. "Professor Kendrick was a genius. I wish Marcus's journal gave the slightest hint as to what truly happened to him; would have been an honor to know such a man. It was his research that made this possible, and it wasn't even complete."

". . . She?" Cazziel rose to his feet. "That's irrelevant. Professor, continue with your research. The Elijah Rings must be operational before our chances elude us."

"I understand, sir. Ever since we've cultivated the creature, there has been some . . . a . . ." the scientist hesitated for a moment, "a response, shall we say, from the rings."

"A response?" Miriam queried, as her eyes carried themselves over to the rings, taking in her own dwarfed size by the sight of them.

The scientist began walking toward the rings, Cazziel and Miriam following behind him.

"Yes, the alignment of the symbols actually came from the creature. We started testing the organism with electromagnetic pulses, attempting to find a tolerance range, and in return, each ring began to rotate until the brackets along the edges of each ring aligned themselves with certain symbols." The scientist pointed his hand up to the bracket of the outermost ring. "Take a look at that there."

Both Cazziel and Miriam let their eyes carry their heads up along the rings and gaze at the bracket above.

"Each of those symbols represents a destination, or a specific time, if you will. The Elijah Rings themselves are actually a mathematical table for calculating any point in history, an exact point in history," the scientist spoke as his eyes ran along the edges of the rings, outlining their shape. "It's all theory at this point, but I suppose the final step would be to simply . . . turn them on."

Miriam's gaze fell back to the scientist. "Professor, continue with your research and update us of any further developments."

The scientist looked back at Miriam. "As you wish, my lady." He stepped away and began to cross back to the other side of the room.

Miriam turned her attention to Cazziel. "Cazziel, when will you be ready for the grafting?"

Cazziel hesitated for a moment before he turned his head toward her, their eyes staring at each other's. "We'll proceed according to schedule. The process will be complete by the time the rings are operational."

Cazziel turned his gaze back to the rings and the future they held for him. Lady Miriam's eyes remained on him, slightly revealing what her heart had felt.

* * * *

CHAPTER 8
~ Ruination ~

THE DOOR OF an old apartment slowly opened, bringing light into a once-dark room.

"Oh . . . I remember this place. It's been a while, huh, Daddy?" Emilia said, holding his hand and slowly looking around. Her expression was that of a child with fond memories.

Brian stepped inside and reached his hand over to the wall beside them. Seconds later, the room was filled with smoldering light as it shined through the dust.

"This place has been about as dormant as the Resistance. I guess it looks less suspicious this way."

Brian stepped inside with Emilia, their feet leaving footprints in the dust-covered floor. Thea walked in behind them, slightly ducking her head as she entered. "This place is a little run-down, wouldn't you say?" She spoke as her eyes slowly danced around the room.

The room they had stepped into wasn't very large; maybe twenty feet by twenty feet. Hanging from the ceiling was a very antique chandelier. The bolts on the left side had come undone and its weight had tilted it to the right. On the left wall was a doorway that led to a room where the light could not reach. Beside that doorway were bookshelves. From the binds of the books, Thea could tell that they were classics: *The Britannica Encyclopedia,* Whitley Strieber, Dean Koontz, Guillermo del Toro, Christian Lee; authors whose works predated the War of Ruin, no doubt.

A slight breeze carried itself through the door and disrupted the environment. The room was filled with a haze as the dust quickly spread into the air. Along the back wall was another doorway, a dim light barely visible on the other side. Beside that doorway was a staircase that extended along the right wall. Thea looked past the staircase and through the doorway at the bottom. The windows of the other room slightly revealed their secrets as dull sunlight shined through the cracks.

Brian stepped farther inside, taking Emilia with him. "Come on. It's been awhile since any of us have been here, and I don't want anybody around us to become nosy," he said as his feet brought him to a stop in front of the bookcase.

Thea watched as he reached to the fourth shelf from the bottom, bringing his hand to a rest on a single book: *Genesis: A new beginning.* As Brian pulled the book from its place, Thea realized that there was no back wall. Brian maneuvered his hand inside, up to his forearm. Seconds later she heard a faint click and suddenly a panel of the staircase behind them slid open. Thea's head snapped around at the unexpected noise. Emilia let out a slight giggle from Thea's reaction as Brian continued to hold her hand.

"Let's go," he added as he stepped around Thea and through the doorway.

She followed him through, leaving the old apartment behind. The air was thick, and she could see a faint light ahead of them, barely illuminating the passageway. The ceiling was low, and moss had outlined the cracks of where the walls came together, along either side.

As they reached the end of the passageway, they entered a room slightly bigger than the one they had left. In the middle of the back wall was a small fireplace. On the wall opposite of them was a cloth drape that had stretched from the floor to the ceiling. The upper right corner of it was tinted blue, a pattern of stars laced throughout it. The rest of the cloth was made of stripes; white and red. There were two lights hanging from the ceiling and a circular table in the middle of the room. Thea looked around and knew it had been a conference room of some sort. After moving over to the table, Brian had placed his belongings down and released Emilia's hand. He walked over to a chair and placed his hand on it, removing the chair from its place. A slight aura of dust emanated from it as the chair creaked across the floor. Brian sat down, looking over at Thea.

"It was so long ago, Brian, so very long ago." Thea's voice grew to a whisper as her hand ran down the side of the drape, her eyes continuing the same motion.

"The Resistance," Brian replied, as his eyes glanced at

it, "of the people that lived before the War of Ruin, it represented freedom. Now for us, it carries that same burden; a symbol the Council could never take."

Thea stepped over to the table and pulled a chair, sitting opposite of Brian. Seconds later, Emilia appeared beside Thea, pulling out a chair of her own. Thea smiled at Emilia's attempt to appear grown-up.

"Brian," Thea said, as she looked back at him, "how is it that you know so much?" She sat back in her chair, folding her arms across her chest.

"None of us 'know' anything, Thea. It's what we're taught that makes us appear to 'know so much.' It all depends on the instructor, I suppose," he finished, as his eyes lingered toward Emilia. "I've just had an excellent tutor."

"I'm sorry, but I'd prefer to waste as little time as possible."

"I understand," he complied, his gaze returning to Thea.

". . . And what of the Elder?" she asked, shifting her weight in the chair.

"I wouldn't worry too much; the Elder is already on his way. He'll be here shortly." Brian leaned forward, placing his arm on the table and rolling his fingers. "You know, if what you speak is true about Evrikh, I'm not sure there is much we can do for him at all."

"There's always something to do, Daddy, it just depends on the path you take," Emilia spoke as her eyes lingered in Brian's direction.

Thea glanced at Emilia, acknowledging her strange intelligence. Brian smiled at her as his eyes slipped into

THE PHOENIX GATE

a more concentrated state. Moments later, Emilia's eyes slowly turned to look back into the passageway they had come from.

Brian noticed her alertness. "What is it?"

Emilia's eyes continued to linger toward the passageway. "We're not alone."

Thea looked up into the passageway, slowly standing up from her chair and taking a defensive position. For a moment, Brian's mind was flooded with a new sensation, something he had never felt before. But before he could indulge in it, his mind was distracted by another presence. Rising from his chair, Brian turned his gaze into the passageway and the secret it now holds. Slowly he moved his hand around to his back when a faint shadow emerged into the dim light of the tunnel. Squinting his eyes, Brian realized who it was.

"Keona?" Brian spoke as his hand retracted from his back. He stepped a little closer, ". . . Keona?"

Seconds later, the figure stumbled into the light, kneeling down from an inability to stand. Leaning against the wall, she slowly looked up through her blood-soaked hair and placed her hand on her shoulder to cover up a wound.

Brian's eyes grew wide. "Keona, you?!" After realizing this, he ran up and knelt down beside her. "Keona, what in the hell happened?"

She gripped her shoulder and tried standing back up, stumbling as she lifted herself. "It's . . . Evrikh," she hesitated for a moment, "something's happened . . . to him."

Brian placed his arm around her and helped her stand

to her feet. "Come on, Keona, let's get you over to the table." Slowly, he guided her to the table, nearly falling as her body gave out a couple of times.

"He has no . . . control over himself," Keona rattled out as Brian lay her down upon the table.

"Who did this to you?" Brian asked as he leaned over her, scanning her body for the severity of her condition.

"The . . . Council tried to take him. But he . . . resisted. Instead . . . they awakened . . . something within him."

". . . Within him?" Brian's eyes were immediately distracted by other thoughts racing through his mind; searching.

"The Elder . . . is the only one . . . who can help . . . him now." Keona's breathing became lighter as she clenched her face, trying to push away the pain.

Brian looked down at the ground for a moment before his gaze turned to Emilia. "I guess we have no choice. We were hoping to avoid a situation like this," he continued as his eyes looked over to Thea. He turned to look back at Keona. "Don't worry, Keona, you'll be all right."

As Brian looked down to Keona, Thea noticed that Emilia had left her chair and walked over to the drape that hung on the back wall. As she stood there, facing the drape, Thea left the table and walked over beside her. Looking down to her, she said, "Hey, sweetie, you all right? You know your dad there . . . well, he's one hell of a guy, and in his care, Keona will be just fine."

As Thea went to place her hand on Emilia, she turned around, her eyes glowing a faint blue. Thea slightly withdrew her hand. "Emilia?" her expression melted into one of wonder.

Emilia looked up at Thea, as her eyes were filled with a seemingly hidden wisdom. "It's all right, Thea. You're right, she'll be fine now; we'll all be fine now."

Thea stared for a moment before she felt the realization within her, like a small cluster bomb had been set off right in the middle of her brain. Leaving every nerve, every thought, every curve, with that same brilliantly burning sensation, "... *You're* the Elder?!"

Emilia developed a faint smile on her face before replying. "Once upon a time I was given that name. Thea, please, I've always preferred my living name; Kendrick."

"Kendrick?!" Thea blurted.

"We've been watching you for some time, you know," Emilia spoke with a soothing voice, almost as if a ghost was laid upon it.

Thea's face retained a puzzled look. "Watching . . . me?"

Emilia smiled again before her eyes wandered over to Brian leaning over Keona. Seconds later, Thea watched as the look of Emilia's face became shattered. Thea quickly turned to Brian's direction, only to see Keona burying some kind of knife into Brian's side, just below his left arm. The knife, riding above his rib cage, went dangerously close to his heart; the splitting sounds of his abdomen were faintly heard. Emilia watched in terror as Brian's face slowly went from shock to stillness; a stillness Emilia had never seen upon him, but was all too familiar to Kendrick. Keona placed her other hand on Brian's chest and leaned forward beside his ear. Although Thea could not hear her, she knew the words Keona had spoken.

"Thank you."

Keona then pushed Brian from the dagger, letting his limp body fall to the floor. She slowly sat up, running the tip of the knife along the grain of the table, blood dripping from its blade. Keona's eyes looked up from Brian's crippled body and stared at Thea and Emilia. They continued to look at Keona, both confused and horrified.

"Oh, I wasn't as hurt as I appeared to be," Keona spoke as a smile slowly crept across her face. "Looks can be quite deceiving. Wouldn't you agree?" she said as her head cocked to the side, her eyes fixated on Emilia.

Tears rolled in Emilia's eyes as she dropped to her knees. Moments later her head lifted to look at Keona. "Why? He was your friend!" Emilia spoke as the tears began to roll down her face. Her eyes returning to Brian, "He was my friend, my mentor; my father." Emilia's voice grew weak.

Thea stepped in front of Emilia. "How could you do such a thing?" her body progressing to a defensive stance.

"Not that it matters, but I'll tell you anyway. The Council has what it's been looking for, so now I'm here to make sure it doesn't receive any outside influence." Keona spoke as she wiped the blade off on her sleeve. "And to think, if you had just let him be in Eden, you wouldn't even be in this situation. And where is he now? He's not even going to come and save you." Keona sheathed the knife as she rose off the table.

"Shut up. Just shut up!!" Emilia spoke, as her head remained lowered. Slowly she stood up, her eyes rising to reveal her anger.

Keona's eyebrow rose for a moment. "Oh? And what do you hope to do trapped in that little girl's body, Elder?" Keona looked down at Emilia in pity. "You're not even a concern anymore."

"SHUT UP!" Emilia screamed as she lunged forward at Keona.

"EMILIA!" Thea yelled, throwing out her arm to try to stop Emilia, but she was already outside her reach.

Emilia shot across the room, her hands extended in front of her. Just as she reached Keona, Keona flinched to the left. Moments later Emilia felt a sharp pain to her gut. The force of the blow had stopped Emilia's movement forward, but her determination kept her arms in front of her. Emilia grunted from the pain as she stretched her arms out, her hands grasping Keona around her neck.

Thea watched as Keona shifted her shoulder, the motion causing Emilia's body to rise slightly higher. The anger in Emilia's eyes grew more intense as her grip on Keona's neck grew tighter. Keona began to struggle as she realized this little girl was actually cutting off her air supply. Bringing her other arm up, Keona slammed it down on Emilia's hands, hoping to break the grip, but her hands remained of stone; unmovable. Keona's face turned a shade whiter as the veins under her skin began to feel the oxygen depleting her body. She began to gasp for air, as Emilia's anger grew stronger, her grip growing tighter. Thea looked closer as she realized blood had begun to flow from Emilia's hands. The movement in Keona's body had grown still, her eyes rolling upward, and soon after, she began to fall backward. As her body hit the floor, Emilia's body landed beside it, her grip breaking from the fall.

Thea ran to Emilia, kneeling down and placing her hands on Emilia's shoulders. As she rolled her over, Thea saw the same knife used on Brian protruding from Emilia's stomach. The blade had been inserted just above her navel, and cut her up to the base of her rib cage. Emilia's breath was faint as her eyes wondered for an answer. For a moment, Thea looked over to Keona's body. Her eyes were wide as they stared into another place. Lacerations remained on her neck where Emilia's fingers had found their place; blood trickling down her neck. Thea's eyes returned to Emilia, only to find her looking up at her. Emilia's eyes were soft, as she knew she didn't have much time. Thea looked down to the knife and grasped it with her hand. Looking back at Emilia's face, she winced as she pulled the blade from Emilia's stomach, feeling the release of tension as the knife came loose. Emilia yelped as her throat gurgled with filling blood. Thea threw the knife aside and looked at the wound on Emilia's stomach.

"Oh God . . . no! No, no, no, no, NO! She's only a CHILD!" she spat at Keona's unconscious body. "Hold on, Emilia, we're gonna get you and your dad to a hospital, OK?" Thea placed her shaking hands on the wound to apply pressure. "God, I'm so sorry." Tears began to swell in her eyes. As Thea applied pressure, the blood kept slipping through; a river that wouldn't be stopped. Thea knew that Emilia's little body couldn't support such a blood loss for very much longer. Brian wasn't doing so well now either, as his breathing had become nothing more than a labored whisper.

As Thea sat there, on the frenzied edge of hysteria, she almost didn't notice the faint hue from the hallway. Looking up, she thought she was on the verge of going crazy as the moss was glowing almost like it was made of green light. Rippling out across the floorboards, the moss was growing, spreading; earthly dirt rising up from beneath the flooring. Almost resembling a small lake of flowing soil, Thea watched as small roots emerged, swaying like that of hair; a woman's face shortly following. Rising to no more than just below her shoulders, Thea couldn't help put be mesmerized by her eyes; were they roses?

"We haven't much time, Thea, but to this I promise you, I am a friend of Evrikh," she spoke as she assessed the condition of the father and daughter before them.

"God, why am I losing my MIND? Get it together, Thea. Emilia can't go . . . not like this!" The tears fell free of their own will as Thea felt that the pressure she kept over Emilia's body was the only comfort she could give.

Emilia's eyes blinked slowly as she struggled to look at Thea. A faint smile spread across her face. "It's all right, Thea," Emilia's face contorted from the pain. "It's up to you now."

"But I don't know what to do," Thea cried as the tears continued.

"The Elijah Rings," Emilia's body compulsively gasped for air as Thea felt her stomach quivering beneath her hand. ". . . the Council. Go to Eden and . . . use the rings . . ."

Thea watched as a foreign hand suddenly guided itself over Emilia's wound; over Thea's hands. She felt the warm rolling sensation of soil spreading around, gently massaging, until the soil was below, and Thea's hands were above. She quickly recoiled herself.

"WHAT THE FU…"

As her eruption trailed off, she watched as a mysterious green aura slowly spread itself across Emilia's little body. Looking up, Thea saw that the same process had already begun with Brian's body. Looking at this woman, or female dirt sprite, Thea believed she was in the company of an Unfamiliar quite possibly the Council wasn't even aware of.

"I am known as Lorelei." Her rose eyes had shifted from magenta to a radiant green. "If you wish for their lives, then this is the only way." She had turned then to look from their wounded bodies, back to Thea. "There is still much left to do. Carry out this little one's wishes. Go to Evrikh and save him, as I will save these two."

With her eyes looming downward again, Thea felt the tiniest bit of despair slip away, thanks to this Lorelei. Maybe she could help them, save them even.

"How will I even—"

"Thea, if you dwell too much about that, then you'll lose sight of what is." Her voice echoed the crackling of firewood, the crashing of waves.

As Thea stepped over to the knife, she knelt down and picked it up, gripping it with a new burning desire engraved within her mind, and she turned to Lorelei one last time. "Just please, do everything that you can for them." She then silently made a vow within herself.

~ ~ ~

As the two strangers walked down the street, they slowly looked up to the old apartment that now contained so many secrets. The female remained a couple of steps in front of the other stranger; a man. As their feet brought them in front of the house, the two of them came to a stop.

"So, now she's free and doesn't even realize it, robbed of that last bit of innocence," the woman spoke as her eyes slowly scanned the exterior of the house.

"How can you accept something you've never known? It will take time, Lashara," the man spoke as his eyes left her and turned to the apartment.

"What's to happen to Brian?" she asked, the apartment appearing lifeless.

"Brian chose his path many years ago. He was never destined to intervene, and neither are we." His voice became a slight whisper as he spoke to himself. "Godspeed, my old friend."

"Tell me, Virgil, if she's the reason we are here, then why do we not end this now?" Lashara asked as she turned back to look at him.

"We are not here to interfere, simply to make sure that everything happens as it has been written." Virgil turned and continued walking down the street. "Come now, Lashara, we are done here."

Lashara turned to follow him, her eyes remaining fixated on the old apartment. "*Beth'da dae lok shiel*; continue to sleep, little lion."

~ ~ ~

The room was filled with scientists who scurried around in preparation. A table remained in the center of the room, a man lying naked on his stomach; a cloth draped over his midsection. He lifted his head, his eyes peering around the room and watching the events unfolding. A woman looked up from one of the monitors and noticed his reaction to the events unraveling around him. She left the monitor and descended across the room.

"Why, Cazziel, if I didn't know any better I would say that you look a little nervous."

Cazziel turned his head in her direction as she floated into the light that was domed around the table. He pivoted his head down upon his arms as a faint smile spread across his face. "Nervous? I think not, my lady. But what if this doesn't work? What could we hope to do against him?"

Miriam stepped around his head and placed her hands on his shoulders, his body tensed from the chill, as her fingers lingered for a moment.

"We will worry about that when it does fail. Either way, you should relax. We've received every indication that this is the point it's to happen. That, in itself, should be reason enough to believe it will work." Miriam spoke as her body continued moving around the table, coming to a halt on the other side. Cazziel turned his head around as another voice entered into the light.

"All right, sir, everything is prepared, and we already

have an organism ready for the grafting. Once again, the decision is yours, Cazziel." The professor spoke as he adjusted his glasses with his hand.

Cazziel lifted his head up from the table and looked into Miriam's eyes. "I am ready." As he spoke, a smile eased across her face, her eyes soft with passion.

The scientist left the table, walking over to the clear box. As he reached it, he picked up a set of gloves lying beside it. Seconds later, a second scientist stepped over to the box, slowly removing the lid. The professor lowered his hands into the box, being careful not to touch anything. As his hands passed down through the box, they came to a rest on the sides of one of the organisms. The professor clamped his hands around the organism; he could feel slight movement beneath his gloves. Slowly, he removed the organism from the case and, while holding it away from his body, turned around to face the table. The organism's multiple tendrils flailed wildly, searching; needing.

Cazziel looked across the room as the professor reentered the light, the organism within his grasp. The professor looked over to Miriam as he approached the table. "My lady, would you please step back from the table. We would appreciate as little interference as possible."

Lady Miriam complied without hesitation and began to step away from the table, her eyes remaining fixated on the organism.

"All right, Cazziel, the organism will not actually begin the cycle until it comes in contact with a biological organism. Are you sure you are ready?" the professor asked one final time as he held the organism above Cazziel's back.

Cazziel looked up at the professor from the table, and then rested his head back on the table, looking out into the light, Miriam returning his gaze. "Please proceed, Professor."

The scientist's eyes shifted their view from Cazziel's head to his back. He took a deep breath as he began to lower his arms. Cazziel felt the chilling sensation of the gloves against his skin. As the organism graced his back, the professor pulled his hands from its sides and slowly began to step away. He looked over his shoulder as his eyes stayed on the organism. "Make sure you monitor everything," his voice carried to the other scientists.

As Cazziel's vision continued lingering out into the shadows, his mind remained fixated somewhere else. A tingling sensation slowly began to pass through his body as he felt a slight movement on his back.

The professor looked over to one of the other scientists at a surveillance monitor. "What's the reading?"

"I'm getting very low residual effects, but nothing too big to notice, sir," the scientist spoke as his eyes continued to read the monitor.

The professor turned his head to the scientist on the other side of him. "What about signal emissions?"

The other scientist looked up from his monitor. "I'm not getting anything either, sir."

The professor turned his head back to the table, his face bringing a look of question. "I don't understand," he spoke to himself. "I'm sure there should have been some kind of reaction by now. The level of compatibility is limitless . . ." At that point the professor had come out of his meditative state and noticed that Cazziel's hands had a firm grip on the table.

Lady Miriam peered into the light and took a step forward. "Cazziel, do you even feel anything yet?"

"My lady, please stay where you are," the professor spoke from across the room. "It's already begun." His arm remained extended in her direction.

The other scientists looked back at their monitors. "But, sir, we're still not getting anything."

"That's because the monitors are looking for a result, not a catalyst," the professor said as his eyes slowly scanned the table.

Cazziel's body began to shake as each muscle tensed uncontrollably. As Lady Miriam looked closer, she could see small veins emerging from the organism. As they came out of the organism, they began to burrow into Cazziel's body, running just below his skin. It was then that Miriam noticed his face. It had become tense and contorted, yet from his mouth there came no sound; only heavy breathing. A new sensation swept through Miriam's body as she realized that this was the first time she had ever seen this side of Cazziel; the side of pain, maybe even fear.

The organism's movement became greater as more veins emerged from its gelatinous shell, indulging themselves in Cazziel's body, invading his skin and massaging the space between his flesh and muscles. The pain had caused him to jerk convulsively. The professor watched as the tentacles quickly spread through his body, running like wild vines beneath the surface of his skin. The organism suddenly clamped down upon Cazziel's back and began to split his skin around its edges, burrowing. Cazziel's face grew weary from the intensity of the pain, and he began to spasm violently as his body arched in an upward motion. Blood ran around his sides and pooled onto the table. Slowly the organism began to pull itself into his body as his skin was forced around it. With the organism continuing to burrow its way to his spine, a pulse of light shot out across the room.

The professor's eyes marveled at the speed of the event taking place before him. "That must be the first tone!"

One of the other scientists looked up from the monitor to the professor. "Sir, the reading on the scale just blew the meter; it's overloading the system!"

"Shut down the differential couplings and engage the synthesizing program!" the professor demanded as he turned his head over to the other scientist. His eyes looked back to Cazziel. "It's time we monitor instead of reproduce!"

As the organism pulled itself farther into Cazziel's body, Miriam noticed that the veins under his skin were now spreading through his head; his face. Cazziel's vision grew wide as small tentacles began to invade his sight, bursting from under his eyelids and running across the marble surface of his eyes. His body lunged forward as another wave of light emerged from the table, consuming the room.

The professor's eyes grew in anticipation. "The second tone!"

The hall had remained empty except for an occasional guard walking past the end opening. A panel on the floor slowly lifted itself a few inches from the surface, and then paused for a moment. Seconds later it continued to move, sliding across the ground and leaving an opening hidden within a shadow. Thea hesitated for a moment before she lifted her head outside the hole. As her eyes came above the floor line, she rotated her head around to glance up and down the hall.

"... Looks pretty good," she whispered to herself.

In a swift motion, Thea climbed out of the hole and ran up along the left wall, her eyes peering down the hall as another guard walked by. As she looked back at the hole, she realized that she had left the panel open. But before her mind had time to worry, the panel began to slide back into place. For a moment Thea became confused but decided she would worry about that panel moving on its own at a more appropriate time. She turned her head back toward the opening of the hallway and quickly descended toward it. As the end of the hallway came closer, Thea was suddenly stopped by a scream she had never heard before, a scream that almost made her want to yell out loud herself. Growing more confused, she whipped her head around as she noticed two more guards approaching in her direction.

Thea quickly looked around for an escape to her situation and noticed another door across the hall from her. The guards came closer as she sat there looking across to the other door. She turned her eyes back to the guards, focusing her thoughts upon them. Her face slightly contorted as her mind began to work in a way that felt a little foreign to her. A slight breeze suddenly picked up through the hallway as the two guards heard a loud noise down the hall, behind them. They suddenly turned away from her direction and quickly ran toward the other end of the hall. Thea leaned back from her aggressive stance with a look of question, or disbelief, on her face. Had she done that? She wanted to believe but didn't really have the time to question anything at this point.

"That'll work," she said as a small grin lingered across her face. After relishing her moment of triumph, her ongoing situation had renewed itself within her mind.

The large door slid open with ease as Thea crept through to the other side. As she looked ahead, the hallway circled down and around the corner; a staircase. Just as the door clicked shut, Thea turned and began to descend the staircase, her mind staying alert for what might lie up ahead, noticing the surroundings had remained a little too silent. The end of the circular staircase revealed a tall wooden door, a light gleaming through its cracks. Voices came from the other side.

Thea approached the door and placed her hands on it, leaning forward. Before her eyes had reached the crack, her mind was suddenly flooded with images. An operating table with a subject lying in the middle, a woman standing on the side as other scientists watched from afar. The subject was writhing in pain as some creature invaded his body. Suddenly the images vanished.

As Thea shook the effects from her head, she leaned

up against the crack of the door, the light blinding at first before she adapted. Looking through to the other side, Thea noticed a man sitting up on a table with a woman standing beside him. As they continued to talk, their faint voices raised a suspicion within Thea; she had known them. Suddenly, another man, dressed as a scientist, came into view walking toward the two at the table. Within his hands he carried papers, and as he walked toward the man sitting down, he looked up to him. Recognition had finally settled in. Cazziel.

~

"Now, Cazziel," the professor spoke, "you may feel a little disoriented at first, but I'm positive you will adapt very quickly. It's nothing to worry about," the professor reassured him.

Cazziel looked down at his hands as he turned them from side to side. "It almost seems like everything is moving in slow motion. I can see that I'm here," Cazziel paused for a moment, "at the same time, it feels like I'm not here."

The professor looked over at Lady Miriam. "I cannot tell you what to expect. After all, it is the first time technology like this has ever been used." He finished as his eyes looked down to Cazziel. "I'm not quite sure how you feel now, Cazziel, but it must feel a little . . ."

". . . funky," Cazziel uttered.

Just then, Cazziel felt a presence, and as if based on instinct, his eyes found their way over to the wooden door. Seconds later, the door exploded inward as pieces of wood lunged forward, flying across the room. As the pieces of wood started heading in Cazziel's direction, he leapt from the table, grabbing Miriam, and landed on the floor behind the table. A firm hand reached back up and ripped the table from the tiles, upturning it and using it as a shield. The professor, while ducking his head, quickly ran from the blast toward the equipment.

"What the hell is going on?" Miriam wondered as her breathing quickened.

"I'm not sure," Cazziel answered as he raised his head above the table.

Just then, he noticed a streak of color duck into the room, hidden by the dust from the explosion. Cazziel turned his attention to Miriam.

"My lady, on my go, I want you to run out that door."

"Cazziel, I'm not leaving you!" Miriam's voice was surprisingly firm.

"I'm afraid you have no choice. If anything happens to you, then I won't be able to carry out our plans."

The professor scrambled across the floor and came around a metal desk.

"An attack—on Eden? ARE THEY CRAZY? Who the hell would be dumb enough to attack Eden directly?" the professor said as he nervously reached into one of the drawers and pulled a gun out. "It doesn't matter. We've come too far; we're not going to lose the project now! My research isn't complete!" His shaking fingers fumbled as he loaded the gun.

"Cazziel, make sure you make it out of here alive! After all, where would I be then?" Miriam said, as a hint of passion slid by her façade.

Cazziel watched her with his eyes as a smile slowly crept onto his face. Just then he heard a voice screaming in the background.

"CAZZIEL! What have you done to Evrikh?!" Thea demanded.

Cazziel turned his head in the direction of the voice. "YOU?" The threat of danger grew stronger at the recognition of her voice. Cazziel's head snapped toward Miriam. "GO, NOW!"

Cazziel leapt from the floor as the table suddenly exploded to life. The professor ducked behind the desk as pieces of metal flew in his direction. The shards of metal embedded into the desk and walls around him. The professor shook as he tightened his grip on the gun, huddled like one of his research projects, lost to the confusion around him.

"ANSWER ME, CAZZIEL!" Thea continued to scream. She suddenly ran from her cover, quickly ducking behind a large clear case.

Cazziel's voice came from above. "Me? I'm sorry, woman, but I have no control over Evrikh. What he's becoming is due to his inability to control himself."

"That's a lie!" Thea yelled as she looked out from the case. She screamed as she threw her hands out in front of her instinctively, launching an orb of estranged energy.

Thea's feet became embedded in the floor as this psychic force left her hands, flying toward the ceiling. Stone and slivers of wood suddenly bloomed into the air as that ball collided with the roof. Thea quickly ducked back behind the case as bits of stone fell around her, ripping into the floor and walls with ease. She carried her eyes up to the hole in the ceiling; nothing. Cazziel wasn't there. Thea suddenly felt a sharp pain graze her arm accompanied by a thunderous boom. As she whipped her head around, the assault was coming from across the room. She crouched up behind the desk as bullets continued to rain in her direction. Just as a shot grazed the edge of the case, Thea noticed that it had cracked and was now draining some kind of fluid.

Thea turned her head around to peer inside. At first it looked like a big jumble of worms, but as they untangled each other, she saw that it was filled with organisms she had never seen before. Another shot.

"Damn it!" the professor yelled aloud. "GET AWAY FROM THERE!" he screamed across the room while reloading his gun.

Thea realized she had an opportunity and readied herself. Just as she ran out from behind the case, the room rapidly came alive as the equipment around her began exploding. Thea ducked her head as pieces of glass and metal zoomed effortlessly through the air. She ran back behind the case.

"NO! CAZZIEL, WHAT ARE YOU DOING?" the professor screamed as he eased off the trigger, his gun pointed toward the case. "We need those organisms for future research!"

"What does it matter? Our concerns lay in the past, Doctor. There's no longer any need for these things." Cazziel's voice echoed throughout the room.

Thea came out from behind the case and began firing wildly. Psychic balls soared through the room, exploding everything they touched as she screamed. The professor leapt from behind the desk as it blew apart at his feet. Landing hard on the ground, he quickly rolled up to a large piece of equipment. Sitting up, the professor leaned against the machinery. Thea immediately ducked back into the cover the case provided.

"CAZZIEL, GO AND JOIN LADY MIRIAM. START THE NEXT PHASE WITH THE ELIJAH RINGS. I'LL HANDLE THINGS HERE!" the professor screamed as his hands held the gun, his body taking over what his mind would choose to neglect.

"Good luck!" Cazziel's voice came from above.

"Go to Eden and use the rings," Thea suddenly remembered what Emilia had told her.

The professor screamed as he lunged out from behind the equipment, firing his weapon wildly. As he ran across the room, he kept his weapon pointed toward the case, uncaring of its contents. His hands cocked the gun, and he fired another round. The bullets began connecting with the case, mystifying the water and spreading shattered pieces of glass into the air.

Thea screamed as she clenched herself, the case exploding all around her. She then felt the cold sensation of liquid running down her back. The case suddenly toppled over, and the contents fell out, engulfing Thea. The professor continued firing his weapon as he reached the other side of the room. Rolling up behind another piece of equipment, he ducked up behind it and pulled his gun aside. Taking a deep breath, he rolled his head back out. The area had grown silent, and what remained of the case was toppled over the backside of the desk from which it fell. What had remained of the desk had fallen to its side. The professor watched as the clear liquid continued to slowly ooze across the floor. Assured that he had won, he slowly stepped out from behind the case, his weapon pointed back at the mess before him.

The lights in the background flickered on and off as the professor approached the center of the room. Drawing closer, he tightened his grip on the gun, raising the sights up to his eye. Moments later his eyes left the mess that lay on the floor, and they carried themselves up to the shadow that cascaded itself on the wall. The professor's eyes slowly grew wider as he began lowering the gun. Loosening his grip on the weapon, it fell from his hands, crashing onto the floor. His body started shaking as he took a step back from the mess. The lights continued to flicker, but suddenly came to a halt as they finally found stable power.

The shadow on the wall was of a human body jerking violently as foreign tentacles burrowed their way under her skin. Flailing convulsively, the organisms began engulfing her body with their tentacles and pulling themselves into her. Screaming came from behind the case, screaming that flooded the professor's ears with confusion. The screams grew louder, but began to die down as her body started choking on the flesh of the organisms. As her body jerked out of control, it lunged out from behind the mess and she rolled down onto the floor, coming to a stop in front of the professor.

At first her body appeared like a mound of flesh, no control over itself. But as the tentacles parted, they slowly revealed Thea's body.

"My God!" the professor said aloud. Watching the horror before him, he continued to move backward.

As the tentacles spread out across the floor, the professor could see Thea's body twisting back on itself, shaking violently. Her screams had become muffles, buried by mounds of rubbery flesh. It was then that the professor noticed the tendrils had stopped spreading out. As they slithered on the floor, he stumbled backward over some debris. After hitting the floor, the professor quickly regained his posture; his eyes never leaving that disfigured mound. The organisms had invaded her body. He watched as they ripped through her clothes, tasting her scent within. The tentacles crammed themselves down into her, and up between her thighs, her ears, her nose, every orifice. They were violating her, penetrating her in every possible way, burrowing their way into a new home, and as a scientist, he couldn't decide if he was appalled or mesmerized.

That moment the tendrils were swiftly retracted, twisting back on themselves and returning to the pile in the center. The professor watched as they began absorbing themselves into Thea's body, the tentacles running beneath her skin. Slowly the pile of flesh grew smaller and smaller as more of the organisms pulled their way into her body. Seconds later, all the tentacles shot in on themselves, disrupting the small debris that lay on the floor; a cloud of dust dissipating outward. As the professor stood back up, his vision was quickly lost due to the increasing thickness of the dusty air.

The professor listened very carefully as the sounds before him grew weaker and weaker, until his heavy breathing was the only noise that filled the room, along with the broken electrical equipment that sparked as though it would return to life. Looking around nervously, he raised his tremblingly hand to adjust his glasses. Very slowly the fog began to thin, and moments later the other side of the room was once again visible. As more of the room became visible, the professor's heart started to calm, but he quickly noticed Thea's missing body, his fear threatening to choke him. Looking down to the ground, he saw the gun rested no more than several feet away.

The scientist looked around cautiously as sweat beaded up on his face, dripping from his chin. Time almost seemed to stop as the rest of the dust fell to the floor; the professor holding his ground. The fluid from the clear case continued to flow across the floor, as creaking noises came from the ceiling above. The room appeared to be deserted. Suddenly, a slight breeze came through the hole in the ceiling, bringing the professor's body to life. Planting his back foot into the ground, the scientist lunged forward for the gun. After only taking two steps, he leapt forward, his body floating toward the resting spot of the gun. Crashing down hard onto the ground, the professor let out a loud grunt as he rolled away, carrying the gun with him. He rolled to an upward position, pointing the weapon aimlessly around the room. His heart continued pounding as his eyes moved frantically for an answer. The room fell silent once more, save for the professor's breathing.

Slowly, the scientist scanned the room with his eyes. As they reached the area of where the clear case once was, more dust fell from the hole in the ceiling. As the dust trailed to the ground, he followed it up to where it fell from. For a moment, the professor just sat there, staring at the beams above. It was then that he strained his eyes, his vision concentrating on those beams. The professor's eyes abruptly widened as he realized that there was something up there. It shifted its weight and slowly moved from one beam to the next. The professor guessed that it hadn't realized he noticed it yet. Slowly it moved across the beams, passing in and out of the light. Its body was transparent, and at times when it stopped moving, it almost seemed to disappear altogether. The scientist continued to aim his gun around the room as his eyes followed the movement above. The figure finally crossed the rest of the beams and into the shadows on the other side. The professor hesitated for a moment before he realized there was no more movement. Slowly he raised his head, looking up to the ceiling. Rain had begun to come down, leaking its way through the hole. The scientist heard the faint rumbles of thunder from outside.

"Where the hell is it?" he said as his body passed into the light, and into the rain. "Did it escape?"

As the scientist looked around the room, rain dripping from his clothes, he felt a slight twitch on his leg, followed by pressure. The professor looked down upon himself; his hair falling around his face. As the rain fell from above, it outlined an invisible object that surrounded his leg.

"What the . . . !"

Before the professor had time to react, his leg was pulled out from under him. Slamming into the ground, the scientist's body was suddenly filled with a horrific pain. He rolled himself over as he saw an object covered in cloth being dragged off behind some equipment. On the verge of shock, the professor looked down and was filled with terror as he saw a severed limb where his leg once was. As blood spread out across the floor, carried by the rain, the professor pushed his hands along the floor, his eyes frantically scanning the room. Just as he reached the other side of the room, the scientist's hand slipped on a piece of glass, diverting his leg pain momentarily. As he looked up, the professor realized that he was lying next to the fallen case of where the organisms were first kept. His body shook violently as he began passing the state of shock, still aware of his surroundings. Pulling himself up to the overturned table, the scientist rested his back up against it. Moments later, he felt a slight nudge from the table. Slowly, the professor began to raise his head as saliva ran from his mouth and a mix of sweat and rain dripped from his face.

As the scientist looked up to the desk, the rain almost dripped into his eyes, but then he knew that the creature was only inches away from his face. Just as he started to scream, he felt incredible pressure around his neck. That pressure soon spread from his neck to his face, and his screams became muffled as his mouth was covered by invisible flesh.

The professor's eyes grew wide as he realized his life was being squeezed out of him. As he looked up into the watery figure, he realized it was a face.

"Now, good Doctor, I believe it's your turn."

Her voice remained unchanged, yet the professor knew who she was. Suddenly he watched as the shape of the figure shifted, and he knew then that she was smiling. The grip around his neck and face grew tighter, and the scientist felt the pressure burst within his head. She was crushing him. His throat began to cave in as he felt his body shaking out of control, screaming for oxygen. The professor's vision started to blur as the pressure on his face intensified, his eyes filling with blood. His head was suddenly set on fire with pain as he felt a quick release of pressure. Feeling his own eyes tumbling down around his face, the scientist's body began giving up. Blood gushed from his empty eye sockets as his bodily convulsions grew less and less.

The air was suddenly accompanied by a quick snap as the professor's life was ended. The invisible flesh slowly left his body as it retracted back behind the desk. The figure hesitated for a moment before it started moving toward the other door. As it crossed the room, the figure's body began taking on color, passing through the rain as though it washed the invisible barrier from her body. Reaching the other side of the room, the color of her flesh finally returned as a flash of light flooded the room. Stepping around the debris, Thea made her way to the other door. Placing her hand on the metal, she looked back once more, another smile growing across her face.

~

From the hole in the ceiling, two faces appeared as they stood above it. Kneeling down to the hole, a female used her eyes to look around the room.

"Well, if you ask me, it looks like she's a little more out of control than Evrikh is," she said as she rose back up to her feet.

"A human body can only do what it knows, Lashara; panic," Virgil said as his eyes lingered down toward the hole before him. "Come now, we are being summoned."

Lashara looked over toward Virgil. "I wonder if this is really the way it went."

Virgil looked at her for a moment. "Is history not the truth itself, Lashara?"

As the rain fell from above, the room became silent once again; its horrors unknown to the outside world.

* * * *

CHAPTER 9
~ History ~

"LADY MIRIAM, WHAT'S going on?"

Miriam, too indulged in her work, ignored the scientist beside her. Her eyes jolted from one side of a screen to the other. "We have no choice. I'm activating the Elijah Rings." She spoke as her eyes remained on the screen, overseeing the data.

"My lady? We haven't even synthesized a test run yet!" the lead scientist spoke, taking a step back. "We're not even sure what to expect!"

Lady Miriam glared over at the scientist as her eyes squinted to a faint blue. "You are paid to work, not question." Her eyes returned to the screen. "Start the process immediately."

"I apologize, my lady; immediately," the scientist said as he stumbled backward.

Just as the other scientists reached their respective machines, the door blew open, crashing into the wall behind it. Lady Miriam and the other scientists quickly looked up, distracted by the sudden blast. After noticing Miriam, Cazziel quickly descended the room to her.

"Miriam, we haven't much time, and the last thing we need are difficulties," Cazziel spoke, as his eyes overlooked her operations.

"Just a few more seconds . . ." She looked up from the screen. "What are you waiting for? Bring the generators online and start the rings!" she yelled across the room to the other scientists.

Immediately responding, the scientists carried out their orders and continued their work.

The base of the rings suddenly came alive as they started energizing. The air was quickly filled with the vibration of a low hum as the base began to supply power to the enlarged monument. The lights slightly dimmed as the Elijah Rings finally found stable power. Lady Miriam approached the base and placed her hand on a large panel, written in a language unknown to the world. Cazziel remained a few steps behind her.

"All we've left to do, Cazziel, is tell it where we are," Miriam said as her hand operated the panel.

Cazziel's eyes turned to her. "Tell it where we are?"

"You see, Cazziel," Miriam left the panel and walked around another panel, along the other side, "time is like an essence, perhaps even a bit of a life-form. It's not going to stop for us, but if we tell it where we are, it just might stop in and say hello. And anything that moves forward always leaves a trail behind it."

"Your point?" Cazziel said as his eyes followed her around the base. "The object is to pass through time; not have it stop in and become buddy-buddy with us."

"Cazziel," Miriam continued in a low voice, "if you were lost in the middle of the forest, would you rather find your way out, or take a road that's already been made?" Just as Miriam finished speaking, she completed her finishing touches. "There, that should just about do it."

Seconds later a scream came from down the hall that quickly died off. Miriam looked over at Cazziel.

"The guards," he spoke.

"Who is it?" Miriam questioned.

"We'll worry about that later," Cazziel spoke as he stepped away with Lady Miriam.

The other scientist looked up from his monitor. "My lady, the preparations are complete."

Miriam returned his look. "Begin the process."

The scientist gazed back down to his monitor and finished punching in the rest of the information. Seconds later the monument slowly began to animate. As Cazziel and Miriam stood at the bottom, very slowly, the Elijah Rings started moving. As the rings began to rotate, the stones cracked where they came together, sending small shards of stone into the air. Their ears were filled with an increasingly deafening hum every time the outermost ring rotated in their direction. Very slowly the rings were gaining momentum. A wind began to flow throughout the room, growing stronger as the rings continued gaining speed. Cazziel and Miriam took another step back.

The outer ring continued emitting a low hum, while the innermost ring began emitting a high-pitched hum. As the rings continued their motion, the force alone slightly shook the room, the vibrations carrying throughout the walls.

"WHAT'S GOING ON?" Cazziel yelled to Miriam as he held his hands out in front of him.

Miriam looked over at him as the emitting force blew her hair back into her face. "THE TONES!" she yelled in return.

The wind grew immensely strong, and Miriam and Cazziel started leaning into it; their grip slightly slipping across the floor. As the outermost ring reached its peak, the rotation caused its shape to blur out into an invisible sphere, spinning impossibly fast. The other two rings remained visible through this transparent sphere. A flash of brilliant light suddenly flooded the room, momentarily blinding everyone. Seconds later the outward force seemed to vanish, Cazziel and Miriam nearly stumbling forward at the realization the force had disappeared.

"What's this?" Miriam said as she regained her balance.

"The first tone," the scientist responded. "In a way, it's disrupting our time."

As Miriam looked around, she realized that the room they were standing in was in a constant state of change. As she concentrated her eyes on the walls, she witnessed them aging, gaining corrosion and remaining normal, all within the same moments of each other.

Within those moments of witnessing the room changing around her, the middle ring reached its peak, blurring out into another transparent sphere within the first. The wind grew so strong it began to vibrate the structures and equipment. As Miriam looked around, she watched as debris slowly rumbled across the floor. It was then that she realized it was moving toward the rings. She turned her attention to the other scientist.

"GIVE ME A REPORT!" she screamed at him, her voice just barely carrying above the wind.

"MY LADY, ACCORDING TO THE MONITOR THE RINGS ARE NO LONGER IN THE ROOM!" he yelled back as his hands braced on either side of the desk.

Lady Miriam's eyes slowly scanned the room as the equipment began to shake more violently. She turned to Cazziel. "Cazziel," her voice almost inaudible to his ear, though mere inches away, "I think something's wrong!"

Just as Cazziel looked over to her, the last ring reached its peak. Before Cazziel had the chance to say something, Miriam turned her attention back to the scientist. Another flash of light flooded the room and slowly faded away. Seconds later the loudness created by the wind grew so strong that Miriam could no longer hear anything else around her; her ears were drowning in a unique unending tone. Very suddenly everything within the room that shook came to a halt—frozen in time.

The doors burst alive as they shattered into the walls they were hinged to, leaving them and floating into the room with a speed that questioned whether or not they were actually moving. As Miriam watched, she saw a figure duck into the room.

"THAT WOMAN!" she muttered to herself, as her eyes filled with anger.

Waiting for a response, Miriam noticed something out of the corner of her eye. Looking over toward the movement, she saw Cazziel hanging onto a piece of equipment, his body horizontal to hers. As the light within the spheres grew more intense, Cazziel's struggle grew harder. It was pulling him to it. A sudden flash came from the other side of Miriam's view, and she jumped out of the way, rolling in Cazziel's direction. As she looked up, Cazziel continued to struggle against this unseen force pulling at him. She began to wonder why she could feel no such thing. She could hear the wind that blew; was it a song? Yet she felt no breeze, and she could see Cazziel struggling, yet felt no force.

"I WILL HAVE ANWSERS!" a voice screamed from the equipment beside the door.

"MIRIAM, I CAN'T HOLD ON!" Cazziel screamed, inches from her body.

Miriam lunged forward, her hands clasping onto Cazziel's. She braced herself against the desk, but turned her head back toward Thea. As she looked across the room, she could see just beyond the other equipment. Concentrating her eyes, she saw that Thea was struggling as well. Feeling Cazziel slip a little, she looked back at him.

"CAZZIEL, YOU HAVE TO COMPLETE THIS MISSION! WITHOUT YOU WE HAVE NO FUTURE!" At that moment, Miriam closed her eyes as a single tear fell from her face; she let him go.

"M...I...R...I...A...M!" Cazziel screamed as his body was being dragged across the floor by this unseen singularity, this immense gravitational wake. As he drew closer, he levitated into the air, swinging his arms and legs helplessly. Screaming for Miriam, his body flew into the sphere, flooding the room with yet another blinding wave of light. As Miriam stood up, she turned herself in the direction of Thea.

"YOU DO NOT UNDERSTAND! THIS IS THE WAY IT HAS TO BE!" she screamed as she raised a hand toward the Elijah Rings. Closing her eyes, she began to concentrate. Slowly her hand became engulfed in a dense blackness, some wild charge of kinetic energy. Consuming her hand, the blackness struck out in waves of lightning, growing more intense. As Miriam opened her eyes, they revealed that same glowing blackness within them.

"I'll wait for you, Cazziel," she spoke to herself. Seconds later she screamed as she launched this dense force toward the rings.

As the force left Miriam's hand, Thea couldn't hold on any more, her grip slipping from her. Thea screamed as her body was being dragged toward the glowing spheres. Lady Miriam watched as Thea and the blackness raced each other toward the spheres. Just as Thea reached the innermost sphere, the blackness reached the outer one. Stretching out around the outer sphere, the blackness began to consume the Elijah Rings, disrupting their rotation. The outer ring began to warp and rotated into the others. Exploding from the colliding force, pieces of stone were flung into the air as Miriam dove for cover. The room was suddenly filled with a thunderous boom as the base of the rings erupted from the collisions above it.

As Miriam lay behind the desk, the force of the explosion flung her, along with the desk, up to the wall. The room quickly filled with a dense fog as dust and debris floated smoothly into the air. Miriam struggled to remain conscious as she heard Thea's screams fading in the distance. Moments later, Miriam felt her own thoughts drifting, taking her consciousness with them. As her last thought slowly drifted from her, she wondered ... Would she ever see Cazziel again?

Miriam fainted.

~

The air was suddenly disrupted as two transparent figures began to transcend into the room. Two blinding lights momentarily flooded the room as the two figures completed their transformation, their transparency vanishing along with the light. The female walked along the broken equipment resting on the floor, bringing herself to a halt in front of Miriam. As she gazed down at her unconscious body, she looked back up to the other figure.

"Well, Virgil," she said optimistically, "this is a twist."

"Indeed," he responded as he stepped toward her.

"What would she have us do?" Lashara asked as she returned her gaze to Miriam.

"This changes nothing. We will not interfere unless we are instructed to do so." Virgil's eyes left Miriam and drifted toward the broken rings.

"You say this changes nothing, yet changes have already been made," Lashara continued as she followed Virgil.

"These decisions are not for us, Lashara. You must remember, this is not our place, nor our time. There is still much for you to learn yet." Virgil brought himself to a stop at the base of the Elijah Rings, Lashara behind him.

"Kovisch says that we are here to push things in the direction they are supposed to go," Lashara said as her eyes remained fixed on the back of Virgil's head.

Virgil let out a sigh before looking over his shoulder. "Kovisch is still young and naïve. This is enough for today, let us return."

Virgil turned around, walking past Lashara. As he descended across the room, the color washed itself from his body, his transparency returning to him. Lashara followed. As the two continued, their bodies appeared to pass through an invisible barrier. Suddenly the room flashed a bright white and the two figures were gone. The room was silent, save Miriam whose unconscious body lay at the edge.

~ ~ ~

The tide rolled in at the edge of the beach as people rested in the sand; picnicking, sunbathing. The air was filled with the faint aroma of barbecue as grills were used to cook food. The sidewalks were filled with people as they strolled around on roller skates and bicycles. Children played at the edge of the water as lifeguards watched from their posts, while other adults walked in and out of the wake of the ocean water. Near the water, a child was building a sandcastle. As he gathered another bucket of sand, there was movement in the water that caught his eye. Looking up from his creation, the movement in the water grew more intense. It looked as though the water had lost control of itself; a jumble of waves. The child slowly stood up in wonderment, stepping toward the edge of the ocean, the water rippling along his toes. Seconds later the child could see a shape forming in the middle. With each new wave, the shape grew more defined, until slowly, the child realized it was a body. Whipping his head around in his parents' direction, the child screamed.

"DADDY!" Turning completely around, he ran up the sand toward them.

Hearing a faint cry in the distance, a man looked around instinctively. As his eyes scanned the beach, they fell upon his son running toward him. Concentrating his hearing on him, his son's words became clearer.

"Daddy! Help! There's someone in the water!" The boy's screams echoed like fainting whispers.

Slowly the man descended from his chair and stepped toward his son. As the boy drew closer, the man looked past him, his eyes falling to the same area of the water. Just as the boy reached his father, the man placed his hand on his son's shoulder.

"I want you to go get the lifeguards!" the man told his boy as he started running toward the water.

Watching his son run for the lifeguards, the man's eyes returned to the water, his feet quickening in haste. The water splashed wildly as his legs brought him tumbling into the wake. Moments later, the man halted his progress as he realized the figure was coming toward him. Growing closer, the man slowly began stepping backward.

As the figure drew close enough to the shore, it stood up from the water, erecting its body. The man was shocked to see a woman. The water dripped from her body as she stepped closer to shore. After some confused short steps, she paused where she stood, hesitating, attempting to free her mind from the disorienting haze that now gripped it. Then her eyes carried over to the man standing at the edge of the beach. As her eyes fell upon him, she began to move in his direction. The man noticed that the only clothes her body wore were ragged pants; a foreign style unfamiliar to him. The top half of her body bore no outer garments and the man noticed she had a tattoo of tiger stripes, which came from around her neck, running down between her breasts. The man followed with his eyes as the stripes wrapped around her breasts, to her back, and brought themselves back around her hips.

As she stepped over to him, the woman wrapped her hand around her hair and slid it behind her. Mesmerized by her beauty, the man almost forgot that she was there, and half-naked. As his mind finally regained control over his eyes, he found himself still staring at her breasts, and then diverted them to her face as embarrassment slowly crept in. Looking around for a moment, the woman let her eyes fall upon the man's.

"You all right, miss?" he asked sincerely, an expression of concern replacing his embarrassment.

The woman faintly smiled. "Yeah. Yeah, I am. But, would you mind telling me where we are?" she asked as her eyes slowly escaped his.

The man's gaze grew more concerned. "Are you sure

you're all right? You were looking pretty helpless out there."

The woman's eyes returned to him. "And am I still appearing helpless? Would you please just tell me where I am?" she lightly rasped, getting annoyed with him.

"Virginia Beach."

"Vir . . . thank you," she quickly finished as she began to walk past him, stepping away from the ocean and onto the dry sand. She continued to take in this crazy new place as the people around her stared in astonishment. Where was all the aftermath? Where the hell were all the people? Was this the only place on the face of the planet that the War of Ruin never reached?

"Hey!" a voice came from behind her.

She stopped for a moment, her vision carrying back over her shoulder.

"You might want to cover up there before you get yourself in trouble," the man yelled out to her from the edge of the ocean.

As the woman looked down she realized her body was bare, save for her ragged pants. *What the hell is this place?* she continued thinking to herself, her own naked body simply an afterthought. Descending across the beach, a child ran up to her with a cloth in her hand. As the woman looked down to her, the child stood there staring, her small mouth gapping.

"Little kids like you shouldn't be staring at people, you know," the woman said as she knelt down beside the child.

After staring for another moment, the little girl finally found her voice. "What's yer name?"

The woman looked at her, slightly bemused by the small girl's curiosity. "My name? It's Thea. What's yours?" A faint smile grazed her face.

"My name's Monica. Here, you can have this." The child raised her hand and held out a small cloth. "I don't need it 'cause I got my bathing suit ... see?" The little girl's hands patted herself on the stomach as her eyes watched the motion with pride, "and Mommy says we're not allowed to walk around without shirts on." She reaffirmed the offer by slightly shaking her hand. "Your mommy should've told you that too, huh?"

Thea accepted the small shirt from the child and held it out in from of her. Appearing like it was made for a child no older than eight, Thea looked at it optimistically. "I'm not sure that it'll fit, but, thank you, Monica," she said as she smiled at the girl.

"Yer welcome," Monica blurted out with a laugh as she ran off toward the water.

Thea slowly stood up as she watched the child running across the beach. Looking back at the shirt, she questioned whether it would actually fit. The style of the cloth was of something she had never seen before, consisting of a montage of colors, spinning altogether toward the center of the shirt. Deciding it was better than nothing, Thea placed her hands inside and grabbed the short sleeves. Slowly pulling it over her head, she struggled to push her arms up through the sleeves. Wiggling her body slightly, Thea managed to pull the shirt below her head, with her arms up through the short sleeves. Wrapping her hands down to the end of the shirt just below her neck, she grabbed the bottom. Pulling the shirt downward, she realized if it had been any tighter, either the stitching would give or her circulation. Slowly the shirt ran down around her breasts, stretching the cloth to its limits. As she finished pulling it down, she saw that it ran inches below her breasts; her nipples leaving faint impressions through the material. The shirt stretched across her breasts, the seams slightly popping as she maneuvered her body within it, hugging her like a glove. The cool sea air felt good against her stomach. Adjusting her breasts within the latexlike cloth, she looked around once more.

"I know you're here, Cazziel." She hesitated for a moment. "I can feel you. Maybe I should look for some clothes first, though."

Thea left the beach as her feet carried her toward the streets. *What the hell am I doing in such a place? More importantly, what the hell kind of language are these people speaking, and how in the hell can I even understand it?* As Thea continued walking, she came across a large metallic box containing paper on the inside. Looking inside, she saw that it was information. Thea placed her hands on the outside of the box as her eyes overlooked the piece of equipment. There remained a name on the front, "Mr. Newspaper Vendor." Running her fingers around a very small slit, she wondered how to get the papers out. Staring at the papers, her concentration grew more intense. Seconds later, the glass window rippled as though it were water. Thea erected herself wondering what had just happened, although she already knew. She reached her hand out in front of her and motioned it forward, her hand passing through the glass. As her arm stretched through the glass, the ripples felt like a cool liquid against her body. Her hand clasped around one of the papers as she began to pull it back out. Reaching the glass, her hand and the paper passed through with ease. Looking at the paper for a moment, her eyes looked back at the glass. The ripples were already gone, and the glass had returned to normal.

"Whoa," a faint sound came from her left.

Thea whipped her head around to the sound and noticed a little boy standing near her. Realizing that he had probably seen what she had done, she smiled at him.

"Magic, little man," she said as she wrinkled her face at him. "Good-bye then."

She turned around and started to walk away as the boy just stood there staring at her, expressionless. Walking along, Thea looked down at the paper and her eyes fell upon the date: MAY 10, 2015. As her mind drew more questions, her eyes traveled further down the paper to the headlines: WORLD'S LARGEST SUPPLY OF PYLORIUM DISCOVERED BENEATH LAKE TANGANYIKA. Thea's eyes grew wide as she threw the paper aside, her eyes becoming crystal clear. As she began running down the street, the color shot off her body, thinning as she traveled away, and within seconds the air almost seemed to absorb her. Vanishing within this invisible breeze, the child stared as the last remaining evidence of Thea disappeared. All that remained was the discarded newspaper.

~ ~ ~

"Tests AGAIN?! Every day it's tests, tests, tests. Yesterday, tests. Tomorrow, more tests," Evrikh repeated as his eyes carefully scanned the room. "I'm TIRED of all these tests."

As the nurse placed one of the sensors upon his chest she looked up to his eyes, her own carrying a sense of monotony. "You know how he can be sometimes, Evrikh. He just wants to make sure you're all right," she continued as her gaze returned to the work at hand.

"If he cares so much, why doesn't he spend more time with me?"

"When you put it that way, you make an exceptionally valid point, Evrikh. And so, when he returns, you and I both will bombard him till he promises to spend more time with you. You do know he loves your company; it's his job that keeps him from you. And, Evrikh, you know that it has to be extremely important; otherwise, all of his time would be spent with you, right?" the nurse finished, as she placed the last sensor upon his body.

"Who matters then? I don't care for his job," Evrikh blurted as a look of anger rippled across his face.

Pieces of plastic, wood, and metal were instantaneously flung into the air as the desktop computer on the other side of the room, along with the desk it rested on, exploded; the sudden eruption momentarily deafening. The nurse immediately ducked instinctively. Moments after the room regained silence, the nurse looked from the small blast radius back to Evrikh.

"This is why it's so important for you to control your anger."

"I didn't mean to!" Slowly he sank further into the bed.

"And what would Kendrick have you do?"

The boy's head turned toward the broken computer as his eyes slowly lifted their gaze, tiny echoes of silver light shimmering throughout. As he sat there, his thoughts became extremely focused, reaching out with lives of their own. The debris slowly began to move across the floor, and seconds later, left it, floating into the air. The nurse watched optimistically as the broken pieces started to realign themselves on the desk from which they came. Everything in the room disappeared, as the pieces became Evrikh's only door of thought. Internally asking them for help, the pieces floated toward each other effortlessly, bringing themselves together and reforming their original shape: the computer. Colliding in a mesh of liquid, it all began to harden, and seconds later the corner of the room remained as it did before; untouched.

Arianna's face looked back at him. "That is amazing. And each time I see it, it shows me how amazing you really are, Evrikh. But that wasn't so hard, was it?"

"Doesn't mean I like doing it, either," he quipped, as the door of the lab suddenly opened.

A man stepped in, placing a folder of papers along with a bag on a desk. Turning in their direction, a slight smile spread across his face, he said, "Hey, Evrikh, what's up with my little guy today?"

Arianna shot off her chair, her lab coat whizzing through the air as she turned. "Kendrick, Evrikh and I have already decided that if you don't spend more time with him, then he's going to make your head explode, here and now. What say you to this, good Doctor?"

Kendrick's arms immediately flew up beside his head as though he were being held at gunpoint. "Innocent, I declare myself INNOCENT ... wait, what're we ..."

". . . guilty," Evrikh's gaze was ablaze with boyish passion.

"GUILTY ... Yes, I'm definitely guilty! I'm guilty, be . . . cause," slowly he let his eyes roll back to Arianna.

"Because you made a dear promise to our boy here, that you'd spend more time with him, right?" Her eyes now reflected the same passionate gaze as Evrikh's did.

"Yes, yes, of course! A promise that I have no doubt you will hold me to, Evrikh!" A small smile began scrolling across his mouth as he witnessed the same smile etching its way across Evrikh's. "Hey, how'd you like to go grab a pizza with me later; maybe even a movie, if you're feeling up to it?" he finished as he slid into the chair next to the boy's table.

"Pizza Hut! Do you promise?" Evrikh queried, as he failed to erase his rapidly growing smile.

"Do I promise?" he asked while looking up at Arianna. "DO I PROMISE?!" His eyes returning, "Tell you what, Evrikh, if I break it, then you can be the one to run the tests on me, and Madam Arianna here will be your witness." A slight look of concern breached his features. "How's that sound?"

Arianna slightly scoffed at the sound of madam coming from Kendrick's mouth.

"All right," the boy responded, retaining the posture of

a maturity that his body lacked.

"I just need you to do this one last test, then that's it for today." The doctor continued, "I need you to go back to that place."

Evrikh's face cringed at the idea. "But that place is so messy! Everything is always together, never alone." His eyes trailed downward. "Sometimes I feel like I get lost there."

"I'm sorry, Ev, but for you to help everyone we need to know more. Besides," he continued as he stood back up, walking toward the readout machines and computers, "you won't need to be there very long; AND ... Pizza Hut awaits!"

~ ~ ~

A strong breeze suddenly flooded an old alleyway as a blinding light shot down the alley. As this miraculous beam vanished, the end of the alley became distorted; the air bending as if reality was misplaced. Outlining the body of a woman, the air stretched around her as she slowly walked through this shift in reality. Completing the transition, another wave of light flooded the alley, and Thea slowly looked around as the distorted reality behind her returned to normal.

"I don't even know how the hell I would describe that to someone, but I'm beginning to think I should name it," she finished with a slight smile.

Stepping up to the end of this secluded street, Thea looked out into the main road. Vehicles traveled up and down that were unfamiliar to her, as she noticed an old building across the way. Walking out into the crowds of people, Thea looked up and down the road taking in her surroundings. The people weaved in and out of the sidewalks as their bodies continued their daily routine. Slowly, she realized that even though these people resembled humans, none of them resembled her. Their eyes were thinner, their skin tone darker, their hair dressed up and stiff in appearance, and their posture slightly hunched. Concentrating on the building across the way, Thea felt a familiar presence. Continuing toward the building, she stepped into the road. Seconds later, her ears were filled with an annoying high-pitched sound as oncoming vehicles slammed on their brakes. Looking at the vehicles racing toward her, Thea's eyes widened with instinct.

Raising her hands in front of her, the vehicles suddenly stopped. As Thea lowered her hands, she looked at the vehicles angled in front of her; the people inside unmoved. Looking around, she realized that everything had stopped moving. While her eyes remained fixed on the vehicle beside her, she continued walking toward the building, her mind questioning what had happened. Reaching the other side of the street, Thea stepped up onto the sidewalk and suddenly the vehicles on the other side of the road shot into motion as they began to collide with one another with irrepressible haste. People jumped out of the way as more vehicles slammed up onto the other sidewalk trying to avoid the accident. Thea stepped backward as she watched everything happening before her. Can she somehow manipulate time? Her mind suddenly flashed back to the incident at Eden and the contents of the clear case.

THE PHOENIX GATE

"The organisms!" she said aloud. She suddenly felt a strange sensation flood her mind. As she pushed it back, Thea could hear voices a little distance from her.

"Hey! HEY!"

Thea slowly turned toward the voices as she pushed away the sensation. Looking forward, she saw three people dressed in uniforms, holding something that was pointed toward her.

"NYPD, PUT YOUR HANDS ABOVE YOUR HEAD!" the uniformed man in front yelled to her.

"Why?" *Who the hell's this guy supposed to be?* "Is that supposed to be how you greet one another?"

"I SAID PUT YOUR HANDS ABOVE YOUR HEAD!"

One of the other men looked toward the other. "Damn, she looks like a friggin' Amazositute."

"Amazos . . . John, what the hell you talking about?"

"Amazon . . . Prostitute . . . Amazositute. Come on, man, you know it's good."

"Both of you, knock that shit off and pay attention!"

"But, Lieutenant, you gotta admit, there's definitely something sensational about this. God, she looks like she doesn't even understand what a uniformed officer is."

"Is something wrong?" Thea asked as she stepped toward them.

"DON'T MOVE!" the last officer screamed out.

"I don't understand," Thea said as she continued walking in their direction.

"DON'T MOVE OR WE'LL BE FORCED TO OPEN FIRE!" yelled the lieutenant in front.

"I'M RIGHT HERE, YOU KNOW; YOU DON'T HAVE TO KEEP YELLING!" Thea mocked, annoyed by their ignorance.

"DON'T MOVE! I WON'T SAY IT AGAIN!"

"Better idea, why don't you find a way to un-retard yourself? Damn!" Thea erupted. "I'm sorry, but I have to get going!" She turned to walk toward the old building.

"STOP!" one of the officers screamed at her.

Seconds later the air was filled with a deafining crackle as the men opened fire. Looking over her shoulder, Thea watched as they pulled the triggers of their guns. Staring at the bullets hurling themselves toward her body, Thea turned around and flinched her eyes at the bullets. Suddenly the bullets slowed almost to a stop as she stepped away from their path, carefully watching them pass her with the speed of falling leaves. Thea then turned her eyes back toward the men. The barrels of the guns kicked up as time was restored to them. A look of question spread across the men's faces as they saw Thea standing outside of the path of their firearms. Moments later they turned their weapons back toward her.

"I'm sorry, but I don't have time for these games," she spoke as she placed her hands on her hips.

"FIRE!" the lieutenant screamed out as he pulled the trigger, unloading a clip of .44-caliber slugs. The other men complied as they pulled the trigger of their guns, a hail of gunfire raining toward her.

Thea let out a deep sigh as she walked along the edge of the sidewalk toward the men who continued to point their guns away from her. As the bullets slowly continued into the street, Thea walked up behind the two men in the back and placed her hands on their heads. Bringing her hands together, she slammed their heads together, and the two bodies went slack. As she placed them back, the two men remained limp, frozen in time. Thea stepped up behind the officer in front when moments later his clip went empty. The man's eyes quickly came alive with instinct as he scanned the streets looking for Thea. His thoughts were quickly interrupted as a loud thud that echoed throughout his ears. Whipping his head around to the sound, the man stared at his partners who now lay on the ground unconscious. After looking at his partners, the man turned his eyes to Thea's.

Leaning forward into his ear, Thea whispered to him, "Don't press it anymore please." Then before pulling away, she placed a gentle kiss on his cheek.

Stepping aside of him, Thea walked past, continuing toward the old building. As the lieutenant watched her walk away, his mind became blanketed with confusion and fear. Thea's mind was suddenly filled with a sensation that screamed louder than any thought she had ever had, filling her mind with confusion. She reached up, grasping the sides of her head with her hands. Hearing voices of a language she's never known, Thea screamed out in confusion, "WHO ARE YOU?"

As her own mind probed the sensation, she realized it was more of a presence than a voice, the presence of a child; a boy.

"Et mulat oot tuban?" the child's voice whispered.

"Boo et cachi demnari?" Thea's thoughts became out of

control as she tried to discover how she understood him.

"Where'd you come from?" the boy's voice continued.

"*Sum panthra* ... far away." Thea could feel the curiosity that came with his thoughts, though his curiosity was not alone.

As Thea rose to her feet, her body loomed forward, her eyes in another place. "*Jun bota hew fenthro* ... Where is this place?" Her eyes looked around; her ears listened as though they have always known the language.

The world around them was the appearance of thoughts brought to life; perhaps chaos brought to life. The air swirled around and seemed as thick as water, almost like a living oil painting.

"I don't know either," the child's voice spoke out in honesty. "I'm told that only special people like us can come here."

"People like us?" Thea wondered.

"It's different when the others are here. They get mad and tell me that I don't belong here." Thea watched as the boy lowered his head. "They say that I'm a mistake."

Thea approached the boy and knelt down beside him. "Who are they?"

The child looked up as sadness filled his eyes. "They call themselves '*Pu et Jumdari*' ..."

"... the Foreseers," Thea's voice faintly whispered.

Thea placed her hands on the boy's shoulders and lifted his head back up; her soft eyes falling upon him. "Well, you don't look like a mistake to me." She spoke as a smile spread across her face.

"*Bet hana,*" the boy replied as he threw his arms around

Thea. "Thank you."

As Thea knelt there for a moment, an overwhelming sensation flooded her mind; she knew him. Feeling his sadness growing inside her, she put her arms around him, holding him close to her.

"... I have to go now," the boy said as Thea held him.

"Do you have a name?" Thea asked, looking down at him.

His intriguing eyes locked with hers once more. "... It's Evrikh."

Thea's eyes suddenly grew wide. Just as she blinked, everything had vanished in a blur of color, bringing the old city and streets back with it. Thea continued to blink as she pushed back the confusion of her sight. Moments later, her body lunged forward as she looked down to the sidewalk. Her eyes looked around hastily as she felt the presence of Evrikh leave her mind. Maybe this explains the mentioning of her name in Marcus's journal. *Damn you, Brian.* The whole team would be much more proficient than just herself as a loner.

For a moment, the lieutenant watched as Thea stumble forward, only to gather herself seconds later. Still lost to his own confusion, he watched as she regained her posture and momentarily looked around.

Thea's thoughts suddenly dwelled on Cazziel and the realization of why he was here. Thea knew that back home Evrikh had become a problem, growing out of control.

Cazziel must have gone back to a time when Evrikh was younger so it would be easier to stop him, she thought to herself, *but the Council didn't even know about Evrikh until after the Great Darkness. Cazziel wouldn't even know what to look for.*

As Thea continued, she thought that if they had actually traveled back through time, using the Elijah Rings, to a point when Evrikh was younger, he might not have come back this far. Cazziel would have to intercept Evrikh sometime after the Council discovered he was the Phoenix Gate. That won't happen for another couple hundred years. *So what brought me here?* Thea's thoughts ran as a river of confusion. Her thoughts suddenly left everything behind as she envisioned Eden . . . the clear case; what had happened to her? As she watched through a new perspective, she remembered the organisms that were being held in the case. She then watched in slow motion as the case exploded around her, those organisms falling upon her body. The visions were suddenly gone, but her mind still remembered. She could still feel them; they had become a part of her, and her, a part of them. Thea looked down at her arms as she curled them up. Moments later her skin became active, bulging out as if tentacles had begun running just beneath her skin.

They must be what allow me to do this, she thought to herself . . . *Time, huh?* A faint smile edged itself into the corner of her mouth.

~ ~ ~

As Evrikh sat up, he slowly opened his eyes, allowing them a moment to attune themselves. Dr. Savari stepped into the light as the nurse began removing the electrical pads.

"Evrikh, you all right?" Kendrick asked as he looked down upon him. "You look a little happier than usual."

Turning toward him, with a slight smirk of pride sliding across his face, Evrikh looked up. "I met someone new there."

"New?" Dr. Savari said as he sat back in the chair beside the table. "Tell me about it," he continued, his voice growing in interest.

"I don't know who she was," Evrikh told him as his eyes looked back down, "but she was very pretty!" Evrikh's eyes looked back at Kendrick as he saw a faint streak of devilishness within them.

"She?" Kendrick queried, his voice gained in interest.

"Yeah, but she was different than the others, I could sense it." His vision carried itself across the room as he continued to speak. "She even knew who I was."

~ ~ ~

A woman was patrolling back across the south wing when she faintly heard a strange sound coming from the tunnel entrance. Turning around to the break of silence, she raised her spear. "WHO'S THERE?"

Just as she began taking a couple of steps toward the entrance, the woman saw a shadow leaning against the wall, as if using it as a crutch. "WHO ARE YOU?" she continued, bringing the spear up to a ready position. She watched as the figure slithered along the wall, stumbling along its way. The woman broadened her step and planted her feet into the ground. "YOUR NAME!" she demanded.

As the figure began to enter the light, the woman could see the light glisten from its body, as though it had lost its way from the water. It was then that she noticed it was a woman.

"I'm sorry," her voice was weak, "I need help," she squeezed from her throat just before she collapsed to the ground.

For a moment, the woman stood there, observing the girl who now lay at the entrance of the tunnel. After realizing the girl was no longer moving, she loosened her stance and stepped toward the girl's direction. As she drew closer, she saw that the woman had strange marks running from her neck and down into her shirt; or what was left of her shirt. If the guard didn't know any better, she'd assume the woman had stolen that shirt.

The guard let out a sigh as she lowered her spear. "Must have been banished by the Council. It's amazing she's even made it this far." Slowly the woman's eyes scanned the girl's body. "Maybe Brian should see her. He'd know what to do."

A wooden door snapped open as a young man swiftly walked through. Carrying himself through the crowds of people, he approached a small table occupied by four people. He walked around to the far side, placing one hand on a man's shoulder, and the other onto the table. "Brian, we have a bit of a situation."

Brian's eyes left the other three gentlemen and looked up to the young man, his laughter slowly trailing off. "What is it, Jacob?"

Before Jacob even had a chance to answer, Brian could

THE PHOENIX GATE

already see the seriousness in his eyes. "A woman was found at the entrance of the south wing. We're unsure who she is, and we don't think she's from this camp; or any camp within the region."

"I see," Brian replied as he rose to his feet. His eyes looked back to the table. "If you gentlemen'll excuse me," Brian's head tilted to his left. "Evrikh, will you accompany me?"

"Sure thing," he replied.

As the woman continued her surveillance of the newly arrived foreigner, she could hear the approaching voices of the others. Turning around, she could see Jacob leading Brian along with Evrikh. "OVER HERE!" she cried out, as she waved them along with her hand.

"Sasha, how is she?" Jacob asked, just as they arrived.

"I'm not sure." The others gathered around her as all their eyes looked down at the foreigner. "She hasn't moved since she's fallen there. She might even be dead."

Evrikh watched as Brian knelt down beside the girl and placed his fingers on the girl's neck; checking her pulse maybe? As he moved the hair from her neck, Evrikh was suddenly overwhelmed with grief as he noticed the tattoo.

"BRIAN!" his voice echoed his unrestrained shock. He noticed that Brian had not moved. *Please, God, don't let her be dead, she can't be dead!*

Removing his fingers before he actually took her pulse, Brian stared for a moment before speaking.

"There's no way. She's supposed to be in the western region, keeping tabs on the Council. There's no way she could have made it back here alone; she would never attempt a stunt like that."

Brian placed his hands on her shoulders and took a deep breath before he rolled her, laying her faceup. As her hair fell from her face, the four of them stood in wonderment. Jacob and Sasha unknowing, as Brian continued observing her body; Evrikh watched for a moment before the world around him had faded to the slightest of whispers. It was her, impossibly her. Slowly, he knelt down to her body and took her arm into his hand as his eyes ran over her body. *This is her, damn it, this has to be her. So why is there something off? Does Brian recognize it also? Seriously, Thea, how the hell are you even here?* Her hair was shorter, her body more defined, as well as developed. But her skin had always been softer than any words, perfect in every sense; and only she ever carried a tattoo such as this. Tears began forming in the corners of Evrikh's eyes as he raised a hand to her brow and caressed the only face he's ever vowed to cherish, till death do them part.

"Thea, don't be gone." His whispers carried no farther than her body.

Her body slightly twitched, and as Evrikh quickly looked to Brian, he found shared relief in this small movement of hers.

"Brian, it has to be her. You know it's her!" Evrikh's voice was hard with compassion.

"Maybe so," the words seemed more a personal thought, "but why would she be back here? Why would she come back here? More importantly, has something happened in the western region?"

"That doesn't matter right now," Evrikh practically spat, as he rose to his feet, lifting Thea within his arms. "We take her back and take care of her for now." His eyes looked back to her face. "She's all that matters right now."

The people of the room rose to attention as the doors snapped alive. The mingling and voices quieted down as Brian stepped in ahead of them; Evrikh a mere pace behind, Thea still within his arms. As they walked toward the table, the people began to gather around them, but at the same time, cleared an opening around the table. Brian walked to the far side as Evrikh came around to the end. He could faintly hear whispers from those who stood around. Their minds were wondering, questioning, who was she? Where did she come from? Evrikh thought it understakable that most of them wouldn't know who Thea was; she had been gone for nearly a year now. But he would recognize her; he would always recognize her. *Thea, what the hell have you been through? Evrikh never should've let you investigate the western region alone.*

As he placed her body on the table, he saw a faint shiver spread throughout her. She must be conscious enough for her body to feel the cool metal she lay upon. Very slowly opening her eyes, Thea looked up as though she was staring into two worlds at the same time. Her breathing remained shallow, and as she slowly turned her head, peering at those around her, her eyes never gave her the strength to blink. Evrikh watched as her head leaned toward his direction, and just as her eyes fell upon him, a new expression washed over her face. Her eyes almost seemed to relax, as small tears welled within their corners.

She had become calm, her body flushing itself with a feeling of comfort; this invisible weight placed upon her suddenly removed. At that moment he could see the skin of her lips pulling at each other as they parted. Evrikh had already taken her hand within his own and now leaned toward her, his face lingering within those familiar inches they often shared.

"Rest now, Thea, you're safe," he whispered into her ear, placing a gentle kiss on her cheek, and then lifting his head away.

She closed her lips, and for a moment, it looked as though she was about to smile. But instead, her eyes closed, and from the shallow rhythmic pattern of her breathing, both Brian and Evrikh knew she had slipped into the world of dreams. Their questions would be saved, for now.

~

The voices quickly went from muffles into clear whispers, coming from the other room. Thea swiftly sat up in the small room she had been placed in, her blanket silently falling from her body. With only two candles alight, their faint glow danced around the walls like that of rippling water. Rooms carved of stone, underground, Thea could almost remember this place from times immemorial. As she looked around, there was a small metal cabinet along the far wall, clothes lay folded, resting on top. Looking down, she had noticed that the floor was covered in fur, animal skins. She then noticed she was still wearing the shirt Monica had given her, or at least what was left of

THE PHOENIX GATE

it. That was, however, irrelevant at this point; what had concerned her was whether this was the right time. Was Cazziel here? Would he come now? It was luck that Thea had found Evrikh so quickly, and she couldn't waste all these precious moments pondering it. At the same time, Thea could feel the toll this traveling of hers was taking throughout her body; perhaps something she would become accustomed to over time.

The door creaked to life as Thea watched a figure step into the light. "I see you're awake now."

A welcome presence; it had been so long since Thea had seen him like this that she had almost forgotten who he was, "... Haven't been very long."

"I know," he continued. "I felt it from the other room. You're obviously feeling better too." Evrikh spoke as he lifted the candle from the stand and stepped across the room toward her. "Thea, you know there are questions I have to ask you."

"I know," she said as her eyes silently moistened.

Evrikh had never seen Thea like this; she was always strong in nature and very strong willed. To see her sitting there, lost in whatever confusion this was, he wanted to hold her, be there for her; tell her he loved her. But then, questions had to be asked, and answers had to be given.

Evrikh sat on the end of the bed and placed the candle on the stand beside it, cascading their shadows along that rippling surface of the walls. "Thea," he began in a low, calm tone, "what happened to you out there? Why did you come back?"

"Come back..." she slowly whispered to herself.

He watched as she took a deep breath, and regained her composure. This was definitely Thea, but she was something more, almost something else. As she exhaled, she opened her eyes and sat there staring at him, shimmers of silver streaking across them. Evrikh realized her expression showed no discomfort, no physical trouble at all. She turned herself and hung her legs over the edge of the bed, keeping her hands by her sides.

"Evrikh, I know you want answers. But I might not be able to give them all to you." She turned to look at him. "Whether you know this or not, the Council knows of you."

"Is this why you came back?"

"No," she looked back down at herself, then whispered, "I won't return for another year or so."

"That was the original plan, darling," he placed his hand on top of hers, "but why are you here now?"

That face, that inviting smile, those smoldering eyes; how she could love a man so feverishly, so dangerously. Thea took another deep breath, and as she did, Evrikh could remember every breath of air they've stolen from each other, every kiss he's placed upon those silken lips. She opened her eyes and repositioned herself to face him. Some expression of love echoed through every motion, but he could feel something more than that within her.

"Evrikh, I'm not the Thea you know. She's still out in the western region." Her voice slowly grew in sadness.

"If you're not Thea, then why is almost everything about you exactly the same?" Every thread in his body told him that this was her. How could he be wrong?

Except that he knows it IS you, from the scent rolling off your body, the feel of your skin, even the thoughts intoxicating your every pore. It's like you're flooding your damn body with this image of him. There's only one person who dreams of him the way you do; befitting, since the two of you met in a *dream* all those years ago.

"I am Thea, but from a time very distant from now." She stood up and stepped toward the metal cabinet. As she placed her hand on it, she turned back around, "and, I'm not the only one who came back," her voice conveying more concern.

"Time . . . Thea, what in the hell are you talking about?" That familiar half-smile almost presenting itself, "and you're saying there's someone else here with you?"

She had already removed what was left of Monica's shirt, leaving it atop the metal cabinet, and slid the other shirt left for her around her shoulders. She turned back to face him as she began with the buttons.

Evrikh watched as tears rolled within her eyes. "Yes, but the other one is here to kill you." Thea suddenly crossed the room with a speed that escaped his eyes. Just as Evrikh realized she had moved, her body suddenly lingered inches away from his own. After looming there for a moment, practically absorbing each other, she threw her arms around him and embraced this man of hers. "I love you, Evrikh," she whispered through falling tears.

He probed her mind and body and could feel that she knew he was doing it, at the same time felt that she was allowing him to do this. He could feel her emotions, her sincerity, and as he allowed her emotions to wash over him, Evrikh, in turn, showered her with his own. "It's all right, Thea, I'm not going anywhere."

The two of them made that sacred vow to each other. Thea was his girl now, then, and forever. Evrikh knew she felt it, their hearts, beating within the same rhythm, two halves of the same whole. One thing's for damn sure, he's diggin' this new look, or style.

Moments later, Thea pulled herself away from him, and sat back on the bed; their hands remaining interlocked.

"The other who came back, his name is Cazziel," she began as her voice cleared up. "He's what the Council calls a Relic in my time: *Rasheen Ezmunda Lantan Ih Cilish'cia*. They're a race that the Council has bred to weed out Unfamiliars and separate us from normal citizens."

"CAZZIEL!" Evrikh suddenly belched out.

"You know of him?" she asked gently.

"Of course . . . a name that's appeared all throughout Marcus's journal."

Evrikh looked at her optimistically, their hands remaining together. "So if this is true, then the Council is still around in the future?"

"Not just around, Evrikh, they control everything; control everyone. Most Unfamiliars have been banished to the Outlands. But not all of us live out here. Most of us have camps in the towns, some even in the Council's own religious cities."

Slowly Evrikh pulled his hand away from Thea's as he stood up, looking down at her. "Am I still around?"

"Yes, you are," she added before he nearly finished the question, "which is why the Council sent Cazziel here.

Even then, they don't have you," she finished as she stood up beside him. "I came back to help you."

As Thea finished speaking, her body loomed closer to his until he felt the warmth of her breasts pressing up against his chest. Their faces drew closer; and then just as their cheeks touched each other, "Evrikh, I've . . ."

He pulled her to him, and their lips embraced; the oldest of rituals. As he held her, Thea's kiss became more passionate as she heard him within her mind. "I already know, luv, I already know . . ." Their arms swallowed each other up, cocooning themselves, and their bodies molded to each other, flooding with the primal urges they had always felt for each other. Evrikh had never known Thea like this, so passionate, determined, radiating; so powerful. As they finished, their lips parted, and Thea looked back into his eyes.

"I shouldn't have come here, but I had to see you." Her eyes contained a look Evrikh thought he would never see within them; as though she had already lost him.

"Could you not see me in your time?" he found himself asking.

"There were complications toward the end," Thea included, keeping the details of the last time she saw him locked deep within her mind. She would not allow him to share in this sadness.

"Complications?" His upper body slowly erected itself.

"I can't stay any longer, Evrikh. I had to see you, to tell you that I love you. Always remember that." As she finished speaking, she pulled herself from his hands and stepped backward.

Moments later the door creaked open, catching both of their attention. Jacob stepped into the room quietly and laughter from the other room slowly died off. After taking a few steps and realizing that they were both standing, he stopped moving.

"Oh! Evrikh, I see everything's all right. Miss, I trust you're feeling better?"

"I'm feeling rather fine now, Jacob, thank you," Thea reassured him as a faint smile slid into place.

"Well, then, I guess I'll retire to the other room once again."

As Evrikh sat himself back onto the bed, he watched as Jacob turned and stepped back toward the door. Just as he placed his hand back on the handle, he spoke once again. "Tell me, miss, if you were unconscious when we picked you up, then how is it you know my name?" His gaze remained facing the door.

"Sometimes we just know things, Jacob, you should know that."

Just as Thea was speaking to him, Evrikh had never thought of probing Jacob. He had been banished to the Outlands about three years ago, and had barely lived by the time Brian and his team had found him. But he felt a sense of uneasiness growing within him, and as if by instinct, Evrikh had sent out a probe. Within those few short moments that passed, his uneasiness grew even stronger when he felt that everything was normal with Jacob. So normal, that he was not even an Unfamiliar. As Evrikh looked up at him, he saw that Jacob had removed his hand from the handle, and it now rested at his side.

Why, Jacob? Why in the devil would you need to lie to them? Are you trying to hide something? Protect something? What is it you're being so overly cautious about?

~

Thea watched as Jacob quickly spun his body around, the knife had barely caught the light in his other hand. His eyes were full of anger as he planted his feet into the ground and lunged toward Evrikh. Just as Thea had even thought to react, she felt an entirely different sensation occurring within her; she felt the presence of those organisms. Suddenly Jacob's lunge almost slowed to a stop, and the look on Evrikh's face remained that of a surprise. Thea stepped toward Jacob as his arm moved forward with what seemed more like an idea than actual movement. She looked toward the candlelight and watched as the flame sat practically frozen in air. As Thea looked around the room, she noticed that of the three figures, hers was the only one not casting a shadow onto the wall. Looking down upon herself, she saw that her body had returned to its transparent state, flowing like a pool of water imprisoned beneath her skin. As she stepped to the other side of Jacob, she took the knife from his hand, the blade was seven inches long easily, the edge serrated, and the end slightly curved upward. Evrikh had already told her about Jacob not long after she had returned, what seemed like more than a lifetime ago. She remembered how he had kept most of the details to himself; maybe he had wished things could have ended differently than they did.

A sudden feeling of terror overwhelmed Thea, as she

now felt another presence close by; but not a terror for herself, for Evrikh. She had known this presence and knew what he was here for. She knew Cazziel was out there, but she couldn't tell where, or how close he was. She walked around behind Jacob and slipped the knife into his thigh, gliding it into his flesh, splitting it with little more than the ease of a piece of paper, leaving the tip lightly protruding from the other side; droplets of his blood floated into the air as though they were tiny ornaments floating around his leg.

"All right, Jacob, maybe now it's time for a couple of answers of your own . . ." Thea spoke as the flow of her transparent body slowed and color began rushing back through it.

~

A moment later Jacob spun around and as his body turned, Evrikh had already noticed the weapon within his other hand. Just as he started to lunge forward, Evrikh caught a flash of light out of the corner of his eye. Suddenly, the blade was ripped from Jacob's hand, vanishing as though it were made of gas. Within that same moment the same distortion had occurred behind his leg, and now the knife was plunged all the way through Jacob's thigh; the brilliance of lightning echoing for a moment. Jacob blurted out a scream at this sudden pain, and from the momentum of his lunge, he toppled over, surprised at this sudden twist. As he fell to the ground, Evrikh noticed the expression on his face, in his eyes. What had happened, what in the hell just happened?

Evrikh stood up with such speed it was hard to believe he was ever sitting in the first place. Then, as Jacob rolled on the floor nursing his leg, Evrikh looked up and saw Thea standing behind him. He watched her kneel down beside Jacob as her hand grabbed his neck and she forcefully sat him up. Jacob's face contorted from the pain, as the blade protruded from his leg, blood dripping wildly from its edge.

"Thea, *you* did this?" Evrikh asked, almost confused himself by what had happened.

"That's not important right now, but I'll explain it to you later if it comes to that." She stood up, Jacob's neck still within her grasp.

Lifting his body looked as though she had lifted a mere twig, maybe something lighter. This was definitely Thea, just not the one Evrikh had known. They would address this later as well. He returned his attention to Jacob.

"Jacob, I don't understand. Why would you do something like this?" Evrikh's eyes had grown dark, his pupils radiating a slight red.

As Jacob hung from Thea's hand, he gritted through his teeth; sweat beaded on his forehead. "None of you deserve to live!" he grunted; then continued, "You are the reason why the world is what it is!"

"Who are you working for?" Evrikh demanded, that redness radiating from his eyes slowly growing more intense.

Jacob sat there for a moment, perhaps enduring the pain, perhaps neglecting the question. Thea tightened her grip on his neck, and his breathing practically slowed to a stop.

"Maybe you should answer the question, Jacob," she whispered into his ear.

After slightly lifting his head, Thea loosened her grip. "It doesn't matter, we'll never stop coming for you, Evrikh. I could never understand why she would need you. Dead or alive, that's all that matters."

Jacob's face suddenly flushed itself white as his eyes comprehended he was no longer breathing. Thea's grip was strangling him. As she turned her body, Jacob floated within her grasp effortlessly, she flung him from her hand. Slamming hard into the far wall, the thud of his body against the stone was enough to knock the rest of the wind out of him. Falling to the ground, he landed on top of his thigh, shifting the blade protruding from it and opening the wound even farther. Jacob let out another scream with the only air he had the strength to muster. Coughing and gasping for air, blood began to trickle from his mouth; must have punctured his lung with his ribs when he hit the wall. Thea walked up to his huddled body and knelt down beside him.

"Why would you even try when you knew there was nothing you could do? I already know about the Council; you're the first generation of Relics. Actually, there's nothing special about you, with the exception of the advanced training they put you through."

Thea grabbed the edge of the blade that protruded from his thigh, and slowly turned it. The sounds of his femur being raked could faintly be heard throughout the room. Jacob's body grew pale as he slipped into shock.

"You're just dogs for the Council, too blinded by lies to even realize it."

Evrikh stepped over to Thea as she stood up beside him. "He's a Relic, part of the Council's Special Unit. There's nothing to worry about now though. They never started experimenting at this early stage." Looking down for a moment, Thea spat on Jacob in disgust. "How naïve. He should've known he never stood a chance."

After a few seconds, Evrikh knelt down beside Jacob and looked from his leg, to his eyes. "You were sent here to kill me?"

As Jacob wheezed, his eyes remained staring at the floor, "...or take you back." His words were a mere reflection of what sanity remained, the rest of him surrendered to the pain.

The light burning within Evrikh's eyes suddenly shifted to black as he reached behind Jacob's thigh and ripped the knife from his leg. The sound of his relaxed flesh sizzled across its blade, as the scent of warm blood renewed itself within the room. Listening to his body, Evrikh knew that Jacob would die soon; his heart already losing its will to beat, his brain concentrating on little more than the image that rested before his eyes. His body had lost too much blood, and it was his shock that had allowed him to live for now; without that, the pain would have been too unbearable. Lowering the curved tip to his throat, Evrikh looked back at his eyes.

"Don't worry, Jacob, we'll send you back to the Council." As he spoke, Evrikh slowly slipped the curved end into Jacob's neck with intimate precision. "I'm sure the goddess will be glad to see you. So please, allow us to help send you on your journey."

Evrikh pushed the blade in farther, curving it around his trachea until he could see the point of the knife slightly lifting the skin on the other side. Jacob began to choke as blood slipped into his throat from within.

"I'm sorry you couldn't say good-bye to your friends, Jacob. Had you succeeded, would you have afforded me the chance to say good-bye to my own? I'm sure you'll see yours soon enough though." As the tip of the knife stuck from his neck, Evrikh slipped the knife out, and Jacob's throat slipped out as well; a tie of crimson red hanging freely from his neck.

Jacob could feel the release of tension as his throat slipped out of his body. He continued to work his mouth as though he had been gasping for air, but instead, it brought him nothing. His neck spattered blood across the floor as his windpipe leaked the air from his body, the balloon that was his lungs simply deflating. Jacob's body began to shake violently at the loss of his oxygen, and his eyes searched the room for some unseen savior that would never come.

Evrikh slowly stood back up beside Thea and watched as Jacob's quivering body slowed to a stop. "He's been with us for three years now. I wonder how much the Council knows because of him." He stared at Jacob's thigh, the blood still steaming from its exposure to the cool air.

"Because of him, you'd meet the Cazziel of your time, almost two years from now," Thea added as they both sat there looking down at Jacob.

He saw Thea raise her head out of the corner of his eye, and just as Evrikh turned to look at her, he had already begun to feel the same sudden alertness. The air in the room shifted slightly and as they looked at each other, the two knew that we were not alone.

"Well, this turned out to be an interesting twist," a voice came from the shadows behind them.

Thea and Evrikh whipped around to the voice, their bodies alive with instinct, as their posture was already that of two animals ready to pounce, to defend against this would-be assailant.

"You know, back then, it was I who sent Jacob out in the first place. If I remember it correctly, not only did he manage to escape with his life, but he wounded Evrikh. Put that knife in his right side here," his thumb raised to his chest mimicking the point, "breaking his ribs, and rupturing his left lung. You might have even remembered that scar, Evrikh, if she didn't just decide to stop it from happening." He stepped into the candlelight.

"Cazziel, I knew you'd be here. This was when it all started. Three years ago was when you started, you and those damn Relics." Thea's voice was full of anger; never had Evrikh heard such resentment explode from her.

As Evrikh squinted his eyes, they began radiating that familiar redness. "Cazziel!"

"Evrikh," his gesture almost displayed a hint of respect.

"For all your theatrics, you never seem to be much of a threat," Evrikh sneered in return.

Thea looked between the two of them. Had they known each other? Had Evrikh known of Cazziel even before the discovery of Marcus's journal?! Why the hell would he keep this from her?!

Cazziel's glare shifted from Thea to Evrikh. "You haven't even been awakened yet. I'd watch your tongue!" Cazziel regained his posture and looked back to Thea. "Not here, not now. There are too many variables. But you'd better keep an eye on that child of yours. It won't be long before you'll have to say good-bye, and how many times are you willing to do that?"

Through all Evrikh's confusion and sudden anger, he stared at Cazziel's face and within that instant, watched as a smile slowly spread across his face. He then stepped back into the shadows and a blinding flash erupted from the corner. Long moments passed before Evrikh realized he could no longer feel his presence. *He's gone, but where the hell to this time, Cazziel? It's almost starting to feel like fate will never let the two of them be.*

A creaking sound came from behind them, and just as they turned to the sudden noise, Brian was already closing the door. Slowly, his face revealed a look of surprise.

"Evrikh, what happened in here?" he asked through skeptic eyes, which finally fell upon Jacob's body. "What is this?" Brian stepped toward Jacob and looked for only a second. "It seems you both have a lot of explaining to do."

Evrikh turned to look at Thea just as a tear fell from her eye. "What's wrong?"

After capturing his gaze within her own, she opened her mouth as if to speak, and for a moment, she didn't.

"Evrikh, you might not always see me, but know that I'm always with you. And no matter what happens, no matter how things turn out, I'll always love you."

As she finished speaking, he watched Thea slowly step away from him. Looking at her and feeling her sadness, it suddenly and very abruptly became their sadness. The color of her skin, the folds of her clothes, began to bleed together as if it were only painted on. The colors slowly became more translucent as the definition of her body started dissolving in this fluidic state. Evrikh's mind was flooded with shock as his eyes stayed mesmerized by the whole event. After taking her last step away, her entire body was encased by this translucent fluid; she was there, hidden by the water that flowed beneath her skin. She turned her head to Brian.

"Brian, thank you, for the life you've always given him. You were his only true friend." Taking her last step backward, the air began to part around her body as though the air itself was a curtain.

As Thea continued backward, her body started emanating a bright light; must have been the same light with Cazziel. Thea's body moved backward through this fluidic air and blended in with it until there was no definition left, until she was no longer there. Then, as the air's strange motion slowed to a stop, the room suddenly flashed with a bright light, and it was as if she had never been there. For an instant, Evrikh's heart had simply fallen out of his chest, dropping to the floor and shattering into a million unrecoverable pieces. Had he lost her, was she gone? No, she was right, the last couple of hours had been very strange and unusual, but through all the confusion and strangeness, he could still feel her; she was still with him.

Brian turned and his eyes fell upon Evrikh. After adjusting his glasses he began to speak. "Well, my old friend, I guess she wanted you to do all the talking."

Evrikh turned to look back at Brian, his only true friend; wasn't that the truth. "Yeah," a small sigh of relief escaped from his lips. "Maybe it's better this way." He turned and stepped toward him, placing his hand on Brian's back. "Come, we'll use the back conference room."

"And what of him?" Brian's hand waved behind the two turning men as they both looked down upon Jacob's lifeless body.

"For now, no one knows of this. We'll leave him here and take care of it when the timing's better suited for something like that," Evrikh replied, raising his hand toward the door. "For now, let's keep this incident just between the two of us."

Damn it, Jacob! Why? Why would you turn your back on them? Even if you've been with the Council since the beginning, you've still been with them for over three years now! Did it mean nothing—any of it? What the fuck was he supposed to tell Leanor? . . . Oh, sorry, hon, but your husband . . . yeah . . . he was a traitor after all. Damn you for this!

* * * *

CHAPTER 10
~ The Truth Revealed ~

THE EVENING HAD grown late. The sun was departing its home in the sky, its orange glow lingering behind, weaving throughout the clouds like that of lost souls. New Kathesias, the city of old, was a fairly quiet place after the sun had gone down. The streets had their owners, but their business was usually peddled beneath the bricks and within the shadows. While one side of the city had grown quiet, for those who would neglect the nightly world, the other side had grown alive. Neon signs and spotlights had reflected from the clouds above and lit the sky with an intimate dimness. Deep within the city, the quietness had been disturbed; the silence had been broken; and for those who would neglect the night, they would soon not forget this one.

Vehicles were accidentally running into each other on Darby Street as the explosions within Central Park had grown more distracting. As the few remaining civilians were running from the gates, the Council's law enforcers had shown up; the Jem'na. As they disembarked from their speed bikes, the first one had rolled his helmet from his head and screamed out to one of the civilians.

"Hey! You there! What's happening in the park?"

After telling his child to run along with his mother, the husband stepped over to the officer. "A man and a woman were screaming at each other, when suddenly things got out of hand; and by that, I mean, literally, fucking crazy." He paused for a moment before placing his hands on the officer's shoulders. "I've never seen people like these before, Jem'na. It's like they're not fuckin' human or something!"

"Thank you, now please, sir, escort your family to safety. We'll take care of things from here," the first officer spoke with a stern tone. Surprisingly, it provided no comfort to the nearly hysterical man.

The civilian didn't hesitate and found himself following the order with extreme speed, leaving the Jem'na to wonder what in the hell had happened on the other side of those gates. He turned to look at the second officer.

"Notify HQ, let them know we have a situation here and may require special help from the new division."

"Sir, you mean help from the Relics?" the second officer asked as he pulled the radio from his belt and raised it to his lips.

"I hear they're very confident and are very effective at getting their jobs done." As the first officer spoke, his eyes slowly wandered over to the growing illumination from within the park. A sudden spark caught his eye from way up in the sky. Watching carefully, the spark soon disappeared and was replaced by a shaded object. Squinting his eyes, he could see that the object was growing in size and descending at an incredible speed. Turning to look at the other officer, he screamed, "RUN!!"

As both officers began running like speeding missiles, the object came screaming out of the sky and slammed into their speed bikes, sending explosions and metal into the air around them. The Jem'na placed their heads on the ground, and their hands over them as shrapnel soared by their bodies, ripping through the surroundings like live bullets. Moments later, the Jem'na rose to their feet and turned to look at the damage. Lying in place of where their speed bikes once were was a marble statue of the Goddess Miriam, half crumbled from the impact.

"What the hell could have done that?" the second officer asked as he stepped closer.

"I wish I could tell you," the first officer said as his eyes wound back to the disturbances within the park. ". . . I'm not sure either of us really wants to know."

~ ~ ~

A wild breeze rustled the leaves of the ground as a figure dropped from a tree, hidden by the shadows cascaded off the trunk. Carefully it peered around to the other side and watched as another figure stepped along a small stone path and toward the water fountain in the middle of this clearing. For a moment the man hesitated as his eyes scanned the area.

"Thea . . . is it?" His eyes continued their evaluation. "What do you hope to accomplish by this?" His voice echoed throughout the park.

"I won't let you harm Evrikh, Cazziel!" Her voice was carried along by the wind, surrounding him. "Why do you work for the Council? You know as well as I do that if they were to control him, then they would own everything!"

"I care not what the Council's wishes are. I work solely for Lady Miriam. If she wishes to have Evrikh . . . she will have him. There are only two people in existence who have a history with Evrikh longer than you have. Why involve yourself in a game you know so little about?"

A sudden flash jolted out from the trees in front of him, and Cazziel slid to the side as a burst of kinetic energy hit the water fountain, sending fragments of brick and water soaring about. Everything seemed to slow to a stop, as Thea herself erupted from the trees and lunged toward Cazziel. The pieces of brick slowed to a stop and floated motionless in the air, as the water resembled pearls lost in the wind.

Thea's left hand shot out in front of her with such a speed, Cazziel almost hadn't realized what was happening. Almost a moment too late, he had managed to catch her fist in midflight and encased it within his own.

"Now, now, Thea, wouldn't you consider effecting time a lot like cheating?" His face did not break its concentration.

Thea's right leg came around and caught Cazziel upside his neck, sending him off balance and to the other side of the water fountain.

"Did I just sense a bit of complaining in your voice just then, Cazziel?" Her posture returned to a fighting stance.

Cazziel quickly rose to his feet and gathered himself. The blow was heavy, and one he had not expected. *How could she be so fast? Not even Evrikh has ever had speed like this.*

"Tell me something, Unfamiliar, what would you do if the Resistance had control of Evrikh?" Slowly, Cazziel raised his hands in preparation to fight.

"My name is Thea!" She had always hated the name branded to her kind by the Council.

"You all look the same to me. You're savages, not even human . . . *less* than human!" Cazziel screamed as a blue light shot out toward Thea.

Thea's hands appeared to materialize in front of her. She had reacted that swiftly to protect herself, the blue light exploding all around her. There was no impact.

Shit! It must've only been a distraction . . .

Just as her head whipped around to her left, Cazziel was upon her and his right knee had caught her in the ribs. The force alone had lifted her body from the ground and filled the air with a gasp as the wind left her lungs. Simultaneously, he brought his elbow down on her back and struck her between the shoulder blades. A loud crack had accompanied her gasp for air. She had fallen to the ground.

"You know, Thea, it's a shame you don't work for the Council." Cazziel raised his boot and placed the sole on her neck, pressing slightly. "You see, the weak must be ruled by the strong; herded, in a way. This is the rule of nature. Therefore, you might say the Council has the right to rule, Miriam has the right to rule." As Cazziel pressed his boot down harder, a noise had caught his attention from the far right.

Four Jem'na had stepped into the clearing and noticed Cazziel standing there, another figure lying below his foot.

"You there! Step away from the body and raise your hands in the air!" the first officer yelled.

Cazziel removed his foot from Thea's neck and stepped toward the Jem'na. "You realize you people were always more of a nuisance than a help, right?" His expression was loathsome.

"Not another step!"

A moment later, all the other Jem'na had shifted their weapons to Cazziel; their fingers quivered at the tension.

"Actually, I have a better idea," Cazziel began as his arms rose halfway up. "Why don't the three of you lay down your weapons and go home? Your families will thank you when you're still alive tomorrow." He dropped his hands to his sides and lifted his finger to the first officer. "However, and I apologize in advance, I will need you to remain. You might be able to cover up an otherwise messy situation."

Just as Cazziel began his next step toward the Jem'na, the officer farthest away pulled his trigger, the sound of the bullet ripping into the air. Without hesitation, the other officers all joined in and began unloading their clips in Cazziel's direction.

The dirt around Cazziel had exploded to life, spreading into a mist, as pieces of dirt and stone were flung around him. Seconds later, the park grew silent as the only sound left was the officers' triggers of their empty guns. The third officer looked over his shoulder toward the first one; his voice quiet and alert.

"Can you see anything?" The tip of his gun was lowered slightly.

The first officer's eyes did not leave the quickly clearing mist. "Not yet. Hurry up and reload."

"Why?"

As that word was spoken, the first officer realized that it was not the voice of any of his men. Whipping his body around toward the fourth officer, he saw that the stranger was holding him with his arm around his neck, his hand covering his mouth. He had placed his hand over the officer's and had the gun down by his side.

"Why even point your gun at me when you know there are no bullets in it? That's kind of pointless, wouldn't you say?" Even though Cazziel's words were for the first officer, he was still aware of the other two on either side of him.

The first officer slowly lowered his weapon. "You're right, but you don't want to do this. Jake has a family; besides, you did say that you only needed me." The officer's voice was calm and steady.

"I'm sorry, did I say I needed the other officers to stay alive?" As Cazziel spoke, the sound of his decision had already echoed into the air.

Cazziel caught a glimpse of movement from the corner of his eye and realized the officer on his left had pulled a knife from its sheath. Just as the officer threw it toward him with surprisingly acute precision, Cazziel swiftly ripped his hostage around. The knife had slowed greatly as the second officer's hand had remained extended. Bringing the officer's body completely around, the distortion had been restored and the knife had been brought back to life with the rippling of air. A moment later it found its place in the neck of Jake. The sounds of his slit flesh were only noticeable for a moment, and then the second officer realized what had happened.

". . . How the hell can anybody move that fast?!" Her voice had grown shaky at the realization that she had just killed Jake.

"Relax, Wynry, don't provoke him." As the first officer's hand was reaching for his own knife, his mind was searching for answers, perhaps some help.

"Oh, that's all right, Wynry," Cazziel said as he looked in her direction. "You can pretty much consider me provoked."

Just as Cazziel finished speaking, the first officer had lunged in his direction with surprising speed. It was then that Cazziel realized they weren't Jem'na, but the first generation of Relics. Still, Cazziel watched as the first Relic's lunge slowed to a speed that challenged any notion of movement. For a moment it had almost embarrassed Cazziel to think that he was once like them . . . for a moment.

". . . So eager to make mistakes." Cazziel lifted Jake's limp body into the air and threw it at the first Relic. As soon as it left his hands, Jake's body slowed to the same speed as the first Relic, and Cazziel had already pulled the knife from the third Relic, stepping toward Wynry.

Just as he reached her, he gripped the knife and slammed it into her chest. The force of the blade ripping through her flesh had restored time, and Jake's body had lunged forward onto the first Relic and knocked him onto the ground. As Wynry watched them fall, a quick and sharp pain had filled her chest, and she soon realized her breaths felt more like drowning. Looking up, she found Cazziel staring down at her as his hand left the back part of the handle; the other half had been forced through her skin. Wynry retched blood from her mouth moments before her body collapsed on itself, falling sideways.

Upon their arrival and the short moments that ensued, the third Relic had watched as Jake was thrown onto Brandon, and Wynry had collapsed with that knife embedded in her chest. As he went to grab his knife, his body was overcome with shock as he found it was missing. Looking up, he then recognized the handle that protruded from Wynry's chest; his own. *It's not possible for a human to move that fast.* After moments of attempting to gather himself, Jackson looked to his right and was staring Cazziel dead in the eye.

"... why ... Why are you doing this?" Jackson's voice had grown wary.

"I don't know," Cazziel began. "... I just can't help myself sometimes." A small smile had found its way across his face.

Just as Jackson began to lift his right arm, Cazziel's hand slammed into his face and encased it in his palm. Cazziel had already started squeezing, and Jackson's body had flailed out of control as it was overcome by a horrific pain. Cazziel continued to squeeze, and his fingers soon forced their way beneath his skin, Jackson's blood oozing from the edges. Cazziel grinned for a moment before he slightly applied more pressure. The pop could be heard all throughout the park as Jackson's headless body dropped to the ground. As bits and pieces of his cranium lay strewn about, Cazziel's glove steamed from the hot blood painted across it. He stood there for a moment before descending back toward Brandon.

Grabbing Jake with one hand, he picked up the limp body and tossed it into the air, the sounds of his clothes whispering into the sky as his body landed in the trees at the other end of the clearing. Reaching down again, he lifted the first Relic up with his hands.

"Now, where should I begin?" As Cazziel spoke, his eyes looked past the Relic and to the spot of where Thea once was, "...where?" Cazziel's eyes jetted upward.

Releasing the Relic from his hands, Thea dove toward Cazziel with great force, her knee connecting precisely with his inner shoulder, driving him into the ground. The Relic rolled away, as wild shards of earth were thrown into the sky from the impact. As Thea stood up, she grabbed a large stone slab and threw it off of Cazziel. Reaching back in with her hands, she lifted him from the rubble and threw him toward a pillar at the other end of the clearing. Just before Cazziel had collided with it, he could see Thea lunging toward him, his mind lost in a half-conscious state. Colliding into the pillar, it had cracked down the middle and the top half began to slide off when Thea arrived with a second blow, her knees thrusting into

Cazziel's chest. The rest of the pillar had crumbled behind him.

"You and the Council are a plague to this world!" She slipped her hand around his throat and lifted him from the rubble, "... Evrikh will cure us of that plague!"

Cazziel gritted through his teeth as he struggled to open his eyes. "You don't understand, Thea. Man will one day discover ... the essence of God, and in doing so, give birth ... to their destruction." His voice grew weaker.

"What the hell are you talking about?!"

Cazziel struggled to take another breath. "He's not the savior you're looking for. He was genetically created ... by a man named Kendrick Savari."

"You lie!" Thea screamed as her grip around his throat tightened.

Cazziel winced at the tension. "He may have started out as a boy, wait . . . you mean . . . You never knew?" Slowly, he took another breath. "... How interesting."

"The Resistance would have known, that information would've been in Marcus's journal!" her voice tightened. "*I* would have known!" Thea took a step to the side and threw Cazziel to the ground. He landed with a loud thud as his body rolled a few feet away. Thea stepped up beside him. "Cazziel, I'm taking you back to our time so that when I kill you, I know there will be no question."

Cazziel rolled up on his side and winced once more. "The journal never documented the discovery of the Phoenix Gate ... It documented the creation of it." Another breath, "... it would seem then ... your Resistance would have a different plan ... than even you knew about." His breathing had returned to him.

"I will not allow you to spread your corruption any further!" As Thea watched him, her eyes had already begun the transformation; clarifying, invisible.

Cazziel lowered his head to the ground and took one last breath. "... good luck!"

Cazziel rolled away from her at an incredible speed and as his body left the ground in front of her, Thea noticed the symbol he had dug into the soil. Cazziel's words had grown weak as he rolled further away, and seconds later the symbol broke out in flame.

"... *argmentes dul'ha faren crestari!*" As he spoke, Thea recognized it as the language of the gods. But how did Cazziel know this language? More importantly, how did *she* know this language?

Thea turned away to run in the opposite direction. With her feet leaving the ground, she flexed her body for a moment and a sudden wave of light erupted from her body, shooting out like an aftershock. It quickly left her body and flooded the park, passing through everything it came in contact with. Moments later the ground shook as it blew apart from the symbol engraved in the soil. The grass was replaced by weaving flames as large pieces of earth and stone leapt into the air. Just as the flames and debris reached the edges of Thea's feet they slowed to that almost-frozen state. As she continued running from the blast area, Thea turned to watch as the flames moved as though they were made of water, the chunks of earth floating like small planets lost in space.

Thea suddenly felt a counterreaction, and at that

moment she knew time was being restored. Cazziel! She leapt to the side and landed hard on the ground, covering her head with her hands as the debris and explosion suddenly shot back to life. Her body tensed from the stones and flames that soared past her head, some shrapnel catching her left thigh. She grunted as she reached down and pulled the sliver of stone from her flesh. Blood quickly filled the wound and ran from its sides.

As the last of the debris flew past her, Thea quickly rose to her feet and began scanning the area for Cazziel. A sudden voice rose from the trees around her.

"Thea, you're a fool if you think I'd work so hard only to lose to a helpless pawn!" His voice was near, but its destination hidden. "Why don't you ask Brian about the truth?"

Thea's eyes continued scanning the area. "How do you know Brian?"

A slight laugh echoed throughout the park, and moments later began to die down. "My, my. They really did keep you in the dark, didn't they, child?" Cazziel's voice suddenly shifted to her left, but Thea still couldn't pinpoint it. "Brian used to work for the Council. In fact, he led the first expedition into the Savari Ruins and was the main reason for the Council discovering Marcus's journal." Cazziel's voice hesitated for a moment. ". . . Or did he forget to mention that as well?"

"LIES! YOU SPREAD NOTHING BU—" A bright flash of blue light suddenly interrupted Thea's scream. It flooded the park for a moment and continued upward, lighting up the night sky. As it dissipated into the cool air,

Thea could no longer feel Cazziel's presence. He had fled, but he would attempt again, Thea knew this.

Thea stood there for a moment, gathering herself and attempting what recovery she could within that time. Resting at the far end of the park was a statue of the Goddess Miriam, one of the few that remained standing now. Slowly Thea turned to look at it.

"I won't allow you to manipulate the people or rule them."

"... Yes, but then people must be ruled," a male voice stated.

As Thea stared toward the statue, she saw that there were two figures standing behind it. Slowly they stepped around it and into the light; a woman and a man.

"Ooh, he almost got you that time, didn't he, Thea?" the woman spoke.

The two figures stepped in front of the statue and were side by side once again.

"WHO ARE YOU? ARE YOU HERE WITH CAZZIEL?" Thea's voice was harsh and full of anger. "I've," she hesitated for a moment, "I've seen you two before."

The female moved her mouth as if to speak, but the man raised his hand and her mouth fell silent. "Go to Brian and discuss the truth, and then return to your own time. You do not belong here." The man's voice was absolute.

"I won't go back without Cazziel!" Thea yelled back at them.

"Those last blows you gave Cazziel damaged the

organism within him. He had no choice but to already return." The female's voice was demeaning, as if she were annoyed to have to explain it in the first place.

Thea's expression suddenly twisted, and she screamed as she threw her hands out in front of her. The air between them shifted to a watery state as an invisible force lunged at the two that stood in front of the goddess's statue. Just as it reached them, the man diverted his eyes to the left, and the invisible force followed as if it were a part of him. Veering way off to Thea's right, she watched as her attack flew into the trees, bringing another explosion into the air. Burning ash and leaves slowly departed the sky and floated back down toward the earth.

"I would consider it wiser to speak to Brian, Thea." The man spoke as his eyes returned to her.

Thea took a step backward as her body became transparent. Her face remained concentrated as she tried to decide whom they worked for. Moments later, the park air was flooded with yet another blue light, and Thea was suddenly gone.

Looking around for a moment, the woman took a step forward and turned back to look at the man. "Now, Virgil, didn't you say that it wasn't our place to intervene?"

Virgil looked around the park before responding to her. "Yes, but this obviously changes things. Jacob was never meant to die. Had he not, Thea would have known the truth then. The smallest ripple can sometimes fund the greatest wave. His death would seem to be another interesting twist to this changing tale of ours."

"But how does this justify our interaction with Thea?"

the woman continued as she stepped away from Virgil.

"When Jacob was killed, the truth never became revealed, Lashara. But it is something that Thea knows, so it turned out to be us who convinced her to follow Cazziel's words. Otherwise, her hatred for Cazziel would have prevented her from considering the truth."

Virgil took a step forward and after a sudden shift in reality, he was standing next to the dead Jem'na. "The greatest puzzle in the world, Lashara, is the one that is incomplete."

~ ~ ~

Brian left the small marketplace and looked around for a moment before approaching the doorway of a little bakery. After leaning through it for a moment, he stepped back out and moments later, he was accompanied by a small girl. She appeared to be about eight years old, with wild blond hair, a child's pale skin, and eyes that reflected the purity only known to a child.

"Come on now, Emilia, time to go," her father toned.

The little girl looked around attentively and took Brian by the hand. "Daddy, I love the smell of the bakery. It has such a sweet smell." Emilia smiled as she spoke.

Brian placed his bag on the ground in order to lift Emilia and set her on his shoulders. Reaching back down to grab the bag, he saw that another hand was wrapped around the handle. Looking back up, Brian saw that it was a woman, and then he realized who she was.

"Allow me to help you with this, Brian." As she spoke, her voice was level.

"Ah, Thea, I see you haven't left yet," Brian added as he rose back up to his feet. "Evrikh explained to me the situation of both you and Cazziel."

"The situation of Cazziel had been resolved. He's returned to his own time and is no longer a threat for Evrikh now." As Thea spoke, they moved through the people and continued walking down the street.

"Yes, but it is the Council that poses a threat to Evrikh, not just Cazziel," Emilia suddenly interrupted.

Thea turned to look up to her resting on Brian's shoulders. "I'm not sure how much you two trusted me back then, but I do know who you are, Emilia." Her eyes moved down to Brian's. "Or should I call her Kendrick?"

Emilia's face suddenly became flooded with shock as Brian turned to look back into Thea's eyes. "It would seem we have much to talk about."

"Where's Evrikh?" Thea's face looked forward once again.

Brian's eyes turned in the same direction. "I sent him to the Archives. He'll be fine there. He's doing some research on DNA."

After twenty minutes of walking, the three of them had turned down a side street and approached an apartment. Brian had reached up and pulled Emilia from his shoulders. He then produced a key from his pocket and slid it into the lock. After a moment's sound of clicking, the door popped open and Emilia stepped inside as Brian followed her with his bags. Moving into the other room, Brian placed the bags down on a counter.

"Emilia, dear, would you do me a favor and take care

of these?" He removed his jacket and placed it on the counter beside the bags.

A few seconds later, Emilia entered the room. "Sure thing." She opened the bags and started pulling the contents from it.

"We should retire to the other room," Brian spoke as he gestured with one hand, the other finding its way to the small of Thea's back.

The room was quite nice. There were a few paintings that hung from the walls and a couch that ran along the far wall. The window to her left almost ran the same height as the wall and was cascaded by a satin curtain, transparent. There was a table to their right, and a rather comfortable-looking chair resting beside it. A few magazines had rested on the small table beside the chair.

"Come, sit and talk with me now," Brian gestured as he wandered toward the chair and sank into it.

After pulling a small lever on its side, the chair seemed to come alive as the front of it lifted up and raised his legs into the air. Brian let out a sigh of comfort as he seemed to become lost in this chair of his. Thea descended to the other side of the room and placed herself on the couch, resting no more than several feet away from where he sat.

"Now, how is it that you know about Emilia?" he began as he turned to look at Thea.

Leaning forward in her seat, Thea rested her arms on her legs and lifted her eyes to meet Brian's. "I'm not here to play games, Brian. This isn't the way it's going to work."

After hearing Thea's tone, he leaned forward and the front of his chair slid back into place. He had regained the posture of a gentleman. "Oh? And what game is it we are to play then?"

"I ask a question, and then you provide an answer." There came silence for a moment. "Then you ask a question, and I provide an answer. After that, we continue so on and so forth. I'm sure you get the picture."

"Hmm, so you'd like to avoid one game by playing another? OK, then, Thea, ask your question."

She hesitated for a moment before she began to speak. "Is it true you used to work for the Council . . . before the Resistance came together?"

"And here I thought we were only asking one question at a time." A faint smile had entered the curves of his annoying mouth. "Very well, yes, it's true."

"Then why did you never tell any of us?" Thea's voice grew more intense.

"That would be three questions now, wouldn't it?" Brian leaned back into his chair. "And I haven't even asked my first. Now, Thea, you're not very good with this game."

Thea let out a sigh and sat back angrily in the couch. "Fine, then, ask your damn question."

Brian pondered for a moment while his eyes remained fixated on her. "Obviously since you're asking me this now, I can assume that you never knew in your own time." He pondered for another moment as Thea physically grew more impatient. "So then, who informed you of these questions?"

Thea's attention returned to Brian as she leaned forward once again. "A man and a woman I encountered last night."

Brian sighed to himself as his eyes left hers, searching for an answer that was just beyond his sight.

Thea continued. "And is it true you led the first expedition into the Savari ruins and basically discovered Marcus's journal?"

"You ask these questions as if you're conferring the answers. Yes, I did." Brian changed his position in the chair. "When we entered the ruins we discovered a series of journals written by a man named Marcus Celaetas . . . you know as Marcus's journal. They spoke of a project titled the Phoenix Gate, among many other things. A project that could control life and death, and for those reasons, Dr. Savari had hidden the project in hopes that humanity would never again find it."

Thea's expression grew more conflicted with each sentence. It was honest enough that he trusted her this much, to share this information. But why would he keep these secrets for this long, and even in her own time? On the flip side of that coin, why would he suddenly, and so freely, share this information? Damn you, Cazziel; damn you and the Council!

"Working for the Council allowed me to witness many of their designs for the people, and it allowed me to witness much of the corruption growing within it."

"Corruption?"

"Yes; and those journals added to that corruption. The Council had become consumed with this search for the Phoenix Gate. A search I believe they've persued since the very beginning."

"And so you suddenly decided that you'd find it before them?"

Moments later Emilia entered the room with two drinks in her hands. She stepped over to Brian and placed one on the small table beside him, then crossed the room and handed the other one to Thea. "Your mouths must be getting dry by now," she smiled.

"Thank you," Thea said as she watched Emilia step back into the other room.

"Not exactly," Brian interrupted, regaining Thea's attention. "That same evening, I made another expedition to the ruins. My clearance had allowed me to pass through without question." Brian sipped his drink and placed it back on the table. "That same evening I found other journals, Dr. Savari's personal journals, along with some blood and tissue samples that had been placed in an old freezer of sorts."

Thea sipped her drink and sat back in the couch. "And how exactly does that tie in with the Phoenix Gate?"

"His journals spoke of how to use the samples I found and basically resurrect Kendrick," Brian smiled for a moment. "It would seem that even without the Phoenix Gate, he had cheated death."

"So if Evrikh has that kind of power, then why didn't he just use Evrikh to keep himself alive, rather than wait for someone else to resurrect him?" Thea spoke as her head shifted slightly to its side.

"For the sake of Evrikh falling into the wrong hands," Brian added. "Kendrick had stored all of his ideas, and every one of his thoughts into a computer . . . even the whereabouts of the Phoenix Gate." He shifted his position once again and brought his drink to his lips. Moments later, the glass found its way back to the table. "I used the labs available at Jurubian City, used the samples I had of Kendrick, and spliced them with samples I had left from my daughter. The Council knew nothing of my little project."

"So Emilia was genetically engineered?" Thea spoke as her eyes shifted to glance into the other room. "I thought she was an Unfamiliar."

Brian's eyes followed Thea's into the other room. "My original daughter was. It would seem that human DNA does carry everything of the original host." They turned to look back at each other, "and once she was far enough along, I took her from Jurubian City and disappeared from the Council. I burned the journals that spoke of the Phoenix Gate in hopes of slowing down the Council, and I took Kendrick's personal journals with me. Later on, I used the computer at the ruins and restored Kendrick's mind. He's been with me ever since, as both my mentor and my daughter."

Thea rose from the couch and stepped over to the window, peering outside. She watched as people walked by the apartment, vehicles driving up and down the road.

"Those two you met last night? Tell me about them." Brian's voice came from behind her.

"They never told me their names," she spoke. Thea continued to watch the world outside. "They told me to ask you about these things and afterward that I should return to my own time."

"Your own time?" Brian rose to his feet. "Now how would they have known where you're from?"

"I'm not sure." A young child ran by to catch up to his parents. "I never told them, nor have I ever met them before last night."

"Well, when you do return to your own time, tell them I thought interference was forbidden." Brian turned to walk back into the other room.

"Now, Brian . . ." Thea's voice hesitated for a moment, "how would you know them?" She turned her head to look back in his direction.

Brian smiled for a moment before he returned her look. "I'm just a man burdened with a fruitful life."

~ ~ ~

Evrikh leaned back from the books he had been staring at for the past few hours and stretched out his arms, looking around at the walls of artwork, the ceiling far above, the shelves and shelves of old literature; their people had lost so much only to regain so little. He closed the books, setting them aside as he stood up from the table. The sounds of flipping pages whispered throughout the rooms, their knowledge faintly heard. Spreading his hands across the table, Evrikh took the books up into his arms and turned to walk them back to their homes. Walking across the floor, his shoes echoed noisily and his eyes carefully watched those who lingered around. Evrikh had learned from Brian that it's always wiser to know, than be surprised. Reaching the bookshelves at the far end of the room, he turned and walked into one of the aisles, D179–239. Carefully, he pulled one of the books from his hands, as to not drop the others. As the other books parted, *DNA Structuring and Cell Bonding* had been returned to its rightful place. Turning to continue down the aisle, he stopped his movement as his eyes remained focused on the floor. Lying at the far end of the aisle on the floor was a single book; closed. Taking a step backward, Evrikh looked around to see if anyone was near, but everyone had kept their distance, pursuing their own needs and ambitions.

Looking back to the aisle, the book had remained on the floor. He placed the other works he had been holding down on a small table at his end of the aisle, and then turned to walk toward the other end. As he drew closer, he could see that the book was lying with its title facing down; the spine bore no writing. Looking around once more, he knew that he had been the only one in these aisles. Evrikh knelt down beside it, pondering for a moment as his fingers found their way around its edges and slowly lifted it from the ground. Turning it right side up, his hand brushed in an upward motion as the title became revealed to him. *The Art of Tracking*.

Evrikh's vision suddenly shifted as he found himself resting behind the wall of the aisle. Slowly his eyes looked around and their vision carried his thoughts to the far end of the room, to a small table, books scattered across the top, to himself sitting there as he read. They diverted themselves to a shelf that rested at waist height. He then realized that he was watching the movements of another person, through their eyes. A hand reached up and it fell upon a book at the end of the shelf, *The Art of Tracking*. As it slid it from its place, the hand lowered it to the floor, turning its cover down, being careful not to make a single sound. Then as Evrikh rose back up to his feet, he watched as his body turned around the corner and began walking away. A bright flash filled his eyes, and moments later, he realized he was still staring at the book held in his hands.

Obviously someone placed this here for me, but why? Is this some new kind of librarian-style pickup trick? Don't be shy, Thea; you're the only person who'd do something zany like this.

Taking in another breath, his mind suddenly became aware of something more than the people around, more than the whispers faintly heard throughout the rooms; a presence that wasn't there before. Slowly exhaling, he turned and walked back to the end of the aisle, a small sigh of laughter escaping his lips.

So, you damn minx, he'll have to come and find you, is that it? Well, there's one thing Evrikh couldn't wrap his mind around . . . what the hell's the purpose of *The Art of* . . .

Scanning the room with his eyes, Evrikh's mind sent out probes to see everything else his eyes would not. He was still here, watching Evrikh even now. A familiar presence indeed, but this wasn't Thea, this would never be Thea's. Continuing the scan, his heart rate grew faster as he felt more and more presences surrounding him—within the building and outside. Just then he watched as a man stepped into the men's room in the back of the main hall. Quickly descending the room, Evrikh looked around to see if anyone was watching; he saw no one, but could still sense them.

Evrikh placed his hand on the door as he reached it, and luckily, the man was still inside; the only one still inside. Sliding it open with the faintest of sounds, he stepped in, only to close it just as quietly. Stepping across the tiles, Evrikh could see the doors of the stalls lining the left wall, the urinals ran along the right; he had already passed the sinks when he first walked in. The man had noticed him now as he stood at one of the urinals. Slowly, Evrikh turned to approach one of the sinks. As the water began to flow he nonchalantly washed his hands, waiting for the man to finish. Once he did, he took a step backward and adjusted his pants as the urinal started its automatic flushing. Evrikh watched through the mirror as the man approached the sinks, the water popping on.

"Can you believe this heat?" Evrikh watched his hands working methodically.

"News says it's been record high recently. Makes me think I should've changed before I left my apartment this morning." The man's voice was oddly social.

"You wouldn't mind handing me one of those towels, would you?"

"Will do," and as the man had taken it in his hand, he turned to hand it over to Evrikh, ". . . WHAT THE—!" he blurted out as Evrikh grabbed his wrist.

"I sincerely apologize, but this can't be helped."

Just as he finished speaking, Evrikh's fist found its way to the middle of the man's stomach, right below his sternum. Feeling this generated pressure rippling throughout the man's body. Evrikh watched as his expression changed from surprise, to shock, and finally unconscious. Falling toward the floor, he quickly grabbed ahold of the man in hopes of preventing any further damage. Then taking him by the legs, he dragged the body off to one of the stalls, closing the door behind them. The others were still watching, however surveillance would be a more accurate description. There's a chance they hadn't seen him yet, and Evrikh would further play on that chance. As he looked down, he measured the size of the man and his clothes; they would do, for now.

The bathroom door slid open with the slightest of sounds, its aged hinges merely whispering aloud. Peering through just a crack, his eyes looked around for his would-be assailants. Evrikh's eyes saw none, but his mind knew they were out there, felt them lingering. Easing the door the rest of the way open, he stepped into the main hall and began descending across to the far side. His newfound shoes clicked greedily along the floor as he continued his brisk pace, the other people carrying on with their business. As Evrikh drew closer to the other door, his eyes found their way to the far left. After looking the area over for a moment, they then began to scale upward. His speed hastened as they continued their climb; his body instinctively reacting to what his mind paused to process. Moments later, only a few feet away from the main door, his eyes reached the upper floor. His eyes darted between the aisles, but why was there nothing there? Looking down the last aisle along the upper floor, his heart suddenly skipped a beat as he saw a man wearing strange clothing. The figure remained there reading a book for a moment.

Dammit, Evrikh, you're almost there! What the fuck are they waiting for? How long have they even been here? God, what the hell is wrong with you . . . You're letting yourself slip! You should've known it wasn't her, and you should've sensed them before they even got here, dammit!

As Evrikh's hand reached out for the handle, the figure turned to look down in his direction as though he knew Evrikh had been watching him. Pushing through the door to the outside, Evrikh caught a glimpse of his hands as they released the book, letting it fall to the floor.

The main entrance flew open with ease, and he crashed into an older couple as he ran through the archway. He quickly turned to look at them both as his confusion grew more intense. That figure had seen him, but more importantly, was he the only one? Would he alert the others? How much time did he have? Evrikh started descending the stone steps that cascaded toward the sidewalks below. His feet echoed loudly as they pelted the stone, absorbing the shock of his own speed. Reaching the bottom, he turned around to the building once again. Carnegie Hall. Watching for a moment, none of them had appeared through the entrance, but he knew they were close, he could feel them lingering ever closer; hunting him.

The street was littered with people as he began his trek through the mobs. Looking up and down the street for a moment, Evrikh noticed a back alleyway not far up ahead. As his mind looked around with frustration, his eyes abandoned the idea of trust. It would be better to stay away from all these people, considering any one of them could be the ones who were looking for him. As he reached the alleyway, Evrikh turned to look back up and down the street. They were there, but it would be impossible to pick them out through all the people. His vision returned to the alleyway as he quickly walked into its concealment. A slight rustle filled the air as his shin caught a newspaper during its midflight. The garbage cans remained unmoved as he swiftly passed, the smell of their decaying contents seeping into his nose. His eyes caught the attention of a broken-down car resting halfway on the sidewalk and street. The hood was missing, and so were the tires; perhaps the owner thought it simply wasn't worth it. The windows were broken, and the back end had caved in a little, the taillights smashed. Even so, it was abandoned.

As he reached halfway down the alley, Evrikh ran into a wire fence that ran at least fifteen feet up. The poles rested too close to the walls to squeeze through.

"SHIT," he fumbled, as his heartbeat began running out of control, "you gotta be kidding me!"

Suddenly everything in his mind washed away, and his body had become frozen as Evrikh felt the presence of one of them step into the entrance of the alley.

"TURN AROUND SLOWLY!" a voice echoed from behind.

Evrikh turned around to face a figure slowly ascending from the entrance of the alley. Steam from the street vents floated through the air as it thinned until invisible. His uniform was something Evrikh didn't recognize. Through the cloak that broke over his shoulders he wore a seamless, body tight uniform underneath, maroon in color. His lower face was covered by a cloth, hugging it like a second skin; his eyes hidden by shaded eyepieces. The hood from his cloak had been pulled down and rested behind him. As Evrikh watched him, his hands remained raised in front, and what the hell kind of weapon is that?

"Hmm, so it would be you the Council's looking for? How interesting." His voice remained calm.

Although his identity had remained hidden by the things he wore, Evrikh could still recognize his voice from the night before. "CAZZIEL! YOU KNOW THE COUNCIL WILL NEVER HAVE ME!"

"That's a surprise," his position remained fixated, "and here after all this time I thought you wouldn't recognize me."

Moments later, his finger eased on the trigger, and his weapon jumped to life.

"NO!" Evrikh screamed and leapt into the air, his feet carrying him as though he had wings, to the top of the fence. As Evrikh cleared the top and landed on the other side, he noticed that the bottom half of the fence was missing, and the walls on either side were now burnt and discolored. Turning to look back in the figure's direction, Evrikh screamed again and suddenly everything in the alley floated to life; the garbage cans he passed, the old car, some tires, even the street trash had ascended into the air. An unseen force had begun to emanate from the area between the two of them, Evrikh's hair and clothes rustling from the generating winds. Even the small pebbles had left the ground now, obeying his call. His eyes filled with rage as they flowed to the color of white, radiating it like the streets venting their steam. Evrikh screamed again as he raised his arms upward, palms out. Continuing the scream, he threw his arms forward, and as they moved, all the floating debris mimicked their movement and shot toward Cazziel in one great motion.

Within that same moment, everything had collided with Cazziel and consumed the entrance to the alleyway, along with the other street, in a massive explosion. Evrikh watched as a tire shot out from the collision to the second story of the building on the corner, sticking from its melted rubber. Some metal shrapnel from the car ripped through the air, passing through the windows of other buildings.

As the smoke started fading into the flames of the explosion, Evrikh rose back up to his feet. He didn't wait to see if Cazziel survived the explosion. Even had he, at least it would have slowed him down. Evrikh turned to run down the rest of the alleyway.

~ ~ ~

As Thea finished her last sentence, she turned to look back out the window, a streak of color barely catching her eye as it flew up the front porch. Staring out the window for a moment, wondering what she had just seen, the door handle suddenly spun to life. There came a couple rumbles of the door before whatever it was realized the door was locked. Brian had already carried Emilia off to the back, and Thea watched as he quietly closed the door behind them. Thea's attention returned to the door. Concentrating her thoughts on the door, she felt a sudden pain arc throughout her body. Moments later, she suddenly dropped to the floor as she fought back the urge to scream. Feeling her toes and fingers clenching tightly, Thea's body began to convulse uncontrollably. Not now—something was changing within her. She could feel it, but her awareness of the door had remained in her thoughts; its handle shaking more violently now. She could hear a voice coming from the other side of the door, but her pain had caused her to lose the accuracy of her hearing.

Feeling her body tighten and loosen once again, Thea curled her head down and watched through the hair that had fallen over her eyes. The pain arched through once more as her legs shot out from under her. Her eyes slammed shut as she rolled onto her back, bringing her stomach up into the air. As she threw her wrists to the floor, her shoulders left it save her hair, which flowed like running water. Screaming again, the windows in the front of the house shattered outward, flying out onto the sidewalks and streets. The lights along the ceiling above Thea sparked just before exploding outward, and at the same moment slowed to an almost complete stop. The doors of the cabinets all throughout the house continued to vibrate open and closed with a speed that defied movement, as Thea's screams grew louder. Slowly her body lost its definition and flowed into the air around her. She could feel her insides churning, liquefying, and witnessed it just as her skin dissolved into the air. The screams died down as her voice started fading, the transparency of her flesh creeping around the edges of her face. A faint blue light could be seen where her ankles and wrists were touching the ground, but quickly dissipated as her wrists and ankles could be seen no more. Then, just as Thea's eyes flowed into this lifeless air, the debris above shot outward and fell to the ground echoing the room with the sounds of small pebbles colliding with each other.

Seconds later the door finally slammed inward as it embedded itself into the wall behind. The figure walked into the room as he slowly looked around. Leaving the front hall, he stepped into the room that reflected Thea's pain. Debris lay everywhere, and the windows now held empty frames of where the glass once was. Looking around for a moment, the figure's eyes turned to the other rooms.

"BRIAN!" There came a moment of silence. "EMILIA! ARE YOU HERE?"

Recognizing his voice, the back door slowly slid open as Brian's eyes scanned the area outside and eventually rested upon Evrikh in the far room.

Evrikh looked around once more as his mind grew increasingly impatient. While he was outside trying to get in he knew he heard screams, her screams, but they seemed to vanish almost before they even started. What had happened in here? Evrikh could sense the struggle but saw no one injured; no bodies. He turned to look back down the hall to see Brian and Emilia walking toward him.

"What happened in here?" Evrikh ordered, his vision looking past Emilia, to Brian.

"I'm not sure. Your knock had startled us, so I took

Emilia to the back and we left Thea out here," Brian spoke as he entered the room, his eyes just beginning to look around.

"So Thea's back with us?" Evrikh asked, his attention jolting back to Brian.

"Not exactly. Thea's still with the western camp." Brian turned, gesturing his hand toward the window where she had been standing. "That's where we left the Thea you had met yesterday."

As he turned toward the window, Evrikh hesitantly stepped closer, as though he could still see a physical impression of her standing there. "I thought she had to leave and go back." His imagination had already begun to paint her right in front of him.

"It seemed she had business to finish before that," Brian added as he watched Emilia finally enter the room.

". . . I did," a faint voice came from the couch Brian had forgotten about as it cut him off.

The three of them whipped their heads around at the unexpected sound of her voice. Sitting on the couch toward the other corner of the room was Thea, leaning over, and breathing heavily. As Evrikh took a step toward her, he knelt down to the floor, though there was little difference between his body collapsing or his want to tend to her.

"Thea, what the hell happened to you?"

". . . You first," she said, as her breathing grew calmer. She lifted her eyes to meet his. "What happened to you?"

Looking over at Brian and Emilia for a moment, he turned back to Thea. "I encountered Cazziel."

Thea sat up as she placed her hand on her knee, leaning to one side. "That's impossible. He's already returned to his own time."

"Not your Cazziel." His eyes glanced at Brian. "Ours."

"How do you know this?" Thea asked as she finally rose to her feet.

"Because," he rose to his feet with her, "he's . . ." his words cut themselves off.

As Emilia stood beside Brian, her eyes turned upward to look at Thea. "Now that Evrikh's shared his Thea, the truth will out."

Evrikh watched as Thea's glance turned to little Emilia, a faint smile hidden within those lips. "The organisms that allowed me to come here have changed again."

"... changed *again*?" came Brian's eagerness.

"It's a little hard to explain," she began. "Everything that's physical is made up of the same type of material, right?" Her eyes turned from Brian to Evrikh, ". . . protons, electrons, neutrons, blah, blah, blah."

Brian's expression suddenly shifted into what can only be described as ultimate concentration as Evrikh noticed Emilia growing more attentive.

"Well, these organisms have been shifting me in tune with all other materials around, and in a way, I suppose, that would look very much like a vanishing act; albeit an unexpectedly painful one. Now I can feel that the organisms are no longer within my body, but a part of it." She finished as her face took on her own personal understanding. "It's a bit odd to have to explain, considering I'm just catching on myself."

"... So at that level, essentially everything becomes a part of you, and you, a part of it," Brian spoke as his hand rose to his face. "Interesting."

"So," Evrikh watched as Thea's image suddenly faded like an image lost in the water and her voice came from behind them.

"... It has brought me a closer sense of the word *unity*," she finished as other three heads whipped around to see her standing by the open window.

Evrikh watched her for a moment, standing there; confused. His dearest Thea, seeing her in this way, his love for her was somehow greater still. To love her as someone he barely knew; to this person she's destined to become ... What sins have you carried within those eyes of yours, as to never had shared with him, to refuse to share with him even now? The silk layers of her skin, the hidden agenda locked within the blanket of her lips?

And now you would look back to them with even greater sadness. Not your sadness alone; shared sadness ... This is something their eyes could never hide from one another.

"You're leaving us now?"

"Yes," she spoke with a voice that sounded sweeter than the freshest of honey; a single word that emptied the world Evrikh's heart had built around her. "Be with the one you love, Evrikh, do not worry about what's to come." Her eyes shifted to Brian. "The Resistance has great things planned for you, Evrikh, do not fill your heart with sorrow." They now looked down upon Emilia. "You will be taken care of, and of all the things she longs for in this world," her eyes turned back and met his, "... is to be back in your arms. I would know this better than anyone."

Although Thea was leaving them, Evrikh knew whom she spoke of. The thoughts of being with his Thea flooded his body and the overwhelming feeling shocked his face into an irresistibly slight smile.

As Thea watched them for a minute, the room around her shifted in a strange manner, an almost fourth-dimensional manner. Looking more closely, she realized the transition had already begun. Her eyes could focus on the cells that made up the people in front of her. Soon after that, it was the atoms; electrons and protons shooting around as though the soul is nothing more than the released energy of overly excited atoms. Looking up to where Evrikh's face would be, Thea watched atoms shoot around aimlessly, but could still manage to distinguish Evrikh's face through the excitement.

"Good-bye, my love."

Staring with that same sadness, he watched as Thea slowly faded away, blending in with the broken window behind her, as if she was nothing more than a dream; perhaps that's all she was. Closing his eyes, Evrikh could still see her standing there, in all her beauty. Her lips untouched by the sadness of the world, her eyes that held the deepest of oceans and how he longed to feel that warm nectar encase his soul. Skin as soft as the petals of a cherry blossom and as pure as the flower from which it came. He had felt her within him, then just as a breath enters the body, they would forever remain a part of each other. As he opened his eyes, his reality had returned and he was robbed of all that she was . . . just a dream.

~

Thea stayed there for a moment, gazing back at her love; her very life. What did her own time hold for her, what would she return to, if there were anything to return to? A thought of Cazziel breezed through her mind and for a moment she thought, had anything even changed? The atoms around Evrikh's eyes slowly closed, and Thea could sense the longing in his heart; she would return to him, as he once had returned to her.

The figures in front of her suddenly grew brighter, and as she looked around, so did everything else. Looking back at Evrikh, she whispered "Good-bye." Seconds later, the atoms within the room shot to life, flying out in every direction. Thea stared as everything lost its shape, the atoms around her getting lost in their own excitement. She then felt Evrikh's atoms intertwine with her own, and for a moment, they were closer than the far reaches of heaven could take them; they were one. Growing with both intensity and brightness, Thea suddenly felt herself projected forward, lunging into a sea of elements. They raced by as though they were set on some destination lost long behind her, some hinting at images, others carrying lives. Looking beyond the glimpses of atoms in front of her, she could see the others in the distance; the stars that longed to move but remained frozen, their movement hidden by the distance between them. She could feel the presence of familiar things to her, some elements aging, others becoming anew. Her journey forward continued, inclining to a pace of both confusion and speed. The only sight that remained was of the lightning that now streaked by her eyes and in the distance around her. Shots of purple and white exploded everywhere; a burst of yellow. Looking forward, the lightning seemed to come from a single point to far ahead for her eyes to focus on. Then as Thea turned to look out to her left, the lightning had streaked across her eyes, reminding her of the trees she used to watch floating by when she rode in vehicles.

Her life had been a mix of so many pleasures, so many intense moments. They all flooded her mind now, the adventures, the experiences; her love. What plot did life hold for her? And yet, through all the thoughts in her mind, there remained one lingering in the back ... Who were those two she had met before? Their presence had seemed familiar to her, but from where? An image suddenly raced across her mind, and as she continued looking out to her left, she saw the atoms form a dream, a memory; her memory.

Watching Brian continue to walk forward, Emilia's hand within his, Thea remained a few steps behind. As Thea followed Brian, her eyes began to move as though they were controlled by something else. Her eyes carried their sight back to a restaurant placed on the other side of the street. For a moment, Thea stared as a female and a male returned her look. As Thea blinked, she realized that the tables were empty and Brian was calling to her.

Had they been following her this whole time, watching her? But if they didn't work for the Council, then who?

MICHAEL S. VISCHI

The atoms collided with such an impact that the radiating light blinded her and flooded her ears with deafening silence. Thea felt herself traveling at a forbidden pace. There came another burst of light; the cellular level.

Within that same instant, Evrikh too had experienced an impact; had felt a specific emptiness. Thea had truly left them.

* * * *

CHAPTER 11
~ The Cry of Hope ~

THE FLOOR WAS checkered, its tiles made of polished ivory, its white color softened with age. The walls stretched impossibly high to the ceiling, a dome resting at the top; a rich canopy that foretold the history of the world. Works of art rested against the walls, some paintings, and others, tapestries. Mere echoes of civilizations lost to the world, some forgotten, and others that had never been discovered. Windows laced about the walls rested far enough above that the only visible world outside was that of the sky, allowing the softest of light to dance along the floor and whisper its hope back up to the ceiling. To those who would bear witness to this place, it would probably resemble a dream should they long for one. There rested a table at the far end of the room, a half moon. There were fourteen chairs in all, a wide mix of the elements of the world; some metal, some wood, ivory, jewels, crystal, and stone. The people mingled among themselves, as this gathering consisted of both men and women. The robes of would-be wise men, spanning the centuries, yet divine in their own nature. Their whispers fell silent as they looked back to the two that stood before them, as if to be judged.

"My brothers, sisters, we cannot allow these people to fall into what so many of us already have," the man had spoken softly as he stepped forward.

"You realize what you ask, Virgil?" an elderly man gestured as he leaned forward onto the table.

"Yes, I do, Melucious," Virgil insisted, turning his attention to the left.

"You would negate our rules so easily?" a woman queried sitting back in her chair of the purest gold, the only pharaoh who would be female.

"Lady Ira, if not for our rules, the world would forever be lost to itself," Virgil replied turning to his right. "As essential as it is, however, there has never been a civilization with two of them. With the first, their path was set. But with the awakening of the second, their time line is forever changing."

Whispers came from those who have yet spoken.

"We have a chance now to break the cycle . . ."

". . . Yes, but by what you ask, it could also mean its continuation," the man in the center chair spoke as he perched his chin upon his folded hands.

"The circle needn't worry," a voice came from the balcony resting halfway up the wall behind them. A woman descended out to its crystal railing, carved of garden vines and roses, softly reflecting the light from within the room. Placing her hands upon it, the edges of her palms became outlined from the railing's warm light.

Her body was encased in a gown of the whitest cloth, too soft to really be named a color. It embraced her shoulders as a new love; shy but caring. Like a glove, it ran down her arms, bound by her wrists, where sashes ran to the floor, becoming lost in the folds of the gown behind her. As the edges of her shoulders were outlined in gold, it ran to her front, teasing the edges of her cleavage and binding into one between her breasts; a pearl rested there. This small trail of gold left the pearl and sank below her belly button, splitting once again and running along the edges of her hips around her backside. Following the curves of her body, the gold strands once again came together at the base of her spine, a blue rose forever binding the gold together.

Looking down at the colleagues before her, her face contained a look of sympathy; perhaps hope. "You will make a decision, for you have always made the decision. The lives of these people will not end, for even I would not speak to you now." She smiled and for a moment, its brightness almost seemed to push back the light.

Stepping up to Virgil, the woman with him began to speak. "But what if we are to make the wrong decision?"

"Lashara, my child, my friends, you are the last of your civilizations, the only true legacy they have left. You were their alpha, destined to be their omega; the Aztecs, the Druids, our beloved Egyptians, my dear Atlantians, all of you, you have all failed your own race, but now redemption lies before you. What would you do? Help these people from a future they know not haunts them, or condemn them as you have mistakenly condemned your own people?" She fell silent for a moment.

"Do not dwell upon your decision, simply make it, and know that you already have."

Virgil watched as she turned from the balcony and her gown slowly drifted away, receding to where it appeared. His eyes lowered to the sages resting before him.

"Virgil, Lashara, we have reached a decision," an elderly man spoke as he leaned in on Lashara's right. "Based on the information that has been laid before us all, we think it would be most wise to stay involved. But recognize that they must not know who you are."

"... And what of Brian?" Virgil began before he was cut off by a voice descending from the door of the other side of the room.

"You know, and it's about time too," a young man said softly as he leaned away from the wall and approached the two standing before the sages, "I've always thought we should be involved and lead the people to the destiny that was given to them." His hands floated through the air as if to beckon the gods.

Lashara hinted a faint smile, amused by his boyish ambition. "Kovisch, you know our rules as well as anyone else. They have been in place since the very first of us, and life has continued because of them," she finished, her faint smile drifting away.

"Well, it wouldn't hurt to have a little fun, would it? I mean, come on, some fun!" As Kovisch looked around the faces of the table, they peered down to him, their expressions unchanged as well as Virgil and Lashara. Kovisch slowly rolled his eyes to a close.

"Bethla dem jun phec et protho cun jeyo ... A foreseer is the hand the cradles God's people ... *Sin et yun werea* ... Know that they are his people." His voice was swift as if annoyed by the words he spoke.

A faint voice suddenly flooded the minds of the people within the room. "Virgil, Lashara, you will take Kovisch with you. This is the way it must be, for it has become a part of his destiny." As the voice faded from their minds, Virgil turned back to look at Kovisch.

"... You see—" Kovisch began.

"Hush now," Virgil spoke, cutting him off. "Understand that you won't so much as even fart unless I give you the word to do so."

"Hey, relax, Virge. This wasn't my call. It came straight from the lady who wears the daddy pants," Kovisch said with his hands raised in the air as a gesture of submission.

Virgil turned to face this board of lost prophets before him, Lashara hesitating for a moment. Measuring Kovisch with her eye, she saw him smiling at her, grinning. Catching a glimpse of Virgil watching her from the corner of his eye, she turned around swiftly to face the board.

"Take your leave of us and go to Helenscia, for this is where history takes us," a woman spoke as her eyes shifted from Virgil to Lashara.

"Immediately, Lady Pjien," Virgil said as he slightly lowered his head in honor of the people before him.

Turning away from them, he walked by Lashara and Kovisch, proceeding toward the door; Lashara and

Kovisch were quick to follow.

Kovisch's whispers interrupted the silence as he spoke to Lashara, "Well, this should be rather interesting, huh?" His grin seemingly burned itself to his face and refused to leave.

The sages' voices faded behind them in anticipation of what's to become of these people so indifferent from their own. Yet Virgil's mind resided on the sudden inclusion of Kovisch. What part would he have to play in this history that changes as though it were never written; or maybe never completely told?

~ ~ ~

The evening had rolled in swiftly, leaving the purity of day behind, and bringing in the mysterious lure of night. Helenscia was truly a remarkable city, one of the few that remains testament to the old-time. Evrikh couldn't help but stare at the buildings in wonderment, the monuments, the past of their people self-betrayed. A faint smile spread through his lips as he thought of the irony. The Phoenix Gate was created to guarantee the continuation of man, yet man continues anyway. Therefore, its creation was made in vain; he was made in vain. Evrikh knew the pain of the world; he could feel it, in the buildings around him, the earth beneath him, the plants that hunger for real air, yet man takes it from them. The world is dying, and man is too blind to see it, to self-indulged. He could see the selfishness of his people ... A loud smack rang clear within his ear as his head turned to witness its origin.

A woman's hand was leaving the man's face as she

turned away from him in disgust and walked away. Her dress would have Evrikh believe her to be a whore denying the man the oldest of sins, his craving for pleasures of the flesh; the perversions of their purpose.

Why put on a show when Evrikh can already smell your heat? Is the pleasure that man wants to share with you any different than the others? Self-righteous bitch ... Maybe now you go for confession. Doesn't matter though, does it? Man could never confess his wrongs. They've all betrayed the very words of God, passed down from father through son, simply by living on ... Who remembers that?!

The gentleman was half-drunk, lost in his haze of delusion and lust. As he turned to leave, probably back to the tavern from which he came, his uncaring of the world around him aroused those deep pleasures of Evrikh's own. Lampposts lined the streets as if to beckon him to the inner city, to embrace its darkness, to feel the vastness of those earthly sins. Once, so very long ago, there had been only several sins. Yet here, Evrikh knew that man had somehow managed to expand those original seven. These humans who plague the very life of the world in which they live ... Why not indulge for a while? Helenscia; the ancient city of London.

The midsection of the museum was vast in height and size. The paintings on the tapestries and been washed away with time and now replaced by lights and speakers; stereo equipment for the club now contained within these walls. The eight pillars that stretched toward the ceiling were made of bricks, some crumbled and replaced with others that radiated neon blue. The ceiling itself was outlined in a faint red, allowing the mural within to be seen but not understood. Resting upon a stone platform toward the back was the DJ, and the equipment he used to flood the ears of the people lost in their world of exotic movement. Bookshelves lined the base of the walls around the room, yet they refused to serve their purpose, but instead, clothing for those who shed them, drugs for those who use them; all the necessities to live a life such as this.

Platforms hung between the pillars, suspended by hidden tracks within the pillars, rising and lowering to beckon new dancers and releasing the old ones. They carried both men and women, their minds lost to a forbidden passion. Their hands teased themselves, probing the edges of their flesh as their bodies danced with the deafening tones of the music. The people below reached up with their arms only to know that their companions had traveled farther into this realm of lust. The floor had become littered with bodies, some fainted or too tired to move, others too dazed to understand why they lack control of themselves.

The grand doors of the museum suddenly burst open as heads turned to peer outside it. The music continued and for a moment there was nothing, but then the people watched as a face slowly appeared, descending to the bottom of the stairs. The man stood there for a moment, watching them, his face searching for some hidden truth. Then he suddenly stepped further in, the crowds near the front moving as though he was their king. Slowly the people stopped their dancing and watched as this man, wearing a long brown trench coat, descended into the room. His pants were of black leather, reflecting the lights of the world around him. As his trench coat hung open, he wore no shirt. His shoes were boots, jet-black in color and laced with metal around the heel. His skin was slightly pale, and his eyes, a certain blackness that was only saved for the intangible evil of man.

These people looked at Evrikh as though he were the answer to their prayers; perhaps their nightmares become real. He could feel the music in his soul, the chaotic indulgences that ached beneath his skin. A woman stepped from the crowd, her feet slowly tracing a path to his own. Evrikh's eyes traveled the roads of her presence, red hair that spiraled downward as though this succubus had finally been set free, swaying at the edges of her breasts. Her shirt, lavender, clung to the front of her body as one lover would embrace another. Each of its cups caressing one of her breasts, only to end as it reached the edges of her sides. From there, a small strap ran around her back, bound between her shoulder blades; this half shirt, outlined in black. She stood before him now, her eyes observing this future conquest of hers. She encircled Evrikh ever so slowly, her eyes now traveling to the depths of his boots.

"Not from around here, are you, stranger?"

Evrikh could smell the sweet smear of passion fruit from her lips, the faint smell of peaches lifting itself from the caresses of her skin.

"Well, now, that all depends," his eyes followed her

trail off behind him, her hand touching the small of his back.

Her feet moved gracefully as she came around the other side of him, her hand continuing around the small of his back. "Depends on what, Mr. Stranger?"

As she came around, Evrikh could feel a faint grin spread itself across his face. Watching it appear as though she had won a prize, this woman spread a smile of her own.

"Whether or not there is still a here when I leave."

Although his mind waited for a reply or a reaction from this girl, his face could not. Evrikh's grin grew in size until it resembled nothing but a chaotic smile, his laugh echoed throughout his mind, yet he kept its sound to himself.

The woman's smile slowly dissipated as though she had lost interest and moments later she moved her lips as though to speak, but his finger found its way to her mouth before she could produce any sound.

"Shh; say nothing, my dear. Instead, offer yourself to me as you have so many others." His other hand found its way between her thighs and gripped the origins of the indulging scent that now flooded his nose.

She raised her hand as if to slap him and just as she did, reached around the edges of his finger and bit into it, drawing blood. Surprised by her movements, she brought her hand down with the force of her body weight, catching the side of Evrikh's face with her palm. A loud pop flooded the air around them, bringing his head back up to meet hers.

"You know, I've always wondered why people do things they know they'll regret later on." As he spoke, his right hand found its way to her right breast and held it within his palm. "For example," he began; his right hand dropped with an incredible speed.

A loud scream suddenly echoed throughout the museum as this woman's hands clasped over where her right breast used to be.

"I'm sure you regret meeting me now . . ." Blood ran from the open cavity down below the edges of her stomach, ". . . as will everybody else."

Evrikh's left hand wisped around her neck, eluding her vision. As he encased her throat within his fingers, his eyes swept around the growing hysteria, passing from person to person.

Is this the way a savior is supposed to act?! Why the hell would his father ever want to save all this?! It's like the further man lives on, the further he regresses as a species. Evrikh's here to help you, help all of you, and what do you do? You fuckin' slap him, and then scream in his face, bitch! Are you worth it . . . Is any of this truly worth it?

Evrikh's hand locked around her neck, squeezing and feeling the small vibrations of her crushing throat tingling the surface of his skin. Then suddenly as he brought his fingers to a close, Evrikh watched as her head left her body, jumping into the air from the force, only to land a few feet away from where they stood. Blood gushed from her neck around the palm of his hand and joined the flow of her missing breast.

Evrikh's eyes left her body and gazed upon her face, ".

.. How interesting."

He turned to look at a man who witnessed this whole experience from within five feet. "Well, now," his smile returning to his face, "I'll bet she sure as hell didn't walk out of her front door this morning thinking her day would end like this, huh?"

As people turned to look at the mess that lay before them, the air was filled with hysterical screams and cries; some were too tweaked off of drugs to even understand why they began screaming.

"Why the fuck are you people so afraid of everything?" a growing annoyance reverberated in his voice. "The Council uses you, the Resistance uses you . . . You even use one another."

Evrikh turned back to the man too horrified to move from witnessing such a gruesome event. His hand quickly slammed onto the man's lower jaw, and in one swift motion, ripped it from his body, exposing the back of his throat to the air.

"Why even have a mouth if you can't keep it closed, eh?" He turned to the rest of the screaming crowd as laughter left his lungs and filled the hazy air floating above them. "Even now you all prance around only concerned with yourselves. Why? It still won't do you any good."

Evrikh's last sentence hung at the very edge of his mind, digging into his past that was never meant to be: Alex's past.

"What's the difference between good and bad? The words, perhaps? Half the world believes in goodness, the light, holier-than-thou, whatever the hell you wanna call it. The other half believes in itself; our so-called *badness*. Isn't it within the instincts of any species to stick to self-preservation? I was created to be without these unbiased ideals; I simply do what must be done. But . . . Is this truly what must be done?" His head ached at such thoughts to the point of kneeling to endure it, his laughter continued in both pain and confusion.

Evrikh looked around at the horrified faces surrounding him. People trying to leave through doors that wouldn't open, windows whose glass wouldn't break; those closest keeping their eyes on him. Evrikh rose to his feet and finished his laughing as he noticed a table no more than ten feet away from him. Stepping over to it, he climbed upon it and looked around the people who trampled each other, yet remained imprisoned; their screams nullifying the ones within him. Looking around for a moment, Evrikh projected a thought of attention that shot out like a wave. Flooding the museum for a brief moment, this wave flew through the air like an invisible layer of water, passing through the people at eye level. Seconds later, the screams stopped and the confusion came to a halt as everybody turned their heads, their eyes, to this devil that now loomed upon the table.

"I apologize for my rudeness . . . but hear me now. If you think I'm bad," his left hand gestured toward the headless woman he left lying near the entrance, ". . . There is a far bigger threat coming than the one I lay before you. And you only need but answer one question . . ." Their faces were full of fear; confusion.

"Why are your lives so important to you," his eyes turned to look at a boy that could not have been more than sixteen, perhaps seventeen, ". . . when they can end so abruptly?"

As Evrikh extended his hand outward, a trail of blackness left it, floating toward the boy as a fog would roll along the ground. Enwrapping the boy's body in this mist, it seemed to pull at his body, asking it for a companion, a young companion that would forever be with it. As the blackness began to leave his body, floating upward, the boy's body went limp, and just as the mist completely left his body, the boy fell to the ground; he would forever remain still. Evrikh could feel the familiar grin slowly spreading through his lips as he gave this demonstration of what it was that was coming, his laughter bolstering out as a thousand banshees would scream from their own torment—Laughter that would flood the city, bringing its vehicles to a halt, the people to a stop, and the animals to a silence—a plague that would purge this city of its life. Evrikh would no longer be a slave or a puppet to any of them; and so it would fall—they would fall.

~

"Did you feel that?" a woman asked as her eyes turned down a street that would lead them to the other side of the city.

"He's already here," Virgil spoke as he himself came to a halt outside an old tavern.

Slowly stepping up beside the two of them, Kovisch looked from one to the other. "Well, then, I understand we have all the time in the world, but why stop when it finally gets exciting?" he finished as his eyes turned toward that uncomfortable feeling, that plague of illness that bellowed forth from an old museum on the other side of the city.

"We wait for Thea," Virgil said as he took a seat at a table outside the tavern. "She's tracked him here thus far, and if I'm not mistaken, she'll be standing behind you, Kovisch . . . right about . . ."

Virgil brought his words to a stop the moment he saw that Kovisch was not moving. Rising to his feet, he saw the arm that wound itself around Kovisch's neck. Stepping over to Lashara, he could see the faint silhouette of this woman standing behind Kovisch.

"What do you people want? First, outside the restaurant, then in the past with Cazziel; now here with Evrikh in this city." Her eyes quickly diverted from Virgil to Lashara. "If you ask me, that's a lot of places to be for someone who claims to be something less."

Feeling a slight movement, Thea watched as Kovisch slowly raised his left hand up as if to gesture, "Do you mind if I ask you . . ."

Tightening her grip around his throat, Thea lowered her lips to Kovisch's ear. "Not only should a child know when to speak, but a child should also know when to be afraid."

"We're not here to do this. We ALL are here for the same reason, and it lies over there," Lashara added in hopes of lowering the tension between the four of them.

Feeling that this man stood no chance against her, yet

still taking her chances with the other two, Thea decided to release her grip. Backing away with an unseen speed, Kovisch jumped over to his companions. Thea's body remained relaxed, but her mind stayed aware of even the slightest of movements around her.

"We are here to help the Phoenix Gate," Virgil said as his eyes measured this woman before him.

"Then you are here to help Evrikh with this destruction?" Thea's head lowered as a predator would stalk its prey.

"God, why are humans so clouded by their own ignorance? Were we all like that once?" Kovisch slipped in while rotating his head from one side to the other.

"Kovisch!" Virgil's expression remained fixed on Thea, "The real Phoenix Gate. The one that was created during mankind's only cry of hope; during the climax of the War of Ruin in 2023 . . ." Virgil's voice was calm and knowledgeable. ". . . More than a thousand years ago, and not by a man named Kendrick Savari."

"Ignorance would have been a blessing, had the world given me that," Thea spoke as her stare left Kovisch. "Whether you speak the truth or you keep it to yourself, I'm here to save Evrikh. And I *will* save him!" Her tone was sharp, reassuring of herself. After a moment of silence, Thea turned to walk down the street, leaving the three strangers behind.

"Thea, wait," Virgil spoke as he took a step in her direction. She continued walking anyway. "You know you can't save him." He watched as her feet slowly came to a stop. "You can already feel it, can't you?"

For a moment only one thought entered her mind: was he really lost to her, for only a moment. "Then you would have him killed?" Her voice was soft, carried along the breeze.

"All we ask is that you take us with you. Let us observe, maybe even help you if it comes to that." Virgil slipped in as though calling for a truce, had they been enemies.

The three watched as her head turned over her left shoulder, the silhouette of her face lit from the lights beyond. "If at any one point you give me one reason—"

"We understand," Virgil finished, knowing the context of her words.

As Thea continued walking once again, the three quickly followed her, Kovisch walking up beside Virgil. "Would this be considered her rebellious stage?"

With Virgil's gaze remaining forward, he spoke softly to Kovisch. "You know, Kovisch, it's no wonder why the Avalonians died off."

With Lashara's eyes leaving Kovisch, she turned to speak to Virgil. "You have to admit though, they must have been an attractive race." Kovisch watched as she slipped him a wink behind Virgil's back.

Ahead of them, Thea remained in her own thoughts. If she could not save Evrikh, she would not allow him to die. And what of Cazziel? His disappearance is only reassurance that she would see him again, but where, when? In fact, the Council has remained at a deafening silence ever since her return. Yet her eyes remained forward, looming toward the other side of the city that would once again unite her with her love.

MICHAEL S. VISCHI

~

The museum and the land around it had become a site of death. Vehicles had crashed into one another, their lights dying from prolonged use, their drivers lying still. The park outside had been emptied of life. A couple sat at a bench, a statuette of a man embracing a woman, their last breaths escaping the two hours before. Their dog lay bloated on the grass a few feet away. The flies would be buzzing around, had they not been robbed of their life. The streets were littered with people who were passing by, some perhaps going home, unknowing of this disease that would slowly lay the city to stillness.

The museum was silent; its screams once heard from blocks away, nothing more than the faint whispers of those damned within its walls. The doors slowly pried themselves open, this bringer of death stepping through, the mounds of people lying still behind him; the treasures of his kingdom. The old museum emanated this blackness that had flowed from his body earlier, its walls filling with his anguish, his indulgence. It had become his sanctuary, his place of deliverance for his people.

As Evrikh left the steps of the museum, he walked out onto the streets of his would-be kingdom, his pillar of blackness stretching up to the heavens mere strides behind him. The area had fallen silent, the air too young to reek of death, yet it loomed so closely.

Evrikh's eyes looked around the silent streets as his darkened hand reached forth throughout the city, his body feeling the passing of each person it touched.

"My flesh of your flesh, and my blood of your blood

. . ." his mind continued to lose itself in this lusty haze, "In creating me, you must have longed for death. Be not afraid, for I offer it to you."

A sudden feeling shot through the concentration of his mind, halting his outreach for a moment, an unforgettable memory of a life he once shared. His darkness enshrouded it with its touch, letting its feelings intoxicate his mind; flood his senses. Evrikh could feel the very signature of its flesh, the lost desires within; those lips he so longed to kiss.

Had she truly returned to him? Of course she has; she's here, isn't she? In the city . . . but where? Evrikh's thoughts subsided for a moment as a new thought emerged from the fade within him. Very close. He know she was there . . . He could feel her.

"Well, I'm not exactly trying to hide myself from you, Evrikh." Her voice was carried by the wind.

Evrikh looked around to her sudden blunt and wild tone, yet there was no one within the distance, no movement, no life; none that he could feel. Then the immediate realization of her presence. She was there; behind him. Evrikh whipped his head around to see Thea standing at the base of the steps, his steps.

". . . And what would a kingdom be without a queen?" he spoke as a sincere look of happiness briefed itself within his eyes, quickly pushed aside by the dormant rage. "Be with me, Thea, the way it should be, like the way it always was."

Thea slowly began walking toward him; her arms extended toward the people lying still, as though she was giving in.

"Like this?" Her eyes looked at the scenery around them. "It doesn't have to be this way, Evrikh. Death should never be the answer." Her eyes returned to meet his. "You can save these people. Why be their hell when you can be their heaven?"

Her feet came to a halt a few inches from his. He watched as she placed her hands upon his shoulders; she was real, here with him now. He could feel his body flood with the feelings of his love finally returned to him. Evrikh closed his eyes absorbing this newfound intoxication, his heart finally beating as though it had found its purpose. Then his mind returned to itself, in all its ideals and glorification.

"I will save these people, Thea, save them from themselves." His hands found their way to her hips and held her as though she would break from even the slightest breath.

Evrikh stepped away from her and looked around for a moment, gesturing with his hand.

"These people created me to guarantee the continuation of man, and yet, here they are," his hand turning around himself, the display for his queen, "...but," he lowered his hand to his side and turned to look back at Thea, "they also created me to bring death. So knowing they'd live on, they must long for death, long to be released, to be cured of their own diseases, their own plagues; cured of their sins."

Evrikh watched as tears formed within the eyes of his true love, could feel the sincerity of her heart. He was truly lost to her; her thoughts had betrayed her.

"You don't have to take that path, Thea, you can still come with me; be my Eve."

She lowered her head as the tears fell from her eyes. Evrikh *had* truly become lost to her. Virgil was right, she could feel that before, but she had to make sure, and now after being beside him she knew that Evrikh could not be saved, yet she loved him so. All the experiences they've shared together, the life they could have lived, the family they could have had. Who was Thea without her beloved Evrikh? Was it merely too much to ask, to hope?

As she once again raised her head, Evrikh saw the glistening trails of the tears that fell from her eyes. He could still feel the love within her, but something had changed now; her eyes were different. Her lips parted as if to speak, but she hesitated for a moment.

"I was hoping I could save you, but I'm starting to see how Virgil was right." Her voice had changed as well; harder. "If this is your choice, Ev, then the man I've loved throughout my whole life is as dead to me as those lying around us." Her tears had slowly vanished.

At the moment she spoke those words, the laughter within him had stopped, the suffering in him seemed dulled, and the rest of the world became but a blur. How could the woman he loved so much betray him like this? How could she betray herself so easily? Had he meant nothing to her throughout their lives? Evrikh suddenly felt the ache of a new sensation pulling within his head, the pain of a wound whose cut seared with the flames of anger, of passion. His face remained expressionless as his eyes began to slowly fill with that familiar blackness, his tears becoming lost within.

"Well, then," Evrikh began to speak as his body flooded with this new feeling, "perhaps you would join them in their death?"

His arms practically raised themselves as he placed his hands upon her shoulders. He could feel a new laughter growing within him, the wild laughter of a broken man. To need nothing from this world, Thea; and for that to mean nothing without you to walk beside him ... and so it falls to him to begin a new foundation. If your love for each other isn't enough to carry you through all this, then what hope is there left for any of them? Was Evrikh truly meant to save nothing?

"And so you must end with everything else, my dearest Thea." The words flowed from his lips, knowing that there would be no other way.

As Thea reached up, she placed her hands keenly on the outside of his. "I am sorry, my love. I still pray for there to be another way."

For a moment their eyes seemed to lock with each other, maybe a new hello, perhaps a final farewell. As this anger grew within Evrikh, he could feel the very threads of sanity being stripped from his mind. She had betrayed him. No one betrays him! Looking back upon her face with this new despair, his eyes flooded with such a profound blackness, it radiated from them as heat would radiate from the earth. A small smile cracked itself on the edges of his mouth.

"How could you turn your back on everything we've

ever been through? How could you betray every single moment we've ever shared?" As he finished his words, Evrikh's eyes conducted the oldest of rituals; he blinked. Within that brief moment, he felt the sudden release of the tension between his hands, and the realization that Thea was no longer between them.

Evrikh's head whipped around, his eyes quickly searching through this world of death he was slowly creating. "I LOVED YOU?" That familiar laughter had returned to his voice.

". . . That's something we'll never lose," her voice had flowed with the wind.

His eyes darted from the trees to the streets; the buildings. Evrikh could feel her all around himself, surrounding him in an unseen cage of delusion, yet she eluded his eyes. "What craft is this?" More whispers; his left. There she was, or at least a blur of her, but gone now. The edge of his mind was being blanketed with insanity from these annoyances.

"ENOUGH!" he screamed as his arms rose up from the ground as though to beckon something from within the earth.

Within that moment, as Evrikh's arms appeared to raise themselves, the earth seemed to slow. The rustling leaves, tempted by his hypnotic movements, floated as though they were lost within an ocean. The low clouds, darkened with hatred, reflected this lifeless canvas, frozen without borders. Even the clothes of the dead swayed with the movement of a lost snail. As this world around him grew to a stop, Evrikh suddenly felt the presence of others; Thea was not alone. She would invite others into her betrayal?

Watching this world around him fueled his anger even more; a world so slow, so incompetent, so uncivilized. Evrikh felt as though his veil had truly been lifted, and for the first time he got to see the human race for what it truly was—unnecessary. His attention was suddenly drawn to a lamppost at the far end of this small park which surrounded the museum. The figure beside the lamppost rested against it, a silhouette that seemed to hold this frozen shaft in its place.

"Evrikh, we've tried so many times in the past to tell you the truth. Was it your ignorance, perhaps the idea that you were created by a species rather than from a species?" He leaned away from the lamppost and turned in his direction, slowly taking a few steps.

As Evrikh watched this clouded figure step toward him, his identity remaining elusive from the distance, old memories suddenly flashed through his mind. Memories of a place so tranquil, knee-high grass, the sky returning from a dream Evrikh once had. His voice was deep and soothing, almost angelic.

He was in his dream from before, but who? Maybe you're one of those bastards from way back when. Makes no difference though; you've mentioned then that he was never meant to be ... perhaps none of you ever were!

"What is this?" he growled, Evrikh's mind already lost in confusion.

Another voice. His head whipped to the right as another figure walked along the sidewalk, running his hand along the metallic fence. "You see, Evrikh, the Chosen One, the Savior, none of these names really matter; every species has one. It's a spiritual cry for hope. Something that might help a race live on as it reaches the brink of extinction." He came to a halt and turned to face Evrikh's direction, his hand dropping from the fence with a ping.

"You people plagued my dreams as a child! Now you wish to plague me in life as well?" His anger grew beyond the threads of self-control, his body as the last unleashing hurtle, save the satisfaction and enjoyment that he would partake in. His hair floated upward as his clothes wisped around from this stagnant hatred emanating from within him.

"But for the first time in the history of all living things, one species, one race, finally made a mistake; Dr. Savari and his grand plans for the Phoenix Gate," his voice was laced with resentment.

"Kovisch!" The other figure's head snapped in his direction. "That's enough!"

"What a dilemma you must find yourself in, ay, Evrikh?" A woman's voice; coming from his right. As he turned to look, his eyes fell upon a statue that stood in the center of the walkway.

The statue was worn and discolored from ages of neglect, its true purity hidden throughout the puzzles of time. A man, kneeling upon one knee, his head held high as if to offer the heavens above something they would never have. His hand extended outward, its contents fallen away, perhaps stolen. But something new rested within his hand now, a woman. Beautiful and serene, the moonlight outlined her body as if an angel had lost its way. Leaping from his hand, she floated to the ground effortlessly.

"Created to help the human race live on, yet live on they do. So without the choice of life, you would choose your other half, and take it away from them. So now you sit here, choosing the destiny of these people when it was never your choice to make."

The other figure's head now turned in her direction. "Lashara, that's enough—from both of you!"

"SHUT UP!" Evrikh screamed as an unseen force rapidly shot out in a circular motion, crackling the cement, the ground shaking. This collided with the three figures and grew more intense as Evrikh's face molded of anger; loathing.

Who the hell were they to judge him? Choices; it was not man who gave him these choices, but God! Maybe it was man who got the ball rolling, but in the end, isn't it all a part of the grand design?

Evrikh's teeth gritted audibly as his body flexed itself, the wave exploding toward the others like a bullet.

The three braced themselves as warriors would embrace a battle rather than run from it. As the fog dissipated from the air, Evrikh could see the three holding their ground, and before long, began to sense the strength of their auras. They were different somehow; somehow almost felt synthetic, as if they weren't real. But the strength of their auras, this raw power he felt emanating from them . . . Evrikh's confusion cleared for a moment as his ears deafened to his own realization. His thoughts betrayed his memories as his eyes found a truth unknown to the physical world.

Evrikh's aura, how could he not have felt this before? This sense of unrealism, it shrouds them, but not from the three standing before him, it's coming from another source; from within himself... So, Thea, is Evrikh to have no destiny, save a man-made one; this warped, laughable, destiny?

"It makes no difference with what choices were made. You do have a point about destiny, though. They have made it my destiny, so now I make it theirs." Evrikh's grin spread with uncontrollable satisfaction. "What would the three of you have me do?" His eyes shifted from one figure to the next. "Run away?"

"Help me show the world a new way of life," her voice whispered from behind him.

As Evrikh spun around, his arm rose as if to backhand her, but Thea was already gone. "Oh, I promise, my dear Thea. I will show them a new way of life!"

Closing his eyes and flooding his senses with life, the world around them shot back to life. Evrikh could feel the grass that swayed hundreds of yards away, the bushes that cracked with age, the bugs that gnawed on the flesh of the dead; even Thea. His hand shot out to the right as an eruption of light ran down from his shoulder, exiting from his palm, forming into a ball of electrical fluid. Lunging forward with a blinding speed, it collided with a group of trees, exploding the air into streaks of lightning and wooden shrapnel. Fiery branches flew across the sky as Evrikh leapt from the ground, flying in its direction;

the ground crackling from the force of his leap. Moments after he reached the point of collision, his hand slammed into the smoke that now surrounds him like a poisonous dream and connected with something.

Pulling himself backward, Evrikh left the cloud of fog as fast as he had entered it, dragging the figure out with him. Stopping, he released his hand from a recognizable throat and watched as Thea dropped to the ground, both surprised and breathless. A moment later his questionable hatred for her returned to him—his hatred for everything. Evrikh brought his left hand around and backhanded her into the air. He watched as her body left the ground and leapt into the air from the impact. Seconds later, she landed again with a dull thud as her body slammed into the cement of the walkway a mere twenty feet away. Feeling the laughter growing stronger within him, he held it back to savor its intoxicating taste. She moved.

"Well, would you look at that," his voice was a mix of pain and relief. "Don't make me do this, Thea . . . not this . . . not you." Evrikh began walking toward her as his eyes remained fixated on her slightly moving body. "It all must fall; the Council . . . the Resistance."

Taking the last few steps, he could see that Thea had managed to roll herself over and lay facedown, "Take your place at my side and let us see this through together." His right foot had found its way to her shoulder as he pushed her sideways, rolling her onto her back.

"Evrikh, were you even designed to be bisexual?"
Kovisch?!
Reaching up with her hands, Evrikh felt them lock

around his wrist and moments later Kovisch's feet connected with his chest, filling it with liquid fire as he watched the world suddenly spiraling around him. Ground, sky, ground, sky... cement. Evrikh slammed hard, feeling the air being ripped from his body. He rolled as he slammed his palms and feet into the dirt to bring himself to a stop; his fingers scrapping, gripping. As he finally rolled up to his feet, Evrikh's head retained only one question... how? That was Thea; Evrikh had always known her body more intimately than even time itself had known the ages. He rose to his feet, his mind lost to the instincts of anger. These strangers were clever, dangerously clever.

Feeling a slight breeze from the left, Evrikh brought his right leg around and caught Virgil by the side of his neck, his body giving way. Kovisch standing no more than ten feet away became motionless, never had anyone touched Virgil. Relishing in a moment of triumph, Evrikh suddenly felt a horrible pain as the side of his body caved in, then his back, his neck. The last blow came to his face, spinning him around as he dropped to one knee, a glimpse of the attacker revealing itself. Lashara.

Evrikh threw out his leg and swept it sideways, connecting with both her feet as gravity worked the rest of her body downward. He leaped from the ground, raging up into the sky like a volcano shooting up into the heavens. Moments later his body turned as Evrikh lowered one knee and shot back toward the earth, bringing thunder to the skies, his body glowing a deep red. Watching the ground grow closer with an absurd speed, he could feel his own hatred pushing him faster. That split second before contact, a sudden wave of light streaked across the ground and Lashara was gone. Evrikh slammed into the ground, pieces of earth expanding outward as though a meteorite had struck the earth. Leaping from this crater he had fashioned, Evrikh's feet brought his body up to the edge of where this impact started.

Watching the dirt settle out of the air, he caught a glimpse of a light from the corner of his eye. Adjusting a little to the right, Evrikh watched as a ball of lightning ripped through the air beside him, its heat singeing the hair of his arm. Another, as he turned to watch it screeching toward him. It struck the right side of his chest, ripping through his flesh and cauterizing the wound as it slipped through. He screamed out from both the pain and his tangible hatred for these nuisances. Evrikh looked down as the remaining ashes floated away from his body. His face twisted with renewed emotion as his eyes radiated a bright red, consuming them until he could feel the heat from the flames around his face; smoldering like fiery embers.

He would avenge himself for their defiance!

As Evrikh's hatred rippled through the remaining flesh of his body, his wound began to glow the same smoldering color as his eyes. He stood back up, screaming as all wounds began to reheal themselves.

"YOU THINK YOU CAN BEAT ME SO EASILY?"

Evrikh's eyes quickly widened as he felt the pressure of a grip around his neck, but how, when? Pivoting his eyes slightly left, he could see Thea standing beside him. Her grip became amazingly tight as he slowly felt his throat closing off. Bringing his right hand around to catch her upside the head, her arm miraculously caught it with an incredible speed and she twisted it around, snapping it in an upward motion. The sounds of Evrikh's cracking elbow flooded his ears as his mouth opened to scream but produced no sound. Within that same moment, the tightness of her grip forced Evrikh's forearm bone to rip through his flesh and jiggle itself up past the joint. The wound in his chest drastically slowed its healing as his body screamed for oxygen.

Her fist suddenly connected with his face as Evrikh felt his right cheekbone shatter from her thrust, setting his head ablaze with liquid fire. Blood ran from the folds of his half-defeated face and flowed down around her wrist bound to his neck. As Evrikh looked up with his dreary eye, he could faintly see the tears that swelled along the edges of hers. Gathering every last bit of energy he could feel flowing within his body, Evrikh brought his knee up with a surprising speed and caught her underneath her chin, releasing her grip around his neck and forcing her to stumble backward.

Evrikh's body fell to the ground, drained, limp from his injuries. As he lay there, his locked mouth ripped itself open as far as it could, bringing in as much oxygen as that sliver of a hole would allow. He could feel his body racing to repair itself as he watched Thea from his one good eye. Slowly she recovered herself as she rose to her feet, her hand rising to her jaw as she moved it around; no broken bones. Her tears were still there.

Feeling his body reeling back to life from its oxygen depletion, Evrikh looked up out of the corner of his eye to see Kovisch peering down at his ragged body. Reaching down with his hands, one gripped Evrikh by the right shoulder, and the other reached just above his broken forearm. Raising him up in the air, Evrikh could see Virgil and Lashara in the distance behind Kovisch; Thea had stopped moving for the moment. Kovisch's face took on a queer expression as he saw Evrikh's lips moving but heard no sound. He stood there for a moment, maybe buying some time, perhaps listening; the whisper came again, very soft, very faint. Leaning in, he brought Evrikh's face closer to his head, his lips resting only inches from Kovisch's ear.

"Your last words, I would presume?" Kovisch spoke as Evrikh's lips reached his ear.

His eyes widened, as he finally understood the whisper escaping from Evrikh's lips, "... thank you."

He let out a scream as his stomach suddenly flooded with a pain he had never known. Looking down in horror, he watched as Evrikh's wrist twisted, his hand buried within Kovisch's body. His expression grew horrific as he felt the sensation of Evrikh's fingers invading the rubbery flesh of his organs; the perverted warmth of his fluids. Releasing his hands from Evrikh's body, he remained standing in front of him. Wrapping both hands around Evrikh's wrist, he tried pulling it from his body, but Kovisch could already feel his life being stripped from his body. All that was his soul, his very being, was leaving him through this hole in his stomach. Feeling his body weakening, Kovisch looked back up at Evrikh, watching his wounds heal themselves at an impossible speed. Never had Evrikh felt a force like this, so pure, so intoxicating; his body hungered for more. It was as though every muscle fiber had been flushed with molten lava, his body had somehow landed on the surface of the sun.

Evrikh felt his forearm pull itself back within his flesh as the skin closed around it, the bones reforming from underneath this newly healed skin. He felt the pulling sensation as the shattered pieces of his cheek echoed back across his face and reconstructed the side of it, allowing his mouth to work once again. Evrikh's socket closed off as his eye rolled back into place, his vision returning. Within the moments that this was all happening, he looked pass Kovisch to see the other three standing in the distance, a look of confusion washing over their faces. Their confusion was quickly replaced with shock as the ever-weary Kovisch rotated his head to look upon them, his hands slowly falling to his sides helplessly.

"KOVISCH!" Lashara screamed as she suddenly lunged forward, Virgil restraining her movements.

Kovisch looked as if to speak, and just before his words left his lips, Evrikh's hand felt it necessary to squeeze the life from his organs, as juice would run from the freshest fruit. His words were replaced by the dying sounds of an animal rather than a man, filling Evrikh's head with music that sounded grander than any orchestra.

"STOP IT! YOU'RE KILLING HIM!" Lashara's screams came helplessly as she watched this horror before her.

"Were the roles not reversed just moments ago?" Evrikh said as he glared toward Thea, ". . . Where were your cries for me?"

The three of them saw the running blood recede from the wounds of Evrikh's face, his skin sizzling to a close as the blemishes faded to nothing more than his skin tone. "Well, now, Lashara, you make it sound as though this isn't justified."

Kovisch's skin began to hang from his body, becoming loose, decaying; resembling a shrinking child whose clothes no longer fit. His eyes rolled freely from their place as his body lost the will to control them. Kovisch's insides had lost their beautiful warmth, their perverted indulgence that breathed such new life into Evrikh.

"You know, Evrikh, there is one thing you neglected to think about in your rush to save yourself," Virgil spoke as he stepped forward, placing Lashara behind him.

"And that would be . . .?" Evrikh asked, just as the bones of his shoulder rolled back into place.

"Could you possibly repair yourself and fight the three of us at the same time?"

A sharp pain suddenly overwhelmed the back of his neck, driving his head into the ground. Evrikh could feel his hand ripped from Kovisch's rotting stomach as his face twisted from this intense pain; a nail that would chisel its way to the center of his spine. Kovisch's lifeless body fell beside him, crackling with dryness, his blood erupting in puffs, as nothing more than powder.

"Hmmm, I guess not." Virgil's voice was almost a whisper.

Rolling over, Evrikh jumped up to his feet, a streak of flesh; pain. Lashara's elbow had connected with his left temple and forced him to stumble away from her.

Damn her; damn all of them! Didn't they understand what Evrikh was trying to do here?! Why would they fight him to save all this? LOOK AROUND! Maybe in some minute way it was all worth it . . . dammit, Thea. Evrikh's stomach knotted with confusion, but this all has to end!

Gathering himself from this assault, Evrikh turned away from his attackers and ran down the walkway, leaping into the air. As he launched upward, his body flew across the park at a blurring speed. Evrikh could still feel the sensations of worms that burrowed beneath his skin in hopes of repairing his body. Flying out toward the city, he turned his head back to see if his entourage of assassins were quick to follow.

A sudden flash of light; Evrikh barely managed to move out of the way as a ball of lightning streaked past his eyes, colliding with a stone fountain up in the distance.

Come on, you little annoying rats, it's time to run your maze!

Feeling a small grin curve itself onto his lips, Evrikh turned to look back out to his front side, his path yet to be decided.

Thea . . . but how? When the hell did she . . .? Of course it's you, how could it ever be someone else?

She screamed as her arms rose in front of her, a blue barrier shooting out to her left and right. As she planted her feet into the ground, the aura around this hidden wall grew brighter, stronger.

Without time to react, Evrikh threw his hands in front of himself and screamed with all the raw emotion unleashed within him. A black light suddenly encased his body as he collided with this invisible wall. The area grew blinding as the explosion flooded the surrounding air, lightning passing in and out. There came other eruptions of blue and black, and the air was vastly filled with smoke from the collision and earth from below. Virgil and Lashara came to a halt, their bodies floating inches from the ground as they slowly descended upon it. Watching from the distance, they could still see mounds of earth falling to the ground, little fires that smoldered alive from the foliage. The explosion had caused some of the surrounding trees to become uprooted, and the others only half remained. As the soil settled from the air, the fog slowly thinned; there was no movement.

"Do you think maybe they killed each other?" Lashara asked, her thoughts still dwelling on Kovisch and his cruel fate.

"Perhaps, but somehow I don't believe this is the way it was written," Virgil finished as he stepped up beside her.

Watching the last of the smoke dissipate into the air, the two of them could see a small figure lying on the ground in the distance. "Virgil, do you think that's—"

Grabbing Lashara by the shoulder, he said, "Wait, you can't tell who that is any more than I can."

There was movement.

The two of them slowly watched as this figure rose

to its feet, weary from injuries. Stumbling forward, they watched as it struggled to remain standing, leaving the damage behind and stepping in to the dim light from the remaining lampposts. Resting at the fountain for a moment, the figure then stepped away from it and into the light. Waves of shimmering black reflected from her hair as it swayed from an oncoming breeze, her body weary from exertion.

"THEA!" Lashara leapt from Virgil's grasp and within moments was standing beside her, holding her in place. Virgil was quick to follow.

Raising her hand, she brought it down upon Lashara's shoulder and leaned against Virgil who now stood on her other side.

"My lady, I'm overwhelmed to see you safe, but what of Evrikh?" Virgil's eyes searched the remaining area, but returned nothing, "What's become of him?"

"I wish I knew," Thea spoke as she raised her eyes and looked forward. "The blast knocked me unconscious. The last thing I remember was seeing his face . . . so full of anger, of hatred." Her face loomed down once again, tears rolling at the edges of her eyes. "Then within that moment, as the world exploded around us, I felt him . . . my Ev. Although it was nothing more than a whisper, I still heard him. 'I love you.'" She lifted her head up to meet Virgil's. "His last words before he used everything he had left to protect me from the explosion." She hesitated for a moment before pressing on. "Even through all his anger and hatred, the life he had forced upon him . . . he still loved me, and I betrayed that."

"Lady Thea, sometimes we are forced to make a decision knowing that it's the wrong one, but also knowing that it's the only one." Lashara's voice was calm, soothing.

Virgil turned away from Thea as his eyes fell upon Lashara and what sounded like her newfound wisdom. Maybe there was hope for her yet. Lashara had some big part to play in destiny, and Virgil could feel that. He's always felt that.

"And now life will go on as it was meant to," he continued to help Thea. "For the first time throughout all the history of life, a species has finally managed to beat its own extinction. And through all its ignorance and self-righteousness, who'd have thought it would be the human race?" Virgil almost laughed at his own slight humor as the three of them pressed on, their legs carrying them toward the front gate. Turning once again to look back through the park, there remained no movement at the point of collision and they watched as the pillar of blackness that stretched up for the heavens slowly dissipated, the aura of death lifting itself from the air around them. And although harmony had not yet returned, maybe new life would bring it here, to this place; this world.

* * * *

PART II
Forgotten Souls

CHAPTER 12
~ Broken Silence ~

"**AND SO NOW** history has been completed as it was written."

"Yes, Virgil, but what of Evrikh? We cannot just assume with history." Lady Ira spoke more of a statement than a direct question.

"My lady, I assure you, there was nothing more before us, save the death he spread with his own hand," Lashara added.

"It was a most unfortunate fate for our young brother Kovisch, as it is for all our people who live to see such times; we share in your loss, Lashara," Kamui's voice was soft, sorrowful.

Watching her begin to lower her head in remembrance of her beloved friend, perhaps would-be lover, Virgil approached this man who resided in the center chair. "Master Kamui, even during these dark times, it's hard to believe our thoughts would betray us."

"This is true, Virgil; however, maybe it's the world

who betrays you." His words, while skeptical, posed an idea unthought of. "I feel as though something is missing from this tale of ours. Perhaps a piece that eludes our eyes yet remains in the back of our dreams."

Turning to look at all the faces of those before him, Virgil's eyes returned to Kamui. "I have felt this as well, but it is possible the cycle has been broken, allowing our unknown fear to bring us doubt."

"What are your feelings on this, Seraph?" Kamui's voice carried off to the right as Virgil's eyes followed to the left.

Leaning into the light, Seraph's face could be seen more clearly. His features were strong, confidant, almost demeaning. Yet his skin was as smooth as silk and as golden as the sun. His eyes were like lost worlds, vast and powerful; surrounded by the fogs of our dreams, what secrets they held.

"A species that finally survived its own extinction? I can't help but feel that you are forgetting an important question." His hands came together as his eyes traveled from Virgil to Lashara. "It pleases me to see that the two of you have returned to us, but are we sure those people were supposed to end at that moment, at that time?"

"Master Seraph, all we know is that Evrikh would be the cause of their fate, and now that cause is gone. What other worry could there be?" Virgil's voice became stubborn, that of a man who secrets were held from.

Seraph leaned back in his chair as his hands floated to their armrests, a small grin barely visible upon his lips. "Perhaps the catalyst for their fate," his eyes were moistened as he blinked, "and yet you speak as if you have proof Evrikh is no longer among them."

"Sir," Lashara began as she stepped forward, "all we have is what we saw, and what we felt." She stood beside Virgil once again. "He is as gone as Kovisch, and we ask that you accept this. We can't allow ourselves to be blinded by our own prejudices."

Whispers began to rise from the others at Lashara's outburst of contestation. But these whispers quickly grew to a silence as Kamui lowered his hand and looked back to Virgil and Lashara.

"We will accept this," his voice reassuring, "once you provide the appropriate proof. You are to return and continue to monitor the flow of Lady Thea's people. This is the decision of the Circle of Reign." His lips fell silent for a moment in anticipation of a reaction, but received none. *"Con du et meshe."*

Kamui watched as Virgil and Lashara turned from the Circle and walked toward the door, receiving their assignment without question. To have faced such a virile enemy, such bravery they have. As they drew closer to the door, Seraph watched them depart with a careful eye. *Maybe it is they who betray us.*

~ ~ ~

The world was renewed as news flowed like an oncoming flood of Lady Miriam and how she, with the faith of the Council of Aurora, brought peace and salvation to the people once again. The damage that had been caused by Evrikh had been restored, and the lives of the people had returned to normal. The floating city of Eden and all its glory had been rebuilt to reflect the purity and holiness masked within its walls. Save the Unfamiliars, the people had lost their doubts of the Council in light of these recent events. Ever since that unforgotten day, the Resistance seemed to have vanished altogether. There had been little uproar, mostly disgruntled civilians who had nothing better to do, but the level of movement from the Resistance had remained at a minimal, leaving the Council with thoughts of nothing more than a removed thorn.

The house in Norwynn had been discovered by the Council, along with the wreckage that remained inside; the body of Keona. She had been removed by the Divine and taken to the Sacred Church of Aurora within Eden to be studied and documented, probably for further augmentation of the Relics. The church had then resolved any documents and involvement that could tie it to the Unfamiliar named Keona, claiming that she was indeed in collusion with the Resistance to defile the Council. Cazziel, along with the Relics, had been commended by the Council for forcing the Resistance to disband and saving the future of the people from damnation, giving birth to the church's newest order, the Protectors of Faith. Cazziel was to remain at Miriam's side.

Thea had been watching the Council more closely than ever now, observing their movements and enjoying this cloak-and-dagger game of chess. She was there, hidden by the shadows of time, as Keona was taken away by the Divine; the last remnants of Brian and Emilia befouled by these grand liars. She was unseen in the crowds. Her eyes gazed up to the balcony where Cazziel and his Relics rested, the church declaring their gratitude and announcing the union of the Protectors of Faith. And now, Thea waited, anticipating her next move, plotting to remove the Council from its power. She stayed in a small apartment now, in the small city of Lenubus along the coast of Phelineous. The people there kept to themselves for the most part and never asked many questions. Thea chose this place because of its lack of business, which meant less traffic, and ultimately, less interaction with the Council. It was here that she made her decisions, that she completed her plans, and waited now for her time.

She had already touched base with what remained of the Resistance, a few outposts scattered throughout the land. Thea also enlisted a few informants, runners, who brought her news of the Council. But of all the information brought to her, Vahn Schiller was, perhaps, her greatest asset; the local purifier of this town's forgotten church. Vahn vowed revenge against the church when he was forced to watch his parents get slaughtered right before his eyes. Declared renewed by the faith of the church and all its glory, Vahn enlisted to become a priest; a Divine, the highest honor one could receive in priesthood. Actually, he wasn't much like a priest at all.

Vahn spent more time in the streets than in his church, where people would rather continue to sin than head into the church and repent. Most of the town knew him from his appearance; black pants whose color almost seemed to elude the light. His shirt just as lifeless, save a single line;

a thin white stripe that ran from within his belt, up past his chest, to the collar running around his neck; a collar that signified a man of the cloth. He wore boots. Black, rugged, and encasing his body was a long white trench coat with flaps that rested upon his shoulders to be zipped into an overly sized hood. The only defining piece of this trench coat were two large black lines on its back. The first, which ran the length of Vahn's back, and the other which ran from shoulder to shoulder; a crucifix.

Being a bringer of peace, Vahn was granted permission by the Council to carry firearms contained within holsters beneath his trench coat. They were both modified pistols, one equipped with high velocity ammo, Godhand; and the smaller of the two equipped with slugs, Savior. Vahn had been instructed by the Council to use them if he encountered the Resistance, or worse, yet, an Unfamiliar. But roughly three years ago, he had encountered the mysterious Thea. Unaware of each other's roles in life, they played off of each other to gain what information they could, using one another. Through that time they had developed an understanding for each other and revealed each other's plans. Their similar lives had allowed them to become close, developing a trust so rarely found in this world of theirs. So together, they laid their plans and tracked the movements of the Council, and over the past three years, the world had almost seemed to have forgotten about Evrikh and the Phoenix Gate.

The church doors had moaned alive with the whispers of ancient wood, their edges brushing the ceiling that loomed so far above. A woman stepped inside, her shoes echoing throughout the church with a feathery touch. Just before reaching the seats, she turned, walking toward the confession booths. Her long white gleaming coat glided along the air. Her pants were white, yet they resembled the comfort of a cloud, and her shirt bore a small collar that rose a half inch above her neckline, the color an exact reflection of her pants. As the shirt hung freely, the V-neck followed her curves downward, slightly revealing the secrets of a woman and the edges of a tattoo. The door to the confession stand turned and opened with a slight pull. As it quietly closed, the woman sat upon the chair and listened just as the window creaked itself open, the wire mesh hiding the man who sat upon the other side.

"Forgive me, Father, for I will sin." Her voice was steady, controlled.

"My child, sometimes our sins are all we have."

"The Council knows something, Vahn."

"I've heard nothing. Besides, Thea, right now, the Council is operating in a most conspicuous manner."

"There are whispers; whispers of Kendrick Savari and the Phoenix Gate." As Thea finished her last sentence, Vahn turned to look through the small window, their eyes meeting each other's.

"I will send Lauren to gather information, and then we'll move."

The doors to the church slid close once again as Thea walked away from its walls; the city around them unaware of their intentions. Vahn stood at the edge of her door as Lauren walked throughout the room, grabbing the things she would need.

"Remember, Lauren, you're going to the Church of Divinity and you've transferred from the Church of Lenubus. That's where you'll stay while in Eden. Gather all the information you can pertaining to Kendrick Savari and the Phoenix Gate. Godspeed, my child." Vahn's voice was that of an operations specialist; void of the faith he represented around his neck.

~ ~ ~

As the four ladies ran their sponges over Lady Miriam's body, the water ran from the curves of her treasures, the steam traveling her intimate roads. Squeezing the sponge and renewing its warmth, Lauren could remember the words spoken by Vahn. *I cannot stress this mission's importance enough, Lauren; get as close as you can.* She placed the sponge over Miriam's knee and watched as the warm water ran from it, falling and caressing her skin. Lowering it, Lauren ran the sponge down her leg and around her ankle.

Noticing the intense delicacy of Lauren's hands, Miriam couldn't help but notice the beauty of her movements, the way her hands glided the sponge so very smoothly over her skin. Perhaps it was Lauren's elegance that should be admired within these moments instead of her own. Miriam surprisingly felt her own face grow warm as these thoughts of Lauren had caught her off guard. Catching an unassuming glance of her emerald eyes, Miriam suddenly realized it was more than her face that had warmed.

A slight breeze drifted into the room as the door slid

open, and then quietly closed. A man walked inside and came to a halt at the edge of the bathing area, being careful not to tread onto its pearly floor.

"My lady, may I speak with you?" His voice was soothing, strong.

Upon his entry, Miriam rose to her feet as the four ladies tended to her needs, wrapping her body in a gown of layered silks. "My dearest Cazziel, and what news would be so vital as to disturb a woman during her bathing time?"

Cazziel had a hard time deciding whether she was trying to be flirtatious or demeaning.

"Lady Miriam, the workers have found another diary." Walking past him, Miriam continued to listen as she prepared herself. "The diary speaks of the true Phoenix Gate, the one behind his theories."

At that last remark, Miriam's movements stopped and she turned to look at Cazziel, their eyes locking for a moment.

As Lauren continued to clean up everything with the other girls, she suddenly flashed back to her conversation with Vahn, *". . . a series of diaries that collectively are called Marcus's journal is what first brought the Phoenix Gate to the attention of the Council. Now, I, myself, have never seen them, but I have it on good word from Brian that they're real . . ."*

"What's more is that it's not part of Marcus's journal . . . but a personal diary of Kendrick's."

"It would seem that in his haste to leave us, Mr. Viseli would also choose to leave behind the chance for further research. It makes me wonder, Cazziel," she thought

THE PHOENIX GATE

aloud as her eyes carried off to the edge of the bathing pool, "what is it you think he read in those pages he stole? What could a man so dedicated have read that would make him abandon everything?" she finished, looking back up to Cazziel with a keen eye.

"My lady, it also has entries dated between the missing pages of Marcus's journal," Cazziel finished, knowing that last remark had absorbed all of Miriam's attention.

Cazziel had never truly been with Lady Miriam, but as he watched her get dressed, her beauty had captivated him, as it had always captured him.

"... And where is this diary now?" Miriam asked with a growing interest peaking in her voice.

Cazziel followed her over to a small table where she picked up a small trinket and used it to pin up her hair. He had always enjoyed seeing this side of Miriam; her vulnerable, graceful side.

"I came ahead, my lady. The diary should be arriving shortly."

"Very well," Miriam stated, her eyes looking into a small mirror. "That's enough, ladies." Her attention turned to the women who had just finished up. Upon hearing their command, they quickly finished and retreated from Miriam's presence; Miriam unaware of would-be listening ears.

"Have them prepare the Level Three Lab below the south wing, Cazziel. I want the contents of every page deciphered within a week."

Cazziel's eyes snapped to Miriam, surprised by her haste. "My lady, the other diaries have been translated over the course of hundreds of years due the nature of the science alone. You couldn't possibly expect to decipher the contents within that short amount of time, let alone hope to understand it all."

He watched as she walked from the small table to a large cabinet, her feet leaving heated imprints that were quick to fade. As its doors swung open, Cazziel could see the clothes that rested within. The gown flowed down from Miriam's body as she slipped it from her shoulders. Falling to the ground, she stepped from its circle and grabbed an evening gown from the cabinet, her skin always softer than the flowers of her beloved gardens. Sorting it through her hands, she glanced over her left shoulder to speak to Cazziel.

"Yes, this is true. However, we have something that we did not hundreds of years ago, and I am sure that he will provide the valuable information that we require to understand this new diary." Miriam's hands gracefully slipped the evening gown over her body as she continued to speak. "And, please, Cazziel, try to make him as comfortable as possible."

Stepping up behind Miriam, Cazziel placed his hands upon her shoulders, his breath warming her delicate neck. "Miriam, this is a dangerous game we're playing. It would be best to walk a path of certainty. This one you choose has too many variables, along with too many consequences."

Leaning into his embrace, Miriam's hands rose up and held Cazziel's within them. "My dearest Cazziel, the only path of certainty is the one without question, with unwavering faith. This is the path I search for our people, no matter the cost."

Holding her within his grasp, Cazziel's arms fully embraced the contours of her body. "Even if it were to cost them their lives?"

She fell silent for a moment. ". . . Even if it were to cost them their Lady Miriam."

~ ~ ~

Lauren had learned her way through the Church of Divinity very swiftly during her short time there. Over the past few months, the maze of catacombs had become no more complicated than her home back in Lenubus. Vahn had chosen her for a peculiar reason. When Lauren was just a child, she was taken from her family. The Council declared that she suffered from the Eye of Kal'Thonnas, named after Jyral Kal'Thonnas as written in the Aurorian Chronicles as being the first human to suffer from this condition. It was a dual standard that allowed her to see the truth behind all things; her mask removed from this world of illusions. A female assassin disguised as a proper woman, Unfamiliars who would try to blend in with the crowds around them, or even they, the Protectors of Faith, hidden among the general populous. Lauren would see one-sided mirrors as windows, their reflections besieged by the contents on the other side. Or even in situations as these, she could see corridors hidden behind walls.

The other half of her condition would be the ability to remember; to remember all things. It allowed Lauren to remember everything that came within her vision, down to the slightest detail unnoticed by the human eye; the cross strokes of paintings from eras immemorial, or the number of grooves within a ceramic pot, foretelling the graceful movements of its creator's fingers.

Soon after their declaration, Lauren's family had an audience with the Council, of which Lady Miriam was present for, her precious Cazziel a moment's reaction behind her. She loomed up there, in her chair made of perfect crystal, softened by the whispers of flower petals. Her faced had looked so gentle to little Lauren, and yet what remained underneath Lady Miriam ... that was the truth hidden from the outside world ... Truth that only Lauren could see.

Cazziel was stern. He stood beside his queen devoted, without question, without fear; what kind of life is it to live for someone else's entirely? The Council had told her family that she had been damned, with her eyes seeing nothing but sin. The Council extended their arms in good faith and told her she must be purified, cleansed of her sins.

"You must be baptized under the holy name of our goddess and review the teachings of the Aurorian Chronicles," they had told her, *"and then you must be relieved of your vision. For the goddess is here to save the pure, not the damned,"* their voices still wrung in the innermost part of her ears, where only whispers were allowed to remain. Lauren and her family were left with two choices: relieve her body of her sight so that she might be saved, or banish her from civilization to save the people from her sins.

As Vahn was returning from the city of Razhein, passing through the southern forest of Lenubus, he stumbled across little Lauren. As he stepped out of his vehicle, walking to the other side, Vahn could tell this child had endured much. She watched him then, with wide eyes, as though death had finally come to take her away. It had been almost three months since the last time Lauren had seen another human. Kneeling down beside her, Vahn's eyes washed over her body; the deep bruises on her arms and legs; she had lost a shoe. This little child also had cuts along her shoulders, the side of her neck, and upper right thigh; must have fallen from somewhere high.

With his eyes traveling back to hers, Vahn could see the fear within them. But he could also see the relief and sorrow. Tears bellowed at the edges of her stare. With the slow extension of his arms, Vahn leaned closer to Lauren until she was within them. He then closed his arms around her and held her; held her as her family once had.

"There, there, my child," he spoke softly, *"your hardships have ended."*

Leaning away from Lauren, he could see the tears growing within her eyes. *"My name is Vahn, Vahn Schiller."* He smiled at her for a moment, such a beautiful smile. *"You can call me Father Vahn."*

". . . laur . . . en," was all she managed to say before her tears ran uncontrollably, and her voice became nothing more than the childish yelps of a confused and scared little girl. She gripped him with her little arms, and she cried as only a child knows how to, robbed of innocence.

It was later that Vahn was given her full name, Lauren Senir, and years before he had learned of her full story. From the moment he first saw her there, he took her in and raised her in the church. After learning of what the Council had done to her, and remembering his own past, he taught her. He taught her how to be quick and how to be strong. Vahn gave her the skills of living in the shadows, hidden by the darkness, and to use that same darkness to move without being seen. By that time, Lauren had grown into a fine woman, and it all but added to the one passion that she and Vahn both shared: revenge. Lauren learned quickly, as she always had, but it was still a miracle that she lasted those three months. Vahn also taught Lauren how to be sly and clever, the two lessons obtained naturally by all women, taken a step higher beyond compare. There had been times when her cleverness had outgrown even his.

Two guards continued their conversation as they finished checking the last door; locked. Speaking of their time with the Protectors of Faith, they continued to tell each other stories of past experiences, their voices, along with their lights, fading down the hall. There was a slight click and the turning of a handle as a door quietly opened into the darkness. Sliding it close behind her, Lauren peered down the hall to see the fading light and faint voices of the patrol guards walking away from her. With the speed of a cheetah and the grace of an angel, Lauren slipped in behind the first guard, mimicking his walking pattern. As the guard continued to walk, they approached another door around the corner. Lauren drew closer. So close, she could taste the musty air rising from his neck. As the first guard stepped over to the door, Lauren drew closer still, her breath like a faint breeze against the small hairs of his neck.

As the door tested correctly, the man turned around to face his partner. Lauren so close now, she whispered, ". . . I see you."

Ripping his light through the air, the guard turned around while stumbling backward. "WHO'S THERE?" his crackled voice demanded.

Stepping away from his stumbling partner, the other guard turned his light in the same direction while aimlessly waving his gun through the air.

"WHO IS IT?"

After the other guard quickly regained his balance, the two hastily bounced their lights throughout the hall, up to the ceiling, down the hall; the far wall. Their perpetrator had vanished, if there ever had been one.

"The hell was that, Ferris?"

"I heard a voice, Ping," he hesitated for a moment, his light steadying, ". . . right behind me."

"Relax, man, it's all in your head," Ping told him as he placed his hand on Ferris's shoulder, "You're just tense. Can't blame you, though, I don't much like this wing either. The guys say they sometimes hear whispers late at night."

The two guards waited a moment after Ferris lowered his gun. Then they turned and continued to walk down the hallway as a shadow leaned around the corner.

"You'll get your turn . . . you all will."

Moving down the hall away from the guards, Lauren reached her door with no more than the grace of a murmur.

With a slight pull, the door eased open and moments later Lauren was inside. The door silently closed as though it was never opened. As she turned around, Lauren's eyes scanned the room, forever writing the slightest of changes, the most hidden of movements within the pages of her mind.

The room was faintly lit by the bluish-white moonlight that stretched in from the windows above. Lauren quickly transcended to the other side of the room, coming to a rest against a full-size cabinet. She had been in this room many times in the past few months, allowing her to know its most intimate secrets. From the time Lauren had begun crossing the floor, she had closed her eyes, for her memories could see much better than this light had permitted, and her mind was sharper than these shadows before her. Glancing around her with her eyes for just a moment, Lauren continued to walk along that wall; her footsteps flooding the air with a deafening silence. Bringing herself to a halt, she rolled to her right and found herself in front of a mirror.

Movement!

Lauren's eyes darted to the left of the reflection, but soon realized she was looking at grand drapes, slightly waving from the breeze above. Lauren continued with the task at hand.

The mirror was larger than most, surrounded by a border of silver angels. Their little bodies intertwining as though pleasure itself is a perversion of the soul. Looking away from its enchanting glow of silver and moonlight, Lauren's eyes returned to the reflections before her.

Raising her hand in front of her, Lauren watched as she pressed against it, the edges of her fingers rippling the image as though the mirror was made of water. Pushing up through to her wrist, she proceeded to follow. Small glares echoed throughout the room as the ripples diffracted the oncoming light; an impossible vertical pond. As the mirror continued to envelop Lauren, she found herself transcending to the other side. The ripples wavered back and forth as they slowly faded away, returning the mirror to its original state; flawless.

A stairwell loomed before her, Lauren's eyes trailing the steps down and to the left, the air carried the scent of a hospital but also of earth. Lit by a faint glow from the secrets ahead, she began her descent. Lauren had used this stairwell many times; she believed it was used as an observation deck at some point, or perhaps still was. Wrapping around, the stairwell finally opened up to a familiar room, which, thankfully, was still empty. The opening to the stairwell was located in the back wall, left corner. Stepping into the room, there were a few chairs that lined the back wall and a map that loomed above them. It was a map of how the world used to be, old text written in a language forgotten long ago. The center of the room contained a rather enticing leather couch, its cushions oversized. There was a small table in front and three more leather chairs around it, yet the couch, along with the chairs, faced forward. Looking forward herself, Lauren slowly stepped over to the front wall. Coming to a rest at about waist height, there were two small stone pillars that ran from this short wall up to the ceiling. Lauren placed her hands on the edges of this stone shelf below them, being careful not to brush any dust or debris into the room below. Bringing her eyes slowly over the edge, she peered down in the room beneath her, a laboratory she would greet yet again.

The floor was made of marble, with the occasional power cord lying about. The floor was an intertwining mix of turquoise and glare, reflecting the lights from the ceiling above. As Lauren looked to the left, she could see a few scientists walking about, some ruffling through papers; they were surrounded by computer terminals, their contents hidden from the distance below. Lauren could also see containers along shelves around those terminals, labeled for various testing. She retracted her hand behind the wall to attend a growing itch along her upper hip, relieving her mind for a moment of the tension at hand. Scanning the room below, her eyes trailed across the floor; more terminals, more scientists, human-size containers along the upper wall. Those containers were a thing of interest. It appeared that only one was in use, and the bottom was emanating steam. After peering a little closer, Lauren could soon tell that it was actually frozen. Too many cables ran from its sides to even contemplate an educated guess, and the glass along the front was too hazed over to see the contents hidden within. Yet the scientists below seemed to be very interested in the contents within. It appeared to have several surveillance systems connected to it, each one reporting a different condition, different information. Lauren's eyes still, trailing to the right, fell upon the entrance of this hidden laboratory, just as she watched the doors swing open and a small crowd of people descend into the room.

The first to come were a couple of other scientists, perhaps doctors of some sort. They quickly transcended the floor and began interacting with the others. Within the confusion of the voices below, Lauren could make out some of it; "condition of the Osiris Project, last readings on the vitals database, progress of the incubation." She then noticed two other familiar figures walk into the room, a woman accompanied by a man; the door closing behind them. Wearing the gown of a lush deep purple, Lauren watched as she moved toward a glass case containing what appeared to be a very old book of some sort. The man came to a halt resting a few feet behind her.

"How's the progress coming on the translation?" Miriam asked as her eyes shifted to the scientist standing beside her.

"Well, Lady Miriam, apparently it dictates his theories on the first Phoenix Gate to walk the earth and the true nature behind it," the small man had said as he moved around to the other side. "His name was Moses, and he freed his people, the Hebrews, from these ... Egyptians." The man adjusted his glasses slightly as he looked up at Cazziel. "Supposedly, when a race is about to die out or become extinct, the soul of that race reaches out to go on ... He speculates much, as though he's attempting to blur the line between science and religion. Sometimes it reads as if they are one and the same."

"The soul?" Cazziel queried.

"A collective, if you will. It's almost like the essence of

that race, a being created for the sole purpose to continue its species at all costs." He seemed to have an insatiable expression on his face from his recent accomplishments. "The problem was that since it was a natural phenomenon, there was no way to synthesize a reproduction. But somehow, Kendrick Savari had discovered the secret. That's what we're working on now." He began to walk toward that human-sized tube and the monitors that rested beside it. From the way the three of them were looking at the screens, Lauren could tell they were reading; damn, and, of course, their mouths had to be turned away from her.

"As far as our guest goes, everything's moving along quite nicely. We've had very few complications, and the reconstruction has been moving along unexpectedly quickly."

As Cazziel turned to look at the tube, he grinned. "Were you expecting something less?"

"I want you to raise the solution to an 80 percent ratio," Miriam said as she turned to look at the scientist. A dulling light flickered in the back corner for a moment.

"But, my lady, we've never operated at such a capacity. Through past test runs we've only used a 4 percent ratio, and in past scenarios, we've never gone above 7, which gave results more than pleasing. Cazziel himself can attest to that." The scientist looked between Miriam and Cazziel in hopes of sympathy; he found none. "To work at 80 percent at this time is madness; it might jeopardize the Osiris Project altogether."

After speaking, the other voices grew to low whispers,

their attention slightly drawn to the confrontation by their precious tube. Cazziel took a step behind Miriam, his stern figure looming above her own. As he cocked his head to look at the scientist, his chin softly grazed the folds of her hair.

"Dr. Rydz, the correct answer would be to do your job. Any other answer would result in another performing it for you." Cazziel's voice was directive, without question; the faint scent of pollen and rosemary flooding his nostrils from her beautiful hair.

"Everything will be ready to go by the end of the week, and the Osiris Project will be completed." Miriam turned her eyes to gaze at the tube once again. "He will walk with us," her voice flowed over her shoulder to the lips of Cazziel. "My dear Cazziel, maybe we have not failed," she whispered.

Upon hearing the timetable allotted, the other scientists and doctors slowed to a standstill, their wide expressions facing Miriam and Cazziel. Growing closer to the door, Miriam proceeded as Cazziel turned back around to face the others.

"It's quite simple. You work, and then you finish ... in one week." Just as he was about to turn, something etched itself into the back of his mind; a feeling, a thought, or worse—a presence. Very swiftly, Cazziel's eyes loomed up to the ceiling above, the overlooking room that they often used for surveillance. He stood there for a moment, his eyes scanning; his instincts piqued at this raw sensation echoing in his thoughts. There was nothing.

Turning himself back toward the door, Cazziel slightly

shifted his hand, pardoning the doors. At his departure, the others continued with their tasks at hand, unaware of the watchful eyes that gazed from above.

~

The Church of Divinity was massive in size, and its grand hall was something perhaps designed for the gods, the intricacies of a perfectionist; Del'Vjirn. Hired by Lady Miriam, along with the Council, he was hired because of his exquisite taste and artistic ability. Not many people were aware that Del'Vjirn had fallen in love with Lady Miriam, and throughout his time staying with her, his emotions became reflective in his work, and his love for her was portrayed as the most graceful, indulging piece the world had ever seen; the Church of Divinity, his church of Lady Miriam.

Miriam was still fond of the days immemorial when the church was being constructed, the faint wisps of incense; the woven intricacies of the tapestries. She watched Del'Vjirn work with the precision and the grace not of a man, but of something more. She had loved to watch him, his hands so beautiful and so masterful. Miriam could remember the many times that she posed for Del'Vjirn, the statuettes that now rest in the grand hall, greeting those that graced these holy doors; the hints of jasmine, and the addicting sweet fresh scent of nectar that flooded its grand halls. On days of the warmest sunrises, the sky's passion of reds and oranges would embrace the windows, and some would say that they've found heaven. Miriam would never forget the faces of her followers when they would enter through her vast doors, only to marvel for hours at a piece of woven tapestry, or playfully run their fingers along the curves of one of her statuettes; such intricate detail. This beautiful creation, her church built for her more than three hundred and fifty years ago.

Lady Miriam watched many people come and go from the church, and her precious Council. She had also watched the slow deterioration of her beautiful church, her Del'Vjirn, fade with time. How she longed for the days when she would sit in one of her gardens as the faint scent of Tuscones would softly caress her lungs, filling her with the taste of beauty. She had emotionally made love to herself back then, lost in Del'Vjirn's intimate world of fanatical art. He was a genius, and she had loved him for that.

Lady Miriam, along with her Council, would have an audience with the Tarben family today. Apparently they have been hiding their son Malseth, in hopes that the Council of Aurora would not discover his sinful nature and brand him an Unfamiliar. The balconies were lined with people along both walls in this room of grandeur, eagerly leaning over their railings in hopes of catching a glimpse of the trial to be. There was a carpet running the length of the floor, an intimate sensation of red, coming to a stop before the doors. The doors slid open with the ease of giants as a child upon the second balcony stretched his arm out to try to touch this wooden god. His mother quickly grabbed his wandering arm and returned it to the confinements of the balcony. Reaching their maximum range, the doors came to a halt with a dulling thud, a boom, to mask the air of thunder. The crowds along the lower level of this cathedral turned in wonderment as guards began to invade this red carpet, the Tarben family faintly visible behind them. As they started their ascent through the grand hall toward the pulpit of the Council and the throne of Lady Miriam, the crowds along the sides watched from their pews in silence. The Tarbens' faces looked throughout the crowds for sympathy, but there would be none. Lauren watched as one of Miriam's maidens, whose chairs lined the back wall, remained poised, ready to carry out the beckoning of her liege. She could see the growing desperation within their faces—the faces of they who have done nothing wrong but would not be given the chance to relish in such truth.

The boy Malseth could not have been older than eleven; perhaps he was as young as nine. By his expression, he appeared confused, but within his eyes Lauren knew that he was scared. As they continued their short journey toward this prospective alter of fates, the faces of the crowds slowly grew into anger, nothing but resentment. How could the Tarbens risk damning the people, with no remorse, no concern? Little Malseth listened as their angry voices were nothing more than mere whispers lost within the confusion of his mind. Looking around, Malseth finally saw the vastness of the hall he was now walking in. He looked past the crowds as his eyes fell upon one of the stone pillars that were used to elevate the balconies above. As his eyes became parallel with the edge of a balcony, they took in the wonderment of a tapestry of such a grand scale that its vision could not all fit within one view. The tapestry dictated the goddess, saving her people from a world of the damned. The detail was so amazingly fresh and vivid, yet the tarnished edges would tell of another story. The face of the goddess, so strikingly familiar.

Malseth's eyes continued about the room, lost in the sea of colors that floated so far above them. As he took in the whole of the nativity, Malseth saw the pictorial story of the birth of the goddess, sent to us from the heavens above after the Great Darkness. According to the Aurorian Chronicles, for a thousand years the world was consumed by darkness due to man's unquenchable thirst for sin. It was the goddess who saved the people from their sins. During her ascension to the people, the Council of Aurora was also birthed in her name, and since then, set on a path to cleanse the world of the hands that sin. Miriam. His eyes had befallen on her, resting on her throne of crystal, besieged by petals, their sweet aroma slowly drifting throughout the church. Such a beautiful woman would have to be understanding of his family. Before her had rested the Council of Aurora, the disciples of the goddess who followed the teachings of Aurora with unwavering faith and devotion. This is where the guards had brought the Tarbens to a halt.

Upon the completion of their small task, the guards had left the Tarbens, exiting to the left and the right, disappearing behind the crowds. The people grew silent and took their seats as the others upon the balcony rose to witness. A man rested up on a separate balcony that loomed above the Council and overlooked the crowd, as well as the Tarbens.

"My liege." He bowed in Miriam's honor. "My brethren," his eyes briefly turned to the Council of Aurora, "how long must these damned be allowed to walk among the purified, the saved?" he spoke as he softly waved his hand toward the crowds. Whispers arose of praise. "These meaningless trials should have ended with the Resistance, and yet we find ourselves drawn back in an attempt to save those who would have destroyed everything Aurora has built and stands for." His gaze returned to that of the Council. "The world should be purged, my brethren, not forsaken."

"And yet, forsaken it is," Miriam spoke. "I will not have the Council drawn into an overbearing search for a meaningless threat and proceed to frighten the people." Her voice, although full of wisdom, was that of absolute.

The man residing in the middle of the Council turned to look upon the faces before him, the Tarbens. "You knew of your son's condition, and yet being children of Aurora, you chose to conceal this abomination? The Council would ask you why." The attention of the Council turned to them as he finished his words.

Looking around for a moment, the man glanced at his wife. He gave her a smile of comfort and completion, forgetting for a moment, this world around them. Then he turned to face the Council.

"My lords," his voice was stern, unafraid. "My son is not afflicted by this plague you speak of. For if he was, surely one of us would have to be," he finished, gesturing between his wife and himself. "My lady, I ask that you reopen the investigation of my son and show him mercy."

Another man of the council rose to his feet upon hearing these words of testimony. "You will not speak to Lady Miriam directly, but through the Council. And now you would choose to befoul the church with your lies? Or is it the church that you accuse of lying?"

Watching the event taking place before her and hearing the words of the Council, Lauren was suddenly drawn back to the shadows of her mind, back to the place where only the darkest of secrets were held. Lauren was suddenly standing before the Council; in the very same spot she had watched Malseth. Through her eyes, she had witnessed the prosecutions laid upon her and her family. Lauren saw through faint tears as her family fought for her, but in the end, it was all the same and she was torn from her family. That was the last time she had even seen them, and now, watching the eyes of young Malseth, she knew that he would have to endure the same fate. Her tears grew at the possibility of another having to suffer as she had.

Lauren's thoughts were suddenly redirected as she watched a man emerge from the crowd and step in front of the family; he turned to face the Council. Silence befell this grand hall at the wonderment of this man as whispers grew among the Council. He seemed like a simple man, with brown hair that ran like the grass of a wild field. He had no facial hair, and his skin was surprisingly smooth. He appeared to be in his mid to late thirties, and contained a rather stocky build, a build that was rather concealed by a long overcoat. He appeared to be a genteel, whose hands rested within the confinements of his coat;

he took two steps and approached the Council.

"My lords, I ask that you let me speak a moment in their good name," he finished as he nodded toward the Tarbens.

The figure upon the foyer lingering above looked down to this dwarfed man. "And what is the name of this man who would choose to speak on the behalf of sinners?"

The man looked up for a moment before his stare returned to the Council, his eyes seeking past to Lady Miriam. "My name is Gale, and I only have but one thing to say, my lords," as he spoke, his shoulders slightly tensed; probably nerves.

"TO THE RESISTANCE!" the man screamed as his overcoat ripped open, and a jumble of cloth-covered arms flew out in an organized manner. It was moments before the Council had realized the man was holding a weapon. Cazziel had known immediately what this weapon was; a particle submachine pistol, but how would a civilian get a hold of one? The man opened fire.

For a moment the world had seemed to revert to slow motion as Lauren's mind finally caught up to the moment. The members of the Council were ripping through the air as they sought cover from the table before them. The bullets from the pistol soared through the air, effortlessly passing through the folds of cloth from the aid-seeking members of the Council. The trail of fire streaked across the table, pieces of wood glowing into the room around them. It quickly rose, leaving the table, and rising to the throne of the goddess, Miriam.

As the first bullet cracked alive from the pistol, Cazziel

had already set his instincts into motion. Tearing himself from his position, he leapt in front of Miriam, as his hand landed on her shoulder. Gently he pushed her to the floor as he watched this trail of fire leaping up from the table in their direction. The women of the chairs, Miriam's maidens, immediately rose to this threat, surrounding her as she lay upon the floor, Lauren among them.

Damn, she had thought to herself, *did Vahn send him, or is he working alone?* Lauren's mind became clustered with questions as she retained her cover, a maiden of the priestess. Instantly, her protectors rose Miriam to her feet, keeping her body hidden among their own as they attempted to rush her to safety. Blood suddenly streaked through the air in front of Lauren's eyes. Ripping her head around, her hands remained encasing Miriam's shoulders. She watched as one of her fellow maidens' body danced into a jumble of oily clothes, her scent of blood and rippling flesh infusing the air.

How could he be so naïve? Doesn't he know they have operatives working on the inside? Lauren's desperation was quickly replaced with anger.

The man continued to fire his weapon, even as he watched one of those women around Miriam crumble to the floor. The crowds behind him had watched, as within moments this audience with the Council had become a scene of horror. It was then that the crowds had realized this man might turn on them next, and so they ran. The doors immediately became flooded with people as they struggled to save their precious lives. None, however, knew the man only had one target, and he would take her no matter the cost. He gripped his pistol with the anger of an animal and the determination of a hunter. A ball of female bodies and woven silks was all he could see, even though he knew she was in there, somewhere. His eyes cocked to the right. A glimpse.

Cazziel had leapt from his position, flying through the air toward this man with the pistol. Hearing the ripping of the bullets as the air forced its way into his speeding ears, Cazziel watched at the last moment as the man's head twitched, his eyes catching a glimpse of him. A moment more and Cazziel would be upon him. Oh, how he would rid this man of his little, pathetic life. The pistol tore itself around, the barrel spinning into the view of Cazziel's eyes. No human can move that fast. With the speed of a ghost, Cazziel's hand rippled through the air, reaching out for the pistol. He would tear it from this man, and then cripple his body, one piece at a time. The weapon was gone. Cazziel's eyes quickly moved through the room around him as they finally landed where the man once stood, but he had somehow vanished now as well. Who is this man?

Cazziel heard the faint click of a trigger behind him. Without turning his head, within that same moment, he reached back his hand with a surprising speed that caught the man unaware. He watched as Cazziel's feet left the ground, spinning him into the air over his head. With a speed that almost eluded him, the man felt the ripping sensation of his pistol being robbed from his hands. Rolling up over his shoulder, he heard the sound of Cazziel landing behind him, the blunt end of the barrel driven into his back.

"First you would betray my sister," the man spoke as his voice carried over his shoulder.

Dropping with the speed of lightning, the man turned, producing the sheer reflection of a blade. Grasping its handle firmly, the man thrust it upward as Cazziel watched the contours of his body begin to dissolve into the air. Twitching inward, Cazziel caught the knife with his side, bringing in his arm and locking the man's wrist. Rotating his shoulder backward, the air was suddenly filled with a pop as the man's elbow became dislocated, the ping of the blade dropping to the floor.

". . . Your sister?" Cazziel queried, just as he brought his hand up under the man's shoulder. "How interesting. And who would this presumed *sister* be?" With the force of a giant, Cazziel pulled his arm down, the crackling of flesh and spurting blood tumbling into the air.

The man screamed in horror, and he felt the bones within his shoulders spreading farther, his skin bursting open. He could feel the sudden rupture of his flesh as his arm became ripped from his body, his blood coating the ground before them. His blood was lush and red; so very red.

As the man looked up, he structured his face to show as little pain as possible. Even now he would deny Cazziel of this pleasure, ". . . my sister," he gritted through his heavy breathing, "Keona."

An image of her small frame streaked through the back of Cazziel's thoughts she always appeared so frail. He remembered all the intimate details of her face. A small grin etched itself into the sides of his mouth.

"How sad. Such failure within the same family. Trust me, it's better this way." His voice was emotionless.

At the same moment, he thrust the barrel of the gun into the man's neck, the bluntness of the metal forcing its way beneath his skin. The sounds of crackling and splitting rose in the air, and the man began to gargle on his own fluids. He worked his mouth as if to speak, but Cazziel, while listening, heard nothing. His grin continued to grow.

Behind him, back behind the safety of the Council, the door that once passed Miriam remained only cracked now. Lauren had watched this treachery, along with the Council. How could they allow such inhumane action? Miriam had never known Keona or her brother, but she grieved them now as tears swelled within the corners of her eyes. She had felt his sadness and shared in his pain, his hatred. She wept.

~

The doors of the lab burst open as Lady Miriam hastily walked inside. She walked to the scientist in charge, with Cazziel appearing moments behind her.

"Now!" she ordered.

"My lady?"

She grabbed the computer terminal and began accessing the database. "I want the Osiris Project brought online now!"

"But, my lady," the man spoke as his eyes widened, "a week hasn't been enough. We still need more time." He looked at Cazziel for assistance. He received none.

"Would you choose to denounce the goddess?" Cazziel's voice carried a sense of disconcert.

Upon hearing his words, the scientist continued to prep the instruments around them, as did the rest of the scientists and doctors, for none of them knew what to expect. Another scientist approached Miriam as he slid in beside her.

"Here, allow me to take over, my lady," his voice was shaky as he grabbed the terminal from her shaking hands.

She turned to Cazziel for a moment before the two of them looked together toward the human-size vessel that loomed against the far wall, its contents hidden within that hazy glass. They approached it as they heard the voices around them grow in precision and speed.

"Bring the incubator online."

"It's already done, sir."

"Vitals-database . . . Give me readings!"

Miriam and Cazziel watched as their room of little mice scurried to carry out their orders. The room began to glow a faint blue as more and more monitors came to life, all in preparation for the activation of the Osiris Project.

". . . Activate the bioamplifiers."

"Sir . . . our readings are showing an 82 percent completion of the reconstruction."

Miriam's eyes were suddenly drawn to the vessel as a slight image echoed itself through the memories of her mind. A low tone spread throughout the room, almost too faint to hear, but she could hear it, and Miriam had no doubt that Cazziel could hear it as well.

"What do you think?" she asked as she stepped beside him, her shoulder brushing his chest.

"My lady," he watched with his perceptive eyes, ". . . he knows." Her head slightly cocked, her cheek slightly shifting toward his mouth.

"Sir, the serum inductors are backing up . . ."

". . . Well then, shut them down!"

". . . We can't, sir, the manual override's been activated!"

The people of the room listened as a female voice suddenly came over the lab's PA system.

"Warning, level two locks are unstable . . . warning, level two locks have been disabled."

Miriam looked back toward the icy glass, its haziness continuing to hide the contents. Was he doing this? Is he trying to revive himself? The two of them watched now as one by one, the cords attached to the container began to snap off; their precious fluid draining to the floor.

"Sir, I'm reading an 86 percent completion rate now . . . 87 percent . . . 89 percent . . . Sir, the process is actually quickening itself!"

They all watched as the ice quickly melted, steam emitting outward through the cracks, condensation rolling down the sides. The sounds of decompression flooded the room as the pressure from within was released. That hazy door, inching its way outward, slightly angled itself, and then began to ascend upward, sliding along its rails. Miriam and Cazziel watched as steam bellowed outward, the small sounds of water trickling downward from this vessel of theirs. Miriam watched with questioning eyes as a faint figure silhouetted itself through the steam. For a moment, there was no movement, and then just before the steam cleared ... His arm twitched.

"There ..."

"I see it," Cazziel finished before Miriam had the time to complete her thought.

Together they watched as the head slightly rolled, the legs twitched, the rising and falling of his chest; he was breathing. Slowly a hand reached up and grasped the edge of the vessel, deliberately caving in its metal chassis; the memory of this hand forever embedded. A foot lifted itself, followed by the movement of his leg. It lurched forward and hit the ground. The movement was so swift that the people of the room were almost thrown into shock as the figure stumbled outward, his body dropping to the floor with a deafening thud. He lay there for a moment.

A scientist approached Cazziel and spoke softly. "Sir, perhaps it still needs more time ..."

"I don't think so," Cazziel slipped in as his eyes remained on the figure lying before them.

"It surprises me that we've only discovered *him* so far," Miriam spoke in wonderment. "This must be so familiar to him."

"My lady, I'm sure this is all as it was the first time he was awakened. It is within the ravines of his memories; perhaps lost, but still there," Cazziel finished.

His hand slid up beside his head, moments before he lifted it from the floor, his face looming there briefly. Very slowly he sat up as his hair seeped downward, encasing his face. *Is he an angel?* Lauren had thought to herself, perched from her vantage point. She was taken by the beauty of this man, such a perfect face, the mirrored smoothness of a pearl. His eyes were seething, so deep, so lush; such a beautiful green. His hair was white, and the structure of his face so engaging, as though he had been sculpted from the mold of a perfectionist.

He looked down for a moment, his face looking toward the hands he held out in front of his eyes; perhaps he looked past them. "My eyes," he hesitated for a moment. "I can't see very well." He shut them as his face slightly contorted. "Why do they hurt?" His hand embraced the floor as he sat there for a moment.

Lady Miriam took a step toward the man as her eyes took in his condition. "Because it's been nearly three years since you've last used them, Evrikh." Slowly, she knelt down beside him. As she did, Cazziel' body slightly shifted; he would be ready.

Raising her hand to his cheek, Miriam embraced it and lifted his face to look into his eyes. "Do you remember anything?"

Just then, the echoes of times immemorial brushed through the edges of Evrikh's thoughts, the sensation of his eyes momentarily twitching. As Miriam knelt there with him for a moment, Cazziel slowly pulled something from his pocket; Miriam hadn't noticed. The faint chimes of silver brushing silver stretched throughout the room. That sound had transcended the memories of time, had reached such a dark forgotten period, that the sound alone had almost knocked Evrikh from where he sat. The lost images of buried times erupted into his memory and flooded his vision with their perverse urgency. Two small crosses drifted in front of his eyes, among the same chain, clinging together as their sound echoed throughout his ears.

Miriam helped him rise up as that faint sound slowly drifted through the room once more. Evrikh had seen them before, such a very long time before. Cazziel's posture had not changed as he sat there mastering his condition. Evrikh could feel his gaze burning itself into him, as though his life has wronged him in some way. Miriam, too caught up in the moment, had not paid attention to the trinket within Cazziel's hands, or the reaction it was having on Evrikh.

The image of a window suddenly flashed before his eyes; such a very small window. It was surrounded by darkness, but not on the other side. On the other side, there had been a lab. Most of the room could be seen, as the window was curved in nature. It had all looked so familiar, but why, and when? The small chime had reached his ears once more; those crosses.

"I just need you to do this one last test, then that's it for today." His voice had come from such a lost period in time; they were *his*. Evrikh watched that day as he walked off to his computers, asking him to go back to that place Evrikh had loathed so much, those same crosses hanging from his neck. Dr. Kendrick Savari.

The window suddenly returned as the room remained empty. He looked out through the glass then, still awake; was he supposed to be? His vision stole across the room as it fell upon a mirror against the far wall, a strange pod resting within its reflection. There had been so many machines and cables connected to it, that it really didn't resemble a pod at all. It was then that he realized it was about the size of a person. As Evrikh's eyes searched through this lost vision, this forgotten memory, they focused on something else; something small. Looking through the glass, toward the pod, going farther, focusing above it, his eyes rested on a plate that loomed just above a small window in the front. His eyes widened as the vision of his memory translated the words engraved in reverse: E.V.R.I.K.H., and they continued to widen as his translation carried to the small words written below: Project Phoenix Gate.

Evrikh stumbled away from Miriam as the room suddenly flashed, and this hue of color faded into the lights. He looked around for a moment as the disorientation drifted from his mind, his eyes shifting from the scientists, to Miriam, to Cazziel. His eyes still wide, turned toward Cazziel and the little trinket contained within his fingers.

"... There was another," he had spoken softly.

"Evrikh," Miriam began, "don't worry, you'll be fine. You just need some rest, and we'll inform you of everything that's happened." Her voice so smooth, so gentle.

"You remember, don't you, Evrikh?" Cazziel spoke, his eyes always hidden behind those mysterious glasses of his.

"... remember." Evrikh's eyes trailed off to that key in his hand, that small silver thing. His vision had returned and continued to look even further still. Out through the very edges of the glass, they fell upon another. The same pod, the same window; the same plate: E.V.E. was all that was written. His eyes turned to look back to Miriam, whose only concern at the moment was for him.

"... You, you were the key," his voice was that of putting the final pieces of the puzzle together.

Cazziel's hand suddenly jumped out in front of him as he jetted across the room, his hand slamming in front of Evrikh's eyes.

"THESE! YOU REMEMBER THESE!" he screamed. "Of course you do," a slight grin sneered across his lips. "I took them!"

As Evrikh watched them, his eyes were consumed by this indulgence, this gleaming color of remembrance. A man had entered the room with a certain sadness lost in his face. He was followed by a nurse.

"I have no choice, Arianna, they're not ready for this. They were never ready for cold fusion, how could they handle this?! This is my life, but in today's world, it cannot be."

"But, Kendrick, there has to be another way. Let him live his life as he was, before any of this," she pleaded.

"I love him just as you do! But this lab will be shut down. It will be secured and locked down; buried in the end." Kendrick's voice was full of despair, perhaps anger.

As he listened to the conversation, the door suddenly opened. Both Arianna and Kendrick looked toward the door, but at first this would-be assailant was hidden by the confinements of the window. Moments later Evrikh saw that it was a boy, probably no more than thirteen or fourteen. As he stepped closer to Kendrick, he looked at the boy as though he was confused. The boy had tears in his eyes as they looked from Arianna to Kendrick.

"Cazziel," Kendrick began, *"what are you doing up?"*

Evrikh watched as the tears within his eyes continued to grow; indulging himself in this hidden memory.

"That most certainly is a question, isn't it, Dad?"

The memory suddenly flashed, and moments later he was staring at Cazziel.

"Yeah, you remember now." Slowly Cazziel lowered his hand as he stepped away from the other two.

"What do you want him to remember, Cazziel?" slight annoyance seeping into her words.

"You've always done what you were meant to do, my lady, simply because that's what you were meant to do. However, you never awakened until the Great Darkness," his voice carried off to the far wall. He then stopped; his body horizontal to theirs. "Do you have any idea what he put me through?" Evrikh watched as his grin grew sharp. "WHAT DID HE EXPECT?"

The memory flashed once more. *"I heard what you and Doctor Arianna said to each other,"* little Cazziel told him.

"He threw me aside when he started with you!" Cazziel's voice was so full of anger. "Said he found a better way to complete the project. He was actually working on a plan to make his previous projects 'disappear.'" Cazziel slowly smiled as his eyes looked toward the floor. "But I wouldn't disappear. He had you make the others disappear, but I wouldn't let you make me disappear."

Evrikh watched as Cazziel slowly trailed off toward one of the monitors that continued to flash information across its screen. "I was the first, you know. But before that, I was a normal boy just like yourself, Evrikh." He gently placed his hand on the side of the monitor. "I even had a family once."

"Cazziel, what are you talking about?" Miriam had asked. "Evrikh doesn't need this confusion. Let him rest for now," her annoyance increasing at Cazziel's theatrics.

"You were never meant for him!" Cazziel retaliated. "You and I were completed at the same time. He was the first one to be made whole, for use without the help of another." His eyes left Evrikh and returned to Miriam's. "YOU WERE DESIGNED FOR ME!" Cazziel suddenly ripped the monitor from its place, throwing it across the room.

The scientists and doctors ran through the doors as small debris and sparks sprang to life from the now-destroyed monitor. Lauren watched from above as this hidden story unfolded itself before her eyes. She had never known any of them, with the exception of Miriam, but she knew this was what she was to report and the reason why Vahn had sent her.

"Cazziel, why are you doing this?" Miriam had momentarily forgotten her concern for Evrikh.

"You see, the problem was that Evrikh was never completed, or I suppose you could say, fully developed. Imagine God as a child, with no idea of what he's capable of. Furthermore, how does any one person begin to teach a god how to be a god? That's what Dr. Savari saw in you; fear." Cazziel had stepped over to another monitor. "But you, my lady, Miriam, had forsaken me. Instead, you became so obsessed with this perversion of yours that it became the only truth you'd accept. And then by freeing him, you showed him exactly everything he wasn't prepared to handle, and it drove him crazy; just as it did before!"

Before!

Flashes of blood soared in front of Evrikh's eyes, and he heard muffled screams of Gavin lost to the bowels of his history. There were many of them then, at least eleven. Miriam was the only one whom he engineered from the start. But something happened back then, something vicious that Evrikh's mind battled to forget.

Just as Cazziel placed his hand upon the monitor, he drove it down fiercely, the monitor shattering along the floor. The pieces of glass reflected the lights above, and for a moment, Evrikh caught a glimpse; someone was watching.

"Evrikh, do you even remember your life before everything they did to us? You had a family once too." The smallest of grins curved onto his lips; he was taking pleasure in this.

The realities and memories passing through his mind had suddenly come to a halt, as though a computer had just crashed. Evrikh's mind was staring at an image that had been lost for over a thousand years. They were on their way back home from school then; Evrikh was only eight then, *he* was eleven. He had watched for a moment as this image of such a forgotten past had reeled into a video. Evrikh was sitting beside a building crouched and holding his stomach, the result of two older boys who had beaten him up. Then as he opened his eyes, he watched as the other two boys were beating up his brother. He had told them to leave Evrikh alone, even jumped in the middle, attempting to save him. Evrikh continued to watch as they beat his brother's body. Minutes later he had fallen to the ground. In light of their accomplishments, the boys stood proud of their victory, and then turned to leave. As his eyes left them, they turned to his older brother who was now curled up on the ground holding himself.

Standing up, Evrikh walked over to him and knelt down as he placed his hand upon his brother's shoulder. As he sat up, Evrikh watched the tears fall from his eyes, then cry. His face was pale, his eyes tired, and his body was shaking. Helping him to his feet, they started to hobble away, but not just before he had remembered what his brother had told him back then.

"Evrikh, whatever you do, Dad always says we can never be slaves to something we know is wrong. We must always be who we are, and nothing else. To be anything else is to fail in everything."

"All right, Cazziel, I promise. But we should get you home to Dad. You don't look very well."

"After the War of Ruin, I guess you could say that we were all lost to each other. Now, let's go ahead and fast-forward a couple hundred years . . ." Cazziel took a step back into the light, "when the Council of Aurora discovered the Phoenix Gate through the journals; the only discovery they focused on was Evrikh!" Cazziel's finger involuntarily jumped out and pressed itself into Evrikh's temple. "And just like a programmed robot, you regurgitated some old memories, and since that moment, believed you were meant to be with Evrikh." Cazziel stepped away and his eyes carried off along the wall, trailing upward. "I have had this conversation with you in my head more times than I could possibly hope to count. I just can't seem to wrap my head around it, Miriam." His eyes turned to hers as he pulled his eyeglasses from his face.

Cazziel's eyes were concealed by nothing but blackness. No definition was even visible; did he even have eyes, ever have eyes? As Miriam and Cazziel stared at each other, their gaze locked, Miriam's mind continued to flood with her own memories that had been lost all those years ago. She had detested Evrikh back when she was first awakened. Even though she had slept for so long, her ears were alive that dreadful day; memories of a project that was deemed superior. Miriam was created before any work had started with Cazziel, the only one of the three to be truly created. But they were brothers. How could Dr. Savari do that to his own children?

Standing up beside Evrikh, Miriam took a step away while her face lingered down at his crouched body. Her own realization of the past had left her momentarily speechless. Cazziel's gaze remained only on Miriam.

"My lady, one gift our father had granted me was to see the world as it truly is; the energy that is around us, the matter that creates us. A side effect he forgot to mention was that my eyes would become useless. But, Miriam, how I wish you could see yourself as I do right now." Cazziel's voice became slight; withdrawn. "Such confusion; such glorious rage. It grows within you. Can you feel it, Miriam? It's almost blinding. The three of us are of the same puzzle, the difference being it takes both you and I to make up the whole that Evrikh already is."

"How could I have let myself become so diluted?" Miriam continued to search her memories for answers.

Cazziel took a few steps toward Miriam as his stare remained unwavering. "How strange it must feel to know that you have spent the greater part of your life searching for something that you loath; for something that you detest, and somehow not even remembering it."

"That's enough, Cazziel!" Miriam's expression had changed, bitter.

He turned, only to be standing beside Miriam a moment later; a speed only this little peculiar race of theirs had shared. As his hand slid up toward her lips, he let it fall along the crevice of her neck only to outline the silhouette of the softest cloud.

"Miriam, I have belonged to you my entire life. You have neglected our purpose, our glory, and our destiny. And so, my lady, now I must be set free." His hand had clamped down around her neck as Miriam felt the pressure of his thumbs sliding under her jaw.

Upon feeling this steel clamp around her throat, Miriam became enraged and her arms shot up, striking Cazziel along his face, both hands gripping his. Evrikh watched as her expression began to grow wild.

"And now this beauty of yours changes again, Miriam. Can you see it?" Her hands pleaded with the iron lock, yet it remained frozen. "... It's fear." Raising up his left arm,

Cazziel twitched his wrist exposing a strange syringe. Lifting it very carefully, he set the needle behind Miriam's ear. "... I had loved you." As he finished his whisper, the needle glided into her flesh, and her eyes widened as she felt the warm sensation violate the back of her neck. While pulling out the needle, Cazziel stepped backward, releasing the grip he had placed around her neck.

As Evrikh slowly stood up, he realized that Cazziel had forgotten about him, it would seem; or perhaps had already decided that he was less of a threat. Miriam had to catch her breath for a minute before gaining enough of her voice back to speak, yet she hesitated for a moment while her hand rubbed the slight burn spreading across her neck.

"Cazziel," her voice was heavy, "... What was in that syringe?!" She lifted her eyes to meet those emotional blurs of his. "What have you done?!"

"Something new, my lady, which I promise has worked on every test subject we've inoculated." Cazziel screamed at another computer, exploding it into the room. "And now, Miriam, you will feel repentance, you will feel abandoned, you will feel neglected, as I have felt."

Evrikh's mind had already made him aware of all the potential exits around the room, but never truly leaving the threat of Cazziel. Yet through all this, a single thought had still lingered above them; who was it that had found all this so interesting?

"You see, Miriam, it is a serum that works on the cellular level. But I suppose it would be more exact to say ... breaks down to the cellular level."

THE PHOENIX GATE

Evrikh watched for a moment as an expression of pain slightly grazed Miriam's face. If what Cazziel was saying was true, then he posed even more of an increasing threat.

As this fairy tale of a story unfolded before Lauren's eyes, she remained well aware that this Evrikh had somehow known of her. For him to just gaze up like that . . . Who was he? Lauren decided it'd be best to finish this conclusion of Miriam and Cazziel, but wise to leave soon afterward.

"That burning is starting to feel more like an unwanted stretch, huh? Go ahead, my lady, stretch," Cazziel spoke with the same grin he had shared with Evrikh so many times before. "As the virus spreads, we've noticed that the skin is usually the first to be affected, soon followed by the ligaments and tendons."

Miriam stumbled forward as the burning within her had continued to grow. Looking up, she watched as her eyes filled with water. "Cazziel, how could you do this to me?" She lingered forward, falling to her knees. Looking down at herself, she watched as the flesh of her arms slowly began to hang, as though slipping from the muscle beneath it.

Looking at the closest exit, a door not more than ten feet or so to his right, Evrikh's eyes returned to Miriam. Only a few moments had passed, and now there she was, resting on her knees, the skin of her arms and hands slacking like a loose blanket. As she lifted her face to Cazziel, Evrikh could barely see her eyes as her forehead started to sink over them; her cheeks running like some unused pastry mix.

"Why, Cazziel?" she asked as blood began to run from her eyes.

Cazziel watched as her skin slid away from her fingers, her nails dropping to the floor. "Because like the rest of the world, Miriam, you share their fate." Her nails had already vanished before they hit the ground. "You see, Evrikh, this serum of ours breaks you down to something even less than the air we breathe." He turned to look at him for a moment. "You wanted Miriam since the first time you saw her, Evrikh, and in moments, you'll be breathing her." Cazziel's stare returned to the terrified Miriam. "Tell me, Evrikh, how does she taste?"

Screaming from where she sat, Miriam lunged at Cazziel with a reserved speed. Almost laughing, Cazziel simply stepped to the side and Evrikh watched as Miriam blew past him, tumbling forward and colliding into his arms. Twisting sideways, they both roared to the floor and Miriam slid a few feet past. Quickly rolling over, Evrikh looked at her as she lay there motionless. Moving toward her, he turned her over, encasing her head and shoulders within his arms. Raising his hand to her hair, Evrikh pushed it aside to see her face, only to watch the hair just vanish from the small breeze alone. This Miriam he now looked at was not the Miriam he had known; how her beauty had blinked away.

"And now," her voice had become loose, "he will take your life as well."

Even now, she would defy him? . . . This disgusting, incomplete mistake? As Cazziel sat there watching, Evrikh leaned in closer to Miriam's ear.

"You are mistaken, my dear. I'm afraid it is the rest of the world that will follow you to wherever it is you are going." Then, just before he pulled his head away from hers, Evrikh blew a gentle kiss into her ear, and watched as it rippled within her head, bursting into a soft reddish breeze erupting from the other side. Miriam's face contorted with pain, her whispering screams hauntingly familiar. Evrikh set her body on the floor and rose in disgust, his mind continuously aware of Cazziel.

Does it truly have to be this way? Look at her . . . being erased right in front of us; like Gavin and the others. Who're we . . . Who the hell are any of us?!

"For a genius, I have spent centuries contemplating how our father could have created such a blind, ignorant creature. And now that she is gone, I find that I am left with even less of an answer." Cazziel turned to look in Evrikh's direction as he slowly revealed another needle of the same serum. "I was not created to destroy you, Miriam, our father, or anyone, for that matter, only to take life as it's needed. You see, Evrikh, that's the fate of the omega . . . You bring ending." Cazziel's eyes looked back at Miriam whose body was convulsing rather than squirming. "And now I believe she is past the point of pain. It must feel more like a dream to her now, a release of the world around her." As he finished, Cazziel's eyes carried down to the other needle within his hand, ". . . should I join her? I have loved her, much the same way I believe you feel for your Thea."

Taking a step back, Miriam's body had disappeared into her clothes, nothing more than a faint cloud to be blown away now. So quickly she had brought confusion to Evrikh's life, and so quickly she has left him with it. Could she have had answers? No, no answers, or at least there would not be any now.

A memory suddenly flashed through his eyes, a memory of that field and those who watched him. *"Look at him ..."*

Evrikh took another step back as his eyes screamed toward Cazziel's direction. Was it he ... that voice? *"He's just like all the others, trying to control you ... trying to own you."* Taking another step backward, his foot slipped across the icy broken glass of the monitors. Catching himself as his palms slammed into the floor, Evrikh's head flew back up in anticipation of Cazziel's attack, yet he stood fast. Why? Why would he choose to watch him like this, rather than attack when his opportunity is clearly before him?

Standing there for a moment, Cazziel watched as he slowly rose back up to his feet. "And yet, Evrikh, there is only one question that I have longed to ask you since the day I took these," with a sluggish toss, the tiny trinkets their father had worn around his neck so many years ago was sliding up against his feet. "Why, brother? Why would you choose to live and kill the rest of us?"

Kneeling down, Evrikh took the trinkets into his hand. Rising back up, his body jolted as another forgotten memory burst into his head and flooded his thoughts. His hand gripped the trinkets harder as he watched these lost thoughts play out before his eyes. They were young then, Cazziel and he, Gavin, Karene, Ganth, Wesler, Thanes, all of them; a big happy family with their father Kendrick, because each other was all they had. Their family had always moved around too much to build any kind of lasting friendships within the communities. Cazziel and he had bonded, bonded as only brothers knew how to, and the connection to their father was no different. Evrikh remembered the games they all used to play and the stories they'd tell each other. Then he remembered his laugh. Cazziel had laughed once, such a long time ago. But his laughter had stopped, and Evrikh had suddenly remembered the events of that day so long ago.

~

During the experiments, it was the first time Evrikh's shift had gone completely through. The stress on his body was more than he could physically handle, and it felt as though something in his mind had burst. It rose from the depths of his darkness, man's oldest of traditions: madness. Their father ran around frantically looking for a way to stop him after his return from the other side. Not being welcomed by the others, Evrikh's mind was flooded with thoughts of how his brethren and he were mistakes, damned since birth, and like a thorn in the side of man, had to be removed. He traveled the building from room to room slaughtering their brothers and sisters; some were sleeping, others were awake, almost as if waiting.

Gavin was the first. He had welcomed Evrikh into his room as his emotionless body had walked right up to him. Slamming his hand around his head, Evrikh stuffed his fingers into Gavin's eye sockets like a kid trying to remove a coin from a jar. While Gavin screamed in horror, Evrikh simply laughed, ripping his jaw from his head and throwing it to the floor; he had asked Gavin to laugh with him. Evrikh tore his eyes open in hopes of not reliving these images, but the words of their father could still be heard within the shadows of his ears.

"Evrikh, I wish there was something I could do, but there was never meant to be two of you." Their father's eyes were so very full of tears as he spoke.

Grabbing his arm with his childish hands, Evrikh searched his eyes for some kind of answer, yet they were void of any. *"But, Dad, Cazziel and I are all that each other have in this world!"*

"No matter what happens, though, either of you would always have me, my son."

When Evrikh had returned, something within him had changed. What had he seen, what had happened to him on the other side? Kendrick had seen the dangerous madness that now lurked beneath his eyes, and Evrikh had never known; had their father used him for it, or was he terrified of it?

~

How could he have placed such a burden on him, given him such a choice. "COULDN'T HE SEE THAT I WAS ONLY A CHILD?!"

"How so very often it seems that these memories come back to you," Cazziel spoke dully.

"Our father loved you! He loved us all, Cazziel! But he stuck me with that decision, and I was only a boy! WHAT WOULD YOU HAVE DONE? WOULD

YOU HAVE CHOSEN DEATH?!" Evrikh took another step backward as he felt the edges of one of the desks brush up against the back of his legs.

"Your answer is this? I have waited centuries, and your answer is that you were *only a boy*?" Cazziel's smirk had changed now, and his familiar rage was beginning to return to his aura. "All that I had given you, all that I had burdened for you, and you still handed me a fate such as that? I WAS THERE, EVRIKH!!!" He finished as he took another step toward him. "I watched that smile spread across your face. Our father abandoned us, and you walked with him. This cannot be forgiven, Evrikh, and it will *not* be forgiven!" Cazziel planted his feet as though an animal ready to pounce. "Unfortunately, I was unable to reach our father before your little vacation into Crazy-Land, and then your little disappearing act. Hmm," Cazziel grinned, "a healer, a magician, and a scientist; bravo, Father, bravo. But you see, Evrikh, every story has a way of finding its own ending, and I believe it's about time we find ours."

Peering at the door behind Cazziel, Evrikh could almost taste the illusion of freedom. A slight giggle rose from within his throat. "You speak as if I ask for your forgiveness. Fact is, we were used as puppets, and they laced us with responsibility so that they wouldn't have to deal with it themselves. As a boy I couldn't choose death any more than an ocean choosing to ripple." Evrikh stood fast, his fingers gripping the edge of the desk behind him. "As for our little story, I suppose an ending would be nice, Cazziel, but then, who're we to write the final pages?"

Evrikh's body ripped itself from the desk into the air with the crackling speed of lightning; the desk launching into the wall behind them. Cazziel slipped himself to the left as Evrikh's body came lunging past. *Even in such a weakened state you are a force to be reckoned with,* Cazziel thought to himself. His right arm came swiftly around to catch Evrikh's legs as they trickled past. In moments his needle would reach Evrikh's calf, and like Miriam, erase him from existence. But then, a hand, neither Evrikh's nor Cazziel's, but he had caught a glimpse of it before his body had slammed into the wall beside the door. Evrikh longed to see who would've done such a foolish thing, though perhaps another time. Gripping the doorway, he threw himself past it, leaving the confinement of the room behind.

Feeling an extraordinarily strong grip around his wrist, Cazziel watched as his vengeance had fled from him yet again. Pulling his arm from the grip that restrained him, Cazziel turned to face the eyes of not one, but two. "You are a fool!" A moment had passed before a realization had hit Cazziel . . . "We've met before."

"Yes," the man replied as he stepped toward the door. "We believed him to be dead before, and now he is just a whisper to us." The man turned to face Cazziel. "And because of your foolishness, the whisper of him will grow. It will grow past the tales that mothers share with their children, past the legends of men. His birth was the beginning, and now his rise will be the end."

It was then that Cazziel felt another hand grasp his wrist, pulling the needle from his fingers. He stepped back in awe of this strength resonating from this woman. "And what did you plan on doing with this, Cazziel?" she asked him stepping away.

"If not for your intervention it would have killed him."

"If his death is what you seek, then why didn't you leave him to die before?"

"Miriam's idea." Cazziel's eyes turned to where her body once lay. "Her perversion and hers alone."

"Lashara, dispose of that. We don't need Evrikh becoming more of a threat than he already is." Virgil's voice was as if he had already known.

Before tossing the syringe to the floor, Lashara gave a questionable look to Virgil. "It was Seraph. He had shared this knowledge with me prior to our departure." Satisfied, Lashara dropped the syringe, shattering its contents about the floor.

"It is you who are a fool. It was luck that had brought Evrikh to his knees before. And now," Cazziel's hand gestured toward the shattered syringe, "perhaps you've wasted my last chance."

A smirk spread across Virgil's face. "You speak as a boy who peers through the veil of knowledge, yet understands nothing."

~ ~ ~

As Lauren reached the main entrance to the west wing of the Church of Divinity, she ran down the stone steps, keeping a watchful eye on the main doors lingering to her side. She slid in behind some brush, hidden among the shadows as her eyes looked about for possible threats.

Given what she had just witnessed, security seemed obscurely minimal. No matter, she would use this to her advantage. Lauren knew that it was imperative this information be relayed to Vahn. Leaping from the shadows of the brush, Lauren ran down the main steps of the church; if she could just reach the main gate. What Lauren did not know was that for a fraction of a second, Evrikh remembered that someone was watching.

Lauren fell hard to her side, her shoulder slamming rigidly into the steps from the momentum, her breath lost to the thump of her body. Seconds later after catching her breath, she looked up to see her assailant.

"Did you enjoy that show of ours?" Evrikh's voice was that of having a mouse by its tail.

Lauren knew that if she ran it would mean her death; but if she stayed, it could mean something worse.

Evrikh's hand slammed into her head, palming it and lifting Lauren to her feet. "Now isn't that interesting, to leave in such hurry implies someone else is expecting you. I'll have to apologize for that; you'll probably be running a little late."

* * * *

CHAPTER 13
~ Ascension ~

THEA WAS ATTENDING business in the small town of Lin'Diel when she received word that Vahn requested her presence back in Lenubus. It was only hours before her preparations were complete, and she paid farewell to her friends. It wasn't safe to take a direct route, rarely would be. For now, the Council believed the Resistance to be dead, and Thea saw no reason to give up this advantage of theirs. So instead, she headed out through the Canyon of Balthus, toward its grand river. Her people were very precise and very quick when traveling this river as she has used it many times in the past few years. Thea knew that she would arrive in ample time to have this meeting with Vahn.

The Council was unaware of it, but the whole town of Lin'Diel had belonged to the Resistance. It was founded by her kind over one hundred and fifty years ago, when its first citizens settled here. The people back then knew that the protection of the canyon and its river, along with the isolation from the rest of society, would allow them to live peacefully out here. But within her heart Thea knew that this little utopia of theirs would not last forever. The Council of Aurora continues to grow in strength, and with it, expand. It's only a matter of time before its hand reaches out to Lin'Diel and discovers its secrets. Thea turned to look back toward the town as they began their journey down the river; but before that time comes, she would indulge this little escape while it lasts. A slow smile crept its way across her lips, almost allowing her to taste the reluctant sweetness of satisfaction.

It had only been half a day's travel when Thea reached the periphery of Lenubus. As she began to walk the streets, she breathed in the rich aroma of stone, the city; pine, the forest, no doubt; and something else, something odd. For a moment she coddled this scent, this slight smell that tingled along the edges of her memories, however, they were not memories of the city; something older. Thea thought it wise to keep this in mind as she headed for her destination.

She made a quick pit stop by her place to change clothes and drop off the burdens of her traveling. Making a quick notion of the time, Thea felt she had made it back in time for a warm shower as well. If Vahn had waited half a day, she saw no reason why he couldn't wait another hour.

As the warm water strewn itself onto Thea's body, it practically revived her. The delicious kneading of the water accompanied by the intense heat was more than enough to help her slip from the reality of the Council.

Then with the turn of a handle, it had all ended. As she slipped into her new clothes she turned her thoughts to more pressing matters and this meeting with Vahn. Vahn knew that it wouldn't be safe to meet in the church at a time like this, so Thea was to meet him in an apartment three blocks away. Beakon Ave. A safe heaven he had picked up a few months back, registered to a Rephil Conus, the guardian of Phelineous. He had frequented Lenubus when Vahn had first been assigned here. As Vahn's importance grew within the Council, Rephil's visits had grown less frequent. Vahn had passed it off to the owners of the apartment that during his visits Rephil would be staying there, and with that, no questions were asked. There would be no concern or inquiries, should the wrong people come asking. Vahn had taken care of it.

As Thea walked up the steps, she used her mind to feel the air around her, but there seemed nothing unusual. Grabbing the handle and turning, an image of Vahn had flickered through her thoughts along with a smile across her face; he had been waiting longer than an hour. Stepping inside, she removed her jacket and placed it on the table beside the door. Breezing through the kitchen, she could taste the bouquet of lunch Vahn had already eaten; her mouth watered.

"I didn't mean to keep you waiting, Vahn," her voice softened as she came around the corner into the quaint living room.

"Didn't mean to, yet you did."

And there he was, sitting in a chair against the wall, enigmatic. Staring at his face for a moment, Thea couldn't tell if he was feeling anxiety or battling constipation.

"Hey, you feeling all right?" she asked as she pulled a chair adjacent to him.

"I have a concern for Lauren. I've heard nothing for thirteen days. However, I have heard that there was a disturbance at the Church of Divinity." Vahn raised a hand to his chin as though to make a gesture to an invisible dream. "The details weren't very clear, mostly covered up, I'm sure. The most I've gotten from it was that there was an attack of some sort."

"One of our people?"

"No, of that, I'm sure."

"Then perhaps an individual group," Thea started as she rose, walking toward the window. "But that would be impossible. Our people aren't even strong enough to assault that church yet."

Vahn looked up to Thea, "... I heard the attack came from the inside." His stare lowered. "Perhaps you understand my concern now."

Thea turned to look back at Vahn. "Maybe yes, but Lauren is smart enough to know that if her position were to be compromised, she would terminate her mission," Thea finished, crossing her arms. "You are right about one thing, though." Her stare loomed into the distance. "Thirteen days is a long time to wait, with no word."

Thea's attention was immediately drawn back out the window. "Vahn!" was the only word she spoke.

"I know!" he added, rising to his feet. "I feel it too."

As they turned to walk back toward the door, Thea picked up her jacket from the table; Vahn quickly followed. After opening the door, Thea stepped outside and proceeded down the steps, halting herself about halfway. Her hesitation was so sudden, Vahn found himself tripping into her back; the blindness of her clothes brushing his eyes.

"Thea," Vahn said abruptly, "perhaps a bit of a warning, or just slowing down, would be much more . . ." As Vahn rose to his feet, his voice just faded. The two of them peered down to the last step . . . and there stood Lauren. A bit ravaged, but more or less it was Lauren. Within those moments the three of them stood speechless. Thea had already begun probing her mind, trying to sift through all her confusion, excitement, and fear. There was the church, Lady Miriam, Cazziel, the hearing, and Evrikh.

"EVRIKH?!" Thea blurted.

"Who?" Lauren questioned breathily.

"The man you saw." Thea gazed over her shoulder to peer at Vahn momentarily. "You may not recognize his face, but your memories reek of his presence. Come." She then turned, "We'll talk inside."

"Wait!" Lauren started. "If that's him you're speaking of, then he's alive." Her voice was shaking, but stern, "He's alive, and he knows of you." Lauren's eyes gleamed to Thea.

Thea proceeded back to the door. "Come, we finish inside."

As they continued into the small apartment, Thea passed the table her jacket once rested on and went into the living room. As Vahn followed close behind, he found himself running into her back once again. Stumbling over the folds of her clothes, Vahn managed to catch himself on the other side of the doorway.

"Damn it! Thea, this is a hell of a bad habit to get into," Vahn finished as he turned to face the living room.

"Now, now, Thea. Why cut her off when she has so much more to tell?" His hand had gestured to Lauren.

Vahn's attention was immediately drawn to the chair he realized that Thea's been staring at it since they first walked in. Then all they heard was Lauren's whisper behind them, "I'm sorry."

~

"Bravo, Lauren, bravo," Evrikh said as he rose to his feet. "Oh, don't be so shocked. Your eyes maybe disbelieving, but your heart knew; your soul knew." His gaze carried over to Lauren. "Wow, you should be proud, you didn't even flinch once."

After standing there for a moment, Evrikh's eyes traveled their way toward Vahn. "You and I will know each other soon enough."

"The Council did this?" Thea asked, her eyes remaining steady.

"Naturally," he began as he turned to look out the window. "The fools! Even in death, I would remain a puppet to them. But you know what I've discovered, Thea?" Evrikh turned from the window. "That in death, we still dream," his eyes finding their way to Vahn once more. "Would you like to know my dreams?"

"Not in particular. After all, you seem like the kind of guy totally enraptured in bad juju. I mean, I've heard of guys with unusually bad luck, even some that trouble seems to just flock to. But when it comes to you, I hear you're the epiphany of it all," Vahn finished as he slipped his coat around Savior.

Evrikh stared for a moment before looking back to Thea. "You know, somehow, I thought you managed to escape all this idiocy."

"Maybe all this idiocy is what separates the sane." Thea's hand gestured toward Vahn. "Vice the insane." Her hand returned in Evrikh's direction.

Evrikh lowered his head, looking at his left hand. Not a single faltered print, not the smallest scar. Like his existence, his hand was perfect. How could he be anything but?

"Kind of an oxymoron, don't you think?" Evrikh began. "If I was indeed IN sane, I would be the very essence of sanity, right?" He made a mental note of Vahn, who was sliding across the room to his left. "And you know what I've decided through all my rational thoughts?" His eyes were at a dead stare into Thea's, "That this will all stop. The Resistance, the Council, the people; even if it must all begin anew. It's not that I want to, just that it's necessary."

Vahn came to a halt as he reached the other side of the room, his hand resting fast beside Savior. "Now I know the world's got some bad habits; very much like Thea's walking emergency brake. But, hey, with no bad habits, there would be no good either, right?"

"Indeed," Evrikh slipped in as his glare journeyed past Thea, to Lauren.

With the reflex of a slingshot, Savior was pulled from its holster and Vahn fired a single round. Vahn's eyes widened as he realized he was aiming at the ceiling and his wrist was locked within Evrikh's hand. Probing his mind for only a moment Evrikh could sense his amazement. He had never witnessed such speed.

"You're an idiot, and slow. I'm amazed you've managed to keep yourself alive this long." His voice ended with a sneer.

"Maybe so, but not many men can claim they have a fourth leg."

As the two of them looked down, there was Vahn's other hand, with Godhand resting firmly in its grip. Just as Vahn pulled the trigger, he let out a marred grunt as his arm was twisted to the side, Godhand now resting on the floor at his feet. He then realized Evrikh was standing beside him. How can any man move that fast?!

"I can see that my presence here is a bad idea." Vahn's voice shook from the pain of his contorted wrist. "You see, Evrikh, this is one of those bad habits we talked about earlier." Vahn suddenly felt the strain on his arm tighten.

Evrikh turned to see Thea who had been watching him so very carefully the entire time. "Evrikh, you know what I did these past three years you spent sleeping?" Her lips parted with the deliciousness of secrets. What suddenly appeared to be at the same moment, Evrikh felt the lustful breath of her whisper behind his ear. "I trained."

Evrikh felt her arm come up under his, and then with the grace of a butterfly flapping its wing, she tore him from Vahn and threw him across the room. He managed to regain his balance about midflight, but not before crashing through the far wall.

"Well, dear Evrikh, you don't seem to be your usual punctual self," Thea added.

"I did say thank you, right?" Vahn trailed off.

As Evrikh rose to his feet, he realized Thea might pose more of a threat than he expected. He brushed some of the dust from his chest. "Perhaps you could ask your friends if you and I could have a moment alone."

A remaining silence overran the room as Thea then turned to look at Vahn. "Please, wait outside with Lauren."

"Thea!"

"Vahn," she paused a moment, "if I need you, you'll be right outside."

Brushing his coat open, Vahn replaced his guns into their holsters. Evrikh watched as he walked between him and Thea, placing his arm around Lauren's shoulder, and preceded toward the door. He turned back to Thea with one last glance, "... just outside."

As they closed the doors behind themselves, Thea turned back to look at Evrikh. Probing her thoughts for only a moment, he couldn't help but sense that she was somehow more relaxed. A ripple of sadness echoed across those lovely eyes of hers.

"Evrikh, why are you doing this?" She carried herself over to the chair and sat down.

As he took a seat across from her, he leaned forward, forever captivated by her beauty. "Thea, it doesn't have to be this way. You can still come with me."

"To where, Evrikh? To what? To bring the world to its

knees?" Her voice laced with sorrow.

"YES! Yes, if that's what it takes!" he finished, rising to his feet. "The Council would choose to use me as a tool to own the world. If not them, then the Resistance, to bring themselves above the Council!" Flashes of anger surged through his body as Evrikh turned to glance out the window.

"The only way I can think of how to cure this illness of man is to remove the scale, rather than trying to tip it. It allows the world the chance to start anew." He found his eyes seeking the floor as despair gripped the edges of his thoughts.

"Evrikh," Thea rose to her feet, "there is another path." Those four words that trickled from her mouth flowed to his ears like the sweet scent of a blossom that brings the morning air. The love that the two shared once, shattering the dreams of the heavens, somehow found its way back to the corners of his thoughts. The kisses that defined the beauty of the sky; her laugh that echoed the splendor of autumn; this woman was once the closest piece of a soul he ever could've had.

"Thea," Evrikh reached up to hold her hand within his own, "I wish I knew how. But the Resistance, the Council, they've flooded every crevice of the world. We'd never be able to live the life that we both want. But nor can the Council be allowed to own the world."

"So we handle it," she began as Evrikh stepped away from his chair to stand beside her. "One step at a time . . . together." She lifted her eyes to within inches of his, her lips a mere breathe away. "We can teach the world to be free, Evrikh, and in doing so, free ourselves."

Thea's lips grazed the edges of Evrikh's; the satin touch of a wild strawberry. The intimacy of his memories flashed across his eyelids as he indulged in this delicious tease of hers. His hands suddenly gripped her shoulders as Evrikh pulled her from him.

"Wait, there's some—"

Evrikh's side ripped into pain as his body was sent across the room, slamming into the other wall. He quickly stood up as he planted his feet into the ground. "YOU!"

"You?" Thea followed with a look of surprise.

The front door suddenly blew off the hinges as Vahn and Lauren came running inside, Vahn's hand gracefully thrusting Godhand to the ready. "Geez, you people are like roaches!"

"Vahn, relax," the words came from the side of her mouth though her eyes did not waver.

"Why are you here?"

Virgil's hand lowered from Evrikh's direction as he regained his posture; the woman Lashara standing behind him. As Evrikh collected himself, he watched as Virgil turned to speak to Thea.

"I hoped our meetings would have ended three years ago, but apparently your fate has a different story to tell."

"He's still here," Lashara added as she stepped forward.

"I remember you!" Evrikh's anger rose in the bowels of his mind. "You're no different than the Council or the Resistance; just more puppeteers looking to control the world with your strings!"

There was a flash of light and suddenly Thea was

standing in front of him. "Together, Evrikh; together."

His anger slowly dissipated as they stood there, looking into each other's eyes. It was almost as if Thea had forgotten the world around them; she would not allow this madness to grip him again. She would lose him to nothing but her own heart. And so she simply stared into his eyes, would stare until she was satisfied that Evrikh knew her allegiance was with him. Almost stunned with the amount of conviction within her eyes, Evrikh almost felt that if he had found a place in the world, it would be beside her.

Feeling a sudden intense soothing burn, Evrikh quickly looked down, to see Thea removing her hand from his side. The hole remained in his shirt, but his side had been completely healed. It was immediately impossible to tell whether Virgil had ever attacked him in the first place. After Thea had felt satisfied, she turned to look back at Virgil and Lashara.

"Once again, why are you here?"

"We believe that the fate of your people rests with Evrikh's life," Virgil turned to face him, "or death."

Lashara's attention drew to Virgil with a queer look on her face. "Weren't you the one who used to preach to me about getting involved?"

"Lashara, we're not doing this right now."

Vahn and Lauren stepped over toward Thea and Evrikh. Just as they reached them, Evrikh watched Lauren's eyes trail toward him. He leaned to her ear, "You can relax now."

"So, Thea, who are they?" Vahn whispered.

"They're—"

"We're foreseers," Vahn interjected. "We're just here to make sure your history plays out the way it was meant to. And to maybe give it the right nudge every now and then."

"You mean manipulate!" Evrikh said, leaning into Thea.

Virgil's face grew to a seriousness Lashara rarely saw. "YOU CAN NOT—"

"Maybe," Thea started, raising her hand up in front of her, "you should just go."

"Fine then," Virgil collected himself. "We'll remain at a distance. In return, we ask that you remember, if *we* found you, Evrikh, then *he'll* find you."

"Are we to report this then?" Lashara whispered to Virgil.

"No, the Circle sent us here as though they already knew. It seems there's more players to this game than we're aware of. For now, we'll watch."

Virgil turned to give the four of them a quick glance. "Evrikh, if you're not to be the end of these people, realize then that the end is still coming."

As he finished speaking, they watched as the air around Virgil and Lashara seemed to liquefy, and then suddenly, a bright flash. Moments later the air became still again, and it was as though they were never there.

"All right, now, who even has the slightest idea of what the hell is going on?" Vahn started as he began looking around.

Lauren grabbed a seat at the side of the room as

Evrikh could sense her thoughts. She didn't know if she could trust him, who those people were, or if she could actually trust Thea. That was when Vahn stepped back in. He took Lauren by the hand and knelt down beside her. Sensing her growing despair, he would comfort her.

"Thea," Evrikh spoke, as she turned around for their eyes to rest on each other once more, "I presume they were referring to Cazziel."

"No doubt," she murmured softly. "He's plagued us even before you became Alex." She paused for a moment. "He plagues us still."

"There was a time when I wanted it all to end," he began, looking down upon their hands. "I didn't think the world should be forgiven; maybe even still. It seems the only care people have is who controls whom." He slowly looked up to Thea's eyes. "But then I knew. Somehow, in all that madness, I knew that if the world needed a reason to be forgiven, it'd be you."

Just speaking those words to her flooded Evrikh's thoughts with the love he knew was branded within him; how could he have let it slip? And as she looked back to him, Evrikh could feel a hint of that same love radiating from her. Gently he began probing her mind, and although she allowed him to taste her feelings, she also let him know she was still more than a bit cautious.

"I've missed you too, Evrikh," Thea gently spoke as her hand slipped around his neck.

"Perhaps we should move more quickly," Vahn spoke as he rose from Lauren's side. "If I know Cazziel, and I really don't, but I'll say that if I were in his shoes, then

I'm sure he himself won't come until they're sure Evrikh's here; which, of course, buys us a little more time." Vahn looked down to grace Lauren a smile.

"... idiot," Evrikh slipped in.

"Thea, why don't you take Evrikh back to your place so you two can reacquaint yourselves," placing his hand upon Lauren's head, Vahn turned back in their direction. "We'll head back to the church and see if there's any news of Cazziel or the Council."

Thea brushed Evrikh a smile before looking back at Vahn. "You and Lauren be careful."

Just as she finished speaking, Evrikh watched as Vahn tossed a disapproving look in his direction. His thoughts betrayed him, for he knew Vahn wasn't as quick to trust Evrikh as Thea was. He sent a quick thought back out to Vahn. *If I find out you're working with the Council to use Thea or me in any way ...*

"Come on, Lauren," Vahn started as he looked away, "let's go see what we can find."

As they opened the door, Thea turned around to look at Evrikh, a familiar look of passion hidden within her eyes. "Come on, Ev, maybe we should go as well."

For the moment they sat there. Feeling Thea's hand within his own, he realized this is where he should have always been—with Thea, beside her. And that same moment, the stone had been set, the heavens bound, the earth itself frozen. He would never lose her again; not by his hand, or any other.

They left.

* * * *

CHAPTER 14
~ The Visitor ~

AS VAHN WALKED about the pews, cleaning up from this morning's preaching, the doors of the church suddenly flopped open as a robed figure graced in, two armed escorts closely behind him. The morning air had scrawled across the floor, kicking up the unseen thin layer of dust. As he drew down the main walkway, Vahn stood up from the pamphlets he was collecting.

"Well, now, what could have possibly happened out here to warrant the arrival of the most exalted purifier in all of Eden?" Vahn condescended.

"It displeases me to have to visit such a speck of a town on the map, Vahn," the man started as he lounged into one of the pews, throwing his feet upon another, "so let's not have a conversation that's equally displeasing."

"But, Solieq, your presence alone is enough to label this as anything but displeasing," Vahn spoke, taking a seat in a pew across from him.

"I'm looking for a man named Evrikh. Where is he?"

"That's a very unique name, belonging to a man I'm sure I've yet to meet. Instead, Solieq, allow me to introduce you to a man in town named Brolly. His pastries are actually quite renowned, and you visit us so rarely." Vahn's face was fierce with sincerity.

"The entire Council of Aurora is in an upheaval over this, and you would like for me to visit your . . . pastry man?!"

"Solieq, you and I both know that for something as important as this man you claim to be searching for, something would have trickled even out here. Yet, I've heard nothing."

"There are people farther up the food chain than either of us, Vahn, people that are looking for this man and have suspicions he could be here. Now," his voice had grown into a sly tone, "why do you suppose that is?"

"As far as the food chain goes, I have head-of-the-line privileges at all the local restaurants, so I'm not worried. And as for your accusations, someone's more than likely grinning at your expense right now, because you have been laughably misinformed."

"Idiot . . ." Solieq belted out.

"Now if you'll excuse me, I have confessions to attend to," Vahn finished.

Pulling his feet from the pew they rested on, Solieq quickly stood up, looking down at Vahn. "One day I will have *you* confessing before the Council." Solieq slammed the railings with his hands and thrust his face to within inches of Vahn's. "Perhaps *begging* before the Council!" he snickered.

Vahn returned a sly smile. "... Perhaps."

Regaining his posture, Solieq stood erect and turned to walk back toward the door. As he moved away, Vahn turned his attention back to the confessionals and the people who sat within. Just as Solieq reached the arc of the doors, a figure caught his attention; the figure of a woman. She was finishing up with the last few pews as she noticed him and looked in his direction; such an interesting face.

"Well, now, this is an interesting turn of events," Solieq added as he stepped in her direction. "With the recent incident that occurred at the Church of Divinity, all the Maidens of the Priestess were accounted for. That is, all but one," he finished as his approach ended beside her.

Looking at the man before her had made her eyes grow wide. During her stay at the church it was impossible not to be noticed when playing such an important role so close to the priestess. She had seen this man many times while at the church; Solieq La'Sarus, as she was certain he had noticed her just as many times. They both turned now, as Vahn's presence beside Solieq was equally startling.

A moment passed before he began to speak. "I see you've found Lauren." Vahn smiled as he slipped in between the two of them. "I'm saddened to hear that Divinity has misplaced one of the Maidens of the Priestess. Lauren has been with us for some time now, and she hasn't even seen Eden, let alone been to Divinity." Lauren watched as the slight smile now left Vahn's face.

"There is nothing for you here, Solieq, as there never

will be. Your place is in Eden, and ours," Vahn gestured between Lauren and himself, "is here."

Solieq leaned closer to Vahn as they locked gazes through moments of tense silence. "I have no idea how, nor do I care, whose nipple you suckled to get this position of yours." Solieq leaned back as he stood erect once more. "You will slip one day, Vahn, and I will be at the top of your pedestal watching you fall."

"May you be blessed by the priestess," Vahn returned with a slight bow.

As he finished speaking, Solieq turned for the door, his robes gracing the pews as they glided over them. The air was filled with a sudden thud as the doors closed behind him, thinning as the tension escaped as well.

"Well, I suppose it's a good thing they've already left, huh?" Vahn slipped out as he turned toward Lauren, that familiar sly smile creeping its way back onto his lips.

"Are you sure about this?"

"My dear, the only assurance in life is the fact that everyone has one, and at some point, it ends. I have no doubt our friends have a plan only known to them, and it'll be interesting to see how it all pans out," he finished, as his gaze slowly turned toward the statuette of the goddess behind Lauren.

"Perhaps this will only hasten things. Either way, those two are on their own now. I'm not sure we can trust Evrikh, but Thea's hands are more than capable." Vahn finished as his eyes rolled back to Lauren.

For a moment, while looking into Vahn's eyes, Lauren had been reminded of *his* eyes; Evrikh. Such determination, ferocity; back at the church during her escape, his presence alone was enough to bind her in place. She had become both captivated, and somehow aroused. Letting her gaze slip from Vahn, she turned to finish with the pamphlets.

"I'm not sure I could ever trust such a man," she spoke as she left Vahn's side.

* * * *

CHAPTER 15
~ Fall of a Tyrant ~

THE GRAND HALL of the Church of Divinity roared with the crowd of people, as the murals of old echoed their cries to the city outside like a chorus. The beautiful tapestries mimicked the flicker of dreams as they swayed against the walls, the wind allowing the slightest of breaths to intimately invade the church.

The crowd's obnoxious cries grew to the silence of whispers as the majestic doors of their beloved goddess slowly opened, their deafening whispers replaced by shock as Cazziel and the Protectors of Faith came forth, proceeding to take their seats where the Council once sat. Slowly Cazziel walked up beside Miriam's chair as his hand came to a rest upon it. Momentarily, his memories were flooded by her presence and the scent of her closeness, a taste he had once nurtured. As he looked around, Cazziel saw a new world had been brought before him; his world.

"People of Eden," Cazziel began, with his hand

outstretched to the crowd. "People of our beloved goddess Miriam," his voice echoed throughout the whole of the church, bringing all others to a silence. "My people . . ."

Cazziel took a moment to look back and forth to the Protectors of Faith, "hear me now, I pray you, for I bring to you the knowledge and the wisdom of our goddess."

More whispers shot out from the crowd as Cazziel eased himself into Miriam's throne, his hands caressing the edges; fingertips deliciously tracing the contours.

"Our goddess sees this lush world we've created, the dreams we've fought so hard to bring to life. She has borne witness to the teachings of Aurora and how they've reached every corner of the globe; every life they've touched." Cazziel's voice was deep and sincere, the richness of a newfound father.

As he spoke, the crowd began to give praise to his words of truth and his faith in the people. Cazziel gestured his hands once more to bring silence and ease to their questions.

"She has granted us the privilege to inform the world that we have achieved what she has helped us rebuild for so long."

More voices murmured from the crowd. "What is he talking about?" "Where's the goddess?" "He's right, you know. Besides, they're the ones who saved us from the Resistance."

Cazziel rose to his feet.

"The goddess has returned to the heavens from which she came. Upon leaving us, she has made two requests. One," Cazziel paused for a moment as he looked around, "she asks that we, the Protectors of Faith, replace the Council of Aurora to ensure its safety and continue its guidance of the people."

A slight roar came from the crowd as they cheered for Cazziel and this new step of their society.

"And two," Cazziel raised a second finger, "she leaves the care of this world we have built to her beloved people."

As Cazziel finished her second request, the crowd roared alive, clapping and cheering. Rising to their feet, the Protectors of Faith watched as the people applauded in praise of their new Council and the hope they have placed in the people. Gesturing his hands once more, Cazziel asked that the people ease into silence.

"Brothers and sisters," he paused a moment, "children of Miriam, after the Great Darkness we have risen from the bowels of New Terra, together, as one." Cazziel stepped down from Miriam's throne and from the Council. He walked upon the red carpet and into the crowd. "And now, I ask, will you heed our goddess's wishes and continue rebuilding our world with me?"

The crowd revered Cazziel's excitement as their praise grew louder. Indulging himself in his own exquisiteness, his own glory, a new smile spread its deception across Cazziel's lips. His World Indeed!

Moments later, Cazziel felt a very familiar feeling. THE CROWD. As his eyes slowly scanned the masses before him, he let the smile slip from his mouth. THE UPPER BALCONY, LEFT SIDE. With a continued look of sincerity, his eyes continued their motion toward the second tier of seats. THIRD ROW, FIFTH SEAT .

..EMPTY!

Turning around graciously, Cazziel departed the crowd and joined back up with the Protectors of Faith; the new Council. "He's here."

"Sir, should we escort you from the hall?" one of the members whispered as he stepped up beside Cazziel.

"That won't be necessary," he began, giving the crowd another look of pride. "He is not that irrational. Instead," Cazziel turned to face the Council, "set up a perimeter around the church. If any of you see something even remotely suspicious, you wait for me. You do *not* engage."

As the members of the Council began filtering out into the crowd, Cazziel scanned once more. His senses toned to a perfect note. He whispered . . . "Evrikh, what kind of fairy tale are you trying to live?"

". . . Mine."

Cazziel whirled around as he startled those in the crowd who sat closest. He practically stumbled over the corner of the table as his eyes searched for the voice that echoed so very closely to his ear. Regaining his posture, Cazziel gave another wave to the people to rest their slight amusement. He then walked past the table toward the chamber doors of his newfound meeting room. Upon grabbing the handle, he took a deep breath and opened. The door graciously clicked shut behind him.

Having a seat at the table within, Cazziel let his fingers ride the exquisite carvings that marked his place . . . the head of all tables. Exhaling, his elbows came to a rest upon the marble top as he massaged his temples. "A few more pawns to play, and then the *real* game begins."

"... Cazziel ..."

WITHIN THE ROOM!

Cazziel's head shot up as his eyes immediately took in the surroundings of the room, his hands gripping the edges of the table. Everything was as it should be ... save one chair; the opposite of Cazziel at the far end of the table. As it began rotating, he could hear the faint sound of gentle clapping; a pair of hands. The chair finished its rotation as the hands came to a rest.

"Bravo, Cazziel; all this just to own the Council ... and the church."

A small grin etched its way onto that disgustingly overconfident face of his. "This is simply the beginning, Evrikh. I thought you would've figured that out by now."

Evrikh watched as Cazziel raised himself from his chair. "Don't even think about it. I'm not here alone."

Cazziel launched himself toward a painting on the wall as his hand slipped through its mirage in search of a weapon contained within this hidden place.

"Don't bother," Evrikh began as he stepped around the corner of the table. "They've all been removed. Tell me, brother, what in the hell would you need eight different weapons hidden for? Surely the years haven't made you *that* paranoid, have they?"

At this slight realization, Cazziel retracted his hand from the painting, turning to face him once more. Slowly, he approached the table and took his seat once again. His mind raced with possibilities, and for an instant Evrikh could almost taste his nervousness. This deliciously raw rarity that Cazziel has not felt in a very long time—perhaps ever—save for a time when they were once kids.

"What is it you're looking for, Evrikh?" His voice contained not even the slightest twitch of this feeling Evrikh was indulging in.

"Give up the church, Cazziel. Disband the Council of Aurora, and allow the world to govern itself." The words fell from his mouth as demands. "Turn the church into nothing more than a house of faith, and allow the people to rule themselves."

"NO!" Cazziel shot up, his hand cracking the marble top as it slammed into it. "NO! Allow these people to rule themselves?" His hand gestured toward the window as he moved toward it. "This would throw the world into chaos—MY WORLD! *I'm* all that these people have now." Cazziel's thoughts had lost their subtlety, and his rage carried over to his words.

"Your world?"

". . . Mine! These people deserve a fate no different than that of Miriam. Their bleeding ignorance appalls me." He continued, turning to face Evrikh once more. "They are like sheep without a herder, lost in these fields of theirs. I stand to correct it all. In the beginning they'll praise me, over time they'll preach about me, and in the end, pray to me."

As Cazziel sat there speaking, Evrikh could sense something else within him, something dark and very grave.

"I will claim these people's faith, Evrikh, and I will destroy it!" That familiar smile gracing his face. "And then I will claim their lives. I'm only finishing what our father started."

"Our father never intended for us to destroy the world!" Evrikh's thoughts had become churned by his common selfishness.

"If that was the case, then the experiments never would have begun." Cazziel took a step in his direction.

"I know that somewhere in your twisted world, you believe our father was a good man. Cazziel, the truth is, he was everything but."

Another step. "And what of your quest you beset yourself upon three years ago? Had you not been stopped, would you have ended it all? Deep down, I know you as well as I know myself. We are brothers!"

"Cazziel, you and I have the power to change our destinies. You don't have to take this path, you could come with us. There's so much we could do for these people," Evrikh gestured his hand toward the drapes of the back window. Cazziel watched as the air around it became stagnant, swirling like a collage of oils. As it thinned out, Thea faded in like a reflection coming into focus, her presence bringing the faint scent of delicious arousal.

"With *her*?" Cazziel erupted. "You would lay your arms with a woman who so fatally wounded you?" His words contained the slight amusement of disillusionment.

Thea smirked. "I suppose you'd have to have loved once to truly understand."

Cazziel turned to face Evrikh once more. "Like the rest of mankind, you are a laughable fraction of existence." Cazziel approached the table as his hands came to a rest upon it. "The only offer is this: surrender yourselves, join the Council, help me bring the world to its knees, and you shall have the rest of your lives to play out." His tone deadened. "What say you?"

"We were brothers once, I'll never forget that. But, Cazziel, if you choose this path, then you walk it alone. Thea and I will end your reign before it has the chance to begin." Evrikh's voice was sorrowful; he was to lose the brother he had only just remembered.

"I see . . . And so it begins."

The doors of the exit in the back were the first to blow in, its opening flooded with Relics tumbling inward. Then there was the main door that led out to the grand hall of the church. With the doors snapping off the hinges, the walls vibrated with life as these wooden pallets slammed into the floor; more Relics swiftly entering. As the drapes slowly swayed from the gentlest of breezes, Thea stepped up beside Evrikh. Looking around this room of engineered assassins, Evrikh absorbed their thoughts along with their doubts. Most of them had known of the Resistance and of Thea. But all of them remembered what had begun and ended with him, three years ago. They were afraid.

Evrikh turned to look at Cazziel, whose expression had become all but doubtful. "You already know they have no chance at stopping us."

"Hmm . . . maybe not," his face glanced downward, "but hopefully enough."

Within the flicker of a light, as though the room itself had blinked, Cazziel pulled a weapon from the folds of his robes. Thrusting it in the other two's direction, his robes rolled up over his shoulders, floating to the floor. The glass of the window on their left suddenly exploded into the room as Evrikh realized Cazziel had turned his aim. He faintly heard Cazziel's whisper as he leapt from the now-gaping hole, "... You have your orders."

"Thea! ..."

"He's yours; I got this," Thea gritted, turning her back to Evrikh to face the Relics. "Evrikh, he's your brother, remember that."

"Thea ... I'll see you soon," he yelled back as he leapt out of the hole after Cazziel.

As the far wall was relieved of its integrity, Cazziel leapt into the hazy mist that was left behind. Leaving Thea to her excitement with the Relics, Evrikh's feet bounded after him, throwing the dust into the air as they gripped the cement. With this stony veil of fog invading his eyes, Evrikh leapt through the hole after him.

The outside wind rushed the irritating fog from Evrikh's vision, quickly blinding him for a moment from the warmth of the sunlight. Turning toward the inevitable provocation of gravity, he could feel the chill of the wind rippling through his clothes. Cazziel was already at least sixty meters below. Even though the land below them was blurry, Cazziel had been close enough for him to see he had already turned, anticipating Evrikh's pursuit. A blinding flash of blue light erupted as Evrikh rolled to the side looking up for a moment to watch the side of his pants drift away. And so once again, the game was on.

Looking back down, his eyes exploded into a lightning blur of red, their bodies soaring past one of the waterfalls descending from another tower. Evrikh's aura ripped to life soon after, Cazziel firing off another three rounds. A comet of red fire shot through the sky above the city as it slammed through the waterfall; pockets of steam erupting along it. Looking back down toward the quickening city below, Cazziel veered off, rolling himself outside of a pillar. Exploding from the far side of the waterfall, Evrikh watched as the edge of the city below moved from beneath them. The murals of the grand hall cascaded past, the stained glass mirroring the used palette of an artist. To see the church from this angle was truly remarkable. His attention returned to Cazziel.

"CAZZIEL! WHY DO THIS?!" Foolish; the chilling wind had already decided to throw his words back at him.

As the streets below echoed their increasing speed, Cazziel suddenly shot right. His body darted along like free ink ripping across an invisible canvas. Following suit, Evrikh torqued his body with as much force as possible, clearing the wall marking the edge of the city and feeling his body uncontrollably slam into the cement of the street. To the people that dotted the walkways, he must have seemed like a flailing fish bouncing along at an incredible speed. With Cazziel only moments ahead, the tumbling began to slow as Evrikh regained control of his own momentum. Dropping at the last second, Cazziel hit the street, the cement spider-webbing from his impact. There was no time; he shot to the left as Evrikh barreled past. Dropping himself, Evrikh thrust his feet and his hands into the street as he skidded away, embedding himself into the gravel below. By the time he managed to stop, Cazziel had already reached the family that huddled together, as the two came tumbling out of the sky.

The man was flung into the air as his body slammed into the side of a building. The shot had been enough to steal his life; he had never felt the impact. The mother, she was brushed aside by the butt of his gun, her head splitting from the blow. Pulling the young child up in front of him, her mother's blood streaked across them both as she fell to the street unconscious. Rising to his feet, Evrikh proceeded to close the distance between them.

"Evrikh, I take it by your motion that you don't seem to understand our little situation here." The voice of an older brother.

"Once upon a time," the words began to dribble from his mouth, "I remember a brother who would've done anything to help his little brother."

"That was a world ago, Evrikh, and a different life for both of us." His words had been steel, void of compassion.

As the child continued to struggle from his grip, she looked at her unconscious mother, unable to see her motionless father. Screams erupted from her little throat as Cazziel lowered his lips to her ear, "Shhhh . . ."

He was no more than twelve meters now. Keeping his line of sight fixated on Cazziel, Evrikh opened his mind to the child.

"Hey, little sweetheart, it's going to be all right. We're going to get Mommy some help, but first I need you to calm down a little bit. Can you do that for me?"

With the child's voice slimming into whimpers, Cazziel pulled his lips away from her ear, unaware of Evrikh's hidden secret.

"Shhhh, you're going to be OK, angel. We're gonna stop this bad man, but to do this I'm gonna need your help." With Cazziel still unaware, he watched as the little girl slightly nodded her head.

Feeling the warmth of his thoughts, the little girl accepted the invitation, and their small journey together began. With her arms falling to a rest, and her legs coming at ease, her pupils dilated out. Moments later there he was, twelve meters away looking back at himself. Damn, Evrikh really was handsome.

"You promised you'd help," the girl said.

"Right, sorry about that."

Throwing his feet into the air, Evrikh reached up and grabbed ahold of Cazziel's arm around them. Bringing their feet racing back to the ground, Cazziel was caught by surprise of this newfound strength inside such a small body. Springing upward, their collective head connected with Cazziel's face and their legs continued the journey into the air over him, rolling them out from within Cazziel's grasp.

Landing behind Cazziel, they thrust their wrist into his left armpit as their right leg swept out, stealing his balance. As Cazziel began tumbling toward the ground, his head spun around to meet Evrikh's. For a moment he seemed confused, and then they saw his right arm thrust his gun in the direction of Evrikh's body.

"You!" Cazziel grunted, his finger easing the trigger to a blast.

Quickly lunging onto his arm, the crack of the bullet deafened Evrikh's ear. A blinding flash of light streaked his eyes, and then it was gone. The connection was gone.

"Get off me!" Cazziel contorted, casting the small girl aside.

While Evrikh gathered himself from the connection with the child, Cazziel was on his feet a moment later, his gun back in Evrikh's direction. The people around them, frightened, had already removed themselves, helping the family Cazziel had already left for dead.

"I can see you've chosen the next life," he started, stepping toward Evrikh's fatigued body, "instead of ruling this one with me."

With his finger resting calmly on the trigger, he slowly compressed it. Hearing the hammer click into place, a sudden crack split the air as a pool of fog erupted off the ground from the impact. Evrikh heard nothing, save the pinging that now echoed within his ears. But there was something. There was Cazziel. Evrikh could feel his aggression, his suffering, but there was something else. A light so dim he had thought it forever consumed by Cazziel's own darkness.

With the fog clearing around them, there it was. A single hole in the ground between Evrikh's foot and his knee. As Evrikh's eyes slowly scanned upward, Cazziel's finger still rested calmly on the trigger, his weapon still pointed at the hole. That face, his face, Cazziel; from times immemorial.

"I'm tired, Evrikh, so very tired."

Pushing his own confusion aside, this was his brother returned to him somehow. Cazziel.

"... Brother," he whispered, slowly rising to his feet.

"Then perhaps you should rest." Thea's voice blew its way into Cazziel's ear as he felt a disturbing prick just behind it.

As Thea stepped back from him, the gun fell from Cazziel's hand as his fingers lightly probed his ear. Looking over his shoulder, he turned as Thea discarded the syringe to the ground behind her. Feeling the effects quickly spreading its way through his neck, a small grin of satisfaction was almost present in his face.

"Ah, Thea, what've you done?" A moment later Evrikh had stepped to Cazziel to catch him as his legs gave out.

"Isn't this interesting," the words trickled from his mouth. "You would lay me to rest as I did Miriam." His gaze crept toward Thea.

"It seemed befitting of you, Cazziel. Perhaps whatever realm you pass on to, she is there waiting."

There was no sorrow within her heart for him. Rather, she had reserved it only for Evrikh, and her love rekindled at the coming loss of his brother.

". . . My brother, it didn't have to be this way."

And suddenly they were kids again. He had been beaten by those other children, and yet there Cazziel stood with all his pride holding his hand out to Evrikh, as he always had back then. His brother.

"Yes, it did, Evrikh." His voice had already weakened to a whisper, the serum working fast. "The world could never have a place for a man such as I."

Evrikh cradled his head within his arm. "Then we begin anew. Create a world where we all have a place." Tears filled Evrikh's eyes as he felt Cazziel's weight growing less of a burden within his arms.

"True fairy tales have such endings, Evrikh." Such a delicate thing he had become in moments. "Please, remove my glasses."

As Evrikh slipped them from around his head, Cazziel's eyes were already gone. His skin was already being breathed away by the wind.

"And look at you, Evrikh, such a resilient color. You finally saved me for once; my little brother." As he took in a breath, Evrikh watched as it would be his last. "It is I who was never meant to be. Take Thea and make this world anew . . . Give to it what Miriam and I could not."

And so like a dream, he faded within those last few moments with Evrikh left kneeling with nothing more than his clothes softly across his arms. Rising to his feet, Thea was already beside him. Taking his hand into hers, she lifted his chin for their eyes to meet.

"We'll rebuild it all, Evrikh, for your brother, and for your father."

Looking back in her eyes, his heart had found its solitude once more. How could he ever be without this woman? They will rebuild it, and the people will finally be free. His eyes fell back down to the empty uniform. Cazziel.

"One day you'll see the world our father meant for us to save." His voice had carried this promise for him. "May you find your peace, my brother."

"Hey!" His voice came from a distance.

Looking up, Thea and Evrikh watched as Virgil and Lashara approached. Stepping up to them, Evrikh slipped his arm around Thea. Virgil had already recognized

Cazziel's empty uniform.

"And so what happens now?" Evrikh's sadness echoed within those words.

"The Circle of Reign tells us it is done, Evrikh. You have saved your people." Virgil's voice had carried with it an overwhelming sense of peace.

Evrikh turned to face Thea once more, his eyes lost to the dreams of her own. "Is it truly over?"

Their lips had touched for a moment; atonement for the betrayal of their love. They had always been one, and this small kiss was the reunion of their hearts; their souls.

"And the Circle tells us there are plans for you both." Such beautiful timing Lashara had.

Dammit, you guys have the most superb timing! Didn't you see him kissing over here?! Evrikh sure as hell doesn't come running at you during your tongue-in-cheek fests, does he, Lashara?! God, you're about as bad as that Vahn idiot!

Thea suddenly passed a smirk in Evrikh's direction, almost as though she had agreed with his comment about Vahn.

Lashara stepped up beside Thea. "Big plans indeed," and Virgil beside Evrikh. He watched as Lashara slipped her hand up to Thea's shoulder.

"Your lives will begin . . . a bit differently."

As Virgil began to speak, the world around them began to glow and swirl. Evrikh felt as though they were fading from this place. A proud look of accomplishment settled into Virgil's face. Looking at Thea once more, Evrikh stared as this light enveloped them; enveloped her.

At that one moment, she appeared to him as his mind had only known her, a dream. His dearest Thea, if ever there was a reason, you were always it.

A sudden wave of light shot out across the streets, and then they were gone, all four of them. Cazziel's uniform had remained lifeless on the ground as people slowly started coming out of their homes and hiding places. Perhaps it had all been an act. It was all so very sudden and very confusing. It was the ending of something witnessed by some who would share this story for years to come. Maybe the Council would cover it up, and brand those vanished four as heretics; or perhaps saviors. Wherever they had gone, maybe they would find a peace unoffered by this world. A peace that could maybe be shared with the world one day.

As a man slowly walked up to the waving uniform, he bent over to pick it up from the ground. Slowly, he turned it over within his hands as he looked back into the shadows of the alley not so far away. There remained a little girl, standing beside a woman who almost appeared to be made of the forest itself. A genuine smile eased into his weathered face. How far they had come together, and how much farther they've yet to go is up to them now. After glancing back to the uniform once more, he turned to the swirling air that was all but nearly gone.

"Godspeed, my friend, Godspeed."

* * * *

Epilogue
~ The Veil Removed ~

THE FLOWERS SPRINKLED about, within this garden, were the lushful color of dreams, the stones of a walking path once laid by hand. There was a small stream running from a fountain within the center, and from the middle of this fountain there was but a single tree. As the tree stretched upward, the base had been carved of a man and a woman whose bodies intertwined, lost to the bliss of their selfless love.

Faint whispers could be heard from beside this wonderful tree as their attention was drawn to the edges of the fountain. Swiftly the air became stagnant as it swirled about into a transparent ocean, bringing forth a man and a woman. As this lifeless color ran from their bodies, the air behind them quickly returned to normal; the two of them stepping up to the source of the whispers.

"That was most definitely a twist I had not seen coming, my lady."

"But, Virgil, if this was not the truth, then where

would that have left Seraph and me?" Thea added with a hint of satisfaction.

Even though Seraph had watched Virgil and Lashara come before them, his eyes still lingered toward Thea. Virgil's expression had become one of final satisfaction; to know the story as it was made to end.

"But, Evrikh, why the name change?" Lashara added, stepping up beside him.

"Thea and I decided when the two of you brought us here that we would leave everything of our world behind, and to lay to rest Evrikh and the Phoenix Gate," he glanced toward Virgil. "We wanted to allow them to live out their lives and for us to live out ours."

"And so, why send Kovisch with us knowing it would mean his life?" Lashara asked, looming her head in his remembrance.

"... Lashara."

"It's all right, Virgil," Thea slipped in. "Dearest Lashara, there are certain things that are sacred to the balance of life, just as death is sacred." She spoke with a voice that brought the warmth of the sun to their lips. "For us to have a whole, there must be pieces, and every piece, however small, is equally important. And so Kovisch's death is what shares with us now everything that is."

"... I'll miss him," Lashara whispered.

"And so, what's to happen now?" Virgil asked as his eyes turned back to Thea and Seraph.

"Of this we are uncertain," Thea started, "this is new ground for all of us. Whatever direction our people take with their lives is theirs to take, just as Seraph and I have taken our direction."

"My lady, perhaps if we had your wisdom back then, my people could've shared in this triumph," Virgil honored.

They all turned their attention to a man who approached rather quickly. As he followed the pathway, bringing himself up beside them all, he leaned over to quickly catch his breath; it was Melucious.

"... My friends, Lady Thea," he took another moment for breath, "apparently there is a new piece to be played," he breathed slowly.

"Melucious, have a seat," Thea gestured as her hand brushed part of the fountain beside her, "and talk with us."

While continuing to catch his breath, he looked back up toward Virgil and Lashara, as though his words could not be said in front of them.

"It's OK, Melucious, they are to now know everything you could share with Seraph and me," Thea reassured.

Taking the seat, Melucious graced the back of her hand to his lips and honored Lady Thea. "Even though power is beginning to balance between your people and the Council of Aurora, they continued to translate the diaries of Kendrick Savari ... his last diary."

As Melucious spoke with Thea and the other three watched in anticipation, Seraph could feel himself slightly tensing; the small hairs throughout his body erecting themselves.

"... And?"

Gracefully Melucious turned from Thea and gazed into Seraph's direction. "Seraph, what do you remember of Avalon's Window?"

Just as he finished his words, the phrase alone was enough to widen Seraph's eyes. How could he have forgotten such a thing as that, and then to leave it there with those people?

"That diary *must* be erased from existence, and perhaps everyone involved," he began as he looked to Thea with despair already within his eyes, "or I fear it'll be everything else that'll cease to exist."

Looking back at Seraph as though their lives had been betrayed, Thea could feel the immediateness within him. Slowly as the sight of compassion, love, left her face, she turned to Virgil once more.

"It seems our tasks are not quite over just yet."

". . . Indeed," he whispered as his eyes carried themselves back in Seraph's direction, "indeed."

"Once, long ago, I visited this place as a boy. Virgil, that was the first time you and I had ever met each other," Seraph spoke as though the statement alone would provide insight. "At that time, I phased to this place much like we pass in and out of their worlds. That was the first time my father had thought to pursue the phenomenon, and the first time he had begun experimenting with it."

"But, Seraph, you returned several years later as a grown man," Virgil spoke as if to ease Seraph's growing alarm.

"Virgil, that was several years later . . . and that was my father you saw."

* * * *

END

Connect with me online:

www.facebook.com/MichaelSVischi